George Griffiths

A History of Tong, Shropshire

its church, manor, parish, college, early owners, and clergy, with notes on Boscobel.

Second Edition

George Griffiths

A History of Tong, Shropshire
its church, manor, parish, college, early owners, and clergy, with notes on Boscobel. Second Edition

ISBN/EAN: 9783337262495

Printed in Europe, USA, Canada, Australia, Japan

Cover: Foto ©Andreas Hilbeck / pixelio.de

More available books at **www.hansebooks.com**

A HISTORY

OF

TONG, SHROPSHIRE,

ITS

CHURCH, MANOR, PARISH, COLLEGE,
EARLY OWNERS, AND CLERGY,

WITH

NOTES ON BOSCOBEL,

BY

GEORGE GRIFFITHS,

OF WESTON-UNDER-LIZARD.

ILLUSTRATED,

BY

EDMUND H. NEW, GERTRUDE M. BRADLEY, AND
CHARLES W. S. DIXON.

———

Second Edition, with Additions.

———

NEWPORT, MARKET DRAYTON, AND STONE:
HORNE & BENNION, "ADVERTISER" OFFICES.
LONDON:
SIMPKIN, MARSHALL, HAMILTON, KENT, & CO., LTD.
———
MDCCCXCIV.

> " Religion never was designed
> To make our pleasures less."
>> *Watts.*

" No entertainment is so cheap as reading, nor any pleasure so lasting."
>> *Lady Mary Wortley Montague.*

> " The knights are dust,
> Their swords are rust,
> Their souls are with the saints we trust."

The Church was old and grey, with ivy clinging to the walls, and round the porch. It was a very quiet place, as such a place should be, save for the cawing of the rooks, who had built their nests among the branches of some tall old trees.

" Let us wait here," rejoined Nell, " the gate is open. We will sit in the church porch till you come back."

" A good place, too," said the schoolmaster, placing his portmanteau on the stone seat.

It was a very aged, ghostly place. The church had been built many hundreds of years ago, and had once had a convent or monastery attached; for arches in ruins, remains of oriel windows, and fragments of blackened walls were yet standing. They admired everything—the old, grey porch, the mullioned windows, the venerable gravestones dotting the green church-yard, the ancient tower, the very weathercock, the brown thatched roofs of cottage, barn, and homestead, peeping from among the trees; the stream that rippled by the distant watermill, the blue Welch mountains far away

>> *Dickens' Old Curiosity Shop.*

This Work is Gratefully Inscribed and

Dedicated to

The Earl and Countess of Bradford,

on the

Fiftieth Anniversary of their Marriage,

April 30th, 1894,

By the Author.

PREFACE TO THE SECOND EDITION, WITH ADDITIONS.

The thousand copies which comprised the first edition of my work on Tong, its Parish Church, and early history, having been exhausted, and the demand for the book by antiquarians and visitors alike continuing, I am persuaded to launch this second and enlarged edition with much confidence and hope of public approval.

The numerous illustrations and additional subjects will, I imagine, increase its general interest and usefulness.

These latter embrace :—

The Hengist Tradition.

Some account of the Earl of Bradford's family and ancestry.

Notes upon the Restoration of the Church, Slabs found, the Stanley Tomb, &c., and numerous revisions throughout.

An account of Tong College and its quaint rules.

A document recording the Perambulation of the Boundary of the Lordship or Manor and Parish of Tong in 1718, with local notes upon perambulations, millers, maypoles, the tithe pig, marlpits, Tong tournament, factory, and clockmakers, surnames, &c.

Memoranda of the Durant family.

Tong Church Registers, and a Proclamation found in the parish chest as to Gunpowder Plot.

Some account of the famous Ladies of Tong, viz. : Venetia Lady Digby, Lady Mary Wortley Montague, Mrs. Fitzherbert, Isabella Forester, Lady Stafford, and Dorothy Vernon.

Some account of Boscobel, which is just outside Tong parish, and particularly of the Royal Oak, the shelter of King Charles II ; the faithful Penderels of Hubbal Grange in Tong. The Nunneries of White Ladies and Black Ladies, immediately on the outskirts.

Early Deeds of the Pemburges, Vernons, and Stanleys, forming a portion of this edition, are of interest to antiquarians, and will help, when time permits a fuller examination, to throw more light upon the ancient history of Tong.

I desire to record my grateful thanks to the Earl and Countess of Bradford for their kind and approving letters written on the publication of the first edition. I must also mention the valuable help rendered me by Mr. Walter de Gray Birch, F.R.S.L,, of the British Museur, and by MS. Notes of the Rev. R. G. Lawrence, a former Vicar of Tong.

To others, whose names are mentioned throughout the work, I am desirous to express my obligations for their courtesy.

GEORGE GRIFFITHS.

Weston-under-Lizard,
30th April, 1894.

PREFACE TO THE FIRST EDITION.

This little book has been printed in the hope that it may be useful in refreshing the memories of those visitors to Tong Church who are already in some degree acquainted with its ancient and historic associations; while to the many tourists from neighbouring towns who resort to the village, it may be not only a "guide" to the building, but a reminder of a pleasant holiday.

The compiler is not unconscious of the importance and delicacy of such a task as the description of Tong Church, but hastens to defend its publication as supplying the great want of a handy comprehensive guide to a much-visited edifice.

He has endeavoured to introduce, where possible, comments upon its rich contents by abler hands, completing the remainder with an ordinary notice of things as they are to be seen at present. He hopes that neither such simple language—nor indeed the existence of conflicting opinions upon matters of remote date—will be allowed to detract from the lustre pertaining to the objects themselves.

He has to express his thanks to those strangers and friends who have favoured him with interesting notes.

GEO. GRIFFITHS.

Weston Bank, Shifnal,
1885.

LETTER FROM THE EARL OF BRADFORD.

Weston, Shifnal, Feby. 6, 1885.

MY DEAR SIR,—Let me thank you very much for the book you have sent me on Tong Church. I think it is very nicely got up, besides the merits of its contents as a guide to Tong Church and Parish.

I have looked through it, and it appears to me to be full of correct information, given in a popular way. I hope it may prove successful, and will certainly recommend my friends to buy it.

Yrs. very faithfully,

(Signed) BRADFORD.

LETTER FROM THE COUNTESS OF BRADFORD.

Weston Park, Shifnal, Sept. 6, 1885.

DEAR SIR,—I am quite delighted with your book, and accept it with much pleasure. I have read a great part of it, and shall study it one day in the Church of Tong. I cannot but think it is a book that will make its mark in the County. I want a copy at once to give away to a friend, and I doubtless shall want several more. With thanks and congratulations on its success.

Believe me,
Yours truly,

(Signed) SELINA L. BRADFORD.

ILLUSTRATIONS.

	Plate on Page
Charles I.	Frontispiece
Tong Church and Vicarage..................	viii
Plan of District	ix
Plan of Church..................	x
Reference to Effigies	xi
Plan of Village..................	xii
Thong Castle and Merlin..................	6
Tong Church from the East, p. 20. .... Stanley Tomb, p. 65	20
East window, 3 Screens, and Pulpit......	26
Seal of Isabella the Foundress, p. 214.... Font, Tong Church, p. 27.................. White Ladies Abbey Ruins and Gate-house, p. 194	27
Sir F. de Pembruge IV. Tomb, p. 30...... Sir Richard Vernon Tomb, p. 37 .... Sir Harry Vernon Tomb, p. 47	30
Brass to Sir W. Vernon	42
Sir Harry Vernon's Tong Castle	50
Brass to Sir A. Vernon..................	53
Sir Arthur Vernon Effigy, p. 54............. The King's Champion, p. 61 .... King Charles II. and the Penderels and Yates, p. 180	54
Tong Church—Choir-Stalls, p. 74 .... Richard and Margaret Vernon Tomb, p 57	74
Duke of Kingston Deed	82
Crystal Ciborium..................	83
Brass to W. Skeffington	84
Brass to Lady Daunsey	86
Tong Castle, as at present	90
Vestry Door	95
Brass to Ralph Elcock	96
Great Bell of Tong, and G. Boden, Clerk	101
Great Bell of Tong..................	103
Sir Thomas More	114
Tong College	122
The Watchman	129
Forge Hammer from a Coin found in Tong Church during the Restoration, p. 142.................. Tong Upper Forge Waterfall, p. 142. ...	142
Hubbal Grange, p 204..................	142
Convent Lodge, Entrance to Tong Castle	156
Dove-house, p. 11 and 160 .... Tong Church from the West, and Alms-house ruins, p. 160	160
Lady Mary W. Montague, p. 166.......... Venetia, Lady Digby, p. 171 .... Dorothy Vernon, p. 177 .... Richard Penderell, p. 180.................. Charles II.. p. 183 .... "Mrs." Jane Lane, p. 182..................	166
Lady Mary, the toast of the Kit-cat Club	167
Mrs. Fitzherbert	169
The Royal Oak, photograph in 1894...... Black Ladies, p. 206	179
The Royal Oak, trunk as at present,......	184
Boscobel and the Royal Oak, copy of a photograph in 1879..................	185
The Royal Oak, with brick wall, p. 187 Tong Golden Chapel Roof, p. 53 .... William Penderell, p. 179 .... Sir Kenelm Digby, p 173	187
White Ladies—slabs, ... White Ladies—from the S. E. Corner of Ruins	200
White Ladies as a Cart Shed, Tiles, North Doorway, Dame Joan Penderill's Tomb .... White Ladies—hinge..................	202
Plan of Stanley Tomb, Tong...............	226

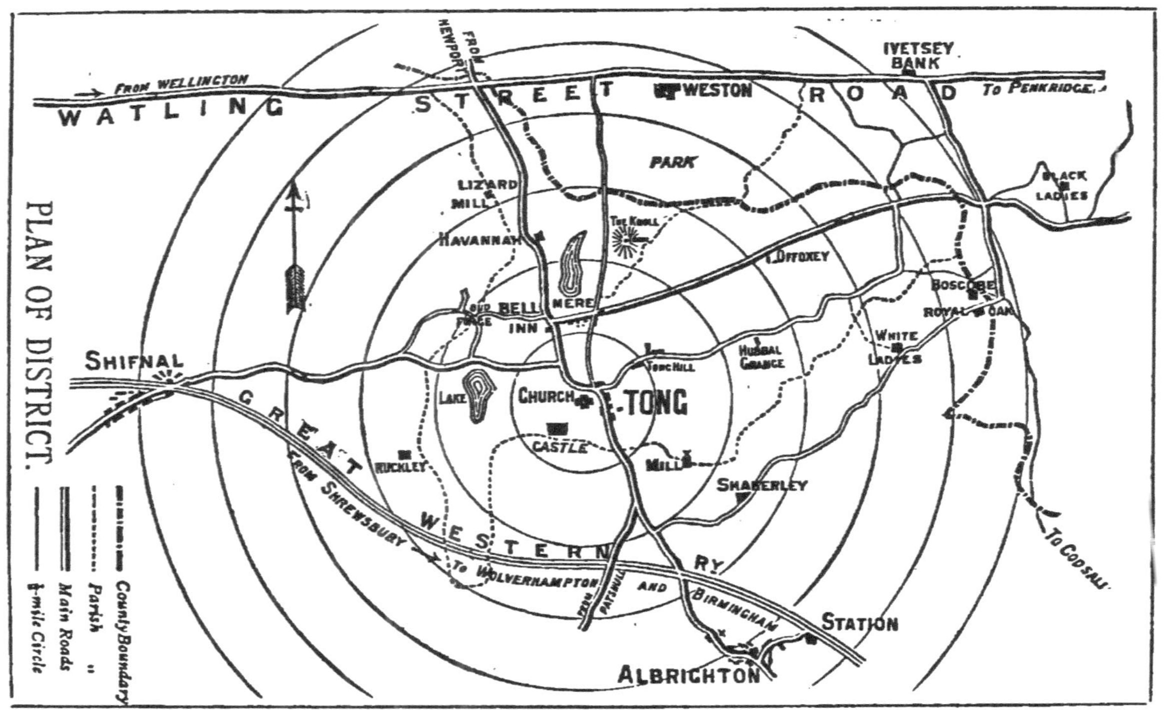
FROM WELLINGTON
WATLING
STREET
WESTON
ROAD
IVETSEY BANK
TO PENKRIDGE
FROM NEWPORT
PARK
LIZARD MILL
BLACK LADIES
The Knoll
HAVANNAH
I. DITTOXEY
BOSCOBEL
OLD BELL MERE
PINE INN
ROYAL OAK
WHITE LADIES
TONG HILL
HUBBAL GRANGE
SHIFNAL
Lake
CHURCH
TONG
GREAT
RUCKLEY
CASTLE
MILL
SHACKERLEY
FROM SHREWSBURY
WESTERN
RY.
TO WOLVERHAMPTON
PATSHULL
AND
BIRMINGHAM
STATION
TO CODSALL
ALBRIGHTON

PLAN OF DISTRICT.

County Boundary
Parish   "
Main Roads
½-mile Circle

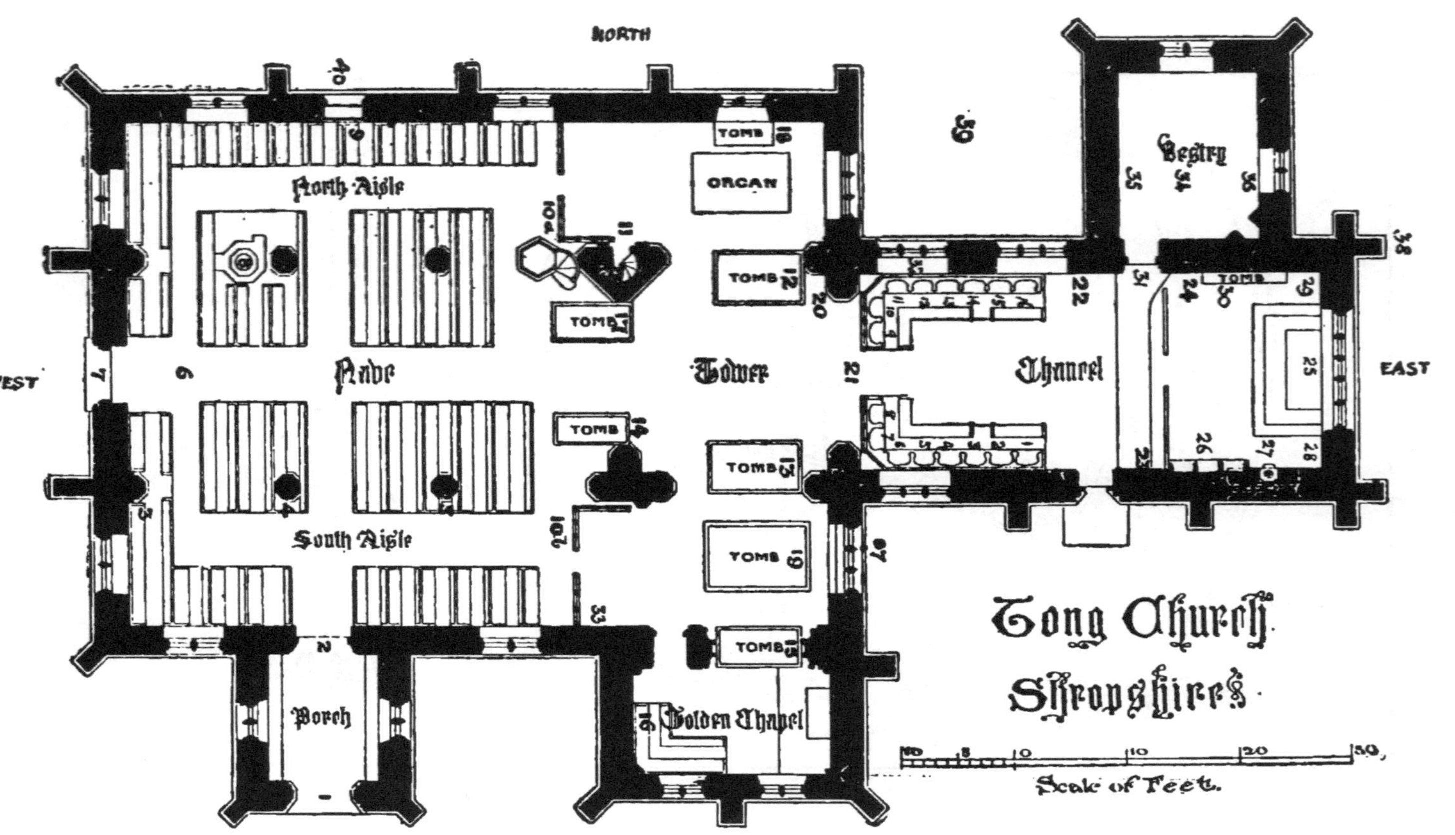

NORTH
WEST
EAST
Tong Church
Shropshire
Scale of Feet.
North Aisle
South Aisle
Nave
Tower
Chancel
ORGAN
Vestry
Porch
Golden Chapel
TOMB

A Concise Reference to ye Effigies.

NOTICE that ye little number placed against each illustrious name refers the industrious reader alike to ye Plan of ye Church, and ye Bodye of ye Boke.

From ye Harcourts of the Blood Royale of Saxony, ye famous De Belmeis familie, and La Zouches descended of ye Dukes of Brittany : came Orabel de Harcourt married to Henry de Pembruge of Pembridge, Co. Hereford ; " my faithfull and beloved Henry," as His Majesty described him : from whom in very direct descent—

Sir Tho := Elizabeth de Lingen = Sir Fulke de Pembruge **12** ... Juliana de = Rich: de Vernon
Ludlow | daughter & heire to Sir Raffe Lingen of Wigmore. She built ye Churche. **12** ... Pembruge sister and heire. | from the Vernons off Normandie

Benedicta de Ludlow = Sir Richard de Vernon, ye Speaker of Lei'ster Parliament, 1426.
13 ... **13**

Sir Will: Vernon = Margaret (Swynfen), heiress of Sir Rob: Pype and Spernor.
14 ... **14**

Sir Harry Vernon = To ye Ladye Anne Talbot, granddaughter to ye Great Earl Talbot.
15 ... **15**
Governor & Treasurer to Arthur, Prince of Wales, elder brother to King Henry VIII., a very worthie Prince.

Margaret (Dymock) = Richard Vernon, Esq. **17** ... Humphrey Vernon, Esq. **18** = Alice de Ludlow, **18** co-heire of her grandfather Sir Richd: de Ludlow. ... Arthur Vernon, Pryst **16**
17
dau: of Sir Robert Dymock, ye King's champion.

Sir George Vernon, buried at Bakewell, leaving two lovely daughters co-heires,

Margaret Vernon = At Haddon, to Sir Tho: Stanley, son to ye Earle of Derbie **19** ... Dorothy = Sir John Manners, from whom His Grace of Rutland.
19

Sir Edw: Stanley = Ye Lady Lucie Percie, daughter to ye Duke of Northumberland.
19

From whom the beautiful Venetia, Lady Digby, and others.

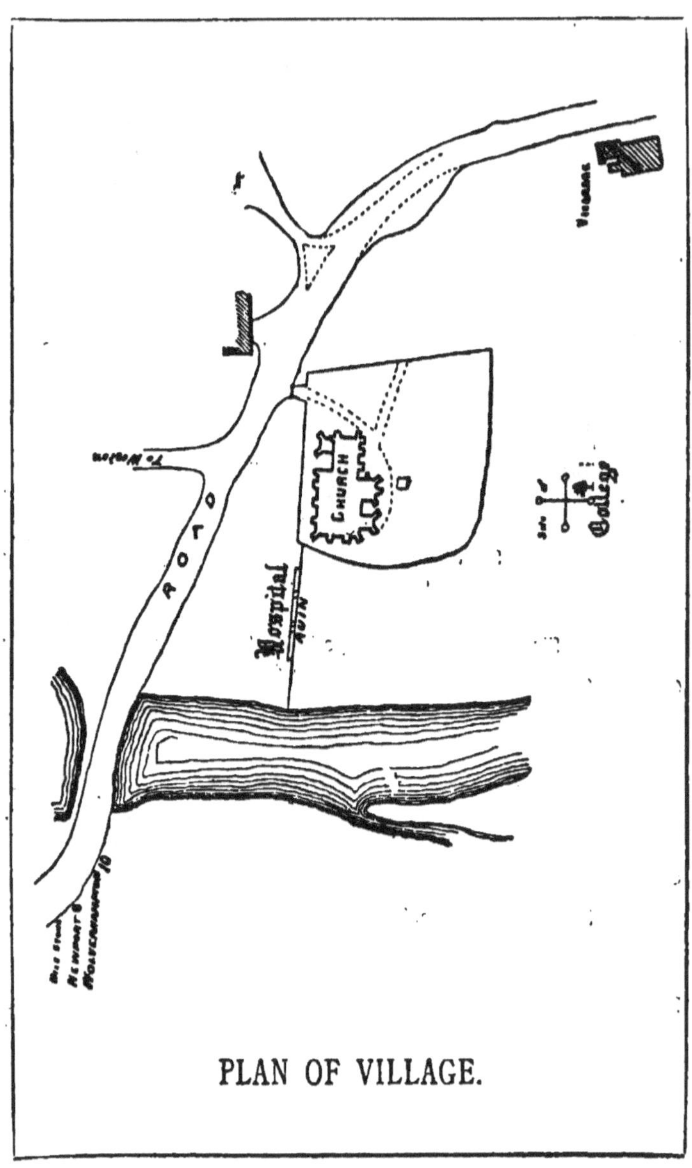

PLAN OF VILLAGE.

TONG—Early History.

THE early history of Tong, from the time of the Conquest till the time of the erection of the present church, about 1411, has been given in the most complete manner possible by Mr. Eyton in his *Antiquities of Shropshire*, a work so scarce and expensive as to be generally inaccessible.

I have therefore extracted from it his preliminary remarks on the place, which form a characteristic preface :—

"Tong was for centuries the abode or heritage of men great for their wisdom or their virtues, eminent either from their prosperity or their misfortune. The retrospect of their annals alternates between the Palace and the Feudal Castle, between the Halls of Westminster and the Council Chamber of Princes, between the Battlefield, the Dungeon, and the Grave. The history of the Lords of the Manor is in part the biography of Princes and Prelates, Earls and Barons, Statesmen, Generals, and Jurists. These are the great names and reminiscences with which the place is associated : The Saxon Earls of Mercia, —brave, patient, and most unfortunate victims of inexorable progress ; then their three Norman successors—one wise and politic, another chivalrous and benevolent, the last madly ambitious and monstrously cruel : then the Majesty of England

represented by Henry I., a Prince who in ability for ruling
almost equalled his father, and has been surpassed by none of
his successors ; then the sumptuous and viceregal pride of De
Belmeis—Bishop, General, Statesman, and withal very Prince ;
his collateral heirs with their various and wide-spread interests,
dim in the distance of time, but traceable to a common origin ;
the adventurous genius and loyal faith of Brittany represented
in La Zouch ; tales of the oscillating favouritism and murder-
ous treachery of King John ; overweening ambition and saddest
misfortune chronicled in the name of De Braose; a Harcourt
miscalculating the signs of his times, and ruined by the error ;
a race of Pembrugges, whose rapid succession tells of youth
and hope and the early grave ; then the open-handed and
magnificent Vernons ; lastly Stanley, a name truly English,
and ever honourable in English ears, yet for one of whom it
was fated to add a last flower to the chaplet of ancestral
memories—to cut short the associations which five centuries
had grouped around his fair inheritance."

THE name of the village has been variously spelt. The
most familiar is Tong, by some attributed to the sound
or " Tong " of a large deep, full-toned bell ; Tonge, as
it was generally spelt in the last century and previously ; and
Tuange, Twange, Tuang, Toang, the sound of a smaller " tang-
ing " bell. The working classes call it " Tung," and the surnames of Tong and Tonge are met with among inhabitants
in the neighbouring town of Shifnal.

On the other hand it is said that Tong or Thong was in
ancient times the stronghold of Hengist the Saxon, and that
the name is derivable from a tradition connected with him, to
the effect that the British King who had hired him and his

followers to fight, in consideration of their success granted to Hengist as much land as an ox-hide would encompass; that thereupon he cut the hide into thongs as narrow as possible, and upon the land thus encircled formed a settlement for himself and followers.

The earliest record, or rather tale, relating to Tong, is connected with Hengist, and is to be found in " The Chronicles of Merry England," of which a translation is given below. Of the state of the country it may be briefly noted that the withdrawal of the Romans to look after their own affairs nearer home, left some parts of Britain destitute of armed soldiers, of martial stores, and of all its active youth; but generally the country was divided into districts under provincial Governors. The attacks of Picts and Scots led to confederations, headed some by British, some by Roman chiefs, which caused civil strife. This, with a religious discussion (arising out of a dispute between the native bishops and Pelagius, a native of Wales), plunged the country into confusion. Application was then made to the Roman General for aid, but in vain. At this juncture, Vortigern, the most powerful of British chiefs, employed mercenaries to aid in fighting his battles. The old Chronicle may now be left to speak for itself. " Now a little before the Hallelujah Victory there had been great strife among the Britons, whether one Aurelius, or his brother Uther, surnamed Pendragon, should reign over them, which a warrior named Vortigern, taking advantage of, he made himself king in their stead, and the two brethren fled into Cornwall. Vortigern, finding his crown red-hot to him by reason of the dis-affection of his subjects, and the fears he had of his enemies, resolved to strengthen himself by alliance with the Anglo-Saxons. A detachment of these enemies of his country in their war-galley had just landed in Kent, headed by two brothers called Hengist and Horsa. To them applied this unworthy king,

with messages of peace, desiring them to repair to his
presence.   Forthwith they comply, and stand before the king.
Like most of the Anglo-Saxon race these men were tall, well-
built and comely, of undaunted yet frank and pleasing aspect,
blue-eyed, fresh coloured, and with pale, brown hair, divided
down the centre, and diffusing itself over their shoulders.
King Vortigern having surveyed them from head to foot, inquired of them (what he knew well enough) whence they
came, and with what object.   Hengist being the mercury of
the twain made answer, according to the Monmouth Book, as
follows :—" Most noble King ! Saxony was the place of our
birth, and our object in coming hither was to offer our services to you, or any other Prince in want of them.   It is a
custom among us, that when our country is over-populated
we should cast lots to decide which of our young and valiant
men shall seek their fortunes somewhere else ; and the lot
having lately fallen upon us—you see us in your presence."
King Vortigern, regarding them earnestly, asked what gods
they worshipped, he himself being professedly, though not
much in practice, a Christian.   " We worship our country's
gods," says Hengist, " the chief of whom are Woden and
Friga."   Then said Vortigern, " I regret your ungodliness,
but am glad of your coming, for I am just now oppressed
with enemies on every side, and if you will aid me in putting
them down, I will entertain you honourably, and bestow upon
you lands and other distinctions."   Hengist and Horsa could
not fail of being satisfied with this arrangement ; and an army
of Picts presently breaking in upon the country from the
North, they went forth with Vortigern against them, and
enabled him to gain a complete victory.   Hengist now
thought he might advance a little on his demands ; and
although Vortigern had already bestowed on him a large
grant of land, he came to him and said " My lord King !
Your enemies are again making head, and your own subjects

love you very little. With your leave, we will send over to our own country for some more to help us; and there is also another thing I shall be glad to mention to you." "What is that?" says Vortigern. "Why," says Hengist, "the possessions you have given me in houses and lands, are certainly very large, but I have no rank conferred upon me suitable to them. I should wish to have some town or city made over to me, that I might take a title from it, and thereby find my proper place among your own nobility. "The thing you ask now is out of my power. You are strangers and Pagans, and my nobility would be highly displeased." "Nay then," says Hengist, "give me at all events so much land in addition to what I have already, as I can compass with thongs cut from a single hide to build a stronghold upon wherein I may shelter if there be need, for faithful I have been to you, and faithful I will be." "Well," said the King, "I will grant you that much." Whereon Hengist cut his thongs as narrow as he well could, and having already selected a strong, rocky position, he compassed it about, and built a strong tower thereupon, to which he gave the name of Thong Castle.

Vortigern married Rowena, the daughter of Hengist who became King of Kent, and died in 488.

Hengist and Horsa, Vortigern and Rowena, are said by some writers to be mythical persons. Nevertheless historians continue to repeat the account of their doings; as there are good reasons for believing that the commonly received accounts of the conquest, are based upon historical facts. (Archeol. Instit., 1849).

The acreage of the parish is now set down as 3,465 acres. The Tong parish in Kent, which reasonably claims to be the one connected with Hengist's stronghold, contains but 1,600 acres, and seems to be now of small account.

A picture of Thong Castle, from Merlin's book, given on another page, shows an extensive fortress occupying a site corresponding somewhat with that of the Tong Castle referred to in these notes.*　　It stands upon a triangular piece of ground formed by two streams which unite immediately below the western tower of the Castle.

THONG CASTLE : from

The Life of Merlin, surnamed Ambrosius.　His prophecies and predictions Interpreted, and their truth made good by our English annals.　Being a Chronological History from Bruti to the raigne of our Royal Sovereign King Charles, by Thos. Heywood.—London : Printed by J. Oakes, 1641.

> "*Merlin* well verst in many an hidden spell,
> His Countries *Omen* did long since foretell,
> Grac'd in his *Time* by sundry Kings he was,
> And all that *he* predicted came to passe."

*Merlin, according to Plot, being " the British Prophet who flourish't about the year 480.'

In the *British Archæological Journal*, Mr. Tucker's Report says :

The Hengist tradition is not only credible, but founded on fact. The Prophet Merlin or Ambrosius was associated with Shropshire. It is worthy of remark that the author gives the venerable Bede, and Wm. de Regibus, as authorities for this tradition. Hengist landed 449, and died 488 ; and flourished contemporaneously with Merlin. When also the locality is admitted, and the strange coincidence of the mention of the building of Tong in his life, and the representation of it on the same print with his portrait is discovered, it appears to me there is not only ground for accepting the tradition but for acknowledging its probability.

In a letter from a Kentish authority on these matters the following passage occurs :

Hengist invaded and subdued Kent. He had nothing whatever to do with Salop. The stronghold of a Saxon Chief was not a stone castle, but an earthen mound, surrounded by a moat. The mound remains at Tong in Kent, and the water remains at its foot, long utilised as a millpool and stream.

In *Domesday* book the word is spelt Tuange, and as early as 1167 the two names occur of Tong and Tong Norton, which were charged with a fine of a merk for an offence their owner had committed against the harsh Forest Laws. Twanga is mentioned by Mr Eyton as occurring 1167, and Thonk 1212; 1284 the Manor of Tugge occurs, but of many references Tong and Tonge are the most frequent. The opinion of an eminent Shropshire archæologist is, however, that the name is simply derivable from Thong-lands, *i.e.*, the lands of Thanes or Barons. May not the solution of these conflicting opinions be that the cunning device of the Saxon in Kent was imitated in Salop in a time when the rewards for great military achievements were generally the lands of the conquered ?

The great Roman Road—the Watling Street --passes through the northern part of the parish, and the spot where it leaves it (at Burlington), crossing the brook that divides the parishes of Tong and Shifnal, was, not long ago, known as Stoneyford, a name, Mr. Hartshorne says, traceable to the Roman occupation.

The first owner of Tong, of whom there is any record,
seems to have been Leofric, called Earl of Leicester, who
governed the North part of Mercia (a) ; he married the
Lady Godiva, who, with her husband, is said to have numbered
Tong among their vast possessions. Their son Algar, Earl of
Mercia (1057) married a sister of the " King of Wales," their
sons were Morcar and Edwin.

The doings of Morcar occupy so prominent a place in the
history of his time, that they may be briefly related :—

The rule of Tostig (Harold's brother) being too severe, the
Northumbrians broke into insurrection (1065) when they
elected Morcar their Earl, which act their king, Edward the
Confessor, confirmed.

The dignity and title of Earl was very rarely held, and
implied much absolute authority ; indeed Earls were little
less than Kings in the districts they governed, which were
called Shires. The Earl's duty was to lead his men to battle,
to preside with the Bishops in the Courts, and to enforce the
execution of justice. He appears to have received one-third
of the fines paid to the King.

After the nobles, in the social scale, there were two classes
of freemen—Thanes and Ceorls—the owners and cultivators
of the soil.

Thanes held lands by honourable tenure of service about
the person of their Lord, or in the field, the law requiring one
combatant from every five hides of land. A hide is said to
be as much land as one plough would cultivate in a year.

At the bottom of the scale were Serfs or born slaves
generally attached to the Manor, and sold with the land and
cattle, or sometimes used as " live money " to purchase or

(a) Mercia extended from Lond m to the Mersey and was the most powerful of the
Seven Kingdoms forming the Saxon Heptarchy.

barter goods, being valued at four times that of an ox.   What
an unhappy contrast with the present state of things !

To return to Morcar.   William I. having won the Battle of
Hastings, and devastated part of London and the southern
counties, Earl Morcar (and his brother Edwin) submitted to
him and swore allegiance at Berkhampsted. They accompanied
the King into Normandy (1067), but returned the end of the
same year.   Edwin for his services was promised the daughter
of William in marriage, but the engagement being broken
they stirred up the people against William I. ; they were
surprised before the affair was ripe, but subsequently pardoned.   Morcar joined Hereward, the banished Saxon, who
came to England, and became a rallying point for all who
were disaffected to the new government.   William I. broke
up their " Camp of Refuge " (1071).   Morcar submitted but
was condemned to perpetual imprisonment ; Edwin was slain
in an attempt to escape; thus the last effort to resist the
Conqueror was overcome, and the conquest became complete.
William I. was now bestowing his new possessions upon his
kinsmen and countrymen who had accompanied him from
Normandy, and so we find he conferred Tong upon Roger de
Montgomery (created Earl of Shrewsbury, Chichester and
Arundel) together with the greater part of the land in the
county of Salop.†

---

† Ex. Ross's History.

OWNERS OF TONG.

EARL MORCAR, elected by his countrymen Earl of Northumberland
in the reign of Edward the Confessor (1042-1066). Tong worth
£11 annually at this time. He forfeited it to the King.

KING WILLIAM I. who conferred it upon

EARL ROGER DE MONTGOMERY, his kinsman, "The Great Earl."[*]
Founded Shrewsbury Abbey. Founded or rebuilt Tong Church.
Tong fully described in Domesday Book about 1086, valued at £6
annually.[†]

EARL HUGH DE MONTGOMERY, his second son, succeeded about
1100.

EARL ROBERT DE BELESME, his elder brother, who rebelled, and
was defeated, forfeiting it to

KING HENRY I.; who bestowed it upon

RICHARD DE BELMEIS I., Bishop of London in 1108, a remarkable
man, a great jurist; he consecrated several Bishops, gave all his
revenue to complete magnificent improvements at St. Paul's Cathedral, died 1127, and was succeeded by his nephews,

RICHARD DE BELMEIS II., as to Church Lands only, He was Bishop
of London.

PHILIP DE BELMEIS (as to other lands). They founded Lilleshall
Abbey. Some of his land between Tong and Brewood was the subject of litigation; the Bishop of Lichfield claimed it—hence probably
the name Bishop's Wood. He granted lands to Buildwas Abbey;
and to Lilleshall tithes of his mills, of his herds, mares and colts,
and free paunage for swine in his woods, also advantage of his woods
for fire and building materials, and lands at Lizard Grange, the once
proposed site of Lilleshall Abbey.[‡]

PHILIP DE BELMEIS his son, died without issue, as also did

RANULF DE BELMEIS his brother, 1167.

ALICE DE BELMEIS, his sister, who married **ALAN LA ZOUCHE,**
descended from the reigning Dukes of Brittany. The land of "Lusard"
is mentioned.

(WM. DE BELMEIS, grandson of Robert, holds land at Tong, Hen. III.)

WILLIAM LA ZOUCHE alias **DE BELMEIS,** d.s.p. Forcibly ejected a
Clerk from Tong advowson, d. 1199.

---

[*] The authority of Earls, within their province, was equal to that of Royalty itself.
They granted the various Manors to Knights (or armed horsemen) whom they undertook
to protect, receiving in return certain military service, generally 40 days every year.

[†] The depreciation was probably due to the devastation attending the Conquest.
Domesday book records that there were then 3 'hides,' may be 120 acres, subject to the
Bishop's tax, and in demesne 4 ox-teams, and 13 slaves and poor people with 3 ox-teams,
an ox-team being said to be as much land as one plough would cultivate in a year.
Here was a league of wood.

[‡] "The grange" of which there are three in this Parish (Lizard, Hubbal, and Ruckley)
and many in this neighbourhood, is defined by Mrs. M. E. Walcott from an old document
of the 13th century, as "the monastic farm, and included a dove-cot, ox-houses, pig-styes,
and stables: sometimes a large one had a hall and two or three chambers abutting on it,
a kitchen and a court enclosed with a stone wall, pierced with a gateway. Some granges
were only thatch'd, others had slatt roofs." [Ex. *Shreds and Patches*, Aug. 16, 1876.]
Mr. Hartshorne also defines it as signifying originally a farmhouse or granary or farm
appertaining to a monastery, or other religious house, and thus in time the term became
identified with the place itself, hence the name, granger or store-keeper, a farmer.
Pigeons are still kept at Lizard Grange, as indeed they are at most Granges.

ROGER LA ZOUCHE alias DE BELMEIS.*   Forfeited Tong 1204 to
KING JOHN, who conferred it upon his favourite
WM. DE BRAOSE, 1204 (he had some undefined interest before in Tong).
Soon forfeited it to King John, and died an exile : his wife and son are
said to have been starved to death.   King John again confers it upon
ROGER LA ZOUCHE (before named), who had returned to allegiance, and
advanced in the King's favour : he accompanied the King on several
journeys : was bound to find 2 men to fight in the King's army in
Wales : was no less faithful to his son, Henry III.; made a grant to
Hugefort, known as the tenure of Chaplet of Roses.* Died 1238.
(HY. DE HUGEFORT, query undertenant only).
ALAN LA ZOUCHE (son of Roger). Distinguished 'for loyalty and
capacity, a great jurist, 1240.   He gave the monks pasturage for their
stock at Ruckley Grange, through all his manor of Tong, and one
swine stall in his wood of Brewde, and eight cart loads of fuel yearly,
1247.   He further gave them leave to take old stumps in Ruckley
Wood, and provided against their stock straying into his manor of
Tong : also leave to make a bridge at Ruckley : the monks gave up
certain privileges before granted, but reserved site for a mill at Timlet
Holloway.   D. 1270.
ALICE LA ZOUCHE, his sister, who married WM. DE HARCOURT, of
the blood royal of Saxony, was in 1256 prosecuted for wasting the
Abbot's trees at Lizard Grange. The Marlpit of Methplckes (? Meashill),
is mentioned.   Died 1272.
MARGERY and ORABEL DE HARCOURT, their daughters and co-
heiresses.
HENRY DE PEMBRUGE married ORABEL.   King Henry granted to his
"beloved and faithful Henry" a weekly market at Tong for three days,
at St. Bartholomew's Day.   The Pembruges came from Pembridge co.
Hereford, a family of high antiquity in that county.
FULCO DE PEMBRUGE I., only son of Orabel : his half-brother insulted
Prince Edmund at Warwick, and was imprisoned in the dungeons of
Wigmore : 1282, is not yet 12 years old, 1284 holds the manor of
Tugge with the vill of Norton.   The capital messuage valued at
5s., the fish in the Vivary (i.e. a place for keeping them alive) at
2s. 8d., the Dovecot at 1s. 8d.,† and the Water Mill at £2 per year.
The Mill was below the Castle in all probability : of rents mentioned, is
the Chaplet of Roses.
FULCO DE PENEBRUGGE II., b. 1292, d. 1326. His mother, Lady of
Tong, 1297, occurs in a return, as liable in respect of her property of
£20 or over, to be summoned to perform military service with horse and
arms, in parts beyond the seas.   Fulco claimed right to fix weight and
price of bread and beer, and to hold a market and fair at Tong.   Of
age in 1312.   In 1314, as a Knight and Lord of Tong, gives to Bishop

---

* He did by a fair deed under his seal on which was his pourtraiture on Horseback in a
Military Habit, grant unto Henry Hugefort, and his Heirs, three Yards-lands, 3 Messuages,
and certain Woods in *Norton* and *Shaw* in this Parish of Tonge, with Paunage for a great
Number of Hogs in the Woods belonging to this, his Manor, also Liberty of Fishing in all
his Waters there, except in the *great Pool of Tonge*, with other Privileges, viz :— of
gathering Nuts in his Woods there, &c., rendering yearly to him the said Roger and his
Heirs a *Chaplet of Roses* upon the Feast of the Nativity of St. John the Baptist, in case
he or they shall be at Tonge, if not then to be put upon the image of the blessed Virgin in
the Church of Tonge for all services, suits of Court, &c [Ex Magna Brit.] In Dukes
Lloyd's Shropshire I find a note that the great Pool was a Meadow in 1736, but I am
unable to identify it.

† A dove-house stands in and still gives a name to part of the Park at Tong, between the
Castle and Church.

of Coventry and Lichfield a plot of wood (? near Brewood).   Confirms
free road for the monks' sheep and animals from their farm (or grange),
at Ruckley, to their pasture at Donington ; also to make a fence and
bridge, and site for a mill at Timlet.   In 1313, he had King's pardon for
joining the Earl of Lancaster.   1319, licence to exchange 10 acres with
Prioress of White Ladies.   1322, a Knight representing Salop at York
Parliament, and later for Gloucester at second York Parliament.
1323-1326, summoned to levy archers, and engaged in several offices
and counsels.   D. 1326, leaving a son, aged 15.

FULK DE PEMBRUGE III., 1333.   Lawsuit against him by his mother
Matilda de Bermingham ; Fulk defeated.

ROBERT DE PEMBRUGE (brother and heir), said to occur 1346-7, occurs
1351.

FULK DE PEMBRUGE IV., see Tomb 12.   1371-1410.

ELIZABETH DE PEMBRUGE, Lady of Tong, his widow, see Tomb 12.

SIR RICHARD VERNON, Fulke's nephew and successor, see Tomb 13.

SIR WILLIAM VERNON, his son, see Tomb 14,

SIR HARRY VERNON, his son, see Tomb 15.

RICHARD VERNON, ESQ., his son, see Tomb 17.

SIR GEORGE VERNON, his son, King of the Peak, owned 30 manors
(buried at Bakewell, near Haddon 1565).

DOROTHY & MARGARET VERNON, his daughters and co-heiresses.
Dorothy eloped with Sir John Manners, upon the night of her sister's
marriage, and conveyed Haddon to the House of Rutland.

MARGARET married HON. SIR THOMAS STANLEY, see Tomb 19.

SIR EDWARD STANLEY, their son, succeeded, and died in 1632.   He
sold Tong to

SIR THOMAS HARRIES, Bart., Serjeant-at-Law.   See referred to under
Tombs 23 and 31.

ANN AND ELIZABETH, his daughters and co-heiresses.   Ann married
John Wylde, Esq., and died 1624, aged 16, see Tomb 23.   Tong
Castle passed to

ELIZABETH, who married THE HON. WILLIAM PIEREPOINT of
Thoresby, Notts., "William the Wise," see under No. 31.   He succeeded, 1640 ; was described as "of Tong Castle."   He died 1679,
and his three grandsons became successively Earls of Kingston, viz :
Robert, died 1682, William 1690, and

GERVASE, LORD PIERPOINT, their youngest son, gained a peerage, see
No. 24.   His only child. Elizabeth Pierpoint, having pre-deceased him,
see under No. 31, Lord Pierpoint died in 1715, when his nephew,

EVELYN, 5th EARL OF KINGSTON, created 1st DUKE OF KINGSTON
succeeded as Lord of Tong.   He was father of Lady Mary Wortley
Montague so celebrated in the literary world.   His son William died
before his father 1713, leaving a son,

EVELYN, last DUKE OF KINGSTON, owner of Tong Castle, and had
his seat there.   He married the celebrated Miss Chudleigh, but left
no issue and on his death in 1773 all his titles became extinct.   He,
in 1760, sold Tong to

GEORGE DURANT, ESQ., of a Worcestershire family, who amassed a large
fortune at Havannah.   Reconstructed the Castle as now to be seen.
See Tomb 30.   He died 1780 aged 46.

GEORGE DURANT, a minor at his father's death.   He had issue a son
George Stanton Eld Durant, who pre-deceased him, but leaving a son,

GEORGE CHARLES SELWYN DURANT, who sold Tong 1855 to the
Earl of Bradford.

THE EARL OF BRADFORD'S FAMILY.

GEORGE A. F. H. BRIDGEMAN, EARL OF
BRADFORD, 2nd Earl of the 1815 creation, D.C.L., descended from Sir Orlando Bridgeman, Kt. and Bart., a lawyer
of great eminence, and Keeper of the Great Seal, 1657, son of
the Right Rev. John, Bishop of Chester, 1619—1657,—a family,
whose seat at Weston Park has passed to them by inheritance
from the De Westons (Knight Templars) of Weston, whose
effigies in heart-of-oak still remain in the chancel of Weston
Church, through the Newports, Wilbrahams, Myttons, and
Peshalls.   The Earl married Georgina Elizabeth only
daughter of Sir Thomas Moncreiffe and Lady Elizabeth
Ramsay.' In 1865 the Earl died, when Tong passed to

ORLANDO GEORGE CHARLES BRIDGEMAN, 3rd
EARL OF BRADFORD, Viscount Newport and Baron
Bradford, of Bradford, co. Salop ; a Baronet, Privy Councillor,
Lord Lieutenant and Custos Rotulorum of Shropshire ; whose
first official appointment was in the administration of the
Earl of Derby ; and later in those of the Earl of Beacons-
field, K.G., having held the high offices of Lord
Chamberlain (1866-8), and Master of the Horse to Her
Majesty the Queen 1874-80 and again in 1885-6. He repre-
sented South Shropshire in Parliament twenty-three years,
until his accession to the peerage. Born 24th April, 1819.
Married 30th April, 1844, the Hon. Selina Louisa Weld
Forester, daughter of Cecil, 1st Lord Forester.

The COUNTESS OF BRADFORD is the youngest
daughter of Cecil, first Lord Forester (created Baron
Forester, of Willey Park, co. Salop, in 1821) by his wife,
Lady Katherine Manners, daughter of Charles, the 4th Duke
of Rutland, K.G.   Her ladyship's brothers, George, second
Lord, and Cecil, third Lord Forester, died without issue,
the present Lord Forester (Orlando Watkin Weld) being a
Canon of York.   This nobleman has an hereditary privilege,
granted by Henry VIII., of wearing his hat in the presence

of the Sovereign. It was made to John Forester, of Upton
and Easthope, in 1520, by licence "to use and were his bonet
on his hede at all tymes and in all places, as well in our
presence as elsewhere."   The name of Forester is derived
from Richard Forestarius, who had charge of the King's
Forest of Wellington Hay in Shropshire, in the reign of
Henry III.—an appointment of trust conferred by the King
when penalties of death were frequently inflicted upon persons
guilty of breach of the Forest Laws. A younger brother of
the Countess of Bradford is the Hon. Henry Townshend
Forester (b. 19 Jan., 1821), the well-known patron of the turf.
Lady Bradford's sisters were:—The Hon. Anne Elizabeth,
who became Countess of Chesterfield; the Hon. Elizabeth
Katherine, married Hon. Robert John Smith, afterwards 2nd
Baron Carrington; the Hon. Isabella Elizabeth Annabella,
married Gen. the Hon. Geo. Anson, and died leaving three
daughters, Countess Howe, Hon. Mrs. George Fitzwilliam,
and the Marchioness of Bristol; and the Hon. Henrietta
Maria, who married Lord Albert Conyngham, created Baron
Londesborough. The Forester arms are *argent*, a bugle horn
sable, garnished with gold, a token of their office. Some
further account of the Forester Family who were owners of
part of Tong Parish will be given later.

. The Earl's eldest son, GEORGE CECIL ORLANDO,
VISCOUNT NEWPORT, born Feb. 3rd, 1845, represented
North Shropshire in the House of Commons from 1867 to 1885,
and is known as a fluent and graceful speaker, and one of the
best shots in England. He lives at Castle Bromwich. His
lordship's Silver Wedding day is in 1894, he having married
on Sept. 7, 1869, Lady Ida Frances Annabella Lumley, second
daughter of Richard George, 9th Earl of Scarbrough, by his
wife Frederica Mary Adeliza Drummond; Lady Newport's
brothers and sisters being the present Earl of Scarbrough,
Lady Algitha, wife of Hon. Wm. Orde Powlett, heir to Lord

Bolton ; the Marchioness of Zetland, Countess Grosvenor, and the Hon. Osbert Lumley. Lord Newport has issue : Sons—the Hon. Orlando (b. 6 Oct. 1873), Hon. Richard Orlando Beaconsfield, (b. 1879, god-son to Benjamin Disraeli, Earl of Beaconsfield), and Hon. Henry Geo. Orlando (b. 1882); daughters—the Hon. Beatrice Adine (b. 1870), the Hon. Margaret Alice (b. 1872, now Countess of Dalkeith), Hon. Helena Mary (b. 1875, god-daughter of H.R.H. Princess Christian), Hon. Florence Sibell (b. 1877). The Hon. Orlando Bridgeman made a voyage round the world in 1893, and all will welcome the attainment of his majority this year ; while the Hon. Richard is a Naval Cadet. The Hon. Margaret married January 30, 1893, John Charles, Earl of Dalkeith, son and heir to the Duke of Buccleuch, and has issue Margaret Ida, born Nov. 13, 1893. Lord Newport accompanied the Duke of Abercorn on his Special Mission from Her Majesty to the King of Italy, in 1878.

The Earl's younger son, the HON. FRANCIS CHARLES BRIDGEMAN, born 4th July, 1846, is a retired Lieutenant Colonel of the Scots Guards, was engaged in the Soudan War, and is M.P. for Bolton. He married 26th July, 1883, Gertrude Cecilia, eldest daughter of George Hanbury, Esq., of Blythwood, and has issue Reginald Francis Orlando (b. 1884), Francis Paul Orlando, Humphrey Herbert Orlando, and Selina Adine. He resides at Neachley. He accompanied the Earl of Rosslyn's Special Mission to the King of Spain.

The Earl's elder daughter, LADY MABEL SELINA, married Lieut. Col. William Slaney KENYON-SLANEY, M.P. for the Newport Division of Shropshire, of Hatton Grange, Salop, and has issue Sybil (b. 1888), and Robert Orlando Rodolph (b. Jan. 13, 1892).

The younger daughter, LADY FLORENCE KATH-ERINE, married in 1881 Henry Viscount Lascelles, and is now Countess of Harewood, having issue a son, Henry Viscount Lascelles (b. 1882), Lady Margaret Selina (b. 1883), and Hon. Edward Cecil (b. 1887).

THE BRIDGEMAN FAMILY.

ORLANDO, 1st Earl of Bradford (who succeeded as
second Baron Bradford, and was created an earl in 1815),
married Lucy Elizabeth, daughter of George, fourth Viscount
Torrington, and Lady Lucy Boyle, daughter of John, Earl of
Cork and Orrery, an old Irish family. Orlando's father, Sir
Henry Bridgeman, Bart., was created first Baron Bradford in
1794. He married Elizabeth, daughter and heiress of the Rev.
John Simpson, of Stoke Hall, County Derby, and her second
son, John Bridgeman, married Henrietta (only daughter of
Sir Thomas Worsley, Bart.), a great heiress, who took the
name of Simpson, and thus founded the Bridgeman-Simpson
family. A delightful miniature of this lady, Miss Worsley, is
in the possession of Lady Bradford, and called " The Heiress
of Appuldercombe."

Sir Henry Bridgeman was the eldest son of Sir Orlando
Bridgeman (of Castle Bromwich and Blodwell, Bart.)
and Lady Anne Newport. She was a sister of the three last
Earls of Bradford, of the Newport family, which title became
extinct on the death of Thomas, fifth Earl of Bradford, in
1762.

. The Newport estates held by Henry Newport, third Earl
of Bradford, Lady Anne's eldest brother, who died without issue, were of enormous extent, but were alienated by him
from the family very largely. Lady Anne's sister, Diana,
Countess of Mountrath, succeeded to a great part of the
London property, including the Park of Isleworth, called the
New Park of Richmond, and also Twickenham Park, with
the mansion-house therein. This lady bequeathed all her
cattle, sheep, and horses, corn, grain, hay, wine, ale, and all
liquors and stores in her house to Lucy, Duchess of Montrose.
Her other properties included Walsall, Tamehorn, Manors of
Newton, Bobbington, &c., some of which happily reverted to
the descendants of her sister, Lady Anne Bridgeman.

Sir Orlando Bridgeman was the son of Sir John Bridgeman, third Baronet, and Ursula, daughter and sole heiress of Roger Matthews, Esq., of Blodwell Hall, Salop, a descendant of the Princes of Powys and Wales. Roger was the son of John Matthews, Esq., of Court, and Jane, elder daughter and co-heir of Morris Tanat, of Blodwell, County Salop. These Tanats, of Blodwell, were seated at Abertanat, and took their name from the sparkling river Tanat, a famous trout stream. A part of the picturesque Tanat Valley in the Marches of Wales, forms a portion of Lord Bradford's ancestral estate.

Morris Tanat was descended from "Einion-Efell," who resided at Llwynymaen, near Oswestry, Salop, and was Lord of Cynllaeth, who died in 1196. He was second son of Madoc-ap-Meredith, Prince of Powys, son and heir of Meredith-ap-Bleddyn, Prince of Powys, 1132. He was son and successor of Bleddyn-ap-Cynfyn and Haer, daughter of Cilin-ap-y-Blaidd Rhud, surnamed "The Wolf." Bleddyn-ap-Cynfyn, Prince of Powys, by inheritance, and Prince of North Wales and South Wales by usurpation, was fourth in descent from Mervyn, King of Powys, third son of Rhodri Mawr (or the Great), King of Wales, A.D., 843, and died 847.

Reverting to the family of Bridgeman, and tracing it a little further it will be seen that Sir John, second Baronet (who bought the Castle Bromwich estate), was son of Sir Orlando Bridgeman, Bart., and Judith Kynaston, daughter and heiress of John Kynaston, Esq., also descended from the great King of Wales. The Kynastons, an ancient Shropshire family, trace back through Humphrey Kynaston "The Wild" (1534), through Griffith (of Cae Howell and Kynaston, Salop), to Jorwerth Goch, surnamed "The Red," son of Meredydd-ap-Bleddyn, Prince of Powys. It is curious that the Newport family also trace through a female co-heiress back to Meredydd-ap-Bleddyn.

Thomas Newport, Esq., ancestor of the Earls of Bradford, married Elizabeth, one of the co-heiresses of Sir John de Burgh, Knight of Mawddy, son of Elizabeth, daughter of John, Lord of Mawddy, son of William-ap-Griffith, son of Griffith-ap-Wenwynwyn, son of Gwenwynwyn, Prince of Powys-wenwynwyn (17 Ed. I.) by Margaret, daughter of Rhys, Prince of South Wales.

Gwenwynwyn was grandson of Griffith-ap-Meredith, son of Meredith-ap-Bleddyn, Prince of Powys. Another sister of Elizabeth, viz., Eleanor, married Thos. Mytton, Esq., M.P., an ancestor of the Myttons, of Weston-under-Lizard, whose heiress is a direct ancestress of the present owner of Weston.

Sir Orlando Bridgeman, the lawyer of great eminence, was successively Lord Chief Baron of the Exchequer, Lord Chief Justice of the Common Pleas, and Lord Keeper of the Great Seal. His father, Dr. John Bridgeman, chaplain to King James I., was, after filling many Church offices, translated to the See of Chester, 1619, but was driven to take refuge with his son, Sir Orlando, at Morton Hall, and died there, the ancestral home of his daughter-in-law, Judith Kynaston, in 1652. During the troublous times of the Civil War, Clarendon tells how "the City of Chester remained true to his Majesty, influenced thereto by the credit and example of Bishop John Bridgeman, and the reputation and dexterity of his son Orlando, a lawyer of very good estimation." Sir Orlando's charge to the jury at the trial of the regicides was highly extolled—indeed, as Chief Justice of the Common Pleas his reputation was at its zenith, and " his moderation and equity were such that he seemed to carry a chancery in his breast."

EARLY CLERGY, &c.

1188-1194 ERNULF . . . . . Chaplain, had the Parsonage.

1215-1220 ROBERT DE SHIREFORD, Parson.

1255 WILLIAM . . . . Parson of Tong : he impleaded a layman as he did not supply boots (?) to his wish. Church of Tong valued at £4.

1410 Church built and College founded : Wm. Shaw or Wm. Mosse, Warden.

1411 WALTER SWAN, Minister.

1416 KING HENRY V. gave the revenues of Lapley town, manor and grange, to the College of Tong, provided Lapley Vicarage be sufficiently endowed, and a competent sum allowed to the poor there.

1454 SIR RICHARD EITON, Priest ; Warden of the College.

1470 MASTER JOHN LYE, Warden of Tong, made - vicar of Idsall. Died, 1515.

1510 RALPH ELCOCK died ; cellarer and co-brother.

1518 SIR ARTHUR VERNON, Priest ; Warden of the College.

1526 THOMAS FORSTER, died; sometime Warden of Tongue and Vicar of Idsall. See curious monument at Shifnal Church.

1535 College valued at £22 8s. 1d. a year.

1546 College sold for £200 to J. WOOLRICH.

1547 Deed of Sale signed by K. EDWARD VI.

1616 Register dates from.

1639 GEO. MEESON, Clerk of Tong.

1641 WILLIAM SOUTHALL, Rector.

1658 ROBERT HILTON, Minister.

1676 RICHARD WARDE, Minister.

1678 WM. COTTON, Curate.

1688 L. PEITIER appointed Minister. Died, 1745.

1694 JOHN HULTER, Curate of Tong, buried.

1765 S. HALL died: 35 years Assistant Curate.

1777 THOS. BUCKERIDGE, Minister of Tong.

1785 THOS. LAWRENCE. Curate of Tong.

1791 CHAS. BUCKERIDGE, D.D.

1806 W. H. MOLINEUX, Perpetual Curate of Tong.

1807 JOHN FLETCHER MUCKLESTON, M.A., afterwards D.D.

1835 THOS. HALL, Curate.

1839 LEONARD HENRY St. GEORGE,

1843 GEO. SHIPTON HARDING.

1855 JOHN WINGFIELD HARDING.

1870 RICHARD GWYNNE LAWRENCE.

1876 CHARLES T. WILSON.

1882 GEO. CLENELL RIVETT-CARNAC who married a granddaughter of the poet Crabbe.

1890 JOHN HENRY COURTNEY CLARKE present vicar, late Major of the Royal Fusiliers. Churchwardens : THOS. MILNER, jun, and G. F. NORTON. Lectors : COL. HON. F. C. BRIDGEMAN, M P., and MR. H. P. SMITH. Clerk : GEO. BODEN. Schoolmaster : THOS. GREENER.

TONG CHURCH.

HE present stately edifice which forms so
pleasing a feature in the village and lands-
cape, is one of few in the country that remain to us without bearing traces of that
destruction which is the natural outcome
of opposing forces of men ; and it is remarkable, looking back upon the struggles
of 500 years, to think there should be
found in a country village so fine a specimen of Gothic
architecture in practically. as good (*i.e.* unrestored) state now
as at the time of its erection ; and this applies almost as well
to the interior as the exterior. The present building, worthily
described as a venerable pile, is a pure and beautiful example
of the Early Perpendicular.

There seems to be no doubt that Earl Roger de Montgomery,
the great Earl (and " a very prudent and moderate man," as an
old chronicle describes him), founded a church here in the reign
of William the Conqueror, within 8 years of Domesday. It is
not clear whether his work was carried on or added to by his
second son and successor, Earl Hugh, or whether the great
bishop and statesman, Richard de Belmeis I., Bishop of London,
who had a grant of Tong a little later, and spent all his resources
in beautifying and improving St. Paul's Cathedral and the
Clerkenwell Priory, had any part in completing the church ;
but in the present building there are traces of work which are

Tong church
from the east

The Stanley tomb
Tong.

E.H.N.

referred, on good authority, to a date at least a century earlier than that of the general fabric as it now stands.

To the pious benevolence of a lady, a widow, we are indebted for this rich and valuable example of Gothic architecture; rich on account of the undisturbed condition of its component parts, thus enabling us to see the church in practically the same condition as that in which it was left by the monkish designer, and valuable in affording the student sufficient concurrent details of the work for his instruction and guidance, with the view to their imitation elsewhere; thus it must awaken a more than ordinary interest in the casual visitor. In short, Tong Church is a building of national interest, and contains monuments rarely to be found in edifices of the like proportions.

Elizabeth, widow of Sir Fulke de Pembruge, Knight, with two clerks, had in the 12th year of King Henry IV., 1411, his license to acquire of the Abbot and Convent of Shrewsbury the advowson and patronage of the Church of St. Bartholomew the Apostle, at Tonge in Shropshire, reserving to the Abbot and Convent an annual pension they were used to receive of 6s. 8d. to convert the said Church into a perpetual college, with warden, chaplains, &c.; the amount paid by Elizabeth being £50, a large sum of money in those days.*

The College stood south of the Church, and seems to have occupied four sides of a square. It must have covered a good deal of ground, judging by the twenty or more people who lived in it, besides the accommodation for the children who were to be taught there. (See account later of Tong College and its rules and regulations.)

The Church thus made over to the widow of the Lord of Tong was made Collegiate, and by her dedicated, as some

---

*Mr. Cox gives the amount £40, paid into the Hanaper, i.e., the King's Exchequer. The Hanaper was a kind of basket used in early days by the Kings of England for holding and carrying the money as they journeyed from place to place.

accounts say, " to the worship and glory of God and in memory of her husband." Built of a durable local stone, evincing little or no decay, it consists as the plan shews of chancel and choir, nave, north and south aisles, vestry and porch. The Golden Chapel adjoining the south transept was added a century later, and is the only part of the building which dates subsequent to the time of Dame Elizabeth. In the centre, supported upon four lofty pointed arches, rises a curious steeple, which above the roof is square, and contains in the lower story the Great Bell of Tong. Upon this springs an octagon, forming the upper bell-story, containing the peal of bells, the whole finished with an elegant spire.

In a report to the *Archæological Journal* of 1845, the following remarks by Mr. Petit occur, and will best complete the description of the edifice :—

" The building affords a striking instance how completely the mediæval architect felt the importance of scale as well as proportion. In a large church the simplicity of detail in this church would have given an unpleasing degree of plainness. In a larger church much that is now excellent would have been meagre and minute. The flattened roof is here a decided beauty, as it not only gives effect to the embattled parapet and pinnacles (which, when the finials were complete, must have been very beautiful), but to the steeple itself ; and had this steeple been of more tapering form, the range of spire lights, which are perhaps nearly unique, would have been out of place.

" The building is essentially a cross-church, yet it neither developes the form of a cross in its ground plan, nor indicates it, as it might have done, by transepts distinguished from the aisles. Such examples are far from common.

" The following discrepancies are remarkable in a building which exhibits so much uniformity in design and carefulness in execution :—

" Difference in north and south ranges of arches in the nave.

" Mouldings at base of piers differ, though the capitals are nearly alike.

" External divisions do not correspond with internal ones, for the parapet along nave is divided by the pinnacles into two equal parts, whereas the interior has three arches between west wall and west pier of tower.

" Width of the two aisles differs a few inches ; and the east window does not stand in the exact centre of the front.

" The base of the tower is not exactly square, nor is the octagon equal-sided ; the equilateral spire is more nearly, if not altogether so, which renders necessary a peculiar construction at its junction with the octagon." This is illustrated in the *Archæological Journal.*

The following interesting note upon Tong Church occurs in Mrs. Halliday's work on the *Porlock Effigies.*

" This is no church of the common order, but a theme for the painter and poet. Situated in a slightly undulating and beautifully wooded country, it is on the whole a building which embodies more of the true mediæval feeling than perhaps any other we still possess. Besides many features of interest, such as the Vernon Chapel, with its beautiful fan-traceried vaulting, the abbatial-looking stalls, with their richly-sculptured poppyheads and western return ends, and several highly-wrought screens, it contains no less than seven elaborate altar-tombs, forming, along with the surrounding architecture, such picturesque groups as true artists like Louis Haghe or David Roberts would have delighted in. Thanks, as I am informed, to the protecting arm of the Earl of Bradford, it has been shielded from the destroying inroads of the dilettante 'restorer,' the interested 'architect,' and the cheap contractor."

THE RESTORATION.

ITH regard to the Restoration of the Church in 1892, it must surely be a great satisfaction to know that no old features have disappeared nor old arrangements been extinguished, but that the work, under the direction of the eminent architect, Mr. Christian, has been done thoroughly and well, and in a true conservative spirit. The cost, about £5,000, has been chiefly borne by the Earl of Bradford, the patron. The Vicar, the Rev. J. H. Courtney Clarke, Mrs. Hartley and her friends, the Churchwardens, and the parishioners all must share in the credit which is due for collecting the monies to commence this great undertaking, and one which the Committee found was too great for their resources. This mediæval fabric, substantially " a gem of the middle ages," is again made good, and the ravages of time are stopped ; and patron, priest, and people are to be congratulated upon the achievement of a noble duty, and one which hands on to posterity a monument alike of the Foundress's bounty, of the Ecclesiastic's devotion to art and religion, and of the present patron's munificence. The performance of such a work earns our present gratitude, it multiplies our inherent veneration, and lovingly consecrates the edifice anew to the holy offices of successive generations.

Traces of one tiny patch of ancient mural painting too indistinct to be of any value whatever, were found on the wall of the nave, when cleaning the walls of the ugly colour which hitherto had disfigured them.

A few modern pews which marred the appearance of the old oak benches have been removed, and the latter with their traceried panels refixed in a little more convenient manner. .

The flooring is entirely new, and the gradual rise of the level of it from the West end to the East, which was so marked and uncommon, has been adhered to.

The various discoveries in the Golden Chapel and elsewhere will be found noted in their places under the headings.

A valuable old book of Homilies was found by the Vicar, and also a note that the Royal Arms in the North Wall cost over £60. The workmen also found two old silver coins, one of Queen Elizabeth's reign, during the restoration.

The builder and contractor for the general work of Restoration in 1892 was Mr. William Bowdler, of Shrewsbury, who also undertook the carving and restoration of the choir stalls and screens, with a success most visible. Mr. Robert Bridgeman, of Lichfield, has re-erected the "Stanley" tomb, and done other work to the altar-tombs. The mediæval stained glass which was all scattered about in a fragmentary way in various windows, has been collected and re-arranged by Messrs. Pepper & Boyd, of London.

The Restoration has consisted of a thorough renewal of the roofs, the old lead having been re-cast, and new oak timbers put in where needed, preserving all old carvings ; the Tower stone-work partly rebuilt, the walls entirely cleaned inside and repaired, as also the damaged tracery of the West window, which was long an eye-sore, and caused many anxieties to visitors. A few missing pinnacles have been supplied, and the parapets, vane, and clock repaired.

Numerous other works have been done, and include heating, with new chamber near the ruins of the ancient Almshouse, the general reflooring, reglazing, new ceiling to tower, &c., &c., and at the close of the work, it was a matter of congratulation to be able to announce that a piece of land had been given by Lord Bradford to enlarge the burial ground.

E

PORCH. Ancient stone seats on either side. Fine old oak ceiling with well-carved bosses, pediment, and shields for arms.

1. Door with considerable mouldings. A two-light window on either side, neither of which Mr. Christian thinks has ever been glazed; old saddle-bars.

2. SOUTH DOOR of Church exhibits some mouldings. Over it is a recessed niche for a statuette of the patron saint.

SOUTH AISLE. Probably the pillars carrying the arches forming the arcade between aisle and nave are older than any other part of the church. Notice dog-tooth ornament on cap of pillar **3**, and the labels of the arches at **4** and **5**. These features, Mr. Petit says, in his report to the Archæological Journal, may be referred to the 13th century (*i.e.*, prior to 1300), and he suspects that the present south aisle originally formed the nave of the earlier church founded by Earl Roger de Montgomery, as the south side of the pillars is more ornamented than the north, which perhaps faced the north aisle of the older edifice. Oak roof with carving. Tracery in windows.

Generally, notice the OLD OAK SEATS and panelling of same with tracery; most of them remain in their proper

Tong Church. East Window and Screens.

Whiteladies
E.H.N.
Font. Tong church
Seal of the
Lady Foundress
E.H.N.

positions, but were rearranged in 1892, when modern seats were removed. The tile flooring is entirely new, but a tiled floor of much older date was discovered in the north aisle when erecting the new organ a few years ago. Tong once possessed a beautiful Gothic organ, described later under " Organ."

6. NAVE. Take a general view of the interior from this spot. Notice old oak roof, with carved bosses at the intersections. The ranges of arches on the right and left are dissimilar, a common occurrence in mediæval work.

7. WEST DOORWAY, formerly closed, but re-opened in 1892. There was found concealed by plaster a very old rough boarding in this doorway, and in it a very small door, 4ft. 6in. high, with double ogee head and rude hinges, and above it, WEST WINDOW. It has five lights, enriched in the upper part with debased Perpendicular tracery, and retains fragments of old stained glass. Subject " We praise Thee, O God."

8. FONT. Old octagonal one of simple design, but good workmanship; each face exposed has a trefoiled arch corresponding with the sedilia arches, and a shield. A hinge and catch still remain, probably appertaining to the old cover. The Font is made a little more accessible, but remains in the same position as usual, viz. : against the north-west pillar. There is a step for the priest, and one for the sponsor handing up the child.

NORTH AISLE, oak roof, carved; old oak seats. Tracery in windows.

A slab found in 1892 beneath the floor of the north aisle bears " Here lieth the body of Thomas Poole, who departed this life Oct. the 21st ano., 1739, aged 51 years." Another slab found near the west door bears " Here lieth the body of Walter Clay, son of Walter and Margaret Clay, who departed this life April ye . . . . 1735, aged 18 years."

There has also been found during the restoration in 1892 an interesting incised slab representing, I believe, a priest, having on his arm the maniple, and a dog at foot. Some large letters

LE WARDE . . . ERC . . . J

are upon it in very old character, which may allude to a Warden of Tong College. Various dates have been assigned to this slab, viz., 8th, 9th, or 12th century. It is now fixed in the floor of north transept, where antiquaries may view, and perhaps enlighten us upon it.

9. NORTH DOORWAY, now closed, and in it notice the fragment of an old tomb now destroyed, comprising a shield of alabaster, with angels supporting it, and at the side some architectural features, twisted column, &c., of stone. The length of fingers and other characteristics have led some visitors to give an opinion that this is the oldest piece of sculpture in the Church. A somewhat, but not exactly similar fragment is to be seen at east end of No. 12 tomb.

10a & b. WOOD SCREENS in north and south aisles dividing them so as to form Chapels in which particular services were said by the Roman Catholics. These screens are in the form of the letter **L** (see plan) and are "of very rich workmanship, with the colours well preserved, and only mellowed and toned down by time," Mr. Petit says. The north aisle screen **10a** is ornamented only on the side facing the west, and was a good deal damaged, but repaired in 1892. It consists of a central arched opening over the path of the aisle, and on each side of it running north and south are three open traced divisions (time of Henry VII.), the piece returned to the pillar of tower consisting also of three divisions; the lower part of screen being of traced panelling, corresponding with the tracery above : the crenulated cornice has carved foliage, and a cresting of Tudor character.

10b. The south aisle screen, the richer of the two, has four openings on either side of the central one, and three returned to the pillar, all of delicate tracery. (Transitional; about 1400). On the side of it facing the west wall is a cornice (acorns and foliage), and below it is a carved string-course of laurel; on the other side the vine. John Babyn is carved in letters 4in. long upon the transom of this screen, in Tudor character. A step is observable from the aisle into the south chapel, but not in the north one.

11. DOORWAY TO BELFRY.

The next object of interest is the oldest altar tomb, and before describing it in detail it will be well to note that the effigies herein described belong to a period of continuous warfare, when the custom of wearing complete armour necessitated the use of heraldic devices; therefore a little note or word has been occasionally inserted, to explain certain objects which at the time of the erection of the monuments had a purpose and signification well known to *all* beholders. Of effigies generally the following prefatory remarks by Mr. C. A. Stothard (author of the *Monumental Effigies of Great Britain*) will enable anyone to appreciate the value of these monuments :—" With very few exceptions, effigies are the only portraits we possess of heroes and others in the ages famed for chivalry and arms. Thus considered they make us acquainted with the customs and habits of the time. To history they give a body and a substance, by placing before us those things which language is deficient in describing."

In the beginning of the 14th century effigies are first met with in full relief. It was generally the custom to bury the dead in the dress which marked the habits of their lives, and so we find Knights who held their lands by so many days military service represented in military costume, their suit of armour descending from sire to son, or sometimes being bequeathed as a rich legacy. The first body armour was composed entirely of " mail," *i.e.*, links interlaced, when the weapons of the rank and file were bows and arrows—" English shafts in volleys hailed "; this was succeeded by a mixture of " mail and plate " armour, and finally " plate " entirely. The head was covered by a steel cap or helmet, having a narrow slit in the form of a cross to allow of vision and respiration.

12. SIR FULKE DE PEMBRUGE AND DAME ELIZABETH. GOTHIC ALTAR TOMB, mostly of alabaster, with recumbent effigies representing Sir Fulke de Pembruge, Knight of Tong Castle, and his second wife, Dame Elizabeth (or Isabella), daughter and heir of Sir Ralphe Lingen, of Wigmore.

This, the first and oldest of the altar-tombs at Tong, is the one under the north arch of tower, and originally beneath the rood loft,—an honourable place of interment, I suppose, for Chaucer relates of a Knight that " He lith y grave under the rode-beem."* It rests upon a sandstone base, and is one of the four monuments described in the *Archæological Journal* before referred to, and in this guide numbered **12, 13, 14, 17.** " They are," the report says, " four monuments *invaluable* as representing a series of Perpendicular work, each specimen being characteristic of the period to which it belongs. The first, though executed with great care (the minutest details of costume being elaborately worked), is comparatively severe and simple in its design, having more a massive than an ornate character."

The Male Effigy :—

Sir Fulke was Lord of Tong 1371, and died May 24, 1409—the last of his line.

---

*Archbishop Courtenay (1396) bequeathed his body to be buried in front of the rood loft, but subsequently revoked that part of his will, by a death-bed codicil, averring that he was not worthy.

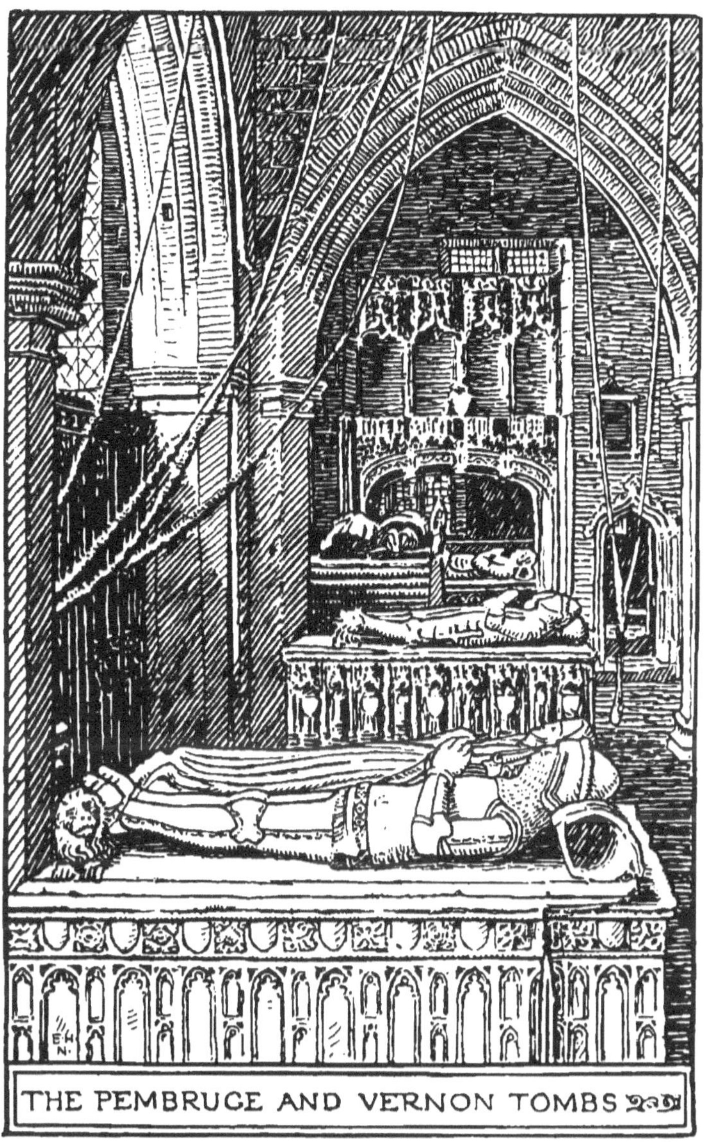

THE PEMBRUGE AND VERNON TOMBS

He is clad in armour, partly mail and partly plate—a fact which helps to fix the date of the effigy closely.

> For men at arms were here,
> Heavily sheathed in mail and plate,
> Like iron towers for strength and weight.
>> *Sir Walter Scott.*

> Ful worthy was he in his lordes werre,
> And thereto hadde beridden, no man ferre.†
>> *Chaucer.*

"The Knight rests his head upon the 'helm' or helmet whereon was the crest, viz.,—a Turkish woman's head, with a wreath about her temples, her hair plaited and hanging below her shoulders." This helmet would completely conceal the Knight's face, and so warriors wore crests upon their helmets, and coats of arms, to distinguish them from one another on the field of battle.

> Then marked they, dashing broad and far,
> The broken billows of the war,
> The plumèd crests of chieftains brave,
> Floating like foam upon the wave ;
> But nought distinct they see :
> Spears shook, and falchions flashed amain ;
> Fell England's arrow-flight like rain ;
> Crests rose, and stooped, and rose again,
>> Wild and disorderly.
>> *Sir Walter Scott.*

Helmets were made of certain different kinds, distinguishing the rank of the warrior. The placing of a helmet beneath the head of the Knight—with his gauntlets laid by his side, as on tomb 17—is suggested by the soldier's actual practice when asleep in camp. Notice the mantlet worn upon the helmet to protect it from stains or rust. The mantlet took the place of the contoise, which disappeared from use about the middle of the fourteenth century. The "contoise" was a coloured scarf, "the lady's favour" or "token" given by her to the knight before he set out to fight. The welding of the joints of the helm is so arranged as to form a cross, a favourite emblem in the middle ages. At the feet of the Knight is a lion, emblem of courage.

---

† *i.e.* further.

The Female Effigy :—

His second (?) wife, Dame Elizabeth de Lingen, described as a widow, and " Lady of Tonge," was the great benefactress of Tong, and survived him. Sir Fulke Pembruge's first wife was Margaret, daughter and eventual sole heiress of Sir William Trussell, of Cublesdon, and of Sheriff Hales, Knight.

Dame Elizabeth, about 1410, caused to be built the present Collegiate Church (except the Golden Chapel), and richly endowed it—as more fully described elsewhere. She died 1446-7, and was buried beside her husband. Her effigy is on his right hand, indicating, Mr. Stothard says,* that she was an heiress. She is in widow's weeds, and on her chin a wimple. At her feet is an animal of the deer kind without a head, collared, and with chain of rectangular links. The lady's head rests upon a two-tiered pillow, an angel at each side supporting it (heads gone). The wimple extends round the chin over the shoulders, where it disappears under a hood. The dress is one long plain garment.

Ful semely hire wimple ypinched was.

For, all for heat, was laid aside
Her wimple, and her hood untied.

It was upon this tomb that the Chaplet of Roses was placed annually on the 24th of June, the peculiar and only rent reserved by one of the La Zouche lords upon granting large privileges in Tong to a De Hugefort (see detailed under Owners of Tong). " Round the neck of one of these Knights I observed a fresh garland of flowers, and was informed that an estate was held by the Tenure of putting such a Chaplet every year about this time on the said Tomb," Mr. Cole says, in 1757.

There seems to be some uncertainty as to this monument, Sir William Dugdale, visiting Tong Church in September,

---

* I think this rule will not apply to the Tong Effigies, as the lady is placed on the Knight's right hand on each of the tombs, and they were not *all* heiresses.

1663, refers to it thus:—" Towards the north side of the Church stands a faire Tombe of Alabaster whereon do lye the figures of a man in armour (partly mail and partly plate armour) and of his wife on his right hand, and on her chin a wimpler. Upon the Helm whereon the man resteth his head is this Crest (upon a wreath), viz., a Turkish woman's head with a wreath about her temples; her haire plaited and hanging below her shoulders, with a tassel at the end of the plaiting. This is sayde to be the monument of Sir Fowke Pembruge, Knight, sometime Lord of Tong Castle. On the sides of this Tombe are divers Escocheons whereon armes *have been* anciently depicted, but I suppose it was since the Vernons became Lords of Tonge Castle, by marriage with the heire female of Pembrugge, for the painting is as followeth :— I., Blank. II., Party per pale,—dexter, barry of six empaling a lion rampant, sinister, blank. III., Barry of six empaling fretty. IV., *Arg.* fretty *sa.* V., *Arg.* fretty *sa.* emp. barry of six. VI., *Arg.* fretty *sa.* VII., Barry of six *or* and *az.* VIII., Barry of six *or* and *az.* IX., Barry of six *or* and *az.* empaling *az.* a bend lozengy *or.* X., *Az.* a bend lozengy *or.* XI., Barry of six. XII., Barry of six." Others including VI. and XI. are repeated.

The above language of Sir William Dugdale does not point to his conviction that the *male effigy* is not Sir Fulke Pembruge's; moreover he says the arms *have been* depicted, implying that they were indistinct even when he saw them.

Mr. Eyton argues from the arms thus recorded, that the tomb must be a Vernon one, but the crest of the knight would throw a doubt upon the conclusion that the entire tomb and effigies commemorate a Vernon, as all the Vernons have a boar's head crest.

The measurements of the panelling (including the shields) on the north, south, and west sides, and part of the east, lead

F

me to venture the suggestion that it originally surrounded a single-effigy tomb, *now destroyed*; and, assuming the arms to be as above, it would seem to have been a Vernon one, upon which the broken alabaster boar's head crest now lying loose about the church would have found a proper place, as also the fragments of angels, and shields of alabaster found in 1892 among the rubbish beneath the church floor. As we have continuous memorials of each generation of the Vernons from Sir Richard, the Speaker, downwards, and as none of them are defective as regards the crest, the thought suggests itself that the destroyed tomb could only have been to the memory of the Richard Vernon, father of the Speaker, whose rebellious conduct resulted in his execution. It seems not unnatural that his loyal descendants should view with indifference the ruin of a monument recalling unfavourable incidents in a distinguished family's career. The sculpture now at the east end of this tomb (17) seems to belong to another destroyed tomb.

Mr. Eyton appropriates the arms above mentioned to Pembruge, Vernon, Ludlow, and Bermingham, and is disappointed at not finding Sir Fulke's first wife's arms among them. Discussing the arms as above recorded, is it possible that the *Arg.* fretty *sable* (Vernon), " the true lover's knot of heraldry," has been mistaken in some shields for *Arg.* a fret *gu.*, for Trussel? And again, the Lingen arms are so similar to Pembruge that they may have been confused—Lingaine, Barry of six *or* and *az.*, on a bend *gu.* 3 roses *arg.*; Lingayne, Barry of six *or* and *az.* on a bend *gu.*, three plates *arg.*

In Hereford Cathedral is a tomb with an effigy to Sir Richard de Pembruge, a benefactor to a priory there, the arms upon it being Barry of six with a bend. He was one of the earliest Knights of the Garter, the 53rd (Edwardian period), and has plated armour and shirt of mail; panache crest to helmet, a very rare example of the kind of plume worn in those times, not flowing but stiff and erect. There is a grey-hound at foot, with shaggy mane, and other details are very perfect and interesting.‡ The effigy has been carefully restored under the late Lord Saye and Sele's directions.

It is probably he, Sir Richard, that is referred to in the *Brantingham Issue of Rolls* :—

" To Henry de Wakefield, Keeper of the King's Wardrobe, by the hands of Sir Richard de Pembrugge, Knight, in dis-charge of £116 19s. 7d., due to the same Richard in the Wardrobe aforesaid, for the expenses of himself, his men-at-arms, and archers in the war, as appears by a bill of the said keeper, cancelled in the Hanaper of this term. 44, Ed. III. (1371)."

" The war " was one of the great military expeditions of Edward, the Black Prince—" the youthful prince who won his spurs at Cressy—that mirror of knighthood, the first and greatest of heroes, whose victories surrounded the name of his country with a lustre which produced strength and safety." †

It is curious that Mr. Eyton makes no reference to a Pembruge so illustrious as to receive the Order of the Garter, whose name might have filled the blank he found when tracing the descent of Sir F. Pembruge IV. from Sir F. Pembruge III., and whose existence would, perhaps, have restrained him from appropriating Sir Fulke Pembruge's tomb to Sir Richard Vernon, alias (as he said) de Pembruge. The records as to the ownership of Tong appear to be deficient between 1335 and 1371*; this would not be surprising if the hero, Sir Richard Pembruge, were the owner, seeing he was absent on the Continent with the Black Prince, whose military career,

---

‡ Note from Lady Saye and Sele.   † Mackintosh.

* See page 12. Under owners of Tong, Robert de Pembruge is mentioned by Shaw as brother and heir of Fulk de Pembruge III., and father of Fulk de Pembruge IV.

commencing in 1346 (Battle of Cressy), kept him almost continuously abroad until his death in 1376.

The will of Fulke Eyton may be here mentioned, as it refers to Sir F. Pembruge's burial, and also gives an idea of the personal effects of a gentleman of that time. It is dated 1454, and directs that his body shall be buried by his godfather, Sir Fowke Pembruge, within the Chapel at Tong. This does not refer to the present Golden Chapel, which was not founded until 1515, but to the Lady Chapel, which sometimes, though rarely, occupies a position near the north aisle.

After directing that prayers, &c., shall be said at 4d. each, he gives £10 to the almshouse of Tong; his best basin and ewer of silver to the priest of the College of Tong; also "to the saide College a Bed called a fedre bed with the honging thereto of blew worstede; to John Eiton "alle myn horse and riding harnes," and "harnes of goldsmythes worke"; to "John the boy an horse and 40s."; to the Chapel of Tonge a "mass boke" and "Chalice," and "blew vestiment of damaske of my arms"; to "Nicholas Eyton one of the good fedre beddis, and a chambre, and a bedde of lynne cloth, steyned with horses"; to Isabella Englefield "another good fedre bedd," which after her decease was to go to John Eiton.

In an old Book in the British Museum, dated 1796, I find "Col. Roper saith Vernon should be a *red* Knot, not *sable*." The same work, in referring to Shottesbrook† (which has the most perfect Gothic Church in its county) confirms the account of a Pembruge and Trussell marriage. It says:—

"Margaret Pembridge, daughter of Sir Wm. Trussell, knight, founded here [Shottesbrook,] 2 Ed. III,* a College and a Chantry for a warden, 5 priests, and 2 clerks. He married Maude, daughter of Sir W. Butler, lord of Wemme. His body was seen by industrious Thos. Hearne (whose father was Parish Clerk of Shottesbrook), wrapt up in lead, and hers at his feet in leather. Their son John died without issue, and then their daughter was married to Sir Fulk Pembrudge."

The arms, *Az.*, a bend lozengy, *or*, for Bermingham, seem more suggestive of the Pembruge family than the Vernon, Sir F. Pembruge II. having married a Bermingham.

---

† Gough's Sep. Mon. v. 2 p. 2.

* If she was wife of Fulk Pembruge IV, this date must be a misprint.

The arms of Ludlow would not be inconsistent with Sir F. Pembrugge's widow Elizabeth's, seeing she married Sir Thomas Ludlow as her first husband, according to an MS. in the British Museum recording the *Visitation* of 1584.

13. RICH ALABASTER ALTAR-TOMB, with the recumbent effigies of a Vernon and Lady, and most probably SIR RICHARD VERNON, and his wife, BENEDICTA, (? daughter of Sir . . . . Ludlow, of Hodnet and Stokesay Castle, Co. Salop, perhaps by his wife, Elizabeth de Lingen).

Sir Richard, born about 1391, created a Knight 1418, was constituted by patent Treasurer of Calais, 4 May, 1444, resigned it in favour of his son 1450, Captain of Rouen, (the place where Joan of Arc was burned to death in 1431), and Speaker of the Parliament held at Leicester 1426, died 1451-2.

The Treasurer of Calais was an important personage. Vast sums were constantly being expended in the protection and maintenance of Calais during the time the English possessed it, and this money all passed through the Treasurer's hands. The office of Captain was almost always held by a great noble or Prince, and the subordinate officers were of corresponding honour and profit with it, the chief one. In the rolls preserved in the Tower of London, mention is made (1) of a safe conduct to Richard de Vernon to Vasconia (Gascony), signed by the King at Westminster; (2) concerning the office of Treasurer of the Town of Calais assigned to Richard Vernon, signed by the King at Westminster, 17th May, 1444; (3) the King appointed Richard Vernon, Knight, and Walter Aumener, Custodians and Receivers of the Mint at Calais, 1 Sep., 1446, and there are many 'safe conducts' for various persons addressed to Richard Vernon, knight.

His father joined in the Rebellion of the Percies, and took part in the Battle of Shrewsbury, July 21st, 1403, for he was executed there two days after, on Monday, July 23rd, Sir Richard being then ten years of age. It was the impatience of Hot-spur (Henry Percy) in attacking the King's forces before his junction with Owen Glyndwr, that cost him his life, and his followers defeat: a contest remarkable for the bravery of the combatants, and described as " one of the most obstinate and bloody battles recorded in English History."

His mother was probably sister and heiress of Sir Fulke Pembruge, who died in 1409.

Of five pedigrees relating to the Vernons no two agree in all particulars, but supposing the above assumption as to Bene-dicta to be correct, and two genealogies confirm it, it is not difficult to discern the exceptional facilities at the command of Lady Pembruge for carrying out the huge task she had set herself, namely, the foundation of a College with its beautiful Church and other accessories, at a place where her own interest was merely as a dowry. Her father, Sir Raffe Lingen, is described in the *Visitation* of 1584, "as of Tong Castle," which is curious. The erection of the Shottesbrook Chantry by Sir Fulke's first wife Margaret (Trussel), was not unlikely the cause of Elizabeth's equal zeal at Tong; and the marriage of her daughter to the Lord of Tong, her husband's nephew, the Speaker (whose influence with the king is marked by the bestowal of the revenues of Lapley upon the College), enabled her to overcome the apparent difficulties in the way of placing upon a permanent footing her College scheme. It seems natural that Sir Fulke's sister, who probably survived her husband, should have had Tong Castle, but I suppose her alliance with the rebel would put her outside the pale of royal sympathy.

The learned antiquary, the Hon. Canon Bridgeman, having found my supposition confirmed in Inq. P.M., I append his letter dated 20 May, 1892 :—

The Hall, Wigan,
20 May, 1892.

Dear Mr. Griffiths, - I told you some time ago that I had come across the inquisition giving the exact connection between Sir Fulke Pembruge of Tong and Sir Richard Vernon.

I do not know that it will be any news to you, but I had lost sight of it and have now found it again.

You know that the last Sir Fulk de Pembruge married two wives. His first wife was the daughter and heiress of Sir William Trussell of Cublesdon and Sheriff Hales, and widow of Nicholas de Whyston, Lord of one-fifth of the Manor of Weston-under-Lizard as being the son of Elizabeth de Weston, afterwards wife of Sir Adam de Peshale. This Margaret died in 1402. You know much more about Elizabeth, the 2nd wife and widow, than I do.

Fulk de Pembrugge died on Friday before the feast of St. Augustin, 10 Hen IV. (May 24th, 1409), and Juliana, wife of Sir Richard Vernon of Hailaston, was found to be his heir. She was then 60 years of age and more.

Sir Fulk held the Manor of Tong jointly with *Isabella* (same name as Elizabeth), his wife yet surviving, with remainder to Richard de P. (Pembruge ?), son of Richard *Vernon*, the nephew of Fulk and Benedicta his wife, yet living, to them and the heirs of their bodies, by charter or settlement.

It would seem from this that the Manor of Tong went straight to this Richard Vernon (or Pembrugge) instead of to his mother, the rightful heir.

The reference for this information is Inq. P.M. 10 Hen. IV. no. 45.

Believe me,
Yours truly,
George T. O. Bridgeman.

The tomb rests upon a sandstone plinth, and is ornamented with rich canopy work, into which are introduced figures of angels and saints alternately. The latter are of remarkable beauty, and doubtless modelled by some Italian artist ; those holding shields, being, on the other hand, of commoner design and execution. Sir Albert Woods, Garter King at Arms, adds a note that these shields are " Not sketched in the Visitation." This is the second of the four tombs in the nave described by Mr. Petit, and of this, in particular, he says, " The second is decidedly florid, yet all its enrichments are of a strictly architectural description."

The knight is on the left, "his face being noble, and very peaceful,—the repose of death."

He rests his head upon a helmet with the Vernon crest thereon, viz., Upon a wreath, a boar's head* couped and tusked. The helmet and crest are placed to the north side. On the Pembruge tomb, the crest is to the south. At his feet is a lion. He is in plate armour, and has a large circlet on basinet of gilt laurel leaves, and probably pearls are intended. There is a gold circlet below on the forehead, and a stud near the ears to fasten the body armour to basinet. The armour on shoulders and chest is crescented. The elbow-roundlets and knee-caps are shell pattern. There is a rich circlet below the waist, from the waist to the hips are four plates, one plate beneath the circlet, and two plates below, and to the lowest plate of the armour are attached straps (4 in front) which form a kind of hinge to the tassets. This arrangement was in order that the armour protecting the thighs should not impede the free movement of the legs when marching. He wears besides a sword-belt and sword, the SS. collar, an honourable decoration to be seen on later Vernon effigies.

The collar of the SS., composed of links of silver gilt, with badges at the centre, containing the shamrock, rose, and thistle, was introduced by Henry IV. The earliest instance of it is believed to be upon the effigy of his Queen, who died in 1397. (See tomb in Canterbury Cathedral of Henry IV. and Queen, in the Thomas A'Becket Chapel, where the letters SS. are often repeated in the ornamentation of the tomb). The King's motto was "Soverayne," and the inference is that the letters were used as the initials of that favourite impress. The king seems to have made this emblem of his sovereignty an honorary mark of distinction ; we find it employed as such, by his son Henry V. at the battle of Agincourt, 1415. " He exhorted

---

* The only colouring left is the animal's red nose.

such of his train as were not noble, to demean themselves well'
in the fight ; he promised them letters of nobility, and to distinguish them, he gave them leave to wear his collar of SS."†

" The sword in the middle ages was a symbol of honour,
an object almost of worship ; the chosen seat and image of
the sentiment of chivalry. ‡ "   On the scabbard of Sir Richard's
two-handed sword, now broken, was the sacred monogram
I.H.S.

In *Stothard's Effigies* those of Sir E. de Thorpe (killed 1418)
and lady, in Ashwell Church, Norfolk, and of Ralph Nevill,
Earl of Westmoreland, and his two wives in Staindrop
Church, are very similar to these Vernon effigies.

Of Sir Richard Vernon's wife little is known beyond that
her christian name was Benedicta.   Rayner suggests that'
she was a native of France, but Mr. Eyton describes her as·
daughter of Sir John Ludlow.

> Woman ! whose sculptured form at rest
>   By the armed knight is laid,
> With meek hands folded o'er a breast,
>   In matron robes arrayed ;
> What was *thy* tale ? — O gentle mate
>   Of him, the bold and free,
> Bound unto his victorious fate,
>   What bard hath sung of *thee* ?
>
> He wooed a bright and burning star—
>   *Thine* was the void, the gloom,
> The straining eye that followed far
>   His fast-receding plume ;
> The heart-sick listening while his steed
>   Sent echoes on the breeze ;
> The pang — but when did Fame take heed
>   Of griefs obscure as these ?
>
> —*Mrs. Hemans.*

The characteristics of her effigy are :— Large head-dress of
the style called " mitred," peculiar to the time of Henry VI.
(illustrated in Mrs. Halliday's work on the *Porlock Effigies* of
Lord and Lady Harrington, who died respectively 1418 and
about 1472), with the fret on each side, laurel band, band

---

† Stothard.   ‡ *Building News*, Aug. 10, 1883.

G

crossing breast and fastening mantle, with enriched lozenge-shaped button on each shoulder. Long cords intertwine across the chest and hang down, with tassels at the end ; several rings are on the fingers, and the hands are folded as if in prayer. At her feet are two dogs collared.* † " These animals, so frequently found with figures on tombs, especially those representing females, are the appendages of high rank. They were indeed the lady's pet dogs." Thus Chaucer (l. 146) says—

> " Ot smale houndes hadde she, that she fedde,
> With rosted flesh, and milk, and wastel brede,
> But sore wept she if on of hem were dede,
> Or if men smote it with a yerde smert,"‡

The lady wears the collar of the SS., and her head rests upon a cushion supported by angels. " The lady's face is lovely, the broad fair forehead, and the well-arched eyebrows, the straight nose, and beautifully-moulded mouth and chin ; and above all, the expression that seems to animate the features, though in stone, and to shine down to us through centuries, fills even a casual observer with admiration and a kind of awe." Somewhat resembling the lady's effigy are those of Sir Humphrey Vernon's wife at Bromsgrove, and Joan, Lady Bardolph, at Dennigton, County Suffolk. This latter lady was daughter of Thomas, Lord Bardolph, whose body was quartered, and parts set upon the gates of Shrews-bury and other towns after the insurrection under the Earl of Northumberland, 1407-8. The attire of Lady Mohun (Joan Burwaschs or de Burghersh) presents us with an example of the fret or reticulated coiffure adopted by Court Ladies of the 14th century.

There is no inscription on the tomb, but in a Gothic window, in the old Chapel forming part of Haddon Hall, is an inscrip-

---

* These dogs are technically called " brackets."
† Stothard.   ‡ i.e. with a stick hardly.

TOMB NO. 14.

SIR WILLIAM VERNON AND MARGARET HIS WIFE.

tion asking the prayers of the reader for Richard Vernon, and Benedicta, his wife, 1427.

"Orate pro animabus Ricardi Vernon et Benedictæ uxoris ejus qui . . . . fecerunt Anno Dni., mccccxxvii."

By this marriage Hodnet came to the Vernons, and the East Window of the Chapel there commemorates the union.

14. FINE ALTAR-TOMB of free-stone, with slab of Purbeck marble inlaid with brasses, to SIR WILLIAM VERNON, of Tong Castle, and MARGARET his wife. He died 1467.

This is the third of the four monuments referred to by Mr. Petit :—" The third, though it has open work canopies, depends much for its richness upon the spaces filled with minute and intricate panelling." There are several stone shields in the panelling, but the arms are defaced. The brasses with the shields form an elegant example of a " mediæval brass." On removing modern woodwork in 1892 from the south side of this tomb it was found to be plain stonework, except one panel at the west end of that side. Solid masonry intervened between it and the pillar near. This and the east end panels are not in their proper positions, but remain as they were found, it being impossible to tell exactly how they ought to be; perhaps antiquarians will examine them and give their opinions.

INSCRIPTION :—

Hic jacent dus Willius Vernon Miles Quondm Miles constabularius Anglie filius et heres dni Ricardi Vernon Militis qui quondm erat Thesaurarius Calesie qui quidem dus Willms obiit bltimo die mensis Junii Anno Domini Millimo cccc lx bii Et Margareta Vxor dici Willi filia Et hereditar dni Roberti Pypis Et Spernores Militis que quidem Margareta obiit . . . . dii Mensis . . . Anno Domini Millimo cccclx . . . quorum Animabus Propicietur Deus. AMEN.

TRANSLATION :

Here lie Sir William Vernon Knight sometime Knight Constable of England son and heir of Sir Richard Vernon Knight who sometime was Treasurer of Calais which Sir William indeed died the last day of the month of June in the year of our Lord 1467 and Margaret wife of the said William daughter and heiress of Sir Robert Pype and Spernore Knight which Margaret indeed died . . . . day of the month . . . . . in the year of our Lord 146-, *on whose souls may God be merciful.   Amen.

It is curious that the inscription should omit the maiden name of Dame Margaret, viz., Swinfen †; she was daughter of William Swinfen and Jocosa his wife.   He was cousin and heir of Sir Robert Pype of Pype Ridware, and Jocosa was younger daughter and co-heir of William Dureversale alias Spermore (or Spernore).   Probably Margaret's father adopted his cousin's name upon his succession to the Pype inheritance. Sir Wm. Vernon and Dame Margaret were married in 1435, when they had grants of her grandfather's (Spernore's) lands. In 1445 she succeeded to her father's estates, Pype Redware, Draycot, and Seile, and the Manor of Wall.

The appellation of " Knight Constable of England " would seem to indicate the deputy of the Lord High Constable, an office next in dignity to the Lord High Steward, who was the first personage in the realm next to the King, but Sir William does not appear to have had a superior.   The Constable's office was, however, more ancient, and at one time more important than the Lord High Steward's.   In the absence of the King, the Constable commanded the army and kept the Constable Court.

---

* She survived her husband, and is described as his executor in 1467.   The inscription is defective as to the day and month, and probably the year was left to be filled up by other hands in the same way, but never was completed.

† The hamlet of Swinfen is near Lichfield, the parish of Pype Ridware being also in that neighbourhood.   I imagine these are the places from which the families of Swinfen and Pype emanated.   Mr. E. Swynfen Parker Jervis is the present owner of a large part of Pype Ridware.

CONSTABLE: To horse, you gallant princes! straight to horse
Shakespeare.

' To the Constable it pertaineth to have cognizance of contracts touching deeds of arms and of war out of the realm, and also of things which touch war within the realm, which cannot be determined nor discussed by the common law." Ralph de Mortimer was the first Constable appointed by King William I. He had the estates of Edric, the Forester, Earl of Shrewsbury, whom he took prisoner in his Castle of Wigmore. King Henry I. made the office hereditary in the family of the Earls of Gloucester; but in Sir W. Vernon's time there appears to have been no *hereditary* constable. Sir William "was the last one who had a grant of the high office, it being looked upon as too important for a subject to be thus entrusted with it," says *Rayner's History of Haddon.*

The brasses inlaid consisted of 26 pieces (well shewn in a print published by Wallers in 1842), viz. :—

1. Sir William, in late chain and plate armour, with sword, dagger, and spurs ; the helmet with mantling in shreds,* his crest a boar's head, and this motto :—

2. "𝔅enedictus deus in donis suis." (Blessed be God for His gifts.)

3. Dame Margaret, wearing a hood and wimple, long cape lined with ermine, hanging from the shoulders, with cords and tassels. At her feet is an elephant.

4. This motto above her head—" 𝔍hu fili dabid 𝔐iserere nob' " (Jesu, Son of David, be merciful unto us.)

5. Shield above the Knight, for Pembruge. Barry of six, *or* and *az.*

6. Shield above the lady for Dureversale.† *Su.*, a fesse chequy *or* and *gu.* between six escallops *arg.*, three above, three below.

7. Shield between 5 and 6 for Pype. *Az.*, two pipes between seven cross crosslets, *or.*

8. Shield in the centre, for Vernon. *Arg.* fretty *sa.*

9. Shield for Ludlow. *Arg.* a lion rampant ducally crowned, *gules,* collared . . . . . langued . . . . .

---

* Latterly mantlings were represented as very much cut and worn, occasioned by the many cuts received about the head, and therefore the more rugged they were, the more honourable, as is the case with our " Colours."

† According to Edmondson. In Ducarell's Book this shield is put down as " Peter de ancerlis.'

10. Shield recording the union of Vernon and Pype. Per pale, dexter, *arg.* fretty, *sa.* sinister, *az.* two pipes between seven cross crosslets *or.*

11. Shield for Camville. *Az.* three lions passant, *or.*

12. [Missing]   Shield, *arg.* a bend engrailed *gules* for . . . . . . [Un-
known.]

13. One son, and this scroll : —

14. " **Spabi in Dno et erepiat me.**"   (I have put my trust in the Lord
and He will deliver me.)

15. One son, and this scroll :—

16. " **FFili Dei memento mei.**"   (Son of God remember me.)

17. One son.

18. One son, and

19. [Place of scroll, missing.]

20. One son, and this scroll :—

21. " **Dne lebabi aiam mea ab te.**"   (Lord, I have lifted up my soul to
Thee.)

22. Two sons (? twins.)

23. Two daughters (? twins)

24. One daughter, and this scroll :—

25. " **Ihu fili marie pietat miserere nobis.**"   (Jesu Son of Mary of Thy
pity be merciful unto us).

26. [Missing.] two daughters (twins ?)

The sons are shown alike in long frocks, and wear pointed
sandals; the daughters wear large fret head-dresses and long
gowns.

Near this tomb is the LECTERN (**L**), given by the Rev.
G. C. and Mrs. Rivett-Carnac in 1890. The old lectern was
an eagle carved in oak, with one leg bent in an unnatural
position.   The Bible upon it is inscribed thus:—"Tong
Church, 1848.   Presented by the Rev. R. H. Leeke."

P. Jacobean PULPIT of oak, hexagonal, exhibits some
good carving. Date and inscription on the side facing the
nave :—"Ex dono Dne Harries Anno Dni. 1622." The gift
of Lady Harries.

15. FINE ALTAR-TOMB with stone effigies commemorating SIR HENRY VERNON KT., (Lord of Haddon and
Tong Castle, Knight of the Bath, Governor and Treasurer to

Arthur Prince of Wales), and his wife LADY ANNE (daughter of John Talbot, 2nd Earl of Shrewsbury), both buried beneath the tomb. He died 1515; his wife in 1494.

The following is the inscription, which, with the shields and base, were until lately partly concealed by modern wood-work in the chapel :—

Hic jacet corpora Henrici Vernon Militis Hujs ecclesie Collegiate fundatoris et Dne Anne Talbot uxoris suis filie Johis Comits Salopie qui quidm Dns Henricus obiit xiii die mensis Aprilis Anno domini millesimo quingentesimo xb° Et dicta dne Anna obiit xbii die mens majj Anno dni millo cccc lxxxx iiijto quor aiam ppicietur . . . .

Translation:—Here lie the bodies of Sir Henry Vernon Knight, the founder of this Chantry Chapel, and Dame Anne Talbot his wife, daughter of John, Earl of Shrewsbury, which said Sir Henry died the 13th day of the month of April in the year of our Lord 1515, and the said Lady Anne died the 17th day of May in the year of our Lord 1494, on whose souls may God be merciful.

The tomb is placed under a wide Burgundian arch, which opens the north side of the chapel to the south aisle.

Above the tomb on the aisle side are four elaborately carved tabernacles, but bereaved of their statues. When this work was richly gilt, and images filled the niches, as no doubt was the case when the tomb was completed, the general effect must have been very striking.

Mr. Cole in 1757, speaking of these, said " There is a very neat small chapel which has a very fine tomb under a most beautiful and richly carved canopy."

A small shield in stone stands between the two central brackets, the arms being :—Quarterly of six, viz. :—1st. Fretty. (Vernon). 2nd. Two lions passant guardant. (.) 3rd.

Gu. a lion rampant *or* within a bordure engrailed *or*. (Talbot). 4th. Barry. (Pembrugge.) 5th. Fretty, a canton . . . . . . (Vernon.) 6th. *az.* Two pipes between nine crosslets *or*. (Pype).

On the north side of the tomb itself are four shields bearing the following coats:—1. Barry of six *or* and *az.* (Pembruge.) 2. . . . . a lion rampant *sa.* within a bordure *gu.* (Talbot.) 3. *Az.,* two pipes between 12 crosslets, *or*. (Pype.) 4. Fretty. (Vernon). And on the south side are four :—1. A lion rampant *sa.* for Ludlow. 2. Fretty for Vernon. 3. . . . . . Three lions passant for Camville. 4. Fretty impaling *Gules* a lion rampant, within a bordure *or* for Vernon and Talbot. The heads of the figures intervening, on the south side, are all broken.

Sir Henry is represented in plate armour and wears the collar of SS. At his head, black plumes surround the helmet, which is large and has narrow ventaille with little ornaments in rows above and below the aperture. The crest of helmet is a boar's head. The knight's figure is of large proportions, and resembles that of Talbot the great Earl of Shrewsbury. The basinet is discontinued and the hair is cropped at the neck. Notice the veins in black lines upon the hands. The shields on this tomb are similar in pattern to the armour hanging down over the thighs. The scabbard of his large sword is coloured red ; upon the hilt is the Vernon crest, a boar's head, which is repeated upon the guard. He also wears a dagger.

Sir Henry was Guardian (or Governor) and Treasurer to Arthur Prince of Wales, eldest son of Henry VII., who lived at Ludlow Castle and held his Court there. In 1489 Prince Arthur was created Prince of Wales, and the nominal government of Wales was vested in him. Probably Sir Henry Vernon was chief of his counsellors. The talents, acquirements, and character of the Prince, are reported to have been

such as reflected honour on himself and on the individual to
whom he was indebted for the direction of his studies and the
cultivation of his faculties.*   He married at the early age of
16 the Princess Katharine of Arragon, and died soon afterwards (in 1502), much regretted by the nation.   Sir Henry
witnessed the marriage contract.

According to tradition Prince Arthur Tudor spent much of
his time with Sir Henry at Haddon, where one of the apart-
ments was called the Prince's chamber.   Sir Henry's seat at
Tong was probably no less honoured by the Prince's presence,
lying as it does a little less than half way between Ludlow
and Haddon, and being within easy distance of Shrewsbury,
where Prince Arthur frequently visited.

Sir Henry was one of " les nobles et vaillants chevaliers "
who gathered round the Royal standard June 6, 1487, and was
M.P. for co. Derby, 1478, and High Sheriff for Derby 1504.
He passed his last days in retirement.

Sir Henry gave the " Great Bell " to Tong, and founded the
Golden Chantry Chapel (both described elsewhere), and in
1500, on the site of the old castle which had become ruinous,
built the second Tong castle.

John Leland's *Itinerary*† thus refers to " The Vernons " at
Tong :

" Many or almost al ly there that were famous
of them sins the Fundation.

Syr Henry
Vernun a late
daies made
the Castel
new al of
Brike.

There was an olde Castel of Stone caullid
Tunge Castel.   It standeth half a mile from the
Toune on a Banke, under the wich rinnith the
Broke that cummith from Weston to Tunge.
Weston is 2 Miles of, and is in Stafordshire."

The bit of very early carved stone now to be seen in the

---

* Vide *History of Haddon*.   † Ordered by K. Henry VIII., and begun in 1538.

H

Castle yard is probably the only remnant of the " olde Castel " of the De Belmeises, La Zouches, and Pembruges.

Lady Anne's effigy is on the right of her husband; she wears a long dress, has a necklet, a mantle with cord and

tassels, and tresses extending below the shoulders. At her
feet, two small hounds hold the hem of her gown. She was
daughter of the second Earl of Shrewsbury, who was a Knight
of the Garter, and Lord Treasurer of Ireland during the administration of his father (Talbot, the " Great Earl "), and subsequently Lord Treasurer of England. He fell at the battle of
Northampton, 1460, fighting under the Red Rose. Lady
Anne's father and grandfather are immortalised by *Shakespeare*
in his *King Henry VI.*, where the reader finds some heroic
yet tender passages addressed by father and son to each
other

> TALBOT (First Earl): Upon my blessing. I command thee go.
> JOHN TALBOT (his son): To fight I will. but not to fly the foe.
>
> JOHN: No more can I be sever'd from your side,
>   Than can yourselt yourself in twain divide:
>   Stay, go, do what you will, the like do I,
>   For live I will not if my father die.
> TALBOT: Then here I take my leave of thee, fair son,
>   Born to eclipse thy life this afternoon.
>   Come side by side together live and die;
>   And soul with soul from France to heaven fly.

A Vernon is also introduced in the play, whose zeal for the
White Rose faction causes him some trouble.

Of Lady Anne's brothers, one, Sir Gilbert Talbot, was High
Sheriff of Shropshire, temp. Richard III., a staunch adherent
of the Earl of Richmond at Bosworth, the right wing of whose
army he commanded. For his valiant conduct he received the
honour of knighthood and the manor of Grafton and other
lands. His son was Sir John Talbot of Albrighton. Leland
says of him : " Syr John Talbot that married Troutbeks Heire
" dwelleth in a goodly Logge on the hy Toppe of Albrighton
" parke. It is in the very Egge of Shropshire 3 miles from
" Tunge "

Of Sir Henry's numerous family, three sons are commemorated at Tong, viz :—Monument No. 16, to Arthur, fifth and
youngest son. Monument No. 17, to Richard Vernon, Esquire,
of Haddon and Tong, the eldest son. Monument No. 18, to
Humphrey, third son, who married the younger daughter of

John Ludlow, Esq., and co-heiress of Sir Richard de Ludlow, Knight, and thus founded the Vernon family " of Hodnet." The second son, Thomas, married (1497) the elder grand-daughter and co-heiress of Sir Richard Ludlow, founding the Vernon family " of Stokesay." In 1509 he, as Sheriff of Shropshire, had a dispute with the burgesses of Shrewsbury, which lasted several years. A daughter Margaret seems to have been Abbess of West Malling 1511.* Sir John, the fourth son, founded the Vernons " of Sudbury." He was one of the King's Council in Wales, and Custos Rotulorum of Co. Derby (died at Harlaston, Co. Stafford, 1542) ; while a daughter Mary married Thomas Newport, Esq., an ancestor of the Earls of Bradford.

---

* See Account of White Ladies and Black Ladies.

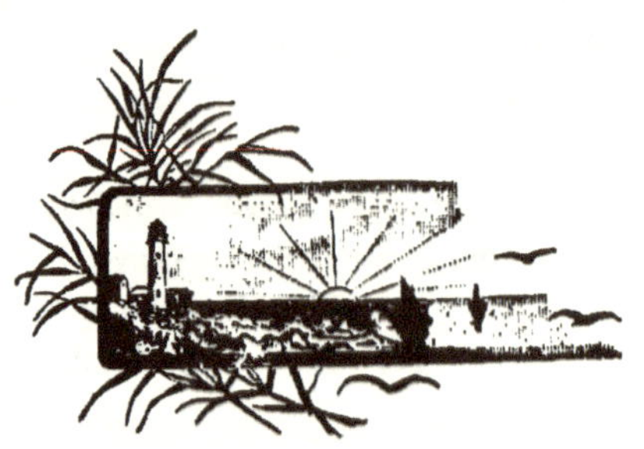

SIR ARTHUR VERNON (*see page 55*).

HE VERNON CHANTRY or GOLDEN CHAPEL is entered by a rich ogee door with finial, the crocket-mound springing from labelled heads. This beautiful chantry, called the Golden Chapel from its once costly ornamentation, is of the latest period of the Gothic, and was described by Walter White as an "exquisite little appendage to the south aisle, which shows what adepts the masons of the 16th century were in the art of fan-vaulting," the roof being of elaborate stone-work, once entirely gilt. From the traceried vaulting hang three graceful pendants, two terminating in foliage, and one in neat shields with arms. The walls were originally decorated in distemper, traces of red and brown colouring being still visible.

On the east wall, in 1757, there was a crucifix in colours, and beneath it the following INSCRIPTION in Gothic letters yet visible .—

"Pray for the Sowle of Syr Harie Vernon Knyght and Dame Anne hys Wyfe whych Syr herie in the year || off owre Lord m ccccc rb made and ffowndyd thys chapell and chawntry and the sayd Sir Harry || departyd the xiii day of Apryll in the yere a bobe sayd and of youre Charite for the soll of Sir Arthur || Vernon Pryst sone of the abobe sayd Sir herry on whos sollys ihs habe mercy Amen.

|| These divide the lines.

There seems to be no doubt that the noble founder was familiarly known as "Sir Harry" or "Herry." *Audelay's poem* affords illustrations of the use of this word in Shropshire in the 15th century:

"On him schal fal the prophecé
That hath ben sayd of kyng Herré."

"Fore hit is mad of kyng Herré."

16. Good half-length figure of SIR ARTHUR VERNON, priest of Tong, in the attitude of preaching, on the west wall of the Golden Chapel; the figure is upright and of stone, beneath a gilt canopy, and rests upon a bracket with pediment apart from the wall. "A monument as singular as it is curious." There is a book in the right hand, the fingers of left hand being raised as if to give emphasis to his reading. Beneath the crockets of the canopy are four shields of arms, viz.:—1. Barry of six (Pembruge). 2. Chequy, the squares raised and depressed alternately (? Reymes): the revenues of the Abbey at Rheims had been conferred on Tong College by King Henry VI. by virtue of an Act passed at Leicester, of which Sir Richard Vernon was Speaker. 3. Fretty (Vernon) impaling a lion rampant, with a bordure *gu.* (Talbot). 4. Fretty (Vernon).

Sir Arthur Vernon was fifth son of Sir Henry Vernon, A.M. of the University of Cambridge, and sometime Rector of Whitchurch, co. Salop. Died 15 Aug., 1517. Buried at Tong.

Mr. Petit says, "the features and expression are remarkably good, and there is a perceptive resemblance to his father, so probably they are faithful portraits."

The prefix Sir or Den, meaning Dean, held by priests before the Reformation chiefly. Mr. Cooper, of Stourbridge, has found his will, of which the following is the commencement :—

In the name of God Amen In the yere of our Lord 1515 the last day of Septembre in the yere of King Henry VIII. the eighth I. Sir Arthur

King Charles making his escape, attended by 5 Penderels and F. Yates

Vernon Prest hole of mynde and of body being in cleue lyfe at the making of this my last Will and in good prosperite often tymes thinking of this wreched lyfe seying by circute of daies and revolucion of yeres the day of deth to fall which nothing lyving may passe therefor of this helefull mynde thus I make my testament &c   [Proved at Canterbury].

Mr. Cole, writing in 1757, says :—

"Time was so pressing [the clock was striking seven, and he had to go seven miles to Newport that evening], yet I conld not resist the Temptation of one [monument] which lies in the very midst of this Neat Chapel, out of regard to beloved Alma Mater, and was only half concerned that I could not stay long enough to take a sketch of it, as on the Grey Marble [*i.e.*, on the floor] was the Figure of a Priest shorn, and in his proper Master of Arts habit as worn at that time, which was different from what it is at present, being more like a Batchelor of Arts with large open Sleeves; over his Head was the Cup and wafer, and at the four corners his coat of arms, viz.: at two corners single for Vernon, viz., fretty; and at the 2 others Vernon and five others, among which I thought I observed one of Trumpington, with two trumpets reversed, etc.*   At his feet was this inscription all in brass :

'Orate specialeter pro Aia Dni Arthuri Vernon In Artibus Magri Unib'sitatis Cantibrigie qui obiit xb Die Augusti Ao Dni mcccccxbii Cnjs Aie p'picietur Deus.'

"On the Floor, just at the foot of his Gravestone, and on the only step in the Chapel, lies the Old Altar Stone [of the chapel] as part of the Pavement of it."

None of these were to be seen until 1892, when on removing the modern woodwork the objects so minutely described by Mr. Cole became again visible. On restoring the Chapel in 1892, there was revealed the grey marble slab, 8ft. 5in. × 4ft. 1in., and Sir Arthur Vernon's brass memorial, with inscription in centre, very perfect and complete ; also four shields of arms in the corners of it, viz. :—Fretty (left-hand top corner), Fretty (right-hand bottom corner). Quarterly of Six : Vernon, Camville, Ludlow, Pembruge, Vernon, Pype. Quarterly of Six : the same. And over his head the Paten sunk in the Chalice, and J.H.S. in brass. The old altar stone, 10 inches deep, was found as part of the pavement. It has 5 Maltese crosses cut in it, viz.: one at each corner, and a larger one in

---

* Error for Pype.

the centre, 5 inches across ; also two other tiny crosses cut in, like the oylets of the Norman castles.   There were indications that this altar was originally against the east wall of the chantry, so it has been fixed again there ; size, 6ft. long, 2ft. 7in. wide.

A piscina, 14½ in. high × 14½ in. wide, in the south wall of this chantry is now seen, though shorn of the projecting mouldings which had been previously cut off; on each side of this piscina have been found Bishop's marks of consecration upon the walls, viz. : a Maltese cross within a circle 14½ inches in diameter, all in colour.   A similar consecration mark is on the north wall of the Chapel, and one on the south wall near the shaft of the vaulting.

The shafts which originally continued from the fan-vaulting of the roof to the floor, had also been cut, and are now restored with greatly-improved effect.   The old chantry flooring was found to be slightly raised in the south-west angle and old encaustic tiles were found, four forming a pattern, of which some similar ones were once seen at White Ladies Abbey. One set of four tiles had each a lion rampant.   Another tile had a yellow shield, and two crosslets in the lower part. Another had a Maltese cross in the first quarter, and a very curious old tile removed from the chancel floor, and now fixed here, is of the Lamb.   The stall end and angle-piece of the old bench to fit this raised floor was found in another part of the Church ; it has now been refixed.   It is probable that this was the high " pew " or seat for the distinguished worshippers, including the Founder of the Chantry, Sir Harry Vernon, and possibly of his princely ward, Prince Arthur Tudor, Prince of Wales, first husband of Queen Katharine.   The Historical Manuscripts Commission has recently discovered among the Duke of Rutland's MSS. a programme by the King's command drawn out, directing how and with what sumptuous array Sir

Harry Vernon and others were to conduct the King's "daughter" Margaret to Scotland for her marriage. A hole, formerly an Aumbry, 15in. high and 10in. wide, was found in the east wall, which contained nothing but a large fungus.

Of the roof of the Chapel, the following notes occur :—

Spaces between fans have circles, to which are attached pendants by ribs of the same moulding with those of the second order in the fans themselves.

Central fan on north side, instead of being supported by shaft (which would have interfered with the Vernon tomb), springs also from a pendant, which is enriched with mouldings and foliage.

H Over the door into the Chapel is a tablet of white marble, surmounted by an urn and bearing a brass plate with the following inscription :—

Near this Place
Is Interred the Body of
Daniel Higgs Gent :
Steward to his Grace of
KINGSTON
Who departed this Life
Oct. 1. 1758
In the 60th Year of his age

———

Few so Honest
None more so.

H And on the south-west pillar of the tower is a tablet—

Near this place lieth the body of Maria Higgs, Daughter of Danl. and Mary Higgs of Tong Castle who departed this life the 9th of May 1748 Aged 19 Months & Ten days.

17. Alabaster ALTAR-TOMB of elegant workmanship with recumbent effigies of RICHARD VERNON, ESQUIRE, and MARGARET, his wife. Mr. Petit, in speaking of the traceried panelling of the Altar which belonged to this very richly-sculptured tomb, says "The front and sides are elaborately worked with open arches, pinnacles, and crocketed canopies with several figures. The round and elliptical arch are freely used, and other marks show it to be of the latest period. The following is the inscription :—

I

Hic jacent corpora Ricardi Vernon de Haddon Armigeri et
Margarete uxoris filie Roberti Dymmok Militis qui habuerunt
exitum Georgium Vernon Qui quidem Ricardus obiit in Vigilia
Assumptonis sancte Marie Virginis Anno dni Millesimo qo decimo
septimo E Et dicta Margareta obiit . . . . die mensis
. . . . Anno dni Millesimo quingentesimo . . . Quorum
animabus omnipotens propicietur des. Amen.

TRANSLATION.

Here lie the bodies of Richard Vernon of Haddon, Esquire, and Margaret
his wife, daughter of Sir Robert Dymmok, Knight, who had issue George
Vernon. Richard indeed died on the * Vigil of the Assumption of Saint
Mary the Virgin, in the year of our Lord, 1517, and the said Margaret died
. . . . . day of the month . . . . in the year of our Lord 15—,on
whose souls may God Almighty be merciful. Amen.

The pannelling on the north side and two ends of this
monument were used for many years to form the altar (No.
25), but were restored to this tomb in 1892. The vault under
this tomb is now filled up with concrete. It is arched with
stone, and appears to have held two coffins only, probably
wooden ones which had perished.

The effigies are somewhat small but finely executed.

The male one is in plate armour and wears the gilt collar of
the SS. His helmet (like Sir Harry's), has the Vernon crest,
a boar's head (lying to the south), with mantlet and armour
very similar to Sir Harry's; an ornamented sword-hilt,
dagger, and gauntlets lying at the side; his feet rest against
the double tail of a lion.

He appears to have died while yet young, soon after his
father, so probably was not knighted (*vide* the inscription) ; we
may imagine him, while we stand by this tomb, a candidate
for knighthood passing the " Vigil of Arms " (pictured in Mrs.
Hemans' poem), the consummation of which honour was
subsequently hindered by some adverse fate.

* Aug. 9. 14 Hen. VIII.

> A sounding step was heard by night
> In a church where the mighty slept,
> As a mail-clad youth, till morning's light,
> Midst the tombs his vigils kept.
>
> He walked in dreams of power and fame,
> He lifted a proud bright eye,
> For the hours were few that withheld his name
> From the roll of chivalry.

The candidate for knighthood was under the necessity of keeping watch the night before his inauguration, in a church, and completely armed. This was called the "Vigil of Arms."

His son and successor was then nine years old, viz., Sir George Vernon,* whose tomb is at Bakewell Church.

His lady on the right has a hood pointed over the forehead and hanging down over the shoulders in short strips. Angels (now headless), support her pillow, and two small hounds at the feet hold her dress in their mouths. There is a circlet at the waist with leaf pattern, and hanging obliquely.

The south side only has shields of arms, and they are:—
1. *Gu.* a fesse dauncettée *or*, between 6 crosslets. 2. *Arg.* fretty *sa.* (Vernon). 3. *Az.* two pipes *or*, between 6 cross crosslets (Pype). 4. *Arg.* fretty *sa.* (Vernon).

Sir Robert Dymmok was king's "champion" at the coronations of Richard III. (1483), Henry VII., and Henry VIII., an office of great antiquity, derived from the celebrated house of Marmion with the feudal manor of Scrivelsby, co. Lincoln, to which the championship is attached. He was a military man, and one of the principal commanders at the siege of Tournay, where, after the surrender of the city, he was constituted king's treasurer. The "championship" has been held by the Dymmok family upwards of 400 years.

The Champion claims on Coronation Day one of the king's great coursers with a saddle, harness, and trappings of cloth of gold, and one of the best suits of armour with cases of cloth of gold, and all such other things apper-

---

* In the side aisle there [Bakewell Church] is a table monument with effigies of a knight, and a lady on each side, and this inscription:—" Here lyeth Sir George Vernon, deceased the . . . . . day of . . . . . . and Dame Margaret his wyffe, doughter to Sir Gylbert Taylebois, deceased the . . . . day of . . . . . . 15, and also Dame Mawde his wyffe doughter to Sir Ralph Langcfofot, deceased the . . . . day of . . . . whose souls God pardon." — *Antiquarian Repertory.*

taining to the sovereign's body, as the sovereign ought to have if personally going into mortal battle.

On Coronation Day, he, mounted on the said courser, trapped and furnished as aforesaid, and accompanied by the Constable and Marshal of England, &c., a trumpet sounding before him, rides into the banqueting hall where the king sits at dinner, and in his presence and the presence of all the people, the herald makes three proclamations to the effect that if any do deny that the sovereign is the rightful heir to the crown, here is his Champion ready by his body to assert and maintain that *he lyes like a false traitor*, and in that quarrel to adventure his life. Thereupon the champion throws down his gauntlet as a challenge, and if none pick it up accepting the challenge, the sovereign drinks to his champion in a gold cup with a cover, which cup the champion has also as a fee for his services.

At Henry IV's coronation, Sir — Dymoke expected an adversary. When dinner was half over, he entered the hall armed, mounted on a handsome steed, richly barded with crimson housings. He was armed for wager of battle, and was preceded by another knight bearing his lance; he himself had his drawn sword in one hand, and his naked dagger by his side.

The canting motto, "Pro Rege Dimico" (I fight for the king), is singularly appropriate to the office of this family.

The scene depicted in Sir. W. Scott's poem, "Marmion," of the approach and entry of Lord Marmion, the Champion, into Norham Castle, may well be imagined as happening at Tong Castle. Sir Robert Dymmok was Champion at the time in which the story is placed, and his daughter, Margaret Vernon, was the Lady of Tong Castle.

The lines so vividly describe the mode of procedure from place to place of a great knight, his retinue, his steed, and habiliments, as well as the occupants of a castle, at the date to which these Vernon monuments refer us, that a rather long quotation may be given.

The sun was setting on the castle when

The battled towers, the donjon keep,
The loophole grates where captives weed,
The flanking walls that round it sweep,
  In yellow lustre shone,
The warriors on the turrets high,
Moving athwart the evening sky,
  Seemed forms of giant height.

The scouts had parted on their search,
  The castle gates were barred;
Above the gloomy portal arch,
Timing his footsteps to a march,
  The warder kept his guard;
Low humming, as he paced along,
Some ancient Border gathering song.

A distant trampling sound he hears ;
He looks abroad, and soon appears
O'er Horncliffe Hill a plump of spears,
  Beneath a pennon gay ;
A horseman, darting from the crowd,
Like lightning from a summer cloud,
Spurs on his mettled courser proud,
  Before the dark array.
Beneath the sable palisade
That closed the castle barricade,
  His bugle-horn he blew ;
The warder hastened from the wall,
And warned the captain in the hall,
  For well the blast he knew ;
And joyfully that knight did call,
To sewer, squire, and seneschal.

Then to the castle's lower ward
  Sped forty yeoman tall,
The iron-studded gates unbarred,
Raised the portcullis' ponderous guard,
The lofty palisade unsparred,
  And let the drawbridge fall.

Along the bridge Lord Marmion rode,
Proudly his red-roan charger trode,
His helm hung at the saddlebow ;
Well by his visage you might know
He was a stalworth knight, and keen,
And had in many a battle been ;
The scar on his brown cheek revealed
A token true of Bosworth field ;   [limb,
His square-turned joints, and strength of
Showed him no carpet knight so trim,
But in close fight a champion grim,
  In camps a leader sage.

Well was he armed from head to heel,
In mail and plate of Milan steel ;
But his strong helm, of mighty cost,
Was all with burnished gold embossed ;
Amid the plumage of the crest,
A falcon hovered on her nest,
With wings outspread, and forward breast :
E'en such a falcon, on his shield,
Soared sable in an azure field :
The golden legend bore aright,
𝔚𝔥𝔬 𝔠𝔥𝔢𝔠𝔨𝔰 𝔞𝔱 𝔪𝔢, 𝔱𝔬 𝔡𝔢𝔞𝔱𝔥 𝔦𝔰 𝔡𝔦𝔤𝔥𝔱.

Behind him rode two gallant squires,
Of noble name and knightly sires :
They burned the gilded spurs to claim ;
For well could each a war-horse tame.

Four men-at-arms came at their backs,
With halbert, bill, and battle-axe :
They bore Lord Marmion's lance so strong,
And led his sumpter mules along,
And ambling palfry, when at need
Him listed ease his battle steed.
The last and trustiest of the four,
On high his forky pennon bore.

Last, twenty yeoman, two and two,
In hosen black, and jerkins blue,
With falcons broidered on each breast,
Attended on their lord's behest :
Each, chosen for an archer good,
Knew hunting-craft by lake or wood ;
Each one a six-foot bow could bend,
And far a clothyard shaft could send ;
Each held a boar-spear tough and strong,
And at their belts their quivers rung ;
Their dusty palfreys, and array,
Showed they had marched a weary way.

Sir Edward Dymoke (brother of Dame Margaret Vernon) officiated as Champion at the Coronations of Edward VI., Queen Mary, and Queen Elizabeth. At the latter. he " came riding into the hall as she sat at dinner in ' faire complete armour,' mounted on a beautiful courser, richly trapped in cloth of gold, and cast down his gauntlet, offering to fight with any one that should deny her to be the lawful Queen of the realm."

ORGAN.

The ORGAN is a modern one, purchased in 1877, with funds the proceeds of some concerts kindly given by Mrs. Hartley and her family at Tong Castle, and voluntary contributions. It was built by J. H. Walker & Sons, of London.

The following accounts of the ANCIENT ORGAN, as seen at the end of the last century, will be read with interest :—

In 1763 :—" In a sort of Vestry close to the Chancel among other old Lumber, is the very same old Organ-case and Bellows belonging to it which was in use before the dissolution of the College, a piece of antiquity hardly to be parallelled in the whole Kingdom. The Organ was small, but the case of Oak is very neat, and of a pretty Gothic Fashion."

" In the Parish Church of Tong (once collegiate), the gallery, with the entrance to the choir, is yet unremoved, and the organ case remains, with little more room than was sufficient for the player. This organ, to judge by what is left of it, seems the most ancient of the sort that has come under my observation, which for the entertainment of your musico-mechanical readers, I will describe. And first the case. It is in the true Gothic, with pinnacles and finials after the manner of ancient tabernacles, and very like the one just finished and erected in Lichfield Cathedral, only on a smaller scale. Now, as to the other parts. The keys are gone, but the sounding board remains, and is pierced for one set of pipes only, seemingly an open diapason, whether of metal or wood could not be determined, there not being a single pipe left; from the apparent position and distance I presume they were of metal. I perceived no registers or slides for other stops, and observed the compass to be very short—only to A in alto for the treble part, and short octaves in the lower bass; therefore, not more than forty tones on the whole. The bellows were preserved in a lumber-room near the vestry, double winded without folds, and made with thick hides, like unto a smith's or forge bellows. Thus simply constructed there could be no transmutation of sounding pipes, nor that variation to be produced from a mixture of different flute and reed pipes, which are made use of in the modern organ. An instrumental machine, whose improvement has been the work of more than one century; at first very plain and uncompounded, like the generality of mechanical inventions. And this remark will serve to establish, in some measure, the antiquity of the Tong Organ."—Quoted from *Gentleman's Magazine*, 1789,—from *Shreds and Patches, Shrewsbury Journal*, Nov. 28th, 1883.

18. Pass behind the organ to a fine TOMB of stone with an INCISED SLAB of alabaster. A soldier (or the right) and his lady (on the left) are represented in black lines inlaid, well defined, except the heads. At the east end of the tomb are the following words in English :—

. . day of August In the yere of oure Lord m ccccc xxx

At the man's feet is a dog with collar and link, short ears, and long tail. At the side of the lady's head is a wingless creature, not a griffin, as has been suggested, but a lion rampant (for Ludlow).

This coat, with the entry and date of decease given below, is doubtless sufficient to warrant the appropriation of the tomb to HUMPHREY VERNON, of Hodnet, and of Houndshill, 2nd son of Sir Harry Vernon (No. 15) and his wife ALICE, younger daughter and co-heir of John LUDLOW, Esq.

He died August, 1542 or 1545,* and was buried with his forefathers at Tong. His funeral is the subject of a curious entry in the Hodnet Churchwardens' accounts for the year 1542 :—

Item.—Rec. at ye burryall of ye Right worshypfull Homfrye Vernon being burryed at Tong, Lyghtes . . . . . . II.

Alice his wife died 28th August, 1531.* The part of the inscription, as above, is much crowded ; the last x is at the corner of the tomb, and it is possible that the final figure i may have been worn off, or perhaps never was put on. Alice was daughter of John Ludlow, and granddaughter of Sir Richard Ludlow, Kt., who married Elizabeth, daughter of Sir Richard Grey, Lord Powys.

Humphrey left two sons, George, of Hodnet, and Thomas, of Houndshill. His great-grandson, Edward Vernon, of Hounds-

---
* *History of Haddon Hall.*

hill, married his brother John's great-granddaughter and heiress, and thus the Houndshill and Sudbury inheritances of the Vernons became united in the persons of Edward and Margaret Vernon. Their son Henry was an ancestor of the present Lord Vernon.†

19. Return to the south transept, where is now the STANLEY TOMB, a fine monument in the Italian style, surpassed by few in Westminster Abbey.

It bears three effigies in very good preservation. Two in the upper or table part,—which is supported by eight pillars of marble—commemorate MARGARET, daughter and co-heir of Sir George VERNON, and her husband, SIR THOMAS STANLEY, second son of Edward, third Earl of Derby, and one in the lower part, beneath the table, SIR EDWARD STANLEY, Knight of the Bath, their son, Lord of Harlaston, and of Tong Castle, and of Eynsham. Dame Margaret's effigy is on the right, and her husband's on the left. The coffin containing Sir Thomas Stanley's remains is in the Stanley vault beneath the chancel, and records the date of his death in 1576. This vault, now filled up with concrete, was found near the altar during the restoration of the Church in 1892, and contained three old-shaped lead coffins, and a small lead box, some of which had been cut open and rifled long years ago. One has an inscription plate of lead, about 8 inches by 7, with the following small quarter-inch letters cut in :—

HIC JACET THOMAS STANL MILES FILVS SECVNDVS EDOVADI COMITVS DARBI MARIIVS MARGARETE FILIE ET VNE HERETVM GEORGII VERNON MILITES QVI OBIIT VICESSIMO PRIMO DIE DECEMBRI ANNO REGNI REGINE ELIZABETH QVINGENTESSIMO SEPTVAGESSIMO SERTO ANIME MISEREATVR DEVS AMEN PER ME JOANNEM LATHOMVM.

---

† I am indebted to Mr. Vaughan for correcting the statement in the first edition to the effect that the Hodnet and Stokesay inheritances became united in the person of Henry Vernon, which was not so.

The following is a translation:—" Here lies Sir Thomas Stanley, Knight, second son of Edward, Earl of Derby, husband of Margaret, daughter and co-heir of George Vernon, Knight, who died on the 21st December, in the 19th year of the reign of Queen Elizabeth, A.D., 1576.   God have mercy on his soul.   Amen.   By me, John Lathom."

Sir Edward Stanley was called by the Puritans an " arrant and dangerous Papist," and died in 1632.   He sold Tong to Sir Thomas Harries in 1623.

The tomb formerly occupied a position at the north side of the altar.   " A monstrous large canopy tomb stands jostling the altar, and before it, placed there, as I should guess, in the indecent reign of Queen Elizabeth," Mr. Cole says, 1757.   It was removed, as I am informed, by Mr. Durant, a late owner of Tong, to make room for the Durant monuments.   The late Mr. Street contemplated restoring it to its original position, as described in the *Gentleman's Magazine*, 1763; but this was impossible, and Mr. Christian wisely contented himself with advising its retention on the present site, simply repairing and re-erecting it parallel with and adjacent to the other tombs of the Vernon family.

Sir Thomas is in heavy plate armour, richly ornamented. Both hands are on his breast.   His helmet plumes are ostrich feathers.   All the effigies recline upon quilted straw-like beds of stone.

Dame Margaret is in black; her head rests upon an embroidered pillow ; the features are delicately cut ; the hair is brushed back off the forehead ; she wears a cap with gold circlet, and a muslin gorget, and narrow Elizabethan collar.

Sir Edward is in plate armour, with right hand on his breast, the left on his sword hilt.

J

The square tapering columns of black marble are now placed upon the tomb ; formerly they were apart from it, and each was surmounted by a white marble figure. The figures are all damaged, and are lying loose about the tomb.

On the arches which carry the upper structure of the tomb and around the sides are the numerous shields of arms quartered by the Stanleys and Vernons.

The eight square alabaster columns supporting the table are carved with elegant narrow ribbon decoration, into which are introduced little centres of compasses, spears, quivers, books, censers, torches, drums, lances, body-armour, helmets, some erect and some inverted. Similar emblems and ribbon decoration were to be seen on the arch of the Goldsmiths, erected by the Emperor Severus. The 32 panels which form the ceiling of the table have been enriched with rosettes or roses, but all are missing. The 8 circular columns, which stand beside each square pillar, are of rich marble, four being black, and four, the centre ones, red.

The present state of the tomb scarcely comes up to the term "magnificent" applied to it by more than one writer, but let us bear in mind that it is now shorn of much that formerly lent elegance to it. The original colouring of the figures representing the deceased as they lived (of which the black hair of Sir Edward is an example), the polished marbles and gilding, the shields of arms, and other embellishments, with the tall columns bearing angels—the whole surmounted by a rich canopy—would give an incomparably different effect from that presented at the present time, though it still exhibits much rich work.

The shields of arms upon the tomb appear to be as follow but the colours are very indistinct :—

1. *Sable* on a bend *azure*, three stags' heads cabossed *or* [Stanley].

2. Stanley 1 impaling a fret *sable* [Vernon].

3. *Or*, a cross engrailed *sable* [   ].

4. *Azure*, a fret *sable*, a canton *gules* [Vernon].

5. . . . . . . a fesse chequy *or* and *az.* between 3 escallop shells [   ].

6. Gone.

7. *Gules*, three legs conjoined in armour proper, garnished and spurred *or* [Isle of Man].

8. *Azure*, three lions passant *sable* [Ludlow].

9. like 1.

10. *Sable*, a lion rampant guardant *gules*, collared *or* [   ].

11. Checky *azure* and *or* [Warren ?].

12. *Azure* a saltier *gules*, on a chief *gules*, 3 escallops *or* [   ].

13. Barry of six *or* and *azure* [Pembruge].

14. *Argent* a lion rampant *sable* langued *gules* [Ludlow].

15. *Or*, on a chief dancettée *azure*, 3 bezants [Latham].

16. *Azure*, two pipes between 7 crosslets *or* [Pype].

17. *Azure*, a fret *sable* [Vernon].

18. *Gules*, a canton sinister and base *azure* [   ].

19. *Gules*, two lions passant in pale, *or* [Strange].

20. *Gules*, a cinquefoil *or.* within 6 cross crosslets *or* [Umfreville ?].

A.   Stanley, impaling *or* a lion rampant [   ].

C.   *Or* a lion rampant *sable* langued *gules* (?) [   ].

B.   *Or* a lion rampant *sable* langued *gules* [   ].

D.   Stanley (?)

E.   Ditto   (?)

F.   Vernon (?)

On the north side of the monument is this INSCRIPTION in gilt lettering (not cut in):—

THOMAS STANDLEY SECOND SOONE OF EDWARD EARL OF DERBIE
LORD STANLEY AND STRANGE DESENDED FROM THE FAMILIE OF THE
STANLEYS MARRIED MARGARET VERNON ONE OF THE DAVGHTERS
AND COHAIRS OF SIR GEORGE VERNON OF NETHER HADDON IN THE
COVNTIE OF DERBIE KNIGHTE

BY WHOM HE HAD ISSVE TWO SOONS HENRI AND EDW: HENRY DIED
AN INFANT & E SVRVIVED TO WHOM THOS LORDSHIPES DESENDED
AND MARRIED THE LA. LVCIE PERCIE SECOND DAVGHTER TO THOMAS
EARL OF NORTHVMBELAND BY HER HE HAD ISSVE 7 DAVGHTERS AND
ONE SOONE SHEE AND HER 4 DAVGHTERS 18 ARABELLA 16 MARIE 15
ALIS AND 13 PRISCILLA

ARE INTERRED VNDER A MONNIMENT IN YE CHVRCHE OF WALTHAM
IN YE COVNTIE OF ESSEX. THOMAS HIS SOONE DIED IN HIS INFANCIE
AND IS BVRIED IN YE PARISHE CHVRCHE OF WINWICKE IN YE COVNTIE
OF LANCA: YE OTHER THREE PETRONELLA FRANCIS AND VENESIE ARE
YET LIVINGE.

At the head of the tomb on west end are these "following verses made by William Shakespeare, the late famous tragedian," says Sir Wm. Dugdale.

ASK WHO LYES HEARE BVT DO NOT WEEP;
HE IS NOT DEAD, HE DOOTH BVT SLEEP.
THIS STONY REGISTER IS FOR HIS BONES
HIS FAME IS MORE PERPETVALL THEN THEISE STONES;
AND HIS OWN GOODNESS WT HIMSELF BEING GON
SHALL LYVE WHEN EARTHLIE MONVMENT IS NONE.

And at the foot of the tomb (*i.e.*, the east end now) these interesting and oft-quoted lines :—

NOT MONVMENTALL STONE PRESERVES OVR FAME
NOR SKY ASPYRING PIRAMIDS OVR NAME
THE MEMORY OF HIM FOR WHOM THIS STANDS
SHALL OVTLYVE MARBL AND DEFACERS' HANDS
WHEN ALL TO TYME'S CONSVMPTION SHALL BE GEAVEN
STANDLY FOR WHOM THIS STANDS SHALL STAND IN HEAVEN.

Underneath was the following line not now to be seen :—

Beati mortui qui in Domino moriuntur.
(Blessed are the dead which die in the Lord)

Mr. Eyton, in his *Antiquities of Shropshire*, writes :—" Sir William Dugdale says positively that this epitaph, ' Not monumental stone,' &c., was written by Shakespeare," and that " the opposite or east end (*i.e.*, the foot) of the tomb exhibits six lines which I cannot help thinking to have been in imitation of them by an inferior poet. Possibly they are in praise of Sir Edward, son of Sir Thomas, for they speak of one who ' lyes here.' Now Sir Thomas is said to have been buried at Walthamstow." This is an erroneous conclusion : Sir Thomas *is* buried at Tong, and he and his wife lie in the same vault. It has been remarked that if Shakespeare wrote the epitaph at the date upon the tomb—(I see no date upon the tomb now)—he could only have been 12 years old, but possibly this tomb, like many others, was not erected for many years after Sir Thomas's decease, and probably not until some time after Sir Edward's decease. May not its beauty of design suggest the artistic taste of Sir Kenelm Digby, Sir Edward's son-in-law?

Sir Edward Stanley was father of the famous beauty Venetia Lady Digby, about whom Johnson wrote a long poem. Her name is mentioned as "yet living" on the Stanley tomb at Tong.

The date of the tomb, and so probably of the inscription also, can be readily traced to a very definite period thus: Venetia Digby was born 1600 and died in 1633, therefore the inscription was put on between those dates. Sir Edward Stanley died, I believe, in 1632.

I have before suggested that this handsome monument was probably due to the refined taste of the husband of Venetia, Sir Kenelm Digby, the "Ornament of England," as he was called. It would seem, therefore, that in attributing the epitaph to Shakespeare's early youth, 12 years, as one writer has done, he may have been guided by its similarity to his sonnets, which, though written in early youth, were not pub. lished till 1603 when he was 39, two of which are given below. I think the doubtful inference has arisen through adopting as its date the time of the death of Sir Thos. Stanley (1576). Shakespeare was born in 1564, and died in 1616. In 1616 Venetia would be a young girl of 16; hence the words "yet living" in the inscription. Shakespeare would then be 52.

There are other lines in Shakespeare's sonnets and elsewhere so similar to these lines attributed to him at Tong, that they, and Sir William Dugdale's record that he wrote them, appear to be conclusive. I choose out these two :—

Not marble, nor the gilded monuments
Of princes, shall outlive this powerful rhyme:
But you shall shine more bright in these contents
Than unswept stone besmear'd with sluttish time.

When wasteful war shall statues overturn,
　And broils root out the work of masonry,
Nor Mars his sword nor war's quick fire shall burn
　The living record of your memory.

. . . .

My love looks fresh, and Death to me subscribes,
　Since, spite of him, I'll live in this poor rhyme,
While he insults o'er dull and speechless tribes,
　And thou in this shalt find thy monument.
　When tyrant's crests and tombs of brass are spent.

As " England's Queen and most chivalrous nobles were his friends," it seems to me most natural that the monument at Tong, which commemorates together the following illustrious names, should bear lines written by the great poet of the time —Margaret Vernon (daughter of the Vernon King of the Peak), Sir Thomas Stanley, son of Earl of Derby, Sir Edward Stanley, K.B., his son, Lady Lucy Percy (daughter of Duke of Northumberland), and Venetia Digby, the beautiful.

I have no doubt the inscription in the 3 compartments, now on the north side, was at first on the south side. The tomb stood in the Chancel on the north side of the altar, and hence the inscription would be only readable if on the south side of the tomb. It seems, therefore, that the table part of the tomb has been twisted completely round. The verse " Ask," &c., originally at the foot of the tomb, and at the east end, is now at the head and west end; and the verse " not monumental," &c., formerly at the head, is now at the foot.

The late Dean Stanley's letter to Mr. Lawrence, regarding the Stanley Tomb, is appended :—

Sept. 8, 1873.
Address Anderfield Dren N.B.

DEAR SIR,—I am much obliged for your kind trouble in regard to the Stanley Monument in your Church. I presume that there is no date on the monument to indicate that it may have been a later epoch than the date of the death of its owner, and so escape the necessity of adopting the impossible youth of Shakespeare, if there were other sufficient points for supposing him to be the author. When in the Church I only read hastily that part of the inscription which is at the west end of the tomb; and, unless I am mistaken, the name was written Standly in the last line, and this made the basis of the play on the words. Is this so?

Yours faithfully,

A. P. STANLEY.

Margaret Vernon by her marriage conveyed Tong Castle to her husband; and her sister Dorothy (who eloped on the night of her sister's wedding, from Haddon Hall, the home of the Vernons, with Sir John Manners) conveyed that grand old pile to her husband. The walk by which the young lady fled the mansion is still pointed out as " Dorothy Vernon's walk."

All Haddon is fragrant with the memory of one fair woman Dorothy Vernon. Her postern, her walk, her rooms, her terrace, her beauty beautifies the whole place ; the charm and romance of the fair heiress linger yet round every part of Haddon. She was daughter of Sir Geo. Vernon, King of the Peak, died 1565, the year that Mary Queen of Scots married the ill-fated Lord Darnley. Dorothy loved one whom her father did not approve, and she determined to elope. And now we must fill in fancy the long gallery of Haddon Hall with the splendour of a revel. and the stately joy of a great ball in the time of Queen Elizabeth. In the midst of mirth and excitement, while " noble lords and stately dames step in the courtly dance," the fair young daughter of the house steals unobserved away. She isues from her door, and her light feet fly with tremulous speed along the darkling terrace, till they reach a postern gate in the wall, which opens. Someone is waiting eagerly for her, with swift horses,—young Sir John Manners, second son of the House of Rutland. The lovers mount and ride rapidly away, and so Dorothy Vernon transfers Haddon to the owner of Belvoir, and the boar's head of the Vernons becomes mingled with the peacock of the Manners of Belvoir.

Sir John was second son of Thomas 13th Lord Ros and Earl of Rutland, and was great-grandfather to the first Duke.

The Hon. (Sir) Thomas Stanley was a Knight, of Winwick, and probably Lieutenant-Governor of the Isle of Man, 1562. The family of Stanley,—an old branch of the Barons Audley, of Audley, co. Stafford, in the time of King John,—is one, the conduct of whose valiant sons has contributed largely to the glorious annals of England. One Sir John Stanley was a K.G., and in 1406 had licence to fortify his new house at Liverpool (Knowsley) with embattled walls, and a grant of the

Isle, castle and pile of Man, with all the isles adjacent, on payment of two falcons to the King on Coronation Day. It was Sir Thomas Stanley's great-great-grandfather who was created Earl of Derby in consideration for his services in the victory of Bosworth, 1485 ; and his placing the crown of Richard III. upon the head of the victorious Richmond (Henry VII) in the field, is a matter of historic record. His great-grandfather George, married Jane, daughter and heir of John, Lord Strange of Knockyn. His father, Edward, 3rd Earl of Derby, K.G., bore the additional titles of Viscount Kynton, Lord Stanley and Strange, Lord of Knockyn, Mohun, Basset, Burnal, and Lacy, and Lord of Man and the Isles. This Earl on the birth of Sir Thomas Stanley's son, Edward, 1562, made a Deed of Settlement declaring that his several manors and lands in the counties of Warwick, Devon, and Oxford, also Dunham Massey, Bowden, Rungey Hale, Æton, and Darfield in Co. Chester, shall appertain and belong to Sir Thomas Stanley for life, with remainder as moiety to his wife Lady Margaret for life, with remainder to Sir Edward for life, with remainder to the Earl's first son, with remainder to the heirs male of Sir Thomas, with remainders to the heirs of Sir Edward. Sir Edward became possessed of all the said lands on his father's death, as well as the Castle of Hornby.

Lady Lucy Percy, his wife, was daughter of Thomas Percy, who was created by Queen Mary, Earl of Northumberland, but conspiring later against Queen Elizabeth, was beheaded at York, 1572. His father, Sir Thomas, a lineal descendant of Hotspur, and other illustrious Percies, was also executed for conspiracy in Henry VIII's reign.

Of Sir Edward Stanley's numerous family only two daughters grew up, viz. :—Frances, married to John Fortescue, Esq., of Salden, Berks, and Venetia, the renowned beauty, married to Sir Kenelm Digby, Knight, the philosopher.

20. Here was formerly an octagonal PEDESTAL attached to N.E. pillar of tower, supposed to have originally supported the image of Saint Bartholomew, the patron Saint of the Church, or perhaps the Virgin Mary; it was called the "pillar of Mary." On the other hand it may have been a pulpit pedestal. Until lately the broken crest from a destroyed Vernon tomb lay upon it.

Tradition says that there once stood in the **Lady Chapel** ("our Lady's" Chapel) "a most beautiful sculptured image of the Virgin, but this was destroyed by some Puritanical hands in the 16th Century; and the pedestal on which it once stood only remains," and is now situated on the north corner under the Belfry tower, close to the foot of the Pembruge tomb, it having been removed there from the Lady Chapel, *i.e.*, supposed to be on the north side of this tomb.† In 1892 this pillar was found to be a modern intrusion of brickwork, and was removed.

CHOIR SCREEN.

21. The CHOIR SCREEN between chancel and tower-space is Transitional, of choice workmanship and design, and in very good preservation for its date. On the side facing the nave, the cornice is composed of oak leaves and acorns, and the string-course or the surbase shews the vine; on the other side are birds, the vine, and other carving, the whole taking up and being continuous with the delicate oak tracery forming the upper part of the choir stalls. Only one piece of the trefoil ornament forming the cresting of the screen remained in 1884, viz., at the end near the chancel door, and that had disappeared a few years later, but fortunately by the aid of a detail in an old photograph belonging to the writer, the cresting has been faithfully reproduced. The reparation of the Choir Screen and Tracery is a very marked improvement, and Mr. H. Bridgman, of Lichfield, is to be congratulated

---

† Note by Rev. R. G. Lawrence.

K

upon his careful execution of the work. The two low doors in this screen separating the nave and chancel were removed in 1892. They were not thought to harmonize with the original work. Perhaps they belonged to the woodwork which is supposed to have run across under the western Arch of Tower, forming part of the rood loft, and which would take up with the two Aisle Screens 10a. and 10b.

In the arch above the screen are to be seen the holes from which were removed the timbers of the rood-cross. The rood-loft gallery doubtless extended from the two east to the two west pillars of the tower-space ; access to the same was gained through the doorway (to be seen over the pulpit) from the stone staircase. Previous to the reign of Edward VI. the rood-loft, or gallery and screen supporting the rood cross, was a conspicuous object in early churches. In the gallery the deacon performed part of the public services of the Church, and at St. Julian's, Shrewsbury, a bottle of claret was placed in it for his use on Passion Sunday on account of an exceptionally long part of the service which he read from there. Upon the gallery was fixed the holy rood, or crucifix bearing the image of Christ. To our ancestors the rood conveyed a full type of Christianity, the nave representing the Church militant, and the chancel the Church triumphant, and thus denoting that they who would go from one to the other must pass under the rood, *i.e.*, bear the Cross.

CHOIR-STALLS.

The CHOIR, though small, contains some original stalls of beautiful workmanship, the carving being well preserved considering its antiquity. They are 16 in number, four adjoining the screen, and six on each side adjoining the north and south walls, and are of the peculiar construction implied by the name " Miserere " (Lord have mercy). The benches are of massive oak, hinged at the back, and when turned up

Tong church, the choir looking west
E·H·N·

against the stall each exhibits a small half-octagon projecting
bracket, carved with floral ornaments or hideous figures, in
very fair preservation. A verger at Chester Cathedral thus
described the use of this uncomfortable bench arrangement,
the misereres there and in many old churches being of exactly
similar construction :—During the long services of the Roman
Catholic Church the monks became wearied from prolonged
standing, and these seats were constructed to give them
partial rest without permitting the comfort of an actual sitting
posture. The occupant is supposed to stand, letting the
weight of his body rest partly upon his feet and partly upon
this little bracket, and so long as he kept awake the little
bracket relieved his tired limbs and served him well ; but the
instant he passed into sleepy forgetfulness his legs ceased to
prop him up, and the increased weight thrown on the bracket
caused it immediately to topple over and nearly precipitate
the drowsy worshipper to the floor. It is difficult to describe
in words the action of this peculiar arrangement, but visitors
may examine the benches for themselves. The stalls were
numbered in Mr. Durant's time (as well as the seats in the
Church), as the following items in an old account book of
Heayse, a wheelwright of Tong, record :—

	£	s.	d.
1806. G. Durrant, Esq., paint and numbering the seats in the Church and Chancel	0	18	6
Altering the Cottage numbers, and in the Church	0	2	6
Numbering the Cottages at Tong	0	1	6
1811. Assisting with the Commandments in the Church and materials ..	0	4	6

The numbers still upon the stalls will be convenient for
reference (see plan).

Detailed notice of choir-stalls :—

Stall 1.—Bracket shews an embattled pattern similar to
parapet on the church. This stall-division differs from the
others, which are single figures, in being a winged male figure
holding a smaller one. The two desk-ends in front of stalls
1 and 2 are the " barbarous repairs " referred to by Mr. Petit.

Brackets of stalls 2, 3, 6, 7, 14, 15, and 16 are generally floral ornaments. Stall 4, a face with foliage springing from the mouth ; this stall must have been the seat of a Church dignitary, for above it a trefoil panel of tracery is enriched with (1) Head of Christ ; (2) an I H S ; and (3) an angel holding a shield, which bears : a heart in the centre, a key horizontally, a spear perpendicularly, a hand in each top corner, and a foot in each bottom corner. Stall-bracket 5.—Winged half-length figure holding shield. Stall-bracket 8, the one upon which most pains seem to have been bestowed, has in the centre the Crucifixion scene ; on each side is an angel holding a scroll. At the foot of the cross are flowers, and on each side of the bracket a bird—perhaps intended for a dove. 9.—A face with foliage springing from each side of the mouth. 10.—A large bird, and a smaller one on either side. 11.—Foliage, a little more elaborate than the others. 12.—A winged half-length figure and shield (same as No. 5). 13.—Modern piece of moulding. The desk-end or poppy-head opposite stall 3 exhibits two figures, and two birds " crewdling." Opposite stall 8 the poppy-head is perhaps for the Ascension scene ; but there are twelve figures, besides the figure upon a bracket above them. Opposite stall 9, the Resurrection scene, Roman soldiers, one large figure sleeping, three smaller, and above them two female figures. Opposite stall 14, two figures, and below two faces. Opposite stalls 15 and 16, two figures, and below two angels with shields.

The elegant tracery of the woodwork above the stalls is composed chiefly of quatrefoils, and is nearly similar to that shewn in the illustration of the Choir-Screen. The numerous birds carved in this woodwork are, I suppose, emblems of watchfulness.

During the restoration in 1892 there were found two Bishop's Marks of Consecration on the walls behind these stalls, one on either side.

WINDOWS IN CHANCEL.

The EAST WINDOW is a fine five-light one, with good Perpendicular tracery, and transom ; it is about 20 feet high, occupying a not exactly central position in the east wall, as before remarked. From north wall, 3ft. 5ins. ; from south wall, 3ft. 1in. Some writers assert that during the middle ages the east window was intentionally placed nearer to one side-wall than the other, in order to typify the Head of the Saviour upon the Cross, which is generally shewn slightly inclined to one side, the east window being the principal light of the chancel, the most sacred part of the Church. In the tracery are some remains of old stained glass, the red and blue colours being especially rich. The following notes roughly record the composition of the glsss until its re-arrangement in 1892.

Referring to the lights by numbers (commencing on the left) :—

Below the transom—

1.—Black and white pieces, chequy. A shield of deep red, in the centre thereof a cross, on dexter side a pair of rings, pincers (white), a hammer (white head, yellow handle) ; on sinister side, three dice (white, black spots), two spears (yellow, white heads). These are the emblems of the Passion, called by heralds the shield of arms of Jesus Christ.

2.—St. Peter and keys (yellow), rich blue foliage.

3.—Some Gothic letters, and yellow and white architecture. A female figure in white.

4.—A shield, same as in No. 1, except that the scourge and a bird appear on the sinister side.

5.—Architecture corresponding very nearly with the arches of the Sedilia, and some old English letters, same as on the tomb of Sir Wm. Vernon (d. 1467).

Above the transom—

1.—Madonna and Child, white and yellow. A rich crown shewing four leaves, yellow ; some deep rich red foliage, and some blue.

2.—Mixture of white and blue, a little red.

3.—Fragments, including a piece of a yellow crown.

4.—Fragments. Three spear-heads held by a white hand, the centre one dark brown, the other two light blue heads, brown handles.

5.—Generally white, some black and white triangles.

Above these again in the tracery were—
Over centre-light (No 3). –

Nearly perfect, left side, a male figure with scroll, Gothic letters ; right side, female figure in white, with hands uplifted, red foliage.

Above light No. 1. –An angel, white head, with censer, and blue foliage. Above light No 2. —A female head, with white covering. Above light No. 4 —Mixture, blue and white. Above light No. 5.—White head, yellow halo; some black and white squares, chequy.

The same glass is now arranged thus :—
Below the transom –
1. - Plain.
2. · Fragments.
3.- Ditto.
4.—Holy face and another, probably St. Anne.
5.—Plain.

Above the transom—
1. - Angel bearing the shield with emblems of the Crucifixion.
2. - St. Peter.
3.—Virgin Mary and Child.
4.—St. Edmund King and Martyr.
5.—Similar to No. 1.

In the 10 panels of tracery immediately above are :—
1, 4. 7 and 10.   Emblems of the Four Evangelists.
2 and 3. - (Larger).   The latter is St Mary Magdalene.
5.—Unknown.
6.—The Angel Gabriel.
8.—The Virgin Mary.
9.—Probably Salome and another Holy Woman.

Of the OTHER WINDOWS in CHANCEL there are two in the north wall, each having three lights, with Perpendicular tracery.   And in the south wall three three-lighted windows with good Perpendicular tracery, the centre one being over the priest's door.*   The graceful black and white flower to be seen in little corners of the tracery of these windows is undoubtedly of Early Fifteenth Century date.

* Mr. Eyton records that in 1663 "the South window of chancel" contained arms as follow :—I. - Barry of 6 *or* and *az* (Pembruge) impaling Barry of 6 *or* and *az*. on a bend *gu*. three roses *arg*. (Lingen). II. - Pembruge). III. -(Lingen). IV. —*Gu*. a lion rampant, (Fitzalan). V. –*Arg*. fretty *sa*. (Vernon). VI.—*Arg*. fretty *sa*., a canton *gu*., (Vernon). VII. —*Az*. two pipes between nine cross crosslets *or* (Pype). VIII.—*Az*. a bend *arg*. cotized between six martlets *or* (De la Bere).
And " the North window of chancel "—I.—*Arg*. fretty *gu*. with a bezant on each joint of the fretty (Trussel), empaling *or* a lion rampant *sa*. (Ludlow). II.—(Ludlow) empaling (Lingen). III.—(Ludlow) empaling *arg*. fretty *sa*. a canton *gu*., (Vernon). IV. (Lingen). V.—(Pembruge). VI.—(Pembruge) empaling (Lingen). VII.—*Arg*. fretty *sa*. a canton *gu*. (Vernon) impaling [blank] VIII.—(De la Bere) empaling *gu*. a lion rampant *or*:

22.   By the commuunion rail and formerly bordered with fossil marble, but now with tiles, was the black marble slab with arms and supporters thereon, to the memory of the Hon. HENRY WILLOUGHBY, youngest son of Sir Thomas, afterwards in (1712), created Lord Middleton of Middleton, who had served in six several Parliaments during the reigns of King William and Queen Anne. Mr. Willoughby died in 1734 at Tong Castle, of which he was tenant. The slab, which was much worn, is now moved for protection nearer to the north wall of the choir : the arms are plainly to be seen, viz. :—Quarterly for Willoughby of Parham and Willoughby of Middleton, with supporters a grey friar and a savage, and the excellent motto " Truth without fear." The inscription is too indistinct to give a verbatim copy, but below the name are some lines which have been preserved :—

> His noble soul and truly generous mind,
> In acts of goodness both were unconfined;
> His charity was free and private too,
> By proper objects felt but known to few.
> His hospitality the poor did share,
> Relieved the widow, dried the orphan's tear;
> Pride with its lures and vain attempting art,
> Hateful to sight, was absent from his heart—
> A friend he was most worthy and sincere,
> There did the lustre of the friend appear;
> And as his merits justly claimed a name
> Inscribed in annals of immortal fame,
> In his just praise to latest times be it said,
> That all who living knew him, mourn'd him dead.

This vault was opened July 3, 1891, when it was found to contain only one coffin, bearing the plate of arms, with a martlet for difference, agreeing with the slab.

23.   On the south wall of the chancel, immediately above the altar rails, is the mural MONUMENT partly of alabaster and partly of marble and stone, to MRS. WYLDE, with female figure in Elizabethan costume, kneeling beside a table. Length of monument, 6ft. 6in. ; width, 3ft. 3in. Inscription :—

HERE LYETH THE BODY OF ANN WYLDE LATE WIFE OF JOHN WYLDE
OF DROITWYTCH IN THE COVNTY OF WORCESTER ESQR ELDEST
DAVGHTER OF SR THO: HARRIES OF TONG CASTLE SERJEANT-AT-LAW
AND BARONET AND DAME ELLINOR HIS WYFE WHOSE VIRTVE
MODESTIE RARE AND EXCELLENT PARTS FAR EXCEEDING HER AGE
HAVE FITTED HER FOR A MORE HEAVENLY HABITATION LEAVING
BEHIND HER THESE SPECTACLES OF GRIEFE AND PLEDGES OF TRVE
AFFECTION SHE DIED THE 6TH OF MAY IN THE YEERE OF OVR LORD
1624, AND OF HER AGE THE 16TH BEING THEN NEWLY DELIVERED OF
HER FIRST-BORNE.

There have been some verses below, which are now
illegible. At the top of the monument is :—

AD TE DEUM CLAMAVI (I have called unto Thee, O God).

There are two shields upon the monument. One, the larger,
has :—Party per pale : dexter—quarterly, first and fourth *arg.*
on a chief *sa.*, 3 martlets (for .... ?), second and third *arg.*
a cross *sa.* (for Wylde) ; sinister—barry of 7 *erm.* and *az.*, over
all 3 annulets *or*, two and one (for Harries). On the smaller,
a lady's shield, the Harries arms are repeated.

John Wylde was descended from Symon Wylde of the
Forde, co. Worcester, by his wife, Ellinor, daughter and co-
heir of George Wall of Droitwich.

Ann was the elder daughter and co-heiress of Sir Thomas
Harries. He was an eminent lawyer, Sergeant-at-Law 1589,
created a baronet 12th April 1623, and died in 1640—the
great-great-grandson of John Harries of Cruckton, Salop, 1463.
Her mother was Elinor, daughter of Roger Gifford, of Lindon,
physician to Queen Elizabeth.

Sir Thomas purchased Tong Castle from Sir Edward
Stanley about 1623.

Among the " prisoners taken at Salop 22nd February, 1644,
were Sir John Wyld, senior, Knight, and Sir John Wyld,
junior, Knight." Sergeant John Wylde was a member of the
Long Parliament in the time of Oliver Cromwell, representing
Worcestershire. At the same time Edmund Wylde, Esq.,
represented Droitwich, and was described as a King's Judge,
i.e., nominated to that office and only in part, or not at all,
risking to perform it.

Mrs. Wylde's sister, and the eventual sole heiress of Sir Thomas Harries, was Elizabeth. She married the Honourable William Pierrepoint of Thoresby, Notts, M P. for Salop, and called " William the Wise," and died in 1656. He was 2nd son of Robert Earl of Kingston, and, in right of his wife, succeeded to the Tong estate in 1640 ; was Member of the Long Parliament for Great Wenlock, Co. Salop, in Cromwell's time, and one of the Commissioners to treat with the King at Oxford, " being one who pressed for an Accommodation with the King ; " while his brother Francis represented Nottingham. At the Restoration, William, as M.P. for Notts, heartily espoused the Royal interest, and was chiefly instrumental in getting rid of the oppressions of the Court of Wards, Reliefs, &c. He died 1679.

In Carlyle's *Cromwell Letters*, Vol. III., occurs the following relating to him :—*

Charles's standard, it would seem then, was erected at Worcester on Friday. the 22nd August, 1651. About sunrise " our messenger " (*i.e.*, the Parliament's) left the Lord General (Oliver Cromwell) at Mr. Pierpoint's house,—William Pierpoint of the Kingston family, much his friend, – the house called Thoresby near Mansfield,—just starting for Nottingham, to arrive there that night.

William's father was Robert Pierrepoint, created Baron 1627, Viscount Newark and Earl of Kingston-upon-Hull, 1628 ; his mother being a daughter and co-heiress of Henry Talbot, 3rd son of Geo., Earl of Shrewsbury. At the breaking out of the Great Rebellion, Lord Pierrepoint was appointed by King Charles Lieut.-General of the Royal Forces within the counties of Lincoln, Rutland, &c. ; subsequently surprised at Gainsborough and made prisoner by Lord Willoughby of Parham, he was sent towards Hull in a pinnace (or small boat), which being pursued by Sir Charles Cavendish (who demanded the Earl and was refused) was shot at by that gentleman with a drake (a small piece of artillery) ; the Earl and his servant

---

* *Ex Tract* printed at London for Edw. Husbands, March 10, 1644}

were placed as a mark to Sir Charles's shot, and were both killed 13 July, 1643.

William and Elizabeth left several sons. The youngest, Gervase, was a considerable benefactor to Tong, and gained the title of Baron Pierrepoint of Ardglass in Ireland, and Lord Pierrepoint of Hanslope in England. (See brass No. 24 to his memory in Tong Church). The eldest, Robert, left three sons, two of whom, Robert and William, became successively Earls of Kingston-upon-Hull, and died without issue 1682 and 1690 respectively. William's elder brother Henry, "succeeded his father as 2nd Earl of Kingston, and was created Marquis of Dorchester 1645; eminent for his learning, a great reader, and well versed in the laws; in 1658 was member of the College of Physicians in London, and became, as Anthony Wood says, their pride and glory." He left two daughters, co-heirs, of whom Anne married John, 9th Earl and 1st Duke of Rutland.

Upon the death of this Marquis, the Kingston titles (except the Marquisate) and estates (including Tong Castle and Thoresby), passed to William's grandson Robert; afterwards to his brother William, Lord of Tong 1690; and afterwards to their brother Evelyn, created Duke of Kingston, 1715. He was father of Lady Mary Wortley Montague (who became so celebrated in the literary world), and grandfather of Evelyn,* last Duke of Kingston, who sold Tong to Mr. Durant in 1762, and died in 1773, when all his titles became extinct. In 1760 the Duke's seat was at Tong Castle.

Lady Harries gave to Tong, about the year 1630, the beautiful and costly Ciborium (see illustration), a sacramental vessel of the time of Henry VIII., said to be the work of the celebrated artist Holbein, and regarded by the highest authorities on such matters as unique. It stands 11 inches high, and is of silver gilt, richly chased, having a central

---

* He married the celebrated Miss Chudleigh.

To all to whome these p[rese]nts shall come I Evelin Duke of
Kingston Cheife Justice in Eyre of all his Ma[jes]t[ie]s fforrests Chases and
Parks Ereut North send Greeting Know Yee That I y[e] said —
Duke doe hereby make Constitute and appoint Jonathan Clay Gen[t] —
to be Clerke of y[e] Swainmote & Attachm[en]t C[our]ts to be held for his —
Ma[jes]t[ie]s fforrest of Sherwood in y[e] County of Nottingham Ereut —
North To hold and Execute y[e] said Office by himselfe or his —
suff[icient] Deputy & to have & take all ffees & dutys to y[e] said Office
belonging dureing my pleasure onely and noe longer In witnesse
whereof I have hereunto sett my hand & Seale this Second day
of September Anno D[omi]ni 1715./

Kingston

DUKE OF KINGSTON'S DEED, 1715.

barrel of crystal 2 in. deep, 2⅜ in. diameter outside, and 2¼ inside.† It probably belonged to the ancient college of Tong,

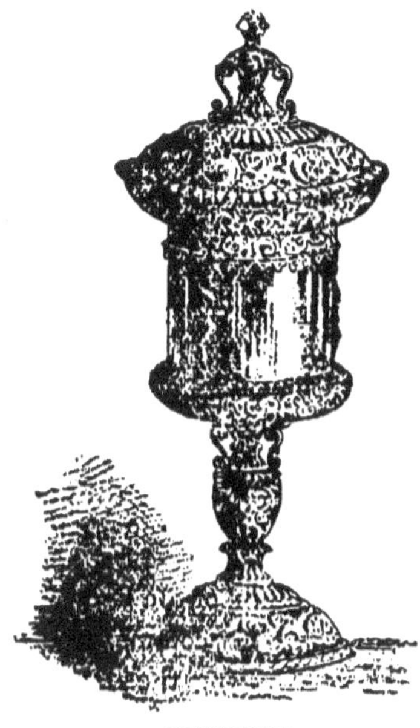

CIBORIUM.

and held the sacred wafers, but is now used to hold the consecrated wine on the high festival days of the Church. It is described among " the guifts of that pious and charitable Lady Eleanor Harries (relict of Sir Thomas)," as " a large Comunion Cup of Gould and Christall and cover."

She also gave the pulpit and " frontal " (see No. 36); besides these, " an 100£ was given by ye vertuous Lady for ye use of ye poore of ye Parish for ever; a yewer and plate of silver; a cloth for ye com'un table of Diaper; a pulpit cloth of black for funeralls; a black cloth for ye bier at all funeralls."

In May, 1645, Tong Castle was one of the garrisons of Salop; and the following other notes of it, about that time, occur :—

" First the King had it ; then the rebels gott it ; then Prince Rupert took it (6 Apl. 1644), and put in a garrison who afterwards burnt it when he drew them out to the battle of York."

" Prince Rupert took Longford at the same time he took Tong Castle."

" Tong Castle shall be speedily released according as Col. Rugelie, Mr. Crompton, and Mr. Stone shall see fit. Apl 16th, ordered that £20 shall be given to the troops which is already paid to Captain Rugelie, and £2 of the rent of Captain Barnsley and Mr. Draycott in Barnhurst, shall be allowed to commanders and officers, a gratuity only to those commanders, officers, and troops, that did so good service in the release of Tong Castle."

Old Vicars relates :—" That Captain Stone, governor of Eccleshall Castle, having intelligence that the garrison of Tongue Castle were abroad, fell upon them with a party of horse, slew many of their officers, took pris ner the Governor of the Castle, and 200 private soldiers."*

Symond's *Diary* gives :—" Saturday, May 17th, 1645. His Majestie marched by Tong, Salop ; a faire Church, the windows much broken,† yet divers ancient coates of armes remaine. A faire old Castle near this Church called Tong Castle, belonging to Pierpoint this 18 years : it was the ancient seat of Stanley, who came to it by marrying Vernon of the Peak at Haddon. Thence through Newport."

" Upon [the Parliament] taking Shrewsbury, the enemy quitted and burned Leahall and Tonge Castle."‡

24. In the Chancel floor is a small BRASS, about a foot square, let into the tile floor, bearing this inscription :—

THE RT. HONBLE. GERVAS, LORD PIERPOINT
BARON PIEREPONT OF HANSLOP, COUNTY BUCKS
AND BARON PIEREPONT OF ARGLAS IN THE KINGDOM OF IRELAND
DEPARTED THIS LIFE MAY THE 22D 1715 IN YE 66 YEAR OF HIS AGE.

This brass was until recently in the centre of the floor, but is now placed near the North Wall. It commemorates Gervase, Lord Pierrepoint, who gave to Tong the valuable library now in the Vestry. A lead plate on a coffin beneath, found in 1892, had this inscription, " The Right Honble. Jervos, Lord Pierpont, died May 22nd, 1715." (See No. 35, under Library). He married Lucy, daughter of Sir John Pelham of Sussex, and had one only child, Elizabeth, who pre-deceased him, and on the north wall of the chancel is a marble tablet, of which the lower part and inscription appear to be to her memory. (See No. 31).

WITHIN THE ALTAR RAILS a handsome new floor and steps have been put. The old flooring tiles have been removed, and the few which could be re-used are laid in the Vernon Chantry. Some were " chequy," corresponding with

---

* Ex *Hulbert's Shropshire.*
† If the Church was garrisoned as an outpost to the Castle, it seems astonishing that more damage was not done.
‡ History of Shrewsbury. p. 39.

TOMB No. 28.—WILLIAM SKEFFINGTON, ESQ.

fragments in the east window; others were quatrefoils, an eagle (yellow on red), a man with sword and shield defending himself against some animal; some Gothic letters were on two tiles, and there were other designs. Size 4¾ in square.

There are two old carved oak CHAIRS. The one on the south side has the letters I.H. upon it.

25. The ALTAR is of wood. It was until 1892 of alabaster, and a part of the very rich tomb to Richard Vernon, Esquire (see under the pulpit, No. 17), to which it has been restored. The new altar cloth, worked by the Sisters of St. Margaret's East Grinstead, is a handsome piece of needle-work, with designs of the Holy Lamb, and the knives of St. Bartholomew. It was exhibited at the Church Congress Exhibition at Folkestone.

26. The SEDILIA, in the south wall, comprise three stone stalls with depressed trefoiled heads. These seats were for the use of the Priest, Deacon, and Sub-Deacon.

27. The PISCINA, in the south wall, is a holy-water basin, carved in stone upon a half-octagon stone bracket; there is a recess, and at each of its two inner corners is a circular shaft supporting a small shelf. This basin was for the purpose of receiving the water used by the priest, which sank through an opening into the rubble of the wall, and was then lost, a method to prevent the water from being applied afterwards to any sacrilegious purpose.

28 & 29. The SKEFFINGTON TABLETS to a mother and son, in the east wall of the chancel, are of Purbeck marble, each bearing plates of copper, inlaid with silver for colour. Over these tablets in the East Wall are shallow recesses, where there appear to have been panels of a date anterior to these tablets, probably having carvings worked in as part of the original walling.

28. The one on the south side of the east window commemorates WILLIAM SKEFFINGTON, Esq., late of the " White Ladies."

The centre plate bears the following quaint lines:—

> Here under lyeth interred the bodye of William Skeffington,
> late of the White Ladies Esquire sonne and heire of Sir
> John Skeffington sometyme of Londo' Knighte.
> Obiit An'o d'ni 1550.

> An esquier he was righte hardye to the fealde
> And faithfull to his Prynce in quiet tyme of peace
> But when his course on earthe he had fulfilde
> The Lord of Worldly woes did him release
> And to his kingdome then his soule did call
> His bodye to dust returned from whence yt came
> Which rayse agayne he will to Joy celestiall
> Where bodye and soule shall ever prayse his name.

The upper plate bears his arms, viz.:—Quarterly of six pieces, 1st *Arg.* three bulls' heads erased, *sa.*, 2 and 1 (Skeffington).   2nd. *Azure*, a bend cotised between six mullets *or* (Ouldbeif).   3rd.........three ravens, two and one (   ) 4th. *Arg.*, a fesse dancettée . . . . . . between three crescents, *gu.*, 2 and 1 (Doyle).   5th. *Ermine*, a bend *az.* (Inglish). 6th. *Ermine*, on a chief indented *gu.*, three escallops *or* (Child) In the fesse point a crescent for difference.   Crest, upon a wreath, a mermaid proper, with comb and mirror *or.*

On the lowest plate are the letters—

G

R   S   T

upon a lozenge ; and this inscription:—

> Posuerunt Pietatis Monumentum.

29. On the north side of the east window is a similar tablet to LADY DAUNSEY (mother of Wm. Skeffington, Esq.), with brass plates.

Here under lyeth interred the bodie of Dame Elizabeth
Daunsey discended of the house & family of p' perkes
first maried to sir John skeffington knighte
somtyme sheriffe of Londō & after married
to s' John Daunsay knighte obijt ā dm 1549.

Thoughe virtues rare did in this knighte abounde
And welthe at will this worthye ladie did possesse
Yet nothinge in y' ende her praise did more resounde
then faithe in Jesus christ with sober godlines
An eie to blynd a lyme to lame she was
To poore a frend of kynne in eche degre
bothe honoured & beloued too loe this dothe virtu pas
To place appointed by the lorde where blessed yt shal be

TOMB NO. 29.—DAME ELIZABETH DAUNSEY.

The centre one bears also a quaint inscription :—

Here under Lyeth interred the Bodye of Dame Elizabeth
Daunsey discended of the house & family of ye Peckes
first married to Sir John Skeffington Knighte
sometyme Sheriffe of Londo' & after married
to Sr John Daunsay Knighte. Obiit Ao dn'i 1549.

Thoughe birtues rare did in this Wighte abounde
And Welthe at will this worthie Ladie did pocesse
Yet nothinge in ye ende her praise did more resounde
then faithe in Jesus Christ with sober godlines
An eie to blind a lyme to lame she was
To poore a frend Of kynne in eche degre
Bothe honoured & beloved too for this doth birtu pas
To place appointed by the Lorde where blessed yt shal be.

On the upper plate these arms :—Per pale : dexter, quarterly
of six pieces (as on monument No. 28); sinister . . . . . .
three eagles displayed . . . . . two and one (Peche), and on
the lowest plate an inscription and initials the same as upon
No. 28.

At Brewood Church, in the east wall of south aisle, there
was in 1680 a companion tablet to Nos. 28 and 29, with
similar initials at foot—

G
R   S   T

and this inscription :—*

Posuerunt Pietatis Monumentum
Here under lyeth the body of Jone, sometime the daughter
of James Levison Esq which Jone was first married to
William Skeffington Esq, secondly to William Fowke,†
Gentleman, et lastly to Edward Giffard Esq. Obiit anno
Dom. 1572.

This virtuous Dame, while that she lived heer,
A godly Matron was, but Christ her chief hold,
Who will he corpse restore to Heaven's cheer,
Where now her soule her Saviour doth behold
To learn of life the course and fatal race
That mortal flesh upon the earth must run
The which both old and young must trace
When as the Lord cuts off the thread well spun

The Skeffingtons of Skeffington, meaning a "sheep town," in Leicestershire, are an ancient family, allied to many Staffordshire families, and in later times had their seat at Fisherwick, co. Stafford.

Sir John Skeffington, Knight, the father of Wm. Skeffington of White Ladies, and husband of 'the Lady Dauntsay,' was an Alderman of London, Merchant of the Staple at Calais. By his will, dated 1524, he gave one third of his property "according to the laudable custom of the city of London to his dear wife Elizabeth," and besides many bequests to relations, friends, and apprentices, gave divers sums to churches, and a vestment with all its appurtenances to be set on the cross at Skeffington Church. He died 1525, seised of lands in the city of London, and the counties of Middlesex and York, leaving, with other children, William his son and heir, 13 years old in 1529, described as of White Ladies, Shropshire. His will, dated 1551, gives £20 to his eldest son, John, £40 each to his other children not married, and the residue to Johanna, executrix with her brother, R. Leveson, Esq., and the said son John: proved at Newport, 1551, the testator calling himself "of the parish of Tong," in which White Ladies was said to be situated.‡

Edward Mytton, Esq., of Weston-under-Lizard, an ancestor of the present owner of Tong and Weston, married Cecilia, daughter of Sir Wm. Skeffington, as a large monument in Weston Church records.

One " Sir Wm. Skeffington, knight, was appointed by King Henry VIII., in 1529, commissioner to Ireland, empowered to

---

* Ex *Hicks-Smith's History of Brewood*, from Ashmolean MSS.
† William Fowke died, 18 February, 1558, and was buried in Brewood Churchyard.
‡ Nichol's *Leicestershire*.

restrain the exactions of soldiers, to call a Parliament, and to provide that the clergy's possessions might be subject to bear their part of the public expense. He was a very distinguished political personage in Ireland, and died in the government of that kingdom as Lord Deputy, 1535."

Lady Daunsay's second husband, Sir John Daunsay, may possibly be the London Alderman of that name occurring about 1542, the founder of the Daunsay Charity at West Lavington, of the Mercers' Company.

30. DURANT monuments in the chancel. The larger one, a handsome marble monument, has sculpture emblematical of grief, Mr. Durant's arms with the motto " Beati qui durant " (Blessed are they who endure, or Blessed are the Durants), besides the following inscription :—

Beneath are deposited the remains of George Durant of Tong Castle, Esquire who died Aug. 4, 1780, Aged 46   He married Maria daughter of Mark Beaufoy Esq and left issue George, born April 25th, 1776 Maria born July 2nd, 1779 who died April 24th 1783 and is interred in the same vault.

His sentiments were liberal
His disposition humane
His manners polished
Happy alike in his mental
As in his personal accomplishments.

In the same vault are deposited the remains of Marianne, eldest daughter of George and Marianne Durant, who was born 22nd November, 1779, and died 18th March, 1800. And of Mark Hanbury Durant, their fifth son, born November 5th, 1808, and died August 22nd, 1815. Emma, their youngest daughter, died in France June 5th, 1829, aged 19, and was buried in the great cemetery called Pere-Lachaise at Paris, in a little chapel built to her beloved memory by her disconsolate father.

The family of DURANT, which has left such traces of itself at Tong and the neighbourhood, came from Worcestershire, and in the Market Place at Worcester is still to be seen an old black and white timbered house bearing the inscription " Love God W B 1577 R D Honour the King." The former half of the inscription having been placed there when the house was built by William Berksley, the latter portion was added by Richard Durant, who lived there at the time of the Civil Wars ; and it was to this house that Charles II. repaired with Lord Wilmot when the disastrous issue of the battle of

M

Worcester was known. He was followed there by Colonel Corbet, a Parliamentarian, and, it is said, effected his escape by the back door as his pursuers entered by the front.

Another of the family was rector of Hagley in the days of Lord Lyttleton of "ghostly fame," and his Lordship seems to have taken a dislike to his son or nephew George, who subsequently became the first Durant of Tong Castle, on account of some difference with one of the Lyttleton family during the time he was holding a position under Government in the West Indies. It was while occupying a situation provided for him by Lord Holland, to whom he had been on a former occasion able to do a kindness, that Mr. George Durant amassed a very large fortune at Havannah, and returning to England determined to locate himself somewhere in the neighbourhood where his forefathers had lived, and with this view he purchased from the Duke of Kingston the Tong Castle estate.

Mr. Durant (about 1764) demolished all but the main block of Sir Harry Vernon's castle, built in 1500. It was a picturesque building of red brick, with stone quoins and clustering twisted chimneys rising above the towers, a very beautiful specimen of the embattled manor-house. Some portions of Sir Harry's building are still left, notably the north and south ends, and the clustered chimneys, as shewn in Buck's View of 1731 (see page 50). The plan of the Castle itself consisted of masses of buildings arranged around three sides of a parallelogram with detached buildings. Mr. Durant seems to have encased the remaining portion of it in stone according to a fanciful design of his own, a mixture of Gothic and Moorish architecture. Surmounted by its lofty domes and pinnacles, the structure is noticeable principally for its massive and stately appearance. This is enhanced in a great measure on the church side by its position at the edge of a broad rich greensward extending uninterruptedly to its very foot, and the pretty low-lying sheet of water winding along the valley;

TONG CASTLE

while on the west side, just below the lawn and shrubberies, this scene of marked repose rapidly changes into one of wilder beauty as the two hurrying streamlets burst away over little falls till they mingle in the dell below.

Mr. G. Durant's son George succeeded him. He was four years old at his father's death. His eccentric character is indicated by the quaint buildings, monuments with hieroglyphics, and inscriptions alike to deceased friends, eternity, and favourite animals, which were then to be found on every path of the demesne. One in the wood still bears " SI MONUMENTUM REQUIRAS CIRCUMSPICE," and of others some further account is given in a later part of this work. He married firstly Miss Eld, of Seighford, by whom he had a son, George Stanton Eld, who predeceased his father, leaving a son, George Charles Selwyn, who succeeded his grandfather, and sold the estate in 1855. He never lived at Tong Castle, and died in 1875 without surviving issue.

DURANT Tablet near east wall.

George Durant remarried ‡September 25, 1830, Celeste, daughter of Monr. Cæsar Lavefve, of Lorraine, and had issue :—

	Born.	Died.	Buried.
Cecil	September 8, 1831	March 25, 1832	Beneath
Celestin	November 22, 1833		
Cecilia	January 20, 1835		
Augustine	January 27, 1837		
Alfred	June 7, 1838		
Agnes	May 2, 1840		

The above George Durant died Nov. 29th, 1844, aged 69.

DURANT Tablet near Vestry Door —

		Died.	Aged.	Buried.
Maria		Apl. 15, 1833	33	Beneath.
Rose		Mar. 24, 1838	32	Beneath.
Bell		Sept. 6, 1835	28	
George	Durant	Sept. 24, 1831	30	In the churchyard.
Hope		Feb. 14, 1836	25	In the churchyard.
Marianne	their mother	Apl. 16, 1829	54	Seighfrd.
Maria	their grandmother	Apl. 28, 1832	74	Dawlish.

Remarried to Major Payne and Colonel Chapman.

Ernest obiit, March 25th, 1846

Ætat 35.

The Vault under the middle of the Choir contains ten coffins of the Durant Family.

HATCHMENTS.—Over No. 30 were until lately two hatchments or mourning shields to members of the Durant family. *Jurisdictions of Courts Leet*, 1675, gives an account of " Trespass brought by Dame Wiche against the Parson for taking down a Coat of Armour with the arms of her husband, when it was decided that a Parson shall not have that nor the Churchwardens, for they are hung there for the honour of the body of him that was buried there."

31. Over the Vestry door is a monument of statuary and grey marble. The inscription upon it records the death of ELIZABETH, only child of Gervase Lord PIERREPONT, aged 11.

A medallion above the inscription shews a finely executed head of a lady, and probably not representing the child referred to in the inscription. There is also some excellent sculpture of drapery, with a shield ; and below are the skull, cross-bones, &c., emblems of death.

In 1763 " there was on the north side of the chancel a *bust* in the wall of a daughter of the Pierpoint family, *but no epitaph*."* May not the medallion be intended to commemorate Elizabeth Pierrepoint, the child's grandmother, eventual sole heiress of Sir Thomas Harries, through whom Tong Castle passed to the Pierrepoint family ? It seems unlikely that there would be no memorial at Tong to one whose protecting arm probably shielded the Church and its monuments during the troublous times of the Commonwealth, and who was buried at Tong, July 1, 1656.

---

* Ex *Shreds and Patches, Shrewsbury Journal*, from the *Gentleman's Magazine.*

Hīc intra

Terrestria Impedimenta

Præmaturius reliquit quasi ad cœlum Properans

Elizabetha Pierrepont.

Ao. Æræ Chrni. cıɔıɔcxcvıı Pridie Kal. Sept.

Annos nata xı

Puella ingenii acuminis & Morum Vrbanitatis

Supra Ætatulæ captum.

Quam multa jam Feliciter edocta,

Nihil non si diutius Parcæ Favissent Assecutura

Parentum Decus Dulce Familiarum Deliciæ

Utrorumque spes gratissima

Filia unica Gervasii Pierrepont Armigeri Dni Terræ de Tong

Nepotis Roberti Pierrepont Comitis Kingstoniæ

Accerimi (ingruentibus sub Carolo Io Rege dissidiis Civilibus) Strategi

Fidelitatis suo Principi debitæ, etiam vitæ dispendio Assertoris :

Cui Genus ortum a Roberto de Pierrepont

Gul'mo Io Regi Expeditionum Comite;

Fratrum natu maximo,

Quorum etiam dum superest in Normannia

Posteritas.

'Ον γ's φιλεῖ Θεος γ' αποθνήσκει νέος.

TRANSLATION :—

Here, below, Elizabeth Pierrepont prematurely has cast off [her] earthly trammels, as it were hasting to heaven, in the year 1697 of the Christian Era, on the day before the Kalends of September [31st August] Eleven years old. A maiden endowed with a mind, prudence, and sweetness of manner far beyond her tender years : How many precepts of her parents would she not have gladly followed if the Fates had spared her longer ! The ornament of her friends, the delight of her family, the most pleasing hope of both : The only daughter of Gervase Pierrepont, Esquire, Lord of the Land of Tong, nephew of Robert Pierrepont, Earl of Kingston, in the civil wars which raged bitterly under King Charles I. the assertor of fidelity due to his Prince, even at the cost of his life: He was descended from Robert de Pierrepont, companion of the expeditions of William I. the Conqueror—the eldest brother—whose posterity even yet survives in Normandy.

Whom God loves dies young.

Mr. Walter de Gray Birch writes me thus: The Greek line should be :—

'Ον οἱ Θεοὶ φιλοῦσιν ἀποθνήσκει νέος.

He whom the Gods love, dies young.

It is a fragment of a poem by Mænander, a comic poet, who died B.C. 290. Plautus says : *"Quem di diligunt adolescens moritur,"* a similar sentiment. The inscription as given herein is slightly altered, and reads : He whom God, etc.

32. Over the stalls, between the two north windows of the chancel, is a white marble TABLET bearing the following inscription :—

Sacred to the memory of the Revd.
Charles Buckeridge D.D.
Archdeacon of Coventry first Canon Residentiary
and Præcentor of the Cathedral
Church of Lichfield
And sixteen years Minister of this Parish
Died 28 Sept 1827 aged 72.

In the same vault are interred the Remains
of his three children
Margaretta born April 1800 died an infant.
Mary Elizabeth born 10 Aug. 1797
Died 7 Septr. 1810 aged 13 years.
Charles Lewis born 3rd July 1802
Died 7 Feb 1812 aged 9 years and 7 months.
Elizabeth relict of the said Charles Buckeridge D.D.
and daughter of the late Richard Slaney Esq.
of Shiffnal in this County
Died 13th Feb. 1832 aged 69 years.

Mr. H. F. J. Vaughan writes : " The Slaneys were much " connected with this neighbourhood, having been Lords of " Donington for many generations, but I do not find one of " them wife of Dr. Buckeridge, who married a Miss Durant, " and had two children buried at Tong."

VESTRY.

 VISITOR to Tong in 1763, describes this as " a detached building, *now used as a Vestry*." The massive door has some carving, and in the upper part, three circular holes four or five inches in diameter (see illustration) ; these are too small for " doles " to be given through, and although Mr. Cole remarked that besides a church and a college there were along the street some almshouses, afterwards called by him a

VESTRY DOOR.

hospital, " *which seems to have a chapel of its own*," there is no reason to suppose it was a hospital for lepers, who, to avoid contagion, were accustomed to receive the consecrated elements through apertures provided for that purpose near the chancel.

The two vestry windows are two-light ones, and differ from all the other windows in having no labels or tracery ; their forms are marked by small sunk triangles similar to the sedilia. The stained glass formerly in the vestry window shewed the half-length figure of a King, very similar to the head of King Edward III. in the great east window of York Cathedral, date latter end of the 14th century, by John Thornton, of Coventry, glazier.*

" The Vestry and Chancel doors have the four-centred arch, and are not later insertions; and these doors alone have spandrils."

33. BRASS in two pieces to RALPH ELCOCK, 1510. This was for a long time in the Vestry, having been detached from the south wall of the south aisle (at the spot marked R E on plan). It is now fixed nearly in its old position.

Hic jacet Radulphs Elcock Celer cofrats istis Collegii qui Natus fuit in billa Stopfordie infra Comitatu Cestrie qui obiit in festo sce katerine Virginis et Marter Anno dni millimo ccccc desima.

Translation of inscription :—

Here lies Ralph Elcock, celerer and co-brother of this College, who was born in the town of Stopford, in the county of Chester, who died on the †feast of St. Katherine, Virgin and Martyr, in the year of our Lord one thousand five hundred and ten.

The " Celerer " had care of the provisions of the College.

34. In the Vestry floor a small BRASS PLATE bears :—

BENEATH
ARE ENTOMBED THE REMAINS OF
ARCHDEACON BUCKERIDGE
AND ELIZABETH HIS WIDOW
ALSO OF
CHARLES: LEWIS, MARY ELIZABETH,
AND
MARGARETTA THEIR CHILDREN.

(See tablet No. 32.)

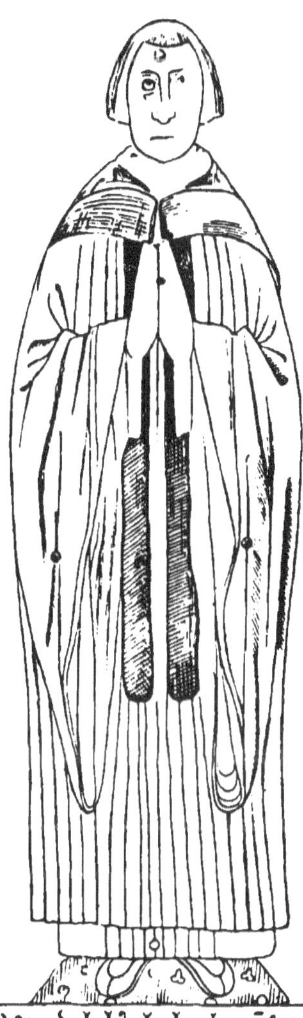

NO. 33.—RALPH ELCOCK (*see page 96*).

35. The LIBRARY, given by Lord Pierrepoint (see No. 24), consisted of 410 volumes, including many scarce and valuable works. A catalogue of them was made under the direction of the late Mr. Beriah Botfield, M.P., F.R.S., F.S.A., and a very few copies of it are in existence. The Duke of Kingston's deed for confirming Gervase Lord Pierrepoint's settlement of several charities in Tong Parish, recites a deed of 23rd October, 1697, by which Gervase granted as to dieting the minister at his own table, and allowing him hay for his horse, and keep; and Lord Pierrepoint granted that the minister should enjoy a chamber in Tong Castle, as the same was then furnished with books and presses, and use of the said books, which were to be inserted in a catalogue.

> Still am I besy bokes assemblinge,
> For to have many is a pleasant thinge.
>
> May I a small house and large garden have,
> And a few friends and many books, both true,
> Both wise, and both delightful too.

Also, the minister to enjoy part of a stable for keeping the horse, and place over same for laying his hay, and between May-day and Michaelmas-day to graze his horse in Tong Park without paying for the same.

In " Heayse's Accompts " occur :—

		£	s.	d.
1806.	Marking Coffers in the Church..	0	2	6
	Printing a large board in the Vestry	1	11	6
1807.	Altering board in the Church ..	0	1	0
1812.	Framing, boarding, and making, and materials; a coal and coak cupboard in the Vestry..	3	19	0
	Making a ladder to go up to Libra	0	9	6
1813.	New bottoming the Bier and repd. it ..	0	5	9
	Painting and lengthening double doors in the Porch	1	7	6
	Do. the Wicket with green	0	11	6

36. In a glass case is an ancient dalmatic or ecclesiastical VESTMENT of red velvet, embroidered and ornamented in gold and coloured silks, with cherubs in raised work, flowers, and other devices, and four scrolls, of which two bear mottoes :—

COR VNVM VIA VNA.   (One heart, one way)

N

and two :—

VSE BIEN TEMPS.   (Use time well)

It is considered a beautiful specimen of needlework, and is supposed to have been made by the nuns at the Cloisters of St. Leonard of the Cistercian Order, for use in their Chapel (now called the White Ladies, and in ruins, a mile or two from Tong). It is said to be 300 years old. It was given by Lady Harries, and was used to a late period as a pulpit frontal. Size about six feet square.

TOWER AND BELFRY.

IMMEDIATELY on opening the door to ascend the steps the following curious lines will be seen in a frame which formerly hung on the outside face of this pillar, but were removed by direction of Bishop Lonsdale.

11.

If that to Ring you doe come here,
You must ring well with hand and eare,
   keep stroak of time and goe not out ;
   or else you forfeit out of doubt.
Our law is so concluded here ;
For every fault a jugg of beer,
   if that you Ring with Spurr or Hat ;
   a jugg of beer must pay for that.
If that you take a Rope in hand ;
These forfeits you must not withstand,
   or if that you a Bell ov'r-throw ;
   It must cost Sixpence e're you goe.
If in this place you sweare or curse ;
Sixpence to pay, pull out your purse.
   come pay the Clerk it is his fee ;
   for one (that swears) shall not goe free.
These laws are old, and are not new ;
therefore the Clerk must have his due.

GEO. HARISON. 1694.

Next to those at Culmington, the above are the oldest version in the county of Salop, of the familiar lines,

"If anyone do wear his hat when he is ringing here."[*]

The BELFRY itself contains eight bells, one, the Great Bell, in the lower stage, and seven in the upper stage of the tower.

The GREAT BELL was given to Tong by Sir Harry Vernon (Governor to Arthur, Prince of Wales), and "a rent out of his Manor of Norton for the tolling of it, when any Vernon comes to Tong." A tradition runs that Sir Harry was once benighted in the immense forest of Brewood, but the bells of Tong led his steps in the direction whence the sound proceeded, and so he reached his Castle in safety, in gratitude

---

[*] Report of visit of Shrop. Archæ. Soc. to Tong, July 8, 1876.

for which he gave "the Great Bell." Mr. Cox (1720), says "the Inhabitants here boast of nothing more at present than a great Bell, famous in these Parts for its bigness."

It originally weighed 2 tons 18 cwt., and measured 6 yards round. It weighed 41½ cwt. in 1892.

Inscription on the upper rim :—

HENRICVS VERNON MILES ISTAM CAMPANAM FIERI FECIT, 1518 AD LAVDEM DEI OMNIPOTENTIS BEATÆ MARIÆ ET STI. BARTHOLOMÆI.[*]

On the lower rim :—

QVAM PERDVELLIONVM RABIE FRACTAM SVMPTIBVS PAROCHIÆ REFVDIT.

ABR RVDHALL, GLOCEST: ANNO 1720. L. PIETIER, MIN., T. WOOD-SHAWT, T. PEYNTON, ÆDITVIS.

Following the precedents of 1518 and 1720, an 1892 inscription has been added in the centre :—

EANDEM VETUSTATE IAM FATISCENTEM DENUO CONFLANDAM ET REPONENDAM CURAVIT ORLANDO GEORGIUS CAROLIUS COMES DE BRADFORD VICARIO JOANNE COURTNEY CLARKE—MDCCCXCII.

TRANSLATION OF INSCRIPTIONS.

Henry Vernon Knight caused this bell to be made 1518 to the glory of God Almighty the Blessed Mary and St. Bartholomew.

Which having been broken through the madness of enemies, was recast at the expence of the parish, [by] Abr. Rudhall. Gloucester, in the year 1720. L. Pietier, Minister, T. Woodshawt, T. Peynten, Churchwardens.

Orlando George Charles, Earl of Bradford, took care that this same bell, now cracked with age, should be cast anew and replaced ; John Courtney Clarke being Vicar, 1892.

The Great Bell was broken by the Parliamentary forces (the Roundheads and Puritans) in the time of King Charles I., probably in 1635, for in the Churchwardens' accounts are entries[*] :—

1635.   " For hanging the Great Bell anew,"
1636.   " For a piece of metal broken off the Great Bell,".....................£1 12s. 8d.
1641.   " Fetching a strike for the Great Bell."
1652.   " Peese of Rope for the Great Bell,"................................   3s.

After being recast at the expense of the parish (as recorded by the inscription), it remained entire until the first Wednesday in Lent [Ash Wednesday], 1848, when, while ringing for divine service, it cracked through the word "Woodshawt,"

---

[*] The words " et Sti Bartolomæi " appeared to have been inserted later, between the beginning and end of the other lettering.

Great Bell of Tong - cracked, taken down 1892.

probably in consequence of a defective clapper having been made to strike the rim too near the edge.

Its weight now is 50 cwt., and diameter 5ft. 2in. The framework has been entirely renovated.

The illustration is kindly furnished by Mr. Taylor, of Loughborough, the Bell-founder who re-cast it.

Once during recent years it was tolled in accordance with the donor's directions, viz. : when the late Lord Vernon came over from Weston Park to Tong Church a few years ago. He was a descendant of Sir Harry. The visits of the Vernons are now so rare that tradition has, I suppose, supplemented Sir Harry's request by requiring the great bell to be rung when " Royalty or a Vernon comes to Tong," and thrice recently have Royal Princesses visited Tong, in company with the Countess of Bradford, whose guests they were, viz : —on December 17, 1872, H.R.H. Princess Christian (Princess Helena, Her Majesty's third daughter), and in the first week of November, 1869, H.R.H. The Duchess of Teck (Princess Mary of Cambridge). The old bell was last tolled upon the death-day of that much-mourned prince, the Duke of Clarence and Avondale. Only a few months before then, the Princess ",May " had visited this church with her mother, H.R.H. the Duchess of Teck, and Lady Bradford, and was shown by the Vicar the interesting features of the place. Since then Her Royal Highness—now gladly known as the Duchess of York—has again been at Tong.

The following lines, which H.R.H. once wrote, give us a glimpse of her kind and sympathetic nature :—

> If each man in his measure
>   Would bear a brother's part,
> To cast a ray of sunshine
>   Into a brother's heart,
> How changed would be our country,
>   How changed would be our poor,
> And then would " Merry England"
>   Deserve her name once more.

In the upper bell story :—

The smallest, and probably the oldest of all the bells, is the one on the south-west side of the octagon, " ye sanctus bell." It is 14in. in diameter, and around the upper rim is a band into which are introduced two fleurs-de-lis alternately with two cross-crosslets, equi-distant. I can find no lettering on the bell, but the French fleur-de-lis and the cross-crosslet suggest its association with Sir William Vernon, Treasurer of Calais, and his wife. [See Tomb 14.] The priest's or " sanctus " bell was generally hung at the west end of the nave, and dates as early as the 13th century. The other six bells form the regular peal, whose melodious notes are heard each Sabbath-day.

Taking the BELLS in the order of their dates :—

On the north side of the octagon is a bell bearing—
PRAISE THE LOROD 1593.

On the bell on the east side —
GLORIA IN EXCELSVS 1623   W.C.
(Glory in the highest).

The initials are probably those of one Chalmer, a bell-founder.

On the east-centre bell—

𝕾𝖜𝖊𝖊𝖙𝖑𝖞 tolling, men do call
To taste on meats that feede the soule.
1605.

and a Latin cross with the letters ℌ.☉. on each side of it, and a crescent and mullet outside those letters.

These initials are believed to be those of a bell-founder, Henry Oldfield, of Nottingham, who helped to re-cast the Great Tom of Lincoln.

On the west bell—
GLORIA IN EXCELSVS DEO 1636.

On the west-centre bell—
PEACE AND GOOD NEIGHBOURHOOD A.R. 1719.

THE GREAT BELL OF TONG.

The initials are those of Abraham Rudhall, the well-known
bell-founder of Gloucester, who brought the art to great perfection in 1684. A bell is also shewn between the above
initials and date. The Eccleston register records a payment
of two shillings for a bottle of wine for Mr. Rudhall, bell-
founder.

On the south bell, the tenor bell—

THOMAS MEARS OF LONDON 1810.

Bells have been in use since the 7th century, and were
anciently prohibited from being rung in time of mourning.
The "passing bell," which in some places still tolls for the
dead (a note for every year of the deceased person's age), was
intended to advertise good Christians to pray for the soul just
departing. .

There seems to be no bell at Tong with a Greek inscription,
as some have said ; nor any bell with a Latin inscription commencing "Virgo regina," given by William Fitzherbert.

A cornice of an old screen, or perhaps a relic of the old
Gothic organ case, remains in the belfry.

It is a peculiar arrangement that the ringers should have to
stand in the centre of the Church floor to ring, but there
is no alternative. Their names are :—George Henry
Boden, treble ; Henry Smith, second ; John Ore, senior,
third ; John Ore, junior, fourth; Richard Bellingham, fifth ;
and Fred Haighway, tenor bell. The great bell of Tong is
toned C sharp, and only rung on certain special occasions ;
it requires two men to set it.

OUTSIDE THE CHURCH.

37. There are some rude CROSSES cut in the stonework
beneath the east window of the south aisle. This window has
a sweeping cornice springing off heads. It may be the chancel
window of the earlier church.

38.   In the buttresses at the north-east corner of chancel are elaborate NICHES, which contained the figures of saints in early days, and were placed at the side ot the church nearest to the high road.

39.   ST. CHRYSOM'S CEMETERY—The burial place of unbaptized children.   A Maltese cross of red sandstone bears the well-known and appropiate verses on the side facing the road :—

> But save the cross'above my head
> Le neither name or emblem spread
> By prying stranger to be read
> Or stay the passing pilgrim's tread.
>
> BYRON.

> Weep not for those whom'the veil of the tomb,
>   In life's happy morning hath hid from our eyes ;
> Ere sin threw a blight on theispirit's young bloom
>   Or earth had profaned what was born for the skies.
> Death chill'd the fair fountain ere sorrow had stain'd it,
>   'Twas frozen in all the pure light of its course,
> And but sloeps 'till the sunshine of heaven has unchained it,
>   To water that Eden where first was its source.
>
> (T. MOORE.)

> Like the last beam of evening thrown
> On a white cloud—just seen and gone.

On the side of this cross facing the church—

G.D.

H. M. E.

1823.

CHRISOME, in the office of Baptism, was a white vesture, which in former times the priest used to put upon the child, saying, " Take this white vesture for a token of innocence."

By a constitution of Edmond, Archbishop cf Canterbury, A.D. 736, the Chrisomes, after having served the purpose of baptism, were to be made use of only for the making or mending of surplices, &c., or for the wrapping of chalices.   The first Common Prayer Book of King Edward orders that the woman shall offer the Chrisome, when she comes to be churched ; but, if the child happens to die before her churching, she was excused from offering it ; and it was customary to use it as a shroud, and to wrap the child in it when it was buried.   Hence, by an abuse of words, the term is now used not to denote children who die between the time of their baptism and the churching of the mother, but to denote children who die before they are baptized, and so are incapable of Christian burial.*

---

* Note from Hook's Church Dictionary; sent by the Rev. J. H. C. Clarke.

40. The north doorway, and indeed the entire north wall of the north aisle, exhibit numerous CANNON BALL MARKS, some of which have been filled up with mortar. These are a lasting record of the Parliamentarian's hatred against the Church. With their cannon well planted on the old mound (now called Castle Hill), at Tong Norton,† they devised the destruction of both castle and church. An intermediate earthwork (by the upper water-carrier) possibly saved the castle from damage, but I cannot help thinking, as before remarked, that the preservation of the castle, and the beautiful monuments in the church, must have been due to the friendship and regard Oliver Cromwell had for Mr· Pierrepoint and his wife Elizabeth. The feeling cannot be mistaken when we call to mind that during the Commonwealth, Christmas-day was ordered to be regarded as a superstitious festival. The holly and mistletoe bough were ordered to be cut up root and branch as plants of the Evil One. Cakes and ale were held to be impious libations to superstition ; and in 1647 Cromwell's party ordered, by the mouth of the common crier, that Christmas-day should no longer be observed, it being a superstitious and hurtful custom, and that in place thereof, and more effectually to work a change' markets should be held on 25th December.

In the churchyard a SUN-DIAL bears—

THOS: ORE
FECIT 1776.

a surname still lingering in the parish in the family of a lusty bricklayer. Thomas Ore was one of the seven jury of the Manor of Tong, who perambulated the Boundary, as described later.

---

† Mr. W. Phillips, F.L.S., of Shrewsbury, is of opinion this is an ancient Tumulus.

o

MINISTER'S LIBRARY AT TONG.

THE chief feature of the Library is a collection of *Councils of the Popes*, 37 volumes, folio, in vellum coverings : " *Conciliorum Pontificum Decretum Miscellaneorum Ab Anno 34 Ad Annum 1623 cum Indicibus* IV. *Paris Typ. Reg.* 1644." The other works are bound in calf, and were chiefly printed in the 16th and 17th centuries ; there are a few of the 15th and 18th centuries also. Mr. Botfield says, " The bibliographer will look in vain for any work of surpassing interest ; they form, however, a useful library of reference for the theological student . . . . . . When the means of locomotion were few, and the sources of information were scanty, this local library argues a degree of intelligence and refinement unknown in other and less favoured districts," and he concludes that this was one of the earliest to enjoy the blessings of religion, and the benefits of learning. Among the other books the following may be named as interesting and valuable :—

Augustino Marlorata. Testamenti Expositio Catholica Ecclesiastica Ex Probatis Theologis, 1593.

Beza, Theodorus (a great Lutheran commentator). *De Trinitate Geneuæ*, 1560.

Brett, LL.D. (an English commentator). Liturgies used by the Church in celebration of the Holy Eucharist. London, 1720.

Carleton. Collection of the Great Deliverances of the Church since the beginning of Queen Elizabeth's reign. London, 1627.

Drexelius, Jeremiah (a famous commentator). 13 volumes, dating 1630 to 1655.

Erasmus (a well-known name). 7 volumes, 1540—1641.

Gaule, John. The Magicall Astrologicall Diviner Posed and Puzzled. London, 1652.

Moulin, Peter. Buckler of the Faith. London, 1623.

Perkins. Declaration showing how near we may come to the Church of Rome, and wherein we must for ever depart from it. Cambridge, 1598.

Ross, Alexander. Mystagogus Poeticus, or the Muses' Interpreter. London, 1648.

Stockwood, John. Disputationes Pueriles. Tunbridgiæ, 1606.

Testamentum Græcum et Latinum cura Th. Bezæ. Genevæ, 1611.

Udall, John. Hebrew Grammar. Amsterdam, 1648.

The Library is referred to under No. 35. It consisted of 554 Volumes and is understood to have been added to by Mr. Peitier, a former Minister.

MONUMENTS FORMERLY IN TONG CHURCH.

Near the spot marked R. E. on plan was a large red stone to the memory of William and Elizabeth SCOTT, who died in 1694 and 1700 respectively. This is not now to be seen. Were these of the familyof Scot of Scot Hall, Cosford, and Tong Norton, otherwise the Heath, Shifnal, whose daughter Mary married Francis Forester, d. 1652 ?

And near the West Door were two other monuments, not now visible. One, an alabaster slab to William CLAY, who died in 1735. The other, to William TAYLOR, of Stapleford, who died at the Castle in 1733.

Mr. Abraham Hare, of Bridgnorth, wrote the following epitaph to the memory of his daughter buried at Tong. He was described by the *European Magazine* of 1789 as " an un-" tutored son of the Muses," and was an excise officer :—

Here lies the the body of Lucy Hare
Who departed this life 1783 aged 19 years.

" In solemn silence, sweet repose,
Virtue and youth these stones inclose,
The sacred path of truth she trod,
Death snatched her hence to meet her God;
Eternal joys, through Christ, to share,
Prepar'd for all as Lucy Hare."

Consists of the Ciborium described on page 60, the gift of Lady Harries.

A Pocket-Service of Silver. The cup about two and a half inches high, engraved with I H S within a gloria. The plate about three inches in diameter, similarly engraved, and having, in addition, the donor's name

𝕲. 𝕯urant, 𝕿ong 𝕮astle, 1839.

A Silver Cup, five inches high, quite plain, on short low stem, and apparently very old.

A Silver Ewer, with dragon-head spout, twelve and a half inches high. Except a little chasing round the base, and the lid-rest, which is a cherub's face, the vessel is a plain one ; probably the gift of Lady Harries.

A Silver Plate, about nine inches across, bears :—" The gift of George Durant, Tong Castle, 1839," beneath a fleur-de-lis, his crest.

A Silver Plate, somewhat smaller, with the shield of the Harries family.

There is also a white enamel portable Font, consisting of an octagonal receptacle, and a lid. The former has, on each face of the octagon, a quatrefoil, and rests upon four feet set cardinally. From the centre of the lid rises a cross (with quatrefoil at the intersection), while from its foot radiate the crocketed divisions of the octagonal lid. Size, seven inches in diameter ; eight and a half inches high.

NOTE.—I believe a few years ago there was, in addition, a handsome walnut or rosewood alms dish, with fret-work cover, and underneath it a brass plate recording the name of the donor. Mrs. Harding, wife of one of the perpetual Curates of Tong.

EXTERIOR OF THE CHURCH.

The following *notes, from the Brit. Archæol. Journal*, are re-counted for the benefit of those visitors more deeply interested in architectural study and pursuits :—

The ground had been terraced up previously.

Base-moulding is varied by breaks, uniform, except at Chapel.

Both ends are finished with embattled parapet ; central raised in two stages.

Vestry is gabled. No parapet.

Pinnacles, square section. Delicate embattled horizontal strings, instead of gables or canopies, their faces being set cardinally. Not crocketed. Well-executed finial, suitable to the building.

Nave has no clerestory.

Aisles have no parapets.

There has been a large pinnacle at each west angle.

Central buttresses had crosses, as the sockets are there.

South porch is embattled. Small pinnacles.

Belfry is rectilinear, and octagonal. On each slope is a small pinnacle. Lower part has the great bell, and a window of two lights, N. and S. Others plain, square-headed. Doors opening on to the leads. No weather moulding to indicate that the Church was ever higher. Octagon contains the peal of bells, and windows of two lights on the cardinal sides.

Spire at half-height is encircled by spire-lights, ending each in a crocketed finial or pinnacle, those only on the cardinal sides being pierced.

Chancel is divided on south side by bold buttresses into three compartments. Each has a beautiful three-light window, the base of central one being slightly raised to allow of a door.

North side is different. It shows the Vestry to be a part of the original design. It is nearly equally divided in two by west wall of Vestry, to which a buttress corresponds.

Principal mullions in Chancel windows are of the first order ; the secondary mullions of the second order. In the rest of the windows throughout the Church, the tracery is of one order.

Arches of windows are mostly two-centred, and differ but slightly in their forms (though less pointed), from the equilateral.

Buttresses of Chancel are finished with a pinnacle, and have well-executed gargoyles, or figures of monsters, with mouths pierced for waterspouts. The east angles of Chancel have each two buttresses, and double pinnacles.

There are 17 gargoyles altogether, viz., 7 to Chancel roof, 2 to the South Porch, 2 to the Golden Chapel, 2 at the West End, and 4 on the Tower.

> And every house covered was with lead,
> And many a gargoyle, and many a hideous head,
> With spouts through, and pipes, as they ought,
> From the stonework, to the kennel rought.
>
> *Lydgate's Boke of Troy.*

The Kennel means crenelle or loophole. As late as Henry VIII's. reign, no man dared to have his house crenellated without royal licence.

TONG COLLEGE.

THE following particulars are extracted from Bishop Tanner's notes, 1744—original date 1695. The Licence for the foundation of the College was in 12 Hen. IV. The Statutes and Ordinances for the Government of the College, dated 9 March 1410, were confirmed by the Bishop of Coventry and Lichfield, 27 March 1411.

King Henry IV., in the 12th year of his reign, in consideration of £50 received, granted his licence to Elizabeth, relict of Fulk de Pembrugge, Knight, Wm. Shaw, Clerk, and William Morse (or Mosse), Clerk, to acquire of the Abbot and Convent of Shrewsbury the Advowson and Patronage of the Church of St. Bartholomew the Apostle at Tonge in Shropshire, of the Diocese of Coventry and Lichfield, for them to have and to hold, reserving to the said Abbot and Convent an annual Pension they were us'd to receive of £0 6s. 8d.

·And the said Elizabeth, Wm. Shaw, and Wm. Morse, when seized of same, to convert the said Church into a perpetual and incorporate College of 5 Chaplains, more or less, one of whom to be by them appointed Warden of the said College. And that the said Persons might assign to the College so founded a Messuage with its Appurtenances in the said Town of Tonge; the aforesaid Advowson and Patronage, as also the Advowson and Patronage of the Parish Church of St. Mary of Orlyngbere in Co. Northampton and Diocese of Lichfield; and two Messuages, 2 roods of Land, and 4 acres of Meadow, with the Appurtenances, at Shameford in

Co. Leicester ; with the reversion of the Manor of Gilden Morton in the County aforesaid, after the Death of Margaret, the wife of William Newport, who had same for her Life ; and the said Master and Chaplains to hold and possess all the Premises, and to be a Body Corporate by the name of the College of St. Bartholomew the Apostle at Tong. Likewise that the said Elizabeth, Wm. Shaw, and Wm. Morse, when the said College was actually founded, might give the Patronage and Advowson of the same to Richard de Pembruge and the Heirs of his Body.

King Henry V, at the Parliament at Leicester,* at the request of Elizabeth, relict of Fulk Pembrugge, gave and granted to the Warden and Chaplains of the Church of St. Bartholomew the Apostle at Tonge, the Town and Manor or Grange of Lappeley, commonly called the Priory of Lappeley, with all appurtenances, and the Church of Lappeley, once part of the Possessions of the Abbot and Monastery of St. Remigius at Rheims, seized into the hands of King Edward on account of the war with France, and had been farmed out to the Prior of Lappeley at 42 marks per annum, free of all impositions whatsoever.

King Henry IV., in the twelfth year of his reign, *i.e.*, 1410, granted the Licence for Tong College. It will be well to re-call a few historical incidents of the time. Henry IV. was not the rightful heir to the Crown, on the deposition of Richard II., although he had been the principal means of the despot's overthrow. The Houses of Parliament, however, admitted his claim, and the House of Lancaster was allowed to add a large share of laurel to British History. It was just at this time that the Commons made a considerable advance in importance and authority. Counsellors were appointed, by whose sole advice the King was to be guided. Various

---

* It will be remembered that Sir Richard Vernon, Elizabeth's son-in-law, was Speaker of this Parliament.

articles were agreed to regulating the grants of money, courts of justice, elections of knights for counties, &c., and other provisions made, which were " of themselves a noble fabric of constitutional liberty." Justices of the peace were first appointed in this reign. Nevertheless the statute book was marred by the Law for the burning of heretics; and in 1401 William Salter, a clergyman, was burned to death in Smithfield, London, because he refused to worship the Cross, and denied that the bread in the sacrament was transubstantiated.

Wycliffe, in order to promote his views, had sanctioned the employment of wandering preachers, called "poor priests," men that, after the manner of the ancient religious orders, traversed the country and preached to the common people assembled at fairs and markets. Hence grew up a sect called "Lollards" (from "lullen," to sing with a subdued voice). The Clergy held that the movement ought to be crushed, and so the statute was passed, and the persecution of the Lollards went on in this and the succeeding reign. In the latter, however, the King was disinclined to persecution. "Many bishops were still accused of slackness in the persecution, and it should be mentioned to their hononr. The prisons in Bishops' houses, which had been simply places of confinement, were now often provided with instruments of torture." At Woburn, in the palace there was a cell in the bishop's prison called "Little-Ease," because it was so small that those confined in it could neither stand upright nor lie at length." "The same law, which transferred to the Church the power of life and death, left a discretion with the ordinary of fine and imprisonment ; and frequently those convicted of heresy were doomed to the sentence formerly inflicted by the Church for homicide, of perpetual imprisonment within the wall of a monastery. It is possible that in such abodes they may have been sometime the blessed instruments of imparting divine truth to the companions of their sojourn ; but if we may judge

P

of the feelings towards them by Walsingham and other
monks of the time, we may well imagine how with such
keepers, they ate and drank the bread and water of affliction.
Others were burned on the cheek with a hot iron, which, if
they dared to hide, they were liable to be burnt as relapsed
heretics; or were condemned to wear the device of a faggot
worked upon the sleeve of their clothing, in token of their
narrow escape from burning.'* Not until the reign of
Charles II. was the practice finally abolished.

The writer has an iron body-ring covered with leather, to
which two wristlets are appended to hold the arms, fixed at
the sides. It seems similar to the rings which victims wore
formerly, when being dragged on a hurdle by a horse to the
scene of execution.

To the credit of Sir Thomas More, the pious statesman and
Chancellor of Henry VIII., Erasmus, his friend, distinctly
testifies, no man was put to death "for Protestant dogmas
while More was Chancellor"; though his staunch adherence
to the Roman Catholic religion, and his denial of the King's
supremacy, as head of the Church in England, brought his
head to the block in 1535.

This period is remarkably interesting to Englishmen. The
year which saw Sir Thomas More's execution sounded the
death-knell of Tong College; it saw the first English translation of the Bible, namely Coverdale's, in 1535; it saw the
commencement of Henry VIII's great act of spoliation, the
destruction of the Monasteries and all their rich treasures;
Tong being one of the 90 Colleges destroyed. The revenues of
the destroyed Colleges, Monasteries, and Hospitals (645 in
number), amounted to £160,000, or one-twentieth of the
National income. The word "protestants" was just coined
from the action of 14 cities and 6 princes in "protesting"

---

* Massingberd.

SIR THOMAS MORE

(From a Painting in possession of the Author).

against further changes in religion; while disciples of Bass and
Allsopp must look back to that period with tender regard as the
date of the introduction of Hops, and the wearers of Mail had
cause to rejoice in the disappearance of Bows and Arrows.
In 1536 Parish Registers were established. Sir Thomas
More, the man of inflexible integrity, whom no motives could
seduce nor honours corrupt, was the guest and retainer of
Holbein, and the famous drawings at Windsor by that artist,
who is supposed to have designed the Tong ciborium,—are
principally of More and his friends. By his indefatigable
application as Chancellor not a cause was left undetermined.
His character has been much mis-represented by Foxe and
Bishop Burnet, while all his contemporaries describe him as
being of a singularly amiable disposition, and unaffectedly
and sincerely pious.

1416. King Henry V. attaches the town or Manor and
       Grange of Lapley in Staffordshire with its Church
       or Priory, and all the Revenues thereunto apper-
       taining being heretofore part of the possessions
       of the Abbey of St. Remigius at Rheimes in
       Champeigne in France, provided that the
       Vicarage of the Church of Laply be sufficiently
       endowed, and a competent sum allowed to the
       Poor of the Parish.

1535. (26 Hen. VIII.) College rated (valued) at £22 8 1

1546. At the dissolution of Religious Houses, Sir Richard
       Manners was appointed Commissioner for the
       Sale of Tong College, and sold it to James
       Woolrich for £200. The deed confirming
       Sir Richard's power to effect the sale—signed by
       King Edward VI. and Lord Protector Somerset
       —was in perfect preservation at Tong Castle
       not long ago.

1649.   J. Woolrich's heirs sold the College to William Pierrepont, proprietor of Tong Castle.

1763.   Visit of Mr. W. Cole. The Duke of Kingston's seat is at Tong Castle. The ancient College where the Clergy lived is mostly demolished, and what remains is partly inhabited by some poor people, and partly converted into a stable. (Gents Mag.) At the West end of the Church there are Alms houses for six poor widows, who have 40s., a shift and gown per annum.

1774.   Duke of Kingston sold Estate to Mr. George Durant.

The above-mentioned Elizabeth, William Shaw, and William Mosse, founders of this College in the year 1410, appointed Statutes and Ordinances to be for ever observed in this College, which were confirmed, 1411, by John, Bishop of Coventry and Lichfield, the Purport whereof is as follows :—

"That there should be in the said College 5 Priests, having no other Benefices excepting the Warden, who might have any One of the Said Priests to be the Warden, and the rest obedient to him, and another Sub-Warden.

That there should be also 2 proper Clerks for the Service of the Church.

Also 13 Poor maintained by the College, 7 of which so infirm that they could not help themselves.

The Warden to be named by the Foundress Elizabeth during her life, and presented to the Bishop of Coventry and Lichfield, and afterwards to be chosen by the Chaplains.

In case the Chaplains disagreeing, a Warden should not be chosen in 15 days, then the right of nomination to devolve to the Patron ; if he name not in 4 months then to belong to the Bishop, who not doing it in a month, it should pass to the

Chapter of Lichfield, and they neglecting it in 15 days, lastly the choice should belong to the Archbishop of Canterbury.

Every Chaplain to be admitted by a majority of the Wardens and Chaplains, and to be in the nature of a novice for the first year, at the end whereof, if found fitting by the greater number, to be received by them.

None to be Warden or Chaplain but a Priest, and of unspotted life and conversation.

If, upon the vacancy of a Chaplain's place, another were not received by the master in three months, the Deficiency to be supplied by the Bishop.

The Poor of the College to be appointed by Elizabeth the Foundress aforesaid during her Life, and after her Death by the Warden ; not to be removed again without just Cause.

Every new Warden before his Admission to swear he will faithfully execute the said office, and observe the Statutes.

Sub-Warden to take the like Oath.

The Chaplains when incorporated to swear Obedience to the Wardens, and to observe the Statutes and defend the rights of the College.

The Warden within 2 months after his admission to make an exact Inventory of all that belongs to the College, and to be afterwards accountable yearly.

The Sub-Warden to have the management of all things when there is no Warden.

The Warden to hear the Confessions of the Chaplains.

The Warden not to be non-resident above two months in a year, nor any of the Chaplains above one, unless it be upon the Business of the College, nor ever to be absent from Divine Service.

The Warden to appoint one of the Chaplains to have the Care of the Parish, and he to be called Parochial Chaplain, and another of them to teach the Clerks and Ministers of the College, as also the Children of that and other neighbouring Towns to read, sing, and their Grammar, for which he to be allowed a Mark a year extraordinary.

The Mattins to be sung early in the morning ; the Mass and other Hours at their proper times ; with many other ordinances about the performing of the Divine Service.

If any of the Poor be so sick and weak that they cannot go to the Church to hear Mass, then a Chaplain to be appointed to say Mass in the Chapel in the House, 3 times a week.

Several Anniversaries to be dutifully kept in the Church.

Every poor person, unless hindered by sickness, to hear one or two Masses every Day.

The Warden and Chaplains to be uniform in their decent Habit in the Church according to the Use of the Church of Sarum, and every Chaplain to furnish himself with Habit, and any of them coming into the Church to Divine Service not so habited, to be punished as absent.

The Warden and Chaplains to live in a Community in the same House, each having a Chamber apart, and if they speak to one another to do it lowly. The Warden to keep the keys of the outward Doors at night. The Warden and Chaplains to eat at one Table, and the Warden to say Grace. Meat and Drink to be modestly distributed. One of the Chaplains to be yearly or quarterly appointed Steward. Provisions always to be laid in at proper seasons. Strangers to be but seldom brought into the house ; and women never, though the most virtuous, or at least very rarely, upon Extraordinary Occasions, and if they be suspicious persons on no account whatsoever.

If any dined there at the upper table, he who invited him to pay 3d. if at the lower 5 farthings. If Provisions should be dear, or the Dignity of the Guest require it, the Charge to be proportionately rated ; but if any person were brought in to eat, for the Benefit of the College, the Charge to be defrayed out of the Public Stock. No Priest to bring any person to Table above one day unless it were a Friend or Relation that came from some remote part.

No Priest or Clerk to use Hunting or Hawking, nor to keep any Dog for sport, and any transgression after three admonitions, to be expelled without Noise.

The Warden and Chaplains to be decently Cloath'd and uniformly, once a year, and the Clerks in like manner.

The Warden to be allow'd 10 Marks a year for his Cloathing and expenses besides Diet ; each Clerk 4 Marks besides Diet, and other profits for Obits, &c.

Clerks and other Choristers to be allowed according to their Ability.

The Sub-Warden, the Chaplain that has the cure of the Parish, the Steward,—½ a Mark above their Constant allowance for a year or in proportion for a shorter time.

The Warden and Chaplains strictly forbid granting or selling any Pensions, Corrodies, or Immovables belonging to the College.

Any one consenting to such Pension, *Corrody, or Alienation, to be expelled the College unless the same were done by the Diocesan for the Benefit of the said College, or upon some other necessary occasion.

The Brethren disabled either by Age or Sickness to be charitably maintained, and not to be expell'd on that account,

---

* An allowance of food and Clothing allowed by an Abbot to the King for the maintenance of one of his servants.—*Halliwell.*

but only for crime committed, or in case anyone have otherwise got temporal Possessions to the value of 6 marks a year.

When the Brethren meet in their Chapter after the business relating to the same, they are to enquire whether any Faults have been committed since their last meeting ; then, and if any appears, the same are to be chastised by the Warden, or Sub-Warden.

Grievous crimes not to be punished but the Warden being present, unless he were long away, and the Delay might be dangerous. But if the case were doubtful, his Return to be expected. Yet if it were such a crime to cause Irregularity, the Party to be immediately expelled as in the case of Murder or the like.

Yet for Adultery, Perjury, Theft, or the like, which might admit of Re-admissions, after due penance performed, the Party having made his humble confession before the Brethren, to be again restored. If it be Fornication, Drunkenness, or the Like, offender to be twice corrected by the Warden or Sub-Warden, and the third time to be expelled.

The same to be observed in relation to the Poor.

If the Warden should be guilty of such offence, the Brothers twice to exhort him to correct the same, and three times to accuse him to the Bishop to be punished by him canonically, and if after such Punishment he does not amend, then to be expell'd by the Ordinary.

If any Chaplain would of his own accord leave the College, he should give 6 months' Warning, and if he did not then, to lose his Allowance for those 6 months.

No seizure to be made by the Patrons or their Heirs during any Vacancy, &c.

The Clerks to serve the Warden at Table, and to eat at a Second Table ; as also to see Harvest brought in at proper season at such Hours as they are not to attend Divine Service. Each poor person admitted into the College to receive Diet, Cloathing, and other necessaries, 1 Mark Sterling in Money or the value, besides their Dwelling house with other profits of the Gift of the Faithful.

A Lamp to be kept burning before the High Altar, and Candles to be furnished for the Divine Service, &c.

The College to have a Common Seal for their Common Business, with the Image of St. Bartholomew the Apostle, as also that of a Knight on one side, and a Lady on the other, kneeling, and the Coat of Arms of Fulk Pembrugge, Knight, and of his wife Elizabeth, the Foundress, in the same Seal, under the feet of the aforesaid Apostle, and about the same written, " The Common Seal of St. Bartholomew at Tonge." The same to be kept under two different Keys in a Chest with the Writings and Treasure of the College.

The above Statutes and Ordinances, dated 2 March, 1410, for the Government of the College, were very salutary and severe.

£50 equal to a large sum of present money.

" Shaw," a name still applied to some of the richest land in Tong Parish, in fact the " Shaw Lane " where there are some old Cottages, is called by " the oldest inhabitant " " The Prior's Road." Fancy pictures " the Rev. William Shaw " sitting with a fellow warden upon the rude old stone seat now remaining in the middle of the Shawfield. Shaw itself means a wood, or cover, a shady place,

Welcom quod he and every good felaw
Whider ridest thou under this greene shaw ?

The immense elms, which lately stood in the Shawfield, testify to the good qualities of the soil for tree or herbage.

2

Two Clerks being mentioned show that even thus early the people of Tong had exceptional religious facilities.

> A worthy clerk, as proved by his wordes and his werk,
> He is now ded, and nailed in his cheste,
> I pray to God to yeve his soule reste.

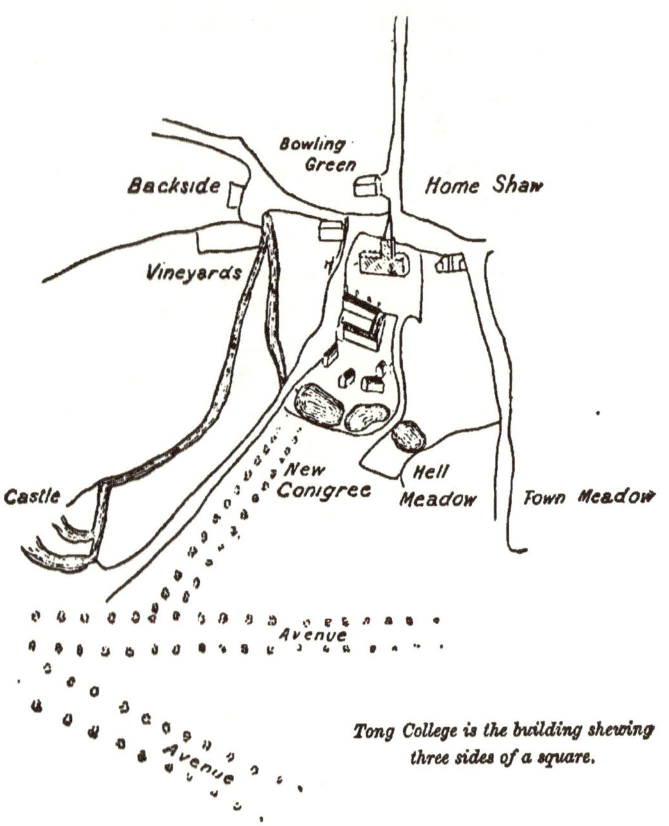

Map made for Evelyn, Duke of Kingston, in 1739.

The exact position of the College is shewn by the sketch which I have taken (by the kindness of the late Mr. Fisher, of Newport, Salop) from a Map dated 1739, when the ancient building was still in existence.   In 1887, a dry summer, the lines of the foundations could be traced in the grass.

The " Town of Tong " is a high-sounding title. certainly not borne out by our present knowledge of it.   We may, how-ever, easily understand the place to have been of considerable importance ; firstly, it had a Royal Grant of a Fair on the Eve-Day and morrow of St Bartholomew the Apostle (24 Aug.) s:condly, the holding of the Manorial Court and View of frank pledge ; and thirdly, from being the centre of religious zeal and means of diffusion of knowledge, its body corporate possessing other towns and manors affiliated to it and in-creasing its income, while the Grange or monastic farm at Lizard, and possibly others, managed and overlooked periodi-cally by one of the chaplains himself riding out, increased its importance and usefulness, and provided employment for the poor.   Thus Chaucer says :—

> This noble Monk of which I you devise
> Hath of his Abbot as him list licence
> Because he was a man of high prudence
> And eke an officer out for to ride
> To seen hir granges and his bornes wide
> For certain bestes that I muste beye,
> To storen with a place that is oures.

It seems as though the officer who had this happy periodical relief from the routine of monastic life may be compared to the favoured boy at a boarding school, who is occasionally sent by his master to perform a little commission for him in the town.

2 messuages or houses, 2 roods of land, *i.e.*, cultivated arable land.

The parish clerk, *i e.*, the priest,

> I trow that he be went
> For timbre, ther our Abbot hath him sent,
> For he is wont for timber for to go,
> And dwellen at the Grange a day or two.

5 priests including the Warden and Subwarden,

2 proper clerks.

13 poor, 7 too infirm to help themselves.

20 inmates in all.

> Upon my faith thou art som officer,
> Som worthy sextein, or some celerer.*
> For by my fadres soule, as to my dome†
> Thou art a mnister, whan thou art at home
> No poure cloisterer, ne non novice.
> But a governour both ware and wise
> And therwithal of braunes and of bones
> A right wel faring persone for the nones.
>
> *Chaucer.*

We may here remark how much greater a blessing a College was than a Monastery. The one a community or assemblage of men invested with certain authoritative powers using their establishment to diffuse learning, promote the education and welfare of the neighbours, and to attend to the wants of the sick and infirm; the other, the Monastery, a place of retirement, a provision for housing and feeding primarily themselves, the monks, without much regard for the rest of the world, an association of men full of the light of learning and blessed with advantages which might have been turned into a blessing to those around them, but one which enabled them to selfishly hem in and bury themselves within the four walls of their habitation, bent only on attaining Salvation themselves, regardless of the rest of mankind.

" The parochial chaplain and another to teach the clerks, " ministers and children of that and other neighbouring towns, " to read, sing and their grammar." Which can the neighbouring towns be ? Tong-Norton, Donnington, Shifnal, Weston.

There appears to have been a little Chapel within the College, besides the Collegiate Church, and Mr. Cole remarked in 1757 that the Alms-house or Hospital had a Chapel of its own. The rules as to their Costume or Habit appear to be

---

* The officer in a monastery who had the care of the provisions.   † In my opinion.

rigid in the extreme, while on the other hand the hospitality to be shown to strangers, although according to rules, was of a full and ample character.

The ambiguous and contradictory regulations for the admission and exclusion of women are truly naïve.

The regulations point to the Clerks' inclination to indulge too freely in matters of sport; however, an offence or two may be overlooked, and if the extreme penalty be enforced, it would be best to say as little as possible about it. Doubtless there was no great harm then as now, but real good in the Clergy joining in the various avocations and diversions of their flock, provided it were not carried too far. The predilection for sporting was manifest too in the ladies of that day, as we shall remark more explicitly in referring to Black Ladies; but it may be that the " Canes Venatici " (Dogs of the Chase) of the Nunnery were frequently instrumental in providing a dinner for the inmates who we read were poor indeed; thus nothing is new under the sun, and the occupation of the lurcher to be seen under every ugly caravan of the present day finds a precedent in the usages of religious zealots of old.

The Manorial Court consisted of the Lord or his Steward and the Jury, duly summoned and warned by the quaint injunction " Oh, yes! Oh, yes! Oh, yes! " At the Court the deaths of various tenants of the Manor, and the fines due to the Lord of the Manor on each death or change of ownership, were declared and recorded.

This custom is still performed in Manorial Courts at the present day—the Jurors and Court being discharged in similar words to the opening exclamation. An old work (referred to previously), and dated 1675, prints elaborate rules of Courts Leet and Courts Baron of the time. One or

two may thus be noted :—"8 Henry VII. The Freehold of
the Church is to the Parson, and the pewes are Chattels unless
they are fixt, but some have pews there by Prescription ; but
the pews fixt there are the Freehold of the Parson."

"A peiw" (says Gough in his quaint History of Myddle,
quoting eminent authorities) "is a certain place in church
incompassed with wainscott or some other thing, for severnl
persons to sitt together. A seat or kneeling (for in this case
they are the same) in such a part of a Pew, as belongs to one
families or person. And a peiw may beelong whoaly to one
family, or it may beelong to the ordinary, and noe man can
claime a right to a seate without prescription or some other
good reason [sic.]. A peiw or seat does not beelong to a
person or to land, butt to an house, therefore if a man remove
from an house to dwell in another, hee shall not retaine the
seat belonging to the first house. . . . .
If a man sell a dwelling house with the appurtenances the
seate in Church passes by the word appurtenances. . . . . .
Wee have a tradition, that theire was noe peiws in Churches
before the Reformation, but I believe that some of the cheife
Inhabitants had peiws in the upper end of the Church before
that time, as appears by certain antient cases in law-books.
Neverthelesse after the Reformation the bodys of the Churches
in most places were furnished with peiws ; or with benches
(which were called forms) for the people to sitt in while the
Lessons were read and dureing Sermon time." And Mr. Gough
proceeds to give a very interesting account of the Parish of
Myddle by taking in order the names of every householder's
pew.

The two pews on the north side of the pulpit in Tong
Church, *i.e.*, in the North Chapel, were claimed a few years
ago as " belonging to the Minister " ; but rights to pews are
—or ought to be—better held in these days by constant use

of them than by any other title. It is the habit, however, of some old people to bequeath the family pew in their Parish Church in the same way as other valuables, although the pew itself may have been already lost sight of in a much-needed re-arrangement of sittings. Such was the case when Mr. Isaac Pugh, a cousin of mine, recently bequeathed ~~Pugh~~ in his will the pew in Oswestry Church. The family came from Llanfyllin, near Oswestry. The name Pugh means son of Hugh, formerly written Ap Hugh, as is Griffiths, for Ap Griffiths (son of).

Harriot. † Two manner of, viz. : Harriot custom, and Harriot Service ; the former after the death of the tenant for life ; the latter after the death of the Tenant in fee.

BREVIATE OF THE CHARGE.

Ill persons for the Commonwealth (inter alia) :—

Of those which Sleep in the day and Walk in the night, and have nothing to live on.

Of those which catch Pigeons in the Winter with Nets or Engines.

Very extraordinary offences !

Herriot. One of the properties belonging to the Tong Charity Trustees is called " Little Harriots Hays," otherwise " Dead Woman's Grave." The connection between the two names is easily surmised. Heriot in " all the Lordship's marches " was the best weapon. Heriot Covenant is such a weapon as an arrow or a sum of money or such a beast or goods as is mentioned in the Covenant. And this the Lord is obliged to take, although it happen to bee worse than the best weapon . . . . . . the best weapon may be but a " pickavill, a trouse bill, or a clubbe staffe, for these are weapons offensive and defensive."

---

† From "here" a lord of herus, and geat or neat, a beast. Quasi dictum "The lord's beast."

TRESPASS.

Of Common Barretors and Scolds.
Of breaking the Common Pound.

" Barretors " or Scolds meant Brawling Women. The ladies charged with this offence were punished by having an iron bridle locked on their heads --part of it, a narrow tongue of iron, one and a half-inch long, much like the bowl of a spoon, was thrust into the mouth, which effectually prevented conversation offensive or even supplicatory.

Pound.—In many a parish the pound is the sole relic of Manorial Authority. All stray animals were impounded, and the fact proclaimed in the Church. There is a pound at Tong Norton, and one at Weston, and at Blymhill.

Constable. To see the Watch kept!

The Community was in very simple hands, if we may judge by Shakespeare's Constable and the men of the Watch.

Dogberry : Well, for your favour, Sir, why give God thanks, and make no boast of it, and for your writing and reading, let that appear when there is no need of such vanity. You are thought here to be the most senseless and fit man for the Constable of the Watch ; therefore bear you the lantern. This is your charge—you shall comprehend all vagrom men ; you are to bid any man stand, in the Prince's name.

Watch : How if a' will not stand ?

Dogberry : Why, then take no note of him, but let him go ; and presently call the rest of the watch together, and thank God you are rid of a knave.

.   .   .   .

Well you are to call at all the ale-houses, and bid those that are drunk get them to bed.

Watch : How if they will not ?

Dogberry : Why then let them alone till they are sober ; if they make you not then the better answer, you may say they are not the men you took them for.

Watch : Well, sir. . . . .

Dogberry : If you meet a thief, you may suspect him, by virtue of your office, to be no true man ; and for such kind of men, the less you meddle or make with them, why, the more is for your honesty.

Each town a century ago had its Watchman, who hourly cried out the progress and atmospheric phases of the night :—

" One o'clock and frosty '
" Two o'clock and raining."
" Three o'clock and fine," &c.

The London Watchman cried the time every half-hour. In addition to a lantern and rattle, he was armed with a stout stick. T. L. Busby, who in 1819 illustrated "The Costumes of the Lower Orders of London," tells us that in March the Watchman began his rounds at eight in the evening, and finished them at six in the morning. From April to September his hours were from ten till five ; and from November to the end of February, twelve till seven. During the darkest months there was an extra watch from six to twelve, and extra patrols or sergeants walked over the beats at intervals.

It is peculiar that the only reference to the farming operations upon which the College must have depended for its provisions is so briefly referred to. " The Gifts of The Faithful " may, however, have been so ample as to provide hard cash with which the Warden could buy the larger portion of the necessaries of life.

R

I have come across no illustration of the Seal of the College.

In the Hon. and Rev. Canon Bridgeman's Account of Marston,* containing some account of Lapley Priory, mention is made that the Master (or Warden) of Tong College was to have a man and a pair of horses kept at the expense of the College to travel about the business of the fraternity ; but, if occasion require it, he might keep more horses when he travelled to more distant parts, and further that the following Masses should be performed :—

> On Sunday, the mass of the Holy Trinity for founders and benefactors ;
> Monday, the mass of the Holy Ghost ;
> Tuesday, *Salus Populi* (the Salvation of all Men) ;
> Wednesday, the Angels' mass ;
> Thursday, the mass de Corpore Christi ;
> Friday, mass of the Holy Cross ;
> And on Saturday, the mass of Rest.

Thomas Forster's tomb is in the north wall of Shifnal Church, a canopied one, with effigy, and this inscription :

> Here lieth the Body of Thomas Forster
> Sometime Prior of Wombridge Warden
> Of Tongue and Vicar of Idsall 1526.

The arms are quarterly (per fesse indented), 1 and 4 *sable* a pheon ; 2 and 3 *argent*, a forester's horn.

Thomas Forster's Will is in the Bodleian Library, dated 1522. Among others, are bequests for the following purposes : "to the prysts and Clerks of St. Andrew of Idsall to kepe the Mass every Friday by rote. x^s to John Hatton to set me in his Bead-roll : every pryst in the parish to have iiis. ivd. to pray for me. Also it is my mynd to have a Trentall-day as soon as may be after my departyng" (*i.e.*, a celebration of Mass 30 days after).

An extract from the *Shropshire Archæological Journal* may be taken, as Forster or the Foresters are further associated with

---

* Staffordshire Archæological Vol., 1884, and Lloyds Duke's Shropshire.

Tong in the person of Isabella Forster referred to later. It says
he was a Pluralist of that date, and one of much dignity ; represented lying in his priestly robes, which consist of a Cassock,
Alb or Tunic, a Chasuble with border, and an Amice round the
neck ; on his head the Tonsure, which was a corona or crown
shewing the mark of his order.   He was one of the family of
the Foresters, presumably of the Royal Forest of the Wrekin,
and a native of the parish, as evidenced by a deed of Richard
Forster of Evelith (temp. Hen. VIII. 20), who granted certain
lands in Alderton in the parish of Great Ness, Co. Salop, to
find a fit chaplain "to pray for the Soul of Thomas Forster,
and for the souls of all his friends and kinsmen."

He was of the same family as Anthony Forster ("Tony
Fire-the-fagot " in " Kenilworth "), whose tomb in Cumnor
Church, Co. Oxford, describes him as "Qui quondam
Ipplethæ Salopiensis erat." Ipplethæ or Ivilith, or Evelith
the paternal Estate, was held by Lord Forester's family
until within the last few years.

A pretty drawing of the Tomb, conveying an idea of its
character, was made by the Rev. J. Brooke, of Haughton.

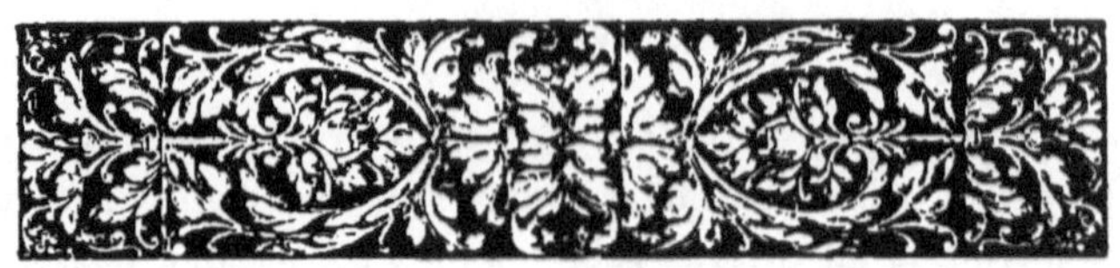

A DOCUMENT DESCRIBING THE "BOUNDARY OF THE LORDSHIP OR MANOR AND PARISH OF TONGE:"—

The 19th and 20th of May in Anno 1718 Memorandum, the days and year above written being Rogation weeke. A Boundery of the Lord-ship, or Mannor and Parish of Tonge was then taken by the Ministor and such of the Inhabitants thereof whose names are hereunto subscribed, and is as followeth :

Impr.

It was begun at Tonge Mill Poole and went Eastward up A Brooke called Kilsall brooke unto A Bridge over the said brooke in the Road from Tonge to Albrington, on the midle of which Bridge was a Gospell Read, and from thence Eastward up the aforesaid brooke unto the upper part of a piece of ground in the tenure of John Cotton, called the Walds, from thence Across the bottom of widdow Harrison's fieald unto the Cornor of Tonge Parke pale then forward adjoyning to the lands of Will. Colemore, Esq., in the tenure of John Yate, and Thomas Ellits four foot on the outside of the Park pale all along, likewise from thence forward on the outside of the Parke pale adjoyning to the Lands Ffitchherbot, Esq. four foot being in the tenure of Thomas Row adjoining unto the Park pale up to the Keepers meadowes, then continuing on by a bond hedge made by Mr How from the Keepers meadows, and also from the Parke fields, from thence unto A marle pitt in mill ti-ld in the tenure of Mr. How being adjudged to be an acre which formerly paid tythes to Tonge, thence returning out of the grounds of Mr. How into Ambling meadowe and still continueing by Mr. How's bond hedge unto Moralls meicell now in the tenure of John Carpentor to A gate place there where there then was A gospell read and from thence Along by the bond hedge of Dennis Field, in the upper part of the aforesaid field is about two Acres of Land in the Parish of Tonge and pays Tithes to the Lord of the Mannor of Tonge as often as it is tilled, from thence returning out of that lands into Bryery hurst and still continuing by Mr. Howes bond he ge unto Pierce Hay lane thence returning to A gate entering into Bishops wood where there then was A gospell read and from thence by a bond hedge dividing from the Parish of Brewood leading to A piece of Land Pertry lessow in the tenure of William Leeke, and from thence by A bond hedge dividing from the Parish of Blimhiil untill we come to Weston Parke Pale Corner, at A gate there was then A gospell read. then goeing seven foot of the outside of the Weston Parke pale westward unto A piece of Land called Cowe haye, then continuing by the Bond hedge of cowe haye in the P-ish of Weston unto Cowe haye gate where there then was A gospell read and from thence continuing

by the Bond hedge belonging to Weston P-ish aforesaid unto A certain gate leading of Norton heath unto Weston new Mill where there then was A gospell read
and from thence by the aforesd Bond henge of Weston unto Windrill
meadow, And from thence continuing by certin grounds called the Windrills unto
Street way still by the P-ish of Weston along certain grounds in the tenure of John
Fox of Lizyard Grange unto to the road from Tonge to Newport were there was a
gospell read. And thence along the lands of John Fox aforesd adjoyning to Street
road in the P-ish of Sheriffehalse unto A certain brooke runing from Burlaughton in
the P-ish of Sheriffhalse And from thence southward downe by the said Brooke
adjoyning to the P-ish of Shiffnall ati* Idsall unto A way and steping stones upon
the same brooke belov Thomas Wenlocks corne Mill where there then was A
Gospell read, And thence along the same brooke unto the upper forge hammor
ditch where there was then A gospell read and from thence along the fforge brooke
unto A way and steping stones where was then a Gospell read And from thence
by the same brooke to A bridge below the lower Forge where there was a Go-pell
read, thence by the same brooke unto Timlett Bridge where there then was a
Gospell read. And from thence by the same brooke unto a certain bridge over
which is a way into Muncke fields from Ruckley Grange near below which bridge
is A bylott or spot of Land over the brooke belonging to the P-ish of Tonge adjoyning to a meadow in the holding of Lancet Jones, then returning to the Forge brooke
aforesd downe to A bridge below Ruckley Grange house upon which there then
was A Gospell read And from thence along the same brooke to the Hole upon A
bridge there then was A gospell read, And from thence by the same brooke round
to Ruckley wood cornor which is the Tenure of Thomas Scott untill it meets the
Brooke that runs from Tonge Mill. Thence returning up Tonge Mill brooke adjoyning to the P-ish of Dunington untill we come to a certain Piece of Land about
half an Acre lyeing over the sd brooke now in the holding of John Horton
which is in the P-ish of Tonge unto a gate upon Worcester Road where there then
was a Gospell read, and from thence returning two and up the saide brooke untill
we come to Tonge Mill, at A gate over the poole Bridge adjoyning to the P-ish o
Dunnington where there then was A gospell read, and the Boundary there
ended :—

<table>
<tr><td>Lewis Peitier, Curate of Tong</td><td rowspan="7">The Seavon of the Jury at the Court Leet & Court Baron held for the Mann' of Tonge the 26th of Oct. 1719 know the Boundaryes.</td></tr>
<tr><td>George Salter</td></tr>
<tr><td>Robert Stones</td></tr>
<tr><td>The mark of Richd   R   Marrion Tent.</td></tr>
<tr><td>The mark of Roger   (ʒ   Masons</td></tr>
<tr><td>Thomas Ore</td></tr>
<tr><td>John Cotton</td></tr>
<tr><td>The mark of George   ℓ   Holmas</td></tr>
</table>

The above was a small paper document 20in. × 16in. found
by the Rev. R. G. Lawrence at Dornington, a neighbouring
parish, and sent by the Rev. H. G. de Bunsen, rector there, to
Mr. Lawrence, Nov. 20, 1872. "This is the Document I told
you of, to which, as far as I can see, not we, but *you* have the
right."

The above old document, describing the Boundary of the Manor and Parish of Tong nearly two hundred years ago, is of much interest, especially to the inhabitants who are acquainted with the roads and places mentioned. It seems that the perambulation took two days to complete, namely, the 19th and 20th of May, 1718, and these no doubt were Rogation days.

Rogation days are the Monday, Tuesday, and Wednesday before Ascension Day; and are said to be so called from the old custom for processions to go out from the Church to various stations in the parish, where hymns, canticles, and litanies were sung, asking for God's blessing upon the fruits of the earth.

The following are words from a beautiful Rogation hymn :—

> Our hope, when Autumn winds blow wild
>   We trusted, Lord, with Thee;
> And still, now Spring has on us smiled,
>   We wait on Thy decree.
>
> The former and the latter rain,
>   The Summer sun and air,
> The green ear, and the golden grain
>   All Thine, are ours by prayer.
>
> Thine too by right, and ours by grace,
>   The wondrous growth unseen,
> The hopes that soothe, the fears that brace,
>   The Love that shines serene.

Why are not out-of-door services revived in the Church of England ? They are very impressive indeed. The service of the Consecration of new burial ground at Tong lately is an instance, and a more striking one was the Volunteer Camp Service at Coppice Green a few years ago.

The walking of the boundaries of the Parish or Manor was a duty zealously performed a century ago in all parishes. The party perambulating included the clergyman, some old men, inhabitants well acquainted with the windings of the boundary, and a certain number of lads " to tell them that come after." Refreshments were provided at certain points on the route, and the proceedings were not infrequently enlivened by practical jokes played upon the boys, to stamp in their memories the day's business, such as where by chance a brook took a doubtful turn or divided in two, in that part of it which remained as the boundary one or two of them would be "ducked." In a place where the boundary ran through a cottage, a small boy was pushed through a little window which defined it ; and in another case where there was no window, money was thrown over for the boys to catch on the other side. †

The Duke of Kingston was Lord of Tong at this time. The parish boundary seems to have been identical with that of the Manor.

"Begun at Tonge Mill Poole." This Mill was probably upon the site of the old Mill connected with the feudal establishment of Bishop de Belmeis, immediately below the Castle. Several mill-stones came to light when the dam of this pool burst a few years ago. It is probable that a small pool on the west side of the Castle fed by the larger Church Pool, supplied the water to drive the mill-wheel, for the document says the boundary went " Eastward up a brooke," thus proving that the Kilsall water was not impounded to form a pool then.

The poet Chaucer (who lived in 1359, and bore arms in Edward's Expedition to Calais), so quaintly describes the miller and other rural characters of the 14th century, that I have quoted his words, in order to bring vividly before us pictures of the country people of those earlier days.

The miller was remarkable for his stout build, and prowess at " wrastling."

Upon the cop right of his nose he hade
A wert, and thereon stode a tufte of heres,
Rede as the bristles of a sowes eres.

---

† Custom on the Hawarden Manorial boundary W.G. says—

> A white cote and a blew hode wered he,
> A bagge pipe wel coude he blow and soune
> And therwithall he brought us out of toun.

A damaging line says

> Wel coude he stelen corne and tollen thries,
> And yet he had a thomb* of golde parde.

It was the boast of old Mr. Bloxham, of Lizard Mill, that he was "*the* honest miller."

"The road from Tonge to Albrington (*i.e.*, Albrighton) "on the middle of which Bridge was a Gospell Read."

Old Plot tells us that—

> "In the skirts of the town [of Wolverhampton] are ranged at determinate "distances a number of large trees, which serve to mark the limits between "the township and the parish. Those are denominated by the inhabitants "Gospel trees, from the practice of reading the Gospel under them, when "the clergy were wont to perambulate the boundaries."

Plot, again in his history of Staffordshire, 1686, says :—

> "They have also a custom in this County, which I observed on Holy Thursday at Brewood and Bilbrook, of adorning their wells with Boughs and flowers ; this it seems they doe too at all *Gospell-places*, whether wells trees or hills ; which being now observed only for decency and custom sake is innocent enough. Heretofore it was usual to pay this respect to such wells as were eminent for cureing distempers on the Saint's day whose name they bore, diverting themselves with cakes and ale, and a little musick and dancing."

There are no wells of this description in Tong, but in the Shaw Lane, at Tong Norton, upon some old half-timbered cottages there, I have seen bunches of yellow May flowers hanging over the doors, some weeks after the 1st of May has passed. And this May-day custom I have observed on John Wilkes's Cottage in the neighbouring parish of Weston.

The May-pole.— The Shaft or Maypole was in former times considered part of the public property of the parish, and as such was repaired by the Churchwardens. Popular amusements were in those days under the patronage of the Church.

---

* Meaning probably that notwithstanding his thefts he was an honest miller, *i.e.*, as honest as his brethren.

May-games, though much older than the Christian Church, were connected with some of its most pleasing rites.

A little nonsense now and then
Is relished by the wisest men.

At Waddingham, before the Elizabethan spoliation, a sacring bell hung from its top. May-poles seem to have existed in most of our villages until the time of the Great Civil War. By an ordinance of Parliament in Cromwell's time, 1644, all May-poles were ordered to be removed as heathenish vanities.

We read that " not long after the restauration of King " Charles II., the young people of Myddle [and others] were " about setting up a May-pole near the church-stile : " whereupon the parish clerk remonstrated. He was brought before a justice of the peace, " when it was deposed on oath that " hee said it was as greate a sin to sett up a May-pole as to " cut of the King's head. (These words hee denied even to " his dying day)." He was, however, subsequently fined 5 marks, " and an order was made that he should louse his place."

" Corner of Tong Parke Pale." There seems to be little doubt that *the* Park belonging to Tong Castle was enclosed with pales, and extended from the present brook at Tong Park Farm northward to Hubball, and possibly to the foot of the Knoll. There is no reason why it should not have done so, as the Offoxey Road is a comparatively new one, happily substituted for the old tortuous way by the Knoll House, passing not far from the old Tithe Barn to White Oak.

This old barn is very large, and was probably the tithe barn of the parish, in which the tithe hay and grain were stored, before the Tithe Commutation Act came into force some 50 or 60 years ago.

In harvest time, when the grain was in mows ready to carry to the stack, notice was required to be given to the person collecting the Tithe-owner's share of grain crops, and he

s

would come to the field and sprig with a twig every tenth mow ; these would be carried to the Tithe barn, for use of the Incumbent, unless he agreed, as was often the case, with one farmer to give him so much money for the tithe crop of the whole parish.

This method was a survival of the practice adopted in the time of the Norman kings to obtain their revenues. The Sheriff was the king's "fermor"; he agreed to give the king so much money from a given County, and anything more he could extract from the people in it was his pay and profit.

By the Tithe Commutation Act there was a certain sum in lieu of tithe apportioned on each field; an Act which often works unjustly at the present day, when the highest-tithed land, *i.e.*, the wheat growing arable land, bears a tithe of perhaps 4/- to 6/- an acre, and the crop itself will not pay the cost of production, while rich pastures are almost tithe free.

Here are some of the words of an old song called "The Tithe Pig" :—

> "Good morning said the Parson," "Good morning Sir to you,"
> "I've come to choose a sucking pig, you know it is my due,
> "I pray you sir, go fetch me one, that is both plump and fine,
> "For I expect a friend or two along with me to dine."
>> With my whack ful the diddle dol the dido.
>
> Then in the stye the farmer went, among the pigs so small,
> And brought him out a little pig, the least among them all.
>
> On seeing this, the parson, how he did ramp and roar,
> He scratched his head and stamped his foot, and almost cursed and swore.
>
> With this outcried the farmer, "Since my offer you refuse,
> "Walk in the stye, you're welcome Sir, now pray go pick and choose."
> Then in the stye the parson went without any more ado,
> Th' old Sow came out with open mouth and at the parson flew.

The other lines of this doggrel are now forgotten, but the old sow tore off the skirts of his coat, not to mention graver ~~grave~~ disasters to other garments,

> And ran her head between his legs, and tumbled him in the mire,
> Then out of the stye the Parson came, all in a handsome trim.
> The farmer almost split his sides with laughing at the fun.

He then demanded his hat and wig (for wigs were worn in

those days), and hurried out of the place, and said he was almost dead, departing with the words—

The " WHITE OAK " overhangs Mr. Murdock's back-kitchen, and is a large tree standing upon an elevated piece of ground midway between Tong and Black Ladies near Brewood, and was probably in the middle of that part of the Forest called Bishops Wood. It was formerly whitewashed, as I am informed. The reason for so doing may have been to render it a more conspicuous signpost, marking the way through the forest, and perhaps denoting that near here was the turn off the main road into the bridle way to White Ladies Abbey, and now the shortest cut to Albrighton Station.

The next name we come to is " Morrall's meicell, at a gate place there, where was a Gospel read," *i.e*, the bridle road to the White Ladies Abbey aforesaid. The " meicell " being spelt with a small m suggests that it was not an uncommon word, but one aptly describing certain lands. Mr. Hartshorne gives : meese, a labyrinth, to turn giddy (from the Anglo-Saxon meuse)—a hole in a fence, a hare's general track. Perhaps the word denotes a part of the old Forest of Brewood, unridded, where the trees were thick, and the way through it puzzling, the underwood growth briery, and good shelter for wild animals.

" Dennis Field "—belonging to the owners of Boscobel. The tithe upon it was apportioned at 6/- per annum, and is still payable to the owner of Tong. St. Denys is the patron Saint of France, and the name suggests a connection-with White Ladies Abbey hard by. The bridle-way field and one adjoining bear the respective names of " White Ladies Close" and " Minerals Leasow "; other old names suggestive of mines are Ores Bank and Small Ores Bank to the North of Meashill house.

"Bryery Hurst." The name is still retained in New and Far Briery Hurst and Briery Leasow some thirty-five acres, lying west of the Meeshill house. A Hurst is defined as a woody place, where trees grow but low.

Mr How's bond-hedge extended to the road to Boscobel, then called Pierce Hay lane.

A well, called Lady Isabel's Well, and a weeping willow over it, are near this spot. At the present cross roads, near a cottage called "Acorn Lodge," was, I suppose, the gate leading into Bishops wood, probably then a wood indeed, and part of Brewood Forest. Near here occurred a famous fight between two pugilists.

Pertry or Pear-Tree Leasow, a name still retained by the field south of Park Pales house.

A bond-hedge divided Blymhill and Tong, "until we come to Weston Park Pale Corner." This is a point in the road leading from Park Pales House towards Ivetsey Bank, not far from the wood to which Weston Old Park extended. The present noble owner, the Earl of Bradford, tells me that Weston Park originally reached nearly to Brewood. A Map in Plot's Staffordshire of 1686 shews this so.

An inhabitant living at Park Pales, named JIMMY TETHERTON, an honest old cottager whose life is bound up with the spot, soliloquized on rent-day in October, 1890, in terms which I paraphrased thus :—

> I want a bit o' paint fur the doo-ers
> It'll do 'em good, Keep the splicings right
> And the nail-holes in the wood ;
> Tisn't much, it'll do for me, I shan't be lung
> Afore I've done with it all, right or wrung
> D'ye know how old I am, why eighty years and more,
> Was eighty-one last birthday, and that's over four score ;

Ten year older than My Lord, cos I know he's seventy-one,
But oh I'm well and hearty, but my work is a'most dun.
I bin' workin at Pyatt's, a harvestin' up at the hill,
Finished six weeks to-day, and some 'ull soon go to the mill.
Farmin's up to nuthin' now, they keep no men,
I never see sich a thing—jest look at it then
When Stockley Squire had the farm, and the stuff they used to grow,
Everywhere like a garden and men he had enow'.
Oh! I bin workin o' *his* garden, Pyatts I mean to say
Fetched all the rubbish and weeds up—ow they dun grow on the clay.
Stockley ee kep it sa nice, an this un ee knows ow ta farm,
But why doant he see to the gardin better from takin' harm.
Well—I must go, good day, you'll see to the paint and stuff,
Better be done afore winter, the weather gits rough.

N.B.—" Meester Norton hasna' sent the paint fur the doo-ers yet !"

A piece of land called "Cowe Haye" in Weston Park. A haye was that fenced or paled part of a forest into which beasts were driven to be caught, as elephants are in India and deer in America. The entrenchments, made by bushes and thickets, were termed hayes.*

"Cowe haye gate." The present Tong entrance Lodge to Weston Park.

Norton Heath. Evidently then unenclosed (1718), as shewn on a Map of Tong, which I have seen dated 1739. It was here that Leslie's 3000 Cavalry re-assembled and offered King Charles their doubtful services again.

Weston New Mill. The mill must have been just erected, in place of a Windmill, which occupied a site on the banky land not far from Streetway or Watling Street. The Windmill was *in situ* in 1686. The Windrills corrupted from "Windmill," a name given to the fields west of Mr. Shaw's farm house, the Woodlands.

The boundary to Burlaughton brook is easily followed in a westerly direction from Pikemere Hollow, the bed of a large sheet of water now dry, but whose outline can be partly followed in the meadows. The present oak trees just inside the field, on the north side of the Watling Street, indicate the boundary of the Parish and County.

---

* Hartshorn's Salop. Antiq.

"Shiffnall, alias Idsall" (Idd's hall ?).—Both names were then in use. Why do not the inhabitants return to the latter and more euphonious name?

> Good lady Ida,
> Hear me, ere I die.
> *Tennyson.*

"A way and steping stones below Thomas Wenlock's corne Mill," *i.e.*, the present Lizard Mill.

"Upper forge hammor ditch," "Forge brooke," "lower Forge," and "Timlett bridge" are names suggesting the important business of the conversion of iron ore, hitherto carried on here, before the discoveries of steam had removed such work to the towns. The ore was brought from the Priors Lee and possibly Wolverhampton districts. The brook lay on a good road between the two, and its rapid fall favored the use of powerful waterwheels. These were constructed either (1) to work a large hammer (as the name of the upper forge implies), or (2) to compress large bellows by which the blast was made constant, and thus the heat became so increased that the operators "had the satisfaction *in three days' time* of seeing the metal begin to run." A token shewing a forge hammer was found at Tong Church during the Restoration in 1892. (See illustration.) A lengthy account of the whole process 200 years ago cannot but interest those engaged in the iron works of the present day.

"When they have gotten the Ore before tis fit for the furnace, they burn or calcine it upon the open ground with small wood, to make it break into small pieces which will be done in three days this is annealing or fiting it for the furnace. In the meanwhile they heat their furnace for a week s time with charcoal without blowing it, which they call seasoning it, and then they bring the Ore to the furnace thus prepared, and throw it in with the charcoal in baskets vicissim *i.e.* a basket of Ore, and then a basket of coal s.s.s. whereby two vast pair of bellows placed behind the furnace and compressed alternately by a large wheel turned by water the fire is made so intense that after three days time the metall will begin to run still after increasing till at length in fourteen nights time they can run a sow and piggs once in twelve hours which they do in a bed of sand before the mouth of the furnace wherein they make one larger furrow than the rest, next the Timp (where the metal comes forth) which is for the Sow from whence they draw 2 or 3 & twenty others for the piggs. It not only runs to the utmost distance of the

Hubbal Grange

farrows but stands boiling in them some time. Before it is cold *i. e.* when it begins to blacken at the top & the red to goe off, they break the Sow and pigs off from one another & the Sow into the same length with the piggs tho' in the runing it is longer and bigger much, which is now done with ease. The hearth of the furnace into which the Ore & Coal fall is ordinarily built square the sides descending obliquely, and drawing near to one another at the bottom where these terminate, which they term the boshes; there are joined four other stones, commonly set perpendicular and reach to the bottom stone making the perpendicular square that receives the metall which 4 walls have the following names—that next the bellows, the tuarn or tuiron wall; that against it the wind wall or spirit plate; that when the Metall comes out the Timp or foreplate; that over against it, the back wall. Tis of importance there should be 5 or 6 soughs made under the furnace in paralel lines to the stream that turns the wheel which compresses the bellows to drain away the moisture from the furnace, for should the least drop of water come into the metall, it would blow up the furnace, and the metall would fly about the workman's ears from which soughs they must also have a conical pipe about 9in. at the bottom set to convey the damp from them into the open air which too otherwise would annoy the workmen even to death." From the furnaces they bring the Sows and piggs when broken asunder to the Forges; these are of 2 sorts, commouly standing together under the same roof, one called the Finery the other Chafery—both open hearths upon which they place great heaps of Coal, blown by bellows like to those of the furnaces and compressed the same way but nothing near so large. In these two forges they give the Sow and piggs 5 severall heats before they are perfectly wrought into barrs. First in the Finery they are melted down as thin as lead, where the metall in an hour thickens to a lump called loop; this they bring to the great Hammer raised by the motion of a Waterwheel and first beat it into a thick square, a half bloom—secondly put it into the Finery for half an hour then bring it to the same Hammer when they work it into a bloom, which is a square bar in the middle and two square knobs at the end, one mu h less than the other the smaller the Ancony the larger the Mocket head. This is all they do at the Finery. Then the Ancony end is brought to the Chapery where after being heated for a quarter of an hour it is brought to the Hammer and beat quite out into such bars as they think fittest for Sale. Whereof those for rodds are carryed to the Slitting Mills, where they first break or cut them cold by the force of one of the wheels into short lengths; next heated red hot & brought singly to rollers by which they are drawn even & to a greater length; another workman takes them whilst hot & puts them through cutters of divers sizes—then another lays them straight whilst hot, and when cold binds them into faggots, then they are fitting for Sale.

Thus I have given an account of the Ironworks of Staffordshire, as they are now exercised in their perfection, the improvement whereof we shall find very great if we look back upon the methods of our ancestors, who made iron in foot blasts or bloomeries by mens treading the bellows, making but a little lump or bloom of iron in a day, not 100 weight leaving as much iron in the slag as they got out; whereas now they make two or three tons of cast iron in twenty-four hours, leaving the slag so poore that the founders cannot melt it again to profit.

The "upper forge hammor-ditch" runs alongside the upper forge pool. Iron cinders still cover a part of the pool embankment.   At "the way and steping stones" is a foot-road still.

"The bridge below lower forge, where was a Gospell read," is now called Upper Timlet Bridge or the Forge bridge.   This road leads direct to the Stone Cross at Tong Norton.   Whether this is the site of an old preaching cross I know not.

Tong Norton had a separate history from Tong as early as 1167, when each was fined for an offence against the Forest Laws.   Stone Crosses were erected first in 653.   When Churches were rare, and clergymen were sent from episcopal monasteries to preach, they did so in the open air at a cross, until the advantages of religion induced the lords to build churches.†   By the will of an Oxford Collegiate Dignitary, dated 1447, Stone Crosses were directed to be put up "of the usual kind, where dead bodies are rested on the way to their burial, that prayers may be made, and the bearers take some rest."*   In Brittany they are common yet.

Timlett Bridge, *i.e.,* Timlett Hollow, the bridge carrying the road from Shifnal to Tong.   An inhabitant of Timlet Hollow informs me that the man who kept horses to do nothing else but cart the ore to the Forge, died about 56 years ago ; and that his father, who lived by the "loom-hole," 2 miles away, used to hear the forge hammer very plainly, "and could always tell when it was a going to rain by its sound."

"Will. Colemore, Esq." was, I suppose, a previous owner of Shackerley property.

"Fitcherbot Esqr.," one of the Fitzherberts, owners of historic Boscobel.

The "Keepers Meadows" are those adjoining the brook, where it bends from a N.E. to an easterly direction on the east side of Tong Park House.   The name is still retained.

---

† Hist. of Hawarden.   * Building News.

Mr. How's bond hedge.—Mr. How seems to have been a large occupier, and without his bond hedge—which may mean a boundary hedge, or one newly pleached down—the boundary would have puzzled Mr. Pietier to describe, judging from the repetition of the name.

Marl is a red earth, brittle when dry, but if wetted becomes adhesive and clayey. "A Marle Pitt in Mill Field." This is in Meashill farm. The dressing of land with marl was very much in vogue years ago, judging by the numberless marl pits in this and the adjoining parishes. Then the profitable production of wheat warranted the farmer in going to considerable expense in preparing his land for that crop ; but now, alas ! this is not the case and agriculture pines. As early as 1260 the Marlpit of Methplekes was referred to in an action against Wm. de Harcourt, as to a tenement in Tong, and as to a Charter of Alan la Zouche, seignoral lord, granting " the land which Robert de Betterton [Beighterton] held in the Barude [Brewood], also his waste near the Pole between the Wood and the Marlpit of Methplekes against the road which passes from Tong towards the Wood, also the Brod-more, &c." The field adjoining the old barn field bears the name of Marlpit Leasow too. The large holes by the roadside indicate the spot whence the earth was taken. The land where these pits are is naturally retentive of moisture. Very likely the marl was carted to other places in the Parish or Manor where the soil is lighter and sandy. I find Neachley was the Grange or Farm of White Ladies Abbey, and the use of marl there would probably be suitable and efficacious.

In the amusing " Chronicles of a Clay Farm," we find an account of some Marl Pits, which puzzled the young farmer :

"Amongst the legacies which the wi dom and labours of antiquity had bequeathed to the Clay Farm and its cultivators, one of the most curious and truly puzzling was a quantity of Marl-pits. In every field of 5 or 6 acres was a great yawning ' pit.'

T

And Sir Anthony Fitzherbert in his Boke of Husbandrie published in 1523, frequently mentions the employment of Marl ; but in his list of Manures omits Lime altogether ; and this is extraordinary when we find a writer on the same subject some 70 years before, declare that " Lime even close to the kiln was dearer than oats "; and when we consider that all produce was carried away by pack-horse, so that lime-drawing would have been too expensive to pay.|

It is thus easy to see that our forefathers had good reason for making the Marlpit do duty for the Limekiln.

"Human instinct and experience had discovered the top of something which neither rain nor sunshine, nor even farm yard manure deprived of their elements could restore, before sulphates or phosphates had been christened ; hence the Marl-pits."

Theory : "This field, for instance, what does it want ?"

Practice : " Lime."

Theory : " Why ?"

Practice : " Because it would *sweeten* it."

Theory : " But why ?" and Practice is silent after centuries of experience.

The Chemist says : "Its effect arises from its avidity for combination ; it searches out free acids, as a ferret does a rat, and instantly *closes with them*. Sulphuric, phosporic, silicic, nitric, humic, and last not least, the 'Great Dissolver,' Carbonic acid ; all these it makes known by seizing upon them and bec m-ing their base ; thus disintegrating, as it were, and reconstructing the elem nts o' the soil, and exciting to a new action the sluggards of Nature wherever ther are lurking. It is the Composer and Decomposer, for nature cannot suffer either process, but fertility must follow : re-composition (growth) has begun ere decomposition is over : does a latent atom of organic matter stand inert for one instant it is *at him* like a Policeman,—' Come, kip moovin' !' "

The ancient De Hugefort deed is translated as follows :—

" And that they [the monks] may have all liberty and free common in woods, in plains, in highways, in paths, in waters, in mills, in heaths, in turbaries, in quarries, in fisheries, in marl-pits, and in all other places, and easements to the aforesaid manor of Tonge belonging, and that they may take marl at their pleasure to marl their land.' *

Here may be mentioned the curious grant of Roger la Zouche to Henry de Hugefort, thus described by Mr. Cox :—

" In after times we find Roger Zouche of Ashby to be Lord of this Manor of Tonge, and that he did by a fair Deed, under his Seal, on which was his

---

* Translation supplied by the late Rev. W. Allport Leighton.

Pourtraiture on Horseback in a Military Habit, grant unto Henry Hugefort, and his Heirs three Yardlands, three Messuages and certa n Words in Norton and Shaw† in this Parish of Tonge, with Paunage for a great Numb-r of Hogs in the Woods belonging to this his Manor ; also Liberties of Fishing in all his Waters there, except in the ‡ great Pool of Tonge, with other privileges, viz. : of gathering Nuts in his woods there, &c , rendring yearly to him the said Roger and his Heirs, a Chaplet of Roses upon the Feast of the Nativity of St. John Baptist, in case he or they shall be at Tonge, if not, then to be put upon the Image of the blessed Virgin in the Church of Tonge, for all Services, Suits of Court, &c."

This quit-rent of a Wreath of Roses is recorded among the rents due from the free tenants of the Manor to Sir Fulco de Pembruge, who died 1296. A visitor to Tong a century ago observed a garland upon the Pembruge tomb. Probably placed then upon the oldest monument of the Lords of Tong on the previous 24th of June, it commemorated the ancient custom, though not in the strict letter, which was impossible seeing that the Image of the Virgin had been removed from the Church. Mr. Lawrence says he renewed the custom.*

The " mill field," about an acre, is not clearly distinguished, but it may be the bit south of the marl pits. The mill must have been the one where Humphrey Pendrell carried on his business, now known as Shackerley Mill, formerly pertaining to the Convent of White Ladies.

"Ambling meadow," possibly where the same ladies of the Nunnery rode their palfreys.

In those days they rode astride like the men. Chaucer tells us how they rode :—

> Upon an ambler esily she sat,
> Ywimpled well, and on hire hede an hat,
> As brode as is a bokeler, or a targe.
> A fote-mantel about hire hippes large,
> And on hire fete a pair of sporres sharpe.

"No sporres sharpe" were needed when the sensational "Sir Hugo" won The Derby for Lord Bradford in 1892, a year in which there were 259 entries, the fourth largest num-

---

† Names still distinguishing part of the Parish.   ‡ The great poole—query, Norton Mere.
* Vide paper read at Archæological Society's visit.

ber on record ; nor can many parishes boast, as Tong can, to have been the galloping ground of a Derby winner, whose owner owned the land and bred the colt.

The Abbies and Convents had to get their own salt made, it seems ; and I read, I think, in an article of Mr. H. F. J. Vaughan's—whether he was quoting from Eyton's Antiquities of Shropshire or not I forget—that the salt works of Lilleshall Abbey were at Donnington near Albrighton. The following letter throws some light on Salt-making :—

Letter from Roger Bedall, 3 Dec., about 1542.

Right worshypple masters, my dewty rememberyd, I have me commendyd unto yow, sertyfying yow that your servanttes hathe demawndyd of me serten salte that the abbye of Bordysley hade yerly, for the whiche sawlte that was laste made I have payd to Mr. Thomas Evans liijs. iiijd. Consytheryng the chargys t'erto belongyng, I thynke hyt be all payd, soo ther ys no more dewe to be payd as yet ; for Bordysley salte ys wont to be made alweys betwene Estur and Penteycoste.

The chargys that beloogythe to the salte makyng

 Item, for the salte makyng...................................xs.
 Item, for the cuttyng of the wod ....ijs.
 Item, for the beryng of the bryne....................xvjd.
 Item, for the drawyng of the bryne .....:.............vd.
 Item, for the reparacyon of the fates [vats]......xvjd.
 Also, for the getheryng of the rent
 and the makyng of the salte, my
 ffee is yerly a lyverye cote and..............vjs. viji

To the ryght worshypple
Mr. Scuddamore and Mr.
Burgoenye   thys   be
delyvered with sped, dd.

With regard to Tong Lake, a sheet of water of some 21 acres in extent, the following old placard has been sent me by John H. Clarke of Tong Norton :—

PROGRAMME

OF THE TOURNAMENT ON THE LAKE AT TONG

MONDAY, SEPTEMBER 16TH, 1839.

The Cecilia, Lotus, and Water Witch, having four Champions and a Bugle man, with the Crew of each Boat in uniform to correspond with the Flags, will start from Vauxhall Gardens at 12 O'clock make a circuit round the Lake, and draw up in front of the Fairy Isle, from whence the Queen of Love and Beauty will give the signal by lowering her flag for the Cannon to fire and the Tilting to commence which will be performed during their procession round the Islands. When the Boats meet the Bugles sound the Charge, and the Champion standing on the stern, with his Lance advanced, will endeavour to overthrow his antagonist.

The Vanquished will be immediately succeeded by another Champion till the whole have been encountered, when the two last will receive the Prizes from the Queen of Love and Beauty.

The Gold Purse to the Champion who has vanquished the greatest number, and the Silver Purse to the other.

When the Tilting is finished the following Coracles—

Neptune-	-	-	-	Colour	-	-	- Red
Nautilus	-	-	-	,,	-	-	- Blue
Mermaid	-	-	-	,,	-	-	- White
Porpoise	-	-	-	,,	-	-	- Yellow
Jim Crow	-	-	-	,,	-	-	- Red & White
Duck 'em	-	-	-	,,	-	-	- Blue & White

Will start from Vauxhall Gardens, make the tour of the Lake, and draw up in front of the Fairy Isle, when the Queen of Love and Beauty will give the signal by lowering her Flag for the Cannon to fire, and the Race to Commence round the Western Island.

The first Coracle that returns to the Starting Post will be entitled to the Ladies Purse.

All the Champions who are overthrown and unsuccessful Competitors in the Race will receive a handsome remuneration.

GEORGE HEMPENSTALL, Seneschal
FRANCOIS DE VOS, Maitre D'Armes
JOHN SWAN } Wardens
JOHN WEDGE }

W. Parke, Wolverhampton (Printer).

There is a grandeur about this programme worthy of old times ! Who were the Champions, and the Bugleman ? The Seneschal we know, and the Wardens are old Tong names ; and was the Fairy Isle the same as the reed bank of to-day ? Above all, who was the Queen of Love and Beauty ? Or were there two Queens ? What a charming "Queen of Love" little Miss Sybil Kenyon Slaney would be.

Four Champions in three boats sounds awkward. Probably they carried long lances and thrust at each other, as was done by Tilting Knights on horseback in old times. The horses were set at a gallop, and the shock of a lance-thrust, received at such a pace, may better be imagined than described. The lance was often broken, or the rider unhorsed. The legend on Marmion's shield, Sir Walter Scott tells us, ran

"Who checks at me to death is dyghte."

A few old tilting lances are preserved in the Tower of London ; they are of light wood, and from memory I should guess them to be about 15ft. long, and 3 or 4 inches through at the butt end.

The Coracle is a small wicker boat, the ancient British Curwgll, which a man can carry on his back, and is rowed with one oar. It requires skilful manipulation, or easily capsizes. Old fishermen on the Severn, near Shrewsbury, are very clever with the coracle, and it is still used on some rivers in Wales and Ireland.

Some names are readily traceable to occupations. Hempenstall, £10 worth of hemp or flax was to be bought by Lord Pierpoint's Will, to be worked up by the poor, and then sold to apprentice poor children. He also bequeathed a sum to buy Staffordshire or "Shalloon" wool to be worked up by the poor, and when woven, to allow each widow a gown. There was a room over the College porch belonging to the Manufactory.

Items in Heayse's accounts occur which probably relate to this factory :—

1803. Mrs Andrews—Repairing the washing mill, 1s. ; a board for the washing mill &c., 2s. 8d. ; webbing for the mill, and nails, 4d.

The work-house or factory was at Tong Norton, a thatched building.

The Wedges are numerous in Tong ; and old John Wedge, who lived at Neachley Brook, a worthy old man, was a walking compendium on Tong parish matters. The name is undoubtedly traceable to occupation at the Forge or Forge hammer, or Wheels. John Wedge it seems won the coracle match and £2, and Abraham Hempenstall the tilting match. There were supposed to be 3,000 persons present and 300 carriages†

---

† Ex. Salopian Journal, 1839.

William Woolley.—He was clerk in 1801, and a clock-maker of no small repute, who carried on his business at Tong Hill. The late Charles J. Horton (who gave me a a curious Tudor Jug, with Medallion of Queen Mary, which belonged to his grandmother) told me that Woolley got the "works" for his clocks from Coventry. The Earl of Bradford has a clock of his make, as also have James Tetherton, of Park Pales, Mrs. Alice Turner (Charles J. Horton's niece), William Stevenson, of Cross Roads, whose parents had it 70 years ago. Woolley was an apprentice of John Baddeley, blacksmith, of Tong, who made Sheriffhales clock, and was "Clockmaker to King George," as I am told. Mrs. George Parker (now Salter) has a clock made by "Baddeley, Tong." She is a daughter of a worthy old Foreman of Labourers, now disabled, named Samuel Greatbach. He found a piece of the old Forge mill-wheel. John Jones, of Tong Lodge ("Rosy Jones"), had a clock made by Woolley & Son, Albrighton. His wife is a Salter, one of the oldest families of Tong. George Salter was one of the Manorial Jury in 1719 who knew the "Manor Boundarye." Benjamin Andrews' father, of Tong Norton, made the frames for these clocks. It seems Thomas Ore was also a Tong clockmaker, and made the present sundial at Tong in 1776. They are "grand-father" clocks, and it was the custom for each young couple who got married to have one of "Woolley's" clocks.

There is a Salter's Hall at Newport, possibly a name derivable in connection with the fish-salting there.

In 1808 Heayse's accounts refer to William Woolley, Esq.: In 1811 he lived at Neachley. In 1808 Heayse put up a bridge at Butters Brook for Mr. W. Jones, of Tong Parish, costing 17/6. Which brook is this? In 1809, James Ellis came to work for him at 1/6 a day. In 1813, Nov. 14, Mr. Smith, of Weston—2 pair of large stocks, £1 5s. 0d.;

Newport, at the Fair, cash 7/-; Easter week, £1 ; Codsall Wake, 5/-; Emingham's cocking, 4/- (what is this ?); stockings, 3/6; Wake, 10/6; cash, Nov. 26, gallowses and ale; cash for a Harper, 4/-; brass for cards, 6d.; cash, £1 1s. 0d., old Nan. "Clew" means a ring at the head of a scythe, from the Anglo Saxon. Mr. Clews was a tenant in Tong, lately, whose father was gardener to Lord Bradford. "Jimmy Beresford, the artist," says "they soul at Tong, and always have done," *i.e.*, on All Souls' Day, and that if you bring the spade or pikel in the house they say "ther'll be a death in the family." Also, "the crows whirling about is a sign of rain !" Milner is a corruption of Miller, and Great-batch from the batch of flour baked at one baking, or brought from the mill. Picken suggests an occupation, and Gamble is from gambrel. Bourne is a boundary stream. Haighway from John "of the highway." Yate and Yates from gate. Crowther a player on an ancient violin.

In 1881, the population of Tong was 498; in 1801, 404 ; in 1831, 510. In 1891, population 445.

Some other local sayings are, "to scratch for the 'adlant," *i.e.*, hurry to reach a place before a certain time ; "hussel," household goods; "with a jaundiced eye," *i.e.*, evil and prejudiced," "twarly," illtempered : "it rained cats and dogs at his funeral," a sure sign of a not very good life ! "By the dumpty derry," a jocular oath; "Wrong way of the Charley," misconstrued or perverted intention ; "gallus," a wag.

Of names we find Leichfield, the field of dead corpses, hence lich-gates to church-yards.—Newport means the new haven, or way; Parker, keeper of a park, or to inclose ; Pierepoint de petra ponte ; Shuker means a bender ; Stanley, a stony hill ; Taylor, from Tailere, to cut ; Twiss, a twin ; Vernon, green-springing, or a town in Normandy.*

____

The name of HARTLEY will long be associated with the tenancy of Tong Castle.   The late Mr. John Hartley died in his 72nd year.   He was a deputy lieutenant for Staffordshire, and J.P. for Stafford and Salop Counties, one of the partners in Chance & Sons' well-known Glass Works, and later a partner with his brother-in-law, Major Thorneycroft, J.P., in Messrs. G. B. Thorneycroft & Co.'s large Ironworks and Collieries, a member of the Royal Coal Commission and chairman of the South Staffordshire Iron Trade, and many years a Director of the L. & N.W. Railway.   Mr. Hartley married in 1839, Emma, a daughter of Mr. G. B. Thorneycroft, of Wolverhampton, the lady who now resides at Tong Castle, and interests herself much in promoting the happiness of her friends, and the cottagers.

There seem to have been four public-houses in Tong, if not more.   There were three at Tong Norton, viz.:—

The Horse Shoes, where George Meddings now lives, near the Smithy.
The Bush, in the hollow, formerly kept by Mrs. Jane Jones.
The Plough, at the north end of the Shaw Lane ; and
The Red House was an Inn in Tong Village.

Birds of some rarity are frequent visitors to Tong, and they have been noted in the *Transactions of the Shropshire Archæological Society* (vol. iii., pt. 4, &c.), from communications furnished by Colonel the Hon. F. C. Bridgeman, M.P. of Neachley, who, like his father, the Earl of Bradford, is an ardent naturalist ; they include Grebes, Herons, Pochards, &c.

Reliable contributions of that kind are always appreciated by the Society, whose operations now are so undervalued, alas !

U

THE DURANT FAMILY.

OME account of Mr. Durant's family is given on pages 89 to 92. The following addenda may be of interest.

Probably few country parishes bear more striking marks of a family's ownership than does that of Tong. Whether these are calculated to increase our respect for the name or other-wise is not for me to say. Certainly many old landmarks were demolished or lost sight of in that time, notably the College, the Almshouses, and Sir Harry Vernon's picturesque Castle itself; but on the other hand, large sums of money were spent greatly in the employment of labour—and there-fore deserving of high commendation—in forming water carriers, in rebuilding the Castle, in razing old and ugly dwellings, and in the erection of new ones. On the whole perhaps a more judicious and discriminating use of his means would have commended itself to all who know the place at the present time. About 1760 Mr. Durant purchased Tong Castle and Estate from the Duke of Kingston, and he appears forthwith to have commenced to chop off the strag-gling parts of the old Castle, and to reface the main building with the mixed Moorish and Gothic exterior forming the im-posing facade which now presents itself to our view, and to carry out his other "improvements."

The ownership by Mr. Durant and his family extended to within a few years of a century, and Mrs. F. O. Durant's decease and her son's change of residence from the neighbouring town of Shifnal sever the last link which associated that name with the district. I append a letter from the elder Mr. Edwin Durant.

Shifnal, 8 Sept., 1884.

My Dear Sir,—I regret it is not in my power to give you any particulars of importance of my "blessed" ancestors.

The tablet giving the names of children who were then alive (and which was erected by my grandfather) does not contain all the names by some half score, as my Father Francis Ossian, and Mav, who are buried in our vault, were then living as well as Ernest Beaufoy and Augustus. (These 3 last, I think, are not buried at Tong. B. and A. are not, but I am not quite sure about Ernest).

Would it not be well to mention that the sketch of "Little Nell" in Dickens's work is taken from Tong Church?

Faithfully yours,

EDWIN DURANT.

It is said (1893) that on the Durant Tomb being opened for the burial of Mr. and Mrs. F. O. Durant there was found half-a-crown on the coffin of one already buried there, it being the legacy left that person by Mr. Durant, and which person refused to receive it during life—so it was placed on his coffin after death, and so paid.

George Durant, Esq., purchased the Castle, &c., in 1750, having married Maria, daughter of Mark Beaufoy, Esq., leaving a large family.

Mr. George Durant, his son, was a minor at his father's death in 1780. He married first Miss Eld of Seighford, and secondly, in 1830, Celeste, daughter of M. Cæsar Lafefve. By his first marriage he had issue a son, George Stanton Eld, who predeceased him, but leaving a son, George Charles Selwyn, who sold Tong Castle Estate in 1855 to the Earl of Bradford.

The following pages are of private rather than of general value, and the result of stray notes made during the frequent sight of these which may be properly termed, "Durant Oddities," dating from the second Mr. Durant's period, called Col. Durant. They may be of secondary interest now, but simple accounts of familiar objects become dignified by lapse of time, and to their happy preservation are we indebted for some valuable details of the domestic history of bygone days. I venture to think that such records also make us regret the less the necessitous removal of those old things themselves, which modern requirements have rendered inconvenient or perhaps valueless.

The Hermitage at Tong, to be seen from the Albrighton Road, is so called from the fact that a miserable poor half-witted man once chose to dwell in a cave-like place cut in the rock behind it. He dressed himself in a kind of tunic or coarse cloth, and wore a long white untrimmed beard. He is said to have been a gentleman who had seen better days. He got together some money at one time, but afterwards lost it, and for several years chose to inhabit this dismal cavern.

Mr. Hubert Smith, in *Shrops. Trans.*, vol. 1, p. 171, says he was called Carolus, but his real name was Charles Evans. He died in a house at the back of the Castle, says the *Gentleman's Magazine* of 1822. "Oct. 6, Shropshire: C. Evans, better known by the name of Carolus, the Hermit of Tong, where he had lived seven years in a lonely and romantic cell, on the domain of G. Durant, Esq."

Near by this place and the Convent Lodge is a handsome octagonal stone Pulpit, six sides of which have open tracery. It is built upon one of the wing walls on the south side of the massive wrought iron Gates, which form the principal approach to Tong Castle.

The pulpit is very similar to the Oratory in the Abbey Yard, Shrewsbury, but is of modern date.

The roof is of stone, and around the outside on each face of the octagon are little emblems carved in imitation, or perhaps ridicule, of heraldry and religion ; such as the following :--a harp, a censer, an hourglass, an axe, flag and spear, cross-keys, a quatrefoil, a mullet, 4 fleur-de-lis with hearts

Entrance, Tong Castle.

thereon, a bell, a crescent, a wreath, cross-spears, lozenges, and a Maltese cross. Inside the Pulpit is a rude stone seat with lion-head ends. The doorway is on the west side, and is reached by steps from the Convent Lodge garden and shrubbery. On one step we are just able to see the well-known lines. I think they are Tom Moore's :—

> *The harp that once through Tara s halls*
> *The soul of music shed.*
> *Now hangs as mute on Tara's Walls,*
> *As if that soul were fled.*

In the West wall of the Lodge itself a stone bears other two verses of the same melody :—

> *No more to Chiefs and Ladies bright*
> *The harp of Tara swells ;*
> *The Chord alone that breaks at night,*
> *Its tale of ruin tells.*

> *Thus Freedom now so seldom wakes,*
> *The only throb she gives*
> *Is when some heart indignant breaks,*
> *To shew that still she lives.*

The gate-pillars and wing-walls of the Entrance Gates are elaborately carved stonework, of fantastic design, the coping being crenulated, and having a continuous rope-like cresting ending in tassels.

Similar emblems to those before named are introduced upon the pillars ; and the faces of the walls on the side next to the high road are relieved by stone entablatures of the Castle, viewed from the East and West respectively, the Durant arms, &c. ; there are also niches, and piercings in the forms of a St. Andrew's and a Latin cross. On the pulpit is this Greek line :—

$$\text{τὸν θεὸν φοβεισθε τον Βασιλέα τιμᾶτε}$$

These piercings appear in other walls built in the vicinity.

The south wing-wall is much the longer of the two, and its terminating pillar at the south end bears this inscription :—

POSTERITATI SACRUM
IMPENSIS
GEO.: DURANT AR.
1821.

(Dedicated to his descendants at the expense of George Durant, Esq., 1821.)

A stone shield in the East Wall of the Convent Lodge has upon it, a bend, between 5 rings (3 and 2). This, I think, is partly a caricature of the arms of Sir Thomas and Lady Harries of Tong Castle, or of their youthful daughter, Mrs. Ann Wylde, whose monument is in Tong Church.

Near to the Convent Lodge and within the Shrubbery is a white stone pedestal surmounted by a ball, bearing this inscription :—

AB HOC
MOMENTO
PENDET
ÆTERNITAS

(On this moment hangs Eternity.)

The two jaw-bones of a whale form an arch over the gateway on the same drive, a little nearer to the Castle. Upon each is a legend. On the north one :—

MORS JANUA VITÆ
(Death the Gate of Life.)

On the south one :—

POST TOT NAUFRAGIA PORTUM.
(A Haven after so many Storms.)

The bones are about 16 feet high, tapering from a foot wide to six inches, and are three or four inches through at the thickest part.

On a stone pedestal surmounted by a well-carved urn of stone :—

GEO: DURANT
OBT. 1780.
ÆTS 46.
SI MONUMENTUM
REQUIRAS
CIRCUMSPICE.

(If you need a memorial [of me] look around.)

This epitaph was inscribed, I believe, by Sir Christopher Wren on St. Paul's Cathedral.

Over the three shutters, through which coals are thrown into the Castle coal-house, is the word :—

MAUSOLEUM.

Other buildings upon the property bear mottoes. The wheelwright and coffin-maker's shop has a stone suitably inscribed :—

IN MORTATE LUCRUM.
(In Death is Gain.)

On Vauxhall Cottage is a semicircular stone bearing in colours a circular shield (......a fesse indented......... a chief ermine) beneath a fleur-de-lis crest and the ' canting ' motto :—

BEATI QUI DURANT 1810,
(Blessed are those who endure ; or, Blessed are the Durants.)

And near this place is a pyramidal Egyptian Fowl-house, into the sides of which are built bricks with encaustic facings, having pictures of birds, and these terse mottoes :—

"LIVE AND LET LIVE."
"SCRAT BEFORE YOU PECK"
"TRIAL BY JURY."
"TEACH YOUR GRANNY."
"CAN YOU SMELL."
"GIVE EVERY (DOG) HIS DUE." (DAY ?)
"HONESTY IS THE BEST POLICY."

Another little pyramidal building at Belle Isle Cottage bears :—

"PARVA SED APTA."
(Small but convenient.)

Upon a classic monument in Tong Priory grounds :—

M.S.

Georgh Hamilton	(Sacred to the Memory
Legione Regis	of George Hamilton of
Armigeri	the King's Guards
In Bollo et Pace	Gentleman. In war and
Virginti Annos	peace he consecrated 20
Georgiam Brittaniæ	years (to the Georges)
Consecravit	of Britain. Born 14
Natum 14 Nov. 1770.	Nov. 1770 died 1832.)
Ob. 1832.	

In the rock below the Castle, near where the old mill stood, is a Dropping Well labelled :—

ADAM'S ALE,
LICENSED TO BE DRUNK ON THE
PREMISES.
1838.

A two-roomed Building (now used as a foreman's cottage) bears :—

LOUVRE,

and another Building near has panels in style in rude imitation of an Egyptian man and woman. A lozenge-shaped shield between them has the Durant crest, arms, and motto, and OB. 18 ÆT :

Upon each pillar of the Gateway to this little yard was an Æolian Harp, which cadenced sweet music to unappreciative animals. One of these instruments still remains in a dilapidated condition. Some eight lines upon a stone in one of these pillars are nearly illegible. They are, I find, after much searching, taken from Sir Walter Scott's " Lady of the Lake."

Harp of the North ! that mouldering long hast hung
And down the fitful breeze thy numbers flung,
Till envious ivy did around thee cling,
Muffling with verdant ringlet ev'ry string—
Oh minstrel harp ! still must thine accents sleep ?
Mid rustling leaves and fountains murmuring.
Still must thy sweeter sounds their silence keep,
Nor bid a warriour smile nor teach a maid to weep.

In the Park of Tong Castle is a pretty Dove-house. (See illustration). There is a similar one at Haughton. Every manor house had its dove-cot in old times.

The north or Rosary Lodge, the Round House at the Forge, and " the Hall," a farm-house in Tong (which latter became Mrs. Celeste Durant's), are examples of fantastic brick structures.

Dovecot
Tong

The church from
the west shewing
ruins

Of Mr. Durant's erections perhaps should be specially . mentioned the Monument, which formerly stood on the Knoll, on a site a few yards east of the Flag Tower built by the present Earl of Bradford in 1883. It was an octagonal cottage of three stories, and had a stone roof finished with a vane, and was occupied, together with a few acres of land, by an industrious cottager, whose children, Lord Bradford informs me, roamed amid the towering bracken. The story goes thus, about Mr. Durant's erection. Built, in questionable taste, to record Mr. Durant's success in a prolonged law-suit against his own wife, her annoyed but powerless sons shared her disgust at its obtrusive existence, and planned its destruction. While Mr. Durant lay upon his dying bed two barrels of gun-powder were placed in the foundations of the monument, and the same night that saw his decease saw the cottage a heap of ruins. A man who now lives at Tong Hill, who was then a keeper at Woodcote (7 miles away), heard the detonation, and was so much alarmed as to attribute the unusual noise to nothing less than a " hearthquake."

Fifty years later, among some débris near, were found some stones, one inscribed—

" FERAMUS,"

another—

An. Jubil. Quia quæ
Reg. Geo. Ter.
Oct. xxv. MDCCCLX. (?)

And a third, which becomes a fitting motto to conclude this paper—

RESPICE FINEM
" Remember the end,"

V

TONG CHURCH REGISTERS.

APTISMS, marriages, and burials are all entered promiscuously down to the death of Thomas Hall, 1765.

We read that registers were begun to be kept in every parish in 30 Henry VIII. (1539,), and by the injunctions of the young King Edward VI. "all parishes were to keep a register booke in the parish chest."

Registers began by being simply labours of love on the part of the clergy, and after many years received partial recognition as public documents. In early times, the Monastic Registers —priceless records, of which too many were scattered during the fanaticism which car.ied everything before it between the suppression of monasteries and the re-organisation of the Church—supplied the place of the Parish Registers. But as the deaths registered were as a rule only those of important persons, the object being to tell when masses became due, their value is limited. Ordinary folk in those ages, and long subsequently, contented themselves with private records, or with entering the births, deaths, and marriages of their families on the fly-leaf of a family Bible, or, when Bibles were scarce, on the blank pages of books of devotion. In 1538 Thomas Cromwell ordained that regular Parish Registers should be kept, in order to meet the needs created by the sup_pression of Religious Houses. This injunction, however, was carried out so carelessly that in 1597 Elizabeth ordered, not only that the Registers should be better kept, but that copies should be sent to the Bishops. During the Commonwealth, the Registers again fell into irregularity, and on the Restoration it was found that many of them were lost, probably having been destroyed. After the Restoration the Parish Registers began to become more interesting, and even entertaining. They contain notices of a host of events, lay as well as ecclesiastical, in addition to the usual entries of births, deaths, and marriages.

The earliest entry in Register now in use is—

Thomas son of Edw. Bistan and Joyce his wife b. Oct. 10 1616

Roger Boult and Jane Wenlock m. May 1, 1636

John Wheeler was bu. May 5 1630, and lyeth 3yds. south from the east corner of the Golden Chapel.

Anne w. of Thos. Scot was bu. June 28th 1636

Frances d. of Wm. Pierpoint was born 1 Sept. 1630, b. 1 Oct.

Eleanor d. of Wm. Pierpoint Esq. and Eliz. his wife was baptized Sept. 4 163 (1 or 2)

Margaret Pierpoint their dau. bapt. Oct. 2 163 (2 or 3)

Dorothy Giffard was bu. Sept. 30 634

Robert son of Wm. and Eliz. Pierpoint b. Sept. 20 1634

Dame Elinor Harries was bu. Apl 9 1635

Mrs. Margt. Harries was bu. Aug 1636

Hy. son of the Hon. Wm Pierpoint and Eliz. his wife was b. Aug 15 1637

Wm. son of Wm. Pierpoint bu. Nov. 13 1640

Elizabeth wife of Wm. Pierpoint of Tong Castle was bu. July 1 1656

1648   Burried was Thos. Lawrence gent.

1692   Burried was Eliz. dau. of the Hon Gervas Pierpoint Aug 30th

1715   Burried was the Hon Gervas Pierpoint June 4th

1738   Burried was the Hon H. Willoughby Dec. 11th

1722   Smallpox raged

1694   Buried was Featherstone of Bromsgrove Oct 11

1777   Geo. son of Geo. Durant Esq. and Maria his wife, of Tong Castle, was born in the Parish of St Margaret's Westminster Apl. 25th 1776 in the presence of Mary Cusin and Mrs. Langley midwifes, and was baptized by me 15 Apl. 1777. Thomas Buckeridge, Minister of Tong.

1780   Aug. 16 Geo. Durant of Tong Castle died Aug. 16

1799   Fras. Humpage unfortunately suffocated

May 15th 1660 there was colected in the Church of Tong s8 11 for Southwold Suffolk

Aug. 25th Collected s5 10 for Willenhall Staffce.

For the Town of Poole [Welshpool] Montgomeryshire, who had suffered a great loss by fire there was colected the sum s2 3 June 16th 1667

Colected in the Church of Tong at the request of the inhabitants of Sheriffhales towards the relief of those that suffered there £3 14 4, 1663

---

b. bapt., m. marr., di. died, bu. buried.

March 14 1717 it began to snow at five o'clock in the afternoon and without any intermission continued till Monday 16th; a strong wind blew at the time; it drove the snow into hollow places to so great a height as to make the roads altogether impassable; snow upon the level of the garden behind the castle 13 inches deep; 16 inches Court before it. It did snow again and freeze all night, and the night following. A vast number of sheep were buried under the snow, 20 and 30 together. The sheep that lay burried 5 or 6 days escaped, but those that continued longer under were found dead. So great a snow in so short a time, and in a season so far advanced, had never been seen by anybody in the Parish. It occasioned as it had done the year before a mighty bright meteor in the air at night, some few days after it had melted away.

In 1715 April 22 there happened to be an eclipse of the Sun which continued total about 2 minutes, during which time several stars did appear ; all things looked much darker than they do during twilight, insomuch that the largest prints could not be read in the open fields, nor hardly anybody be seen in the house.

I have been told that "the Parish Register before Mr. W———'s time [he died in 1596] was written in several pieces of parchment or paper," subsequently transcribed into one book, the latter being attested by two Churchwardens. This refers to the Parish Clerk who answers to that description in the present day, and not to the Clerk or priest of the parish.

Old Gough of Myddle tells us about Parish Clerks :—

The first that I remember was Will. Hunt, a person very fitt for the place as to his reading and singing with a clear and audible voice ; but for his writeing I can say nothing.

On Christmas day in the afternoone when the minister had gone out of Churche this Will Hunt sung a Christmas caroll in the Churche, being assisted by old Mr. ——— who bore a base exceedingly well.

In Will Hunt's successor's time there was an ordinance of parliament that there should bee a parish register sworne in every parish. His office was to publish the banns of marriage, and to give certificates thereof ; and alsoe to register the time of all births (not christnings), weddings, and burialls.

The next was a person altogeather unfitt for such an imployment. Hee can read but litle ; he can sing but one tune of the psalmes. Hee can scarse write his owne name, or read any written hand.

Copy of ye original Proclamation for the observance of the 5th Nov. found among parish papers in ch.wds. chest and deposited by me with other papers in the parish chest for the Registers.

Anno 3 Jacobi Regis (1600).

An Act for a publique Thanksgiving to Almighty God every year on the 5th Novr.

For as much as Almighty God hath in all ages shown His power and mercy in the mysterious & gracious deliverance of His Church & in ye p°tection of Religious Kings and States & that noe nation of yᵉ earth hath been blest wʰ greater benefitts than this Kingdome now enjoyeth, having yᵉ true and frie p°fession of yᵉ gospel under oʳ most Soveraigne Lord King James—the most great, learned & religious King that ever reigned therein inricht with a most hopefull & plentiful p°genie p°ceeding out of his royal loynes, p°mising continuance of his happiness & p°fession to all posterity, the wʰ many malignant & devilish Papists Jesuits & Seminary Priests much envvinge & fearinge conspired most horribly, when the King's most excellent Mᵗ the Queene the Princes & all the Lord spirituall and temporall, and Comⁿˢ shᵈ have been assembled in the upper house of Parliament upon the 5ᵗʰ day Novʳ in the yeare of our Lord 1605 suddenly to have blowne up the said whole house wʰ gunpowder, an invention (invention) so inhumane barbᵣrous, & cruell as the like was never before heard of, and was, as some of the principall conspirators thereof confess, purposely devised & concluded to be done in the sᵈ house. That whereas sundry necessary & religious lawes foᵣ the p°servation of the Church & State were made : that they falsely & slanderously { be r me sevell / teme c virell } lawes enacted against them and their religion, both place and person shᵈ be all destroyed & blown up at once, wh wᵈ have turned to the utter ruine of this whole Kingdome, had it not pleased Almighty God by enspyringe the Kinges most excellent maᵗⁱᵉ with a Divine spirit to interprit some darke p'hrases of a letter shewed to his majesty : above & be-yonde all ordinary construction, thereby miraculously discovering this hiden treason not many hours before ye appointed time for yᵉ execution thereof. Therefore the Kings most excellent Majesty the Lords Spiritual & Temporall & all his Majestys most faithful & loving subjects doe most wisely acknowledge this great & infinite blessinge to have proceeded meardeley fr Gods grate mercie, and to his Holy Name doe ascribe all honor glory and praise.

And to the end this unfaigned thankfullnesse may never be forgotten but be had in a perpetuall remembrance that all ages to come may yielde praise to his Divine Majesty for the same & have in memory this w'full day of deliverance Be (Be) it enacted by the Kings most excellent mᵗⁱᵉ the Lords Spiritual and temporall & the Comons in this p' sent Parliament assembled & by the authority of the same, that all and singular ministers in every Cathedrall & Pᵃʰ Church or other usual place for Com Pry within this realme of England & Dominions of yᵉ same, shall allwaies upon yᵉ 5 day of Novʳ ɪay morning prayer & give unto Almighty God thanks for this most happy deliverance & that all & every p'son & pᶜᵉ some in-habiting it in this realme of England & the dominions of yᵉ same shall allwaise upon that day diligently & faithfully resoɪt to yᵉ Pᵃʰ Ch or Chappell accustomed or to some usual ch or chapell where yᵉ said morning prayer, preaching or other service of God shall be used & then & there to abide, & duly & soberly duringe the time that the said prairs or preaching or other service of God used : And that all & every p'son may be put in mind of this duty & be the better p'pared to the said holy Service, be it inacted by authority aforesaid that every minister shall give warning to his p'shners in yᵉ Ch at morning prayer the Sunday before every such 5 day of Novʳ for the observacion of yᵉ said day, & that after morning praier or preaching upon the said 5 day of Novʳ they reade distinctly & plainly this p' sent act.

GOD save yᵉ Kinge.

FAMOUS LADIES ASSOCIATED WITH TONG.

NOTES upon Tong can hardly be closed without some reference to the celebrated ladies associated with it.

Few country places can boast association with such distinguished ladies. They are VENETIA, LADY DIGBY, (of whom some account is given under the particulars of Monument No. 19), LADY MARY WORTLEY MONTAGUE, and MRS. FITZHERBERT: not to mention Elizabeth Chudleigh, Duchess of Kingston, and Isabella Forester, who married Lord Stafford.

LADY MARY WORTLEY MONTAGUE was daughter of Evelyn, 5th Earl of Kingston, who was in 1706 created Marquis of Dorchester, by Queen Anne, and in 1716, Duke of Kingston; and Tong was the scene of her early years, if not her birthplace (which is claimed by Thoresby). Her youth at any rate must have been passed between these two homes of the Pierpoint family. Her letters form a conspicuous part of the literary productions of her time. Born in 1690, she lost her mother in 1694, and being educated under the superintendence of Bishop Burnet, obtained a high degree of mental cultivation. She married Mr. Edward Wortley Montague by special license. Her father had refused him, because he would not make the necessary settlements; and she had allowed him to encourage another suitor; and matters had gone so far that the wedding clothes had actually been bought; but, only making up her mind the evening before, she decided to run away with Mr. Montague, and was married on August 12, 1712.

CHARLES II

from a portrait
in the possession
of the author

It had fallen to the lot of the Duke of Kingston in 1690 to propose a beauty as the annual toast of the Kitcat Club, and a whim seized him to nominate his little daughter, Lady Mary Pierpoint, then 8 years old. Some of the members demurred, as they had not seen her. The Duke sent for her, and when she arrived, finely dressed, she was received with acclamations, her health drunk, her beauty extolled on every side, and she was petted and caressed by all present, the company consisting of some of the most eminent men in England.

Walpole, writing in 1762, describes his visit to this strange lady :—

"I found her in a little miserable bedchamber of a ready furnished house, with two tallow-candles, and a bureau covered with pots and pans:

On her head she had an old block-laced hood, wrapped entirely round, so as to conceal all hair, or want of hair. No handkerchief, but up to her chin a kind of horseman's riding-coat, made of dark green brocade, with coloured and silver flowers, and lined with furs; bodice laced, a foul dimity petticoat, sprig'd velvet muffeetens on her arms, grey stockings, and slippers. Her face less changed in 20 years than I could have imagined. . . . . She is very lively, all her senses perfect, her language as imperfect as ever, her avarice greater. With nothing but an Italian, a French, and a Russian, all men-servants, and something she calls an *old* secretary, but whose age till he appears will be doubtful, she receives all the world, and crowds them into this kennel. The Duchess of Hamilton, who came in just after me, was so astonished and diverted, that she could not speak to her for laughing.''

Lord Byron, in describing the shores of the Ægean and Bosphorus, thus refers to her :—

> And the more than I could dream,
> Far less describe, present the very view,
> Which charmed the charming Mary Montagu.

The picture on the preceding page of Lady Mary entering the club is supplied by Mr H. Blackburn, author of *Royal Academy Notes*, 1884, by kind permission of Mr. Yeames, R.A.

Edward Wortley Montague was in 1716 appointed Ambassador to the Porte, and she accompanied him to the East, and during his residence in the Levant wrote the well-known Letters, which form one of the most delightful books in our language. In 1718 she returned to England, and settled at Twickenham, where she renewed her acquaintance with Addison and Pope. In 1739 Lady Mary went to Italy for her health, and did not re-visit England till 1761, and died Aug. 21, 1762. During her residence in Constantinople she was enabled to confer on Europe a benefit of the greatest consequence, namely, inoculation for the small-pox, which was at that time universal in Turkey. She had so much faith in its safety that she tried it first on her own son. Lord Wharncliffe has a picture of her which she gave to her god-son. *

---

* Mr. H. A. Grueber says.

MRS. FITZHERBERT.   (*See page 169.*)

Writing in 1730 from Dijon to her husband she says :—

This is a very agreable Town, and I find ye air agree with me extreamely ; herein a great deal of good company, and I meet with more civility than I had reason to expect. I should like to pass ye winter here, if it was not for ye expense. I have been entertained by all ye considerable people, French and English.

MARIA ANNA FITZHERBERT, born 1756, youngest daughter of William Smythe, of Tong Castle, and niece of Sir E. Smythe, Bart , of Acton Burnell, married 1st, Edward Weld, of Lulworth Castle, who died the same year, 1771 ; secondly, Thomas Fitzherbert, of Swinnerton, County Stafford, who died in 1781.

Soon afterwards her beauty and fascinating manners attracted the particular attention of the Prince of Wales (George IV.), and she consented to a marriage with him according to the rites of the Roman Church, which marriage however was not permissible by the law of England, she being a Papist. In her memoirs written by the Hon. Charles Langdale, it is said that there was not one of the Royal Family who had not acted with kindness to her, including the Queen of George III., herself. At the command of the Prince, Fox denied the marriage in the House of Commons.

Earl Fortescue has a portrait of this lovely woman by Gainsborough, which she left to the Hon. Mrs. Dawson Damer ; and the Earl of Portarlington has one by Sir Joshua Reynolds, whose studio she often visited with the Prince of Wales. The accompanying picture is after Cosway, who painted delightful miniatures of her, including two rings belonging to Lord Portarlington, one representing an eye of George IV. as Prince of Wales, and the other an eye of Mrs. Fitzherbert.

Lord Portarlington has also a fine collection of miniatures and relics owned by that lady, one being a gold ring given to George IV. by her, bearing on it the poesy reading " L'ami de mon cœur," expressed by two musical notes, *la mi,* DE MON in letters, and a heart.

W

The *Graphic* of March 5th, 1892, has an article about this lady, commencing with the lines of a ballad, which are said to have some reference to Mrs. Fitzherbert :—

> *I'd crowns resign to call thee mine,*
> *Sweet Lass of Richmond Hill.*

We cannot question the charms of person and mind possessed by Mrs. Fitzherbert ; they enthralled one of the most volatile of Princes, and under their fascination, induced that wayward youth to jeopardise the splendid prospects of heir to the Throne by marrying a lady who had been twice a widow whose religious faith, as well as the restrictions of the Royal Marriage Act, were insuperable barriers ; and who, moreover, had the formidable disadvantage of being seven years the senior of the enamoured swain. The Church of Rome received the pair as man and wife ; the King, Queen, and members of the Royal family consistently treated the lady with respect and consideration. Mrs. Fitzherbert, who was a rigid and devout Roman Catholic, retired to the Continent. The enforced separation failed to allay the Prince's passion. He threatened numerous acts of folly, and, after lengthened absence, the return of Mrs. Fitzherbert was, by her advisers, counselled as the most prudent course in 1785. The Prince proposed the most romantic schemes. One morning affairs reached a crisis ; two of the Royal suitor's friends drove to Park Lane with the urgent request that the lady would hasten immediately to Carlton House, for the Prince lay bleeding to death. This highly-sensational summons sent the lady off in a flutter ; on her way to the Palace, she thought proper to call upon her confidential friend, the Duchess of Devonshire, and they decided to fly to comfort the sufferer, and to receive his last sigh. The agitation of his feelings, the alarming apprehensions of his confidential attendants, backed up by the violence of his passion, his reckless declarations, his moving entreaties, and the melting tears, convinced the lady that there was danger in standing aloof. On December 21st, 1785, in the presence of Mrs. Fitzherbert's connections, the nuptial ceremony was gone through at her house in Park Lane, according to the ritual of the Church of Rome, and also the Protestant service was performed by the Rev. Samuel Johnes. On the death of George IV., his successor authorised Mrs. Fitzherbert to wear royal mourning, and gave her the right of using the royal liveries ; moreover, William IV. proposed to make the lady a duchess, a distinction she, with excellent taste, thought proper to decline. It is said that by his own wish the miniature of Mrs. Fitzherbert was buried with the King, suspended round his neck.

Mr. H. F. J. Vaughan writes to me, Nov. 17, 1884, as follows :—

Mrs. Fitzherbert, the wife of George IV., was born in the Red Room at Tong Castle, having arrived somewhat unexpectedly during a visit of her parents at Tong, as I was informed by the late Madame Durant, with whose family my own was intimate. You are probably aware that her maiden name was Mary Anne Smythe, and that she was thrice married.

One of the dearest friends of Mrs. Fitzherbert, Lady Horatia Seymour, in the last stage of a decline, was advised to go abroad to seek in change of climate her own chance of recovery, and had at that time an infant daughter, Miss Seymour, who became devotedly attached to Mrs. Fitzherbert.

There arose difficulties on account of Mrs. Fitzherbert's religion, and the question of custody became a Chancery suit. The opposing Counsel, the Attorney-General, observed that Mrs. Fitzherbert merited everything that could be said in her favour ; but whatever amiable qualities she might possess, the religion she professed excluded her from the right to retain the custody of a Protestant child. The Lord Chancellor however decided in favour of Mrs. Fitzherbert, and the child, who became Mrs. Lionel Dawson Damer, erected a monument to her memory at Brighton, with the following inscription :—

"In a vault near this spot are deposited the remains of Maria Fitzherbert. She was born on the 26th July, 1756, and expired at Brighton on the 29th of March, 1837. One to whom she was more than a parent has placed this monument to her revered and beloved memory, as a humble tribute of her gratitude and affection."

The hand of the figure had three rings on it, bearing evidence of the triple marriage of her departed friend.

VENETIA STANLEY, OF TONG, married Sir Kenelm Digby. "With the exception of Lady Rich, no woman has been made the theme of so much song that deserves to live as Venetia Digby." Tong Castle was the birthplace and scene of her early years, and she died there in 1633. Lord Clarendon speaks of her as "a lady of extraordinary beauty, and of as extraordinary fame." Her husband was so enamoured with her beauty that he is said "to have attempted to exalt her charms and preserve her health by a variety of whimsical experiments, and to have fed her with capons fed with the flesh of vipers, inventing for her use new cosmetics." Her beauty and fascination were the theme of many an eulogy by painter and poet. Ben Johnson has devoted some lines to her, including one rather long poem called " Eupheme." He tells us how to paint her, so :—

> Draw first cloud all save her neck,
> And out of that make day to break,
> Till like her face it do appear,
> And men may think all light rose here;
> Then let the beams of that disperse
> The cloud, and show the universe,
> But at such distance that the eye
> May rather yet adore than spy.
> The Heaven designed draw next as spring,
> With all that youth as it can bring,
> Four rivers branching forth as seas,
> And paradise confining these,
> Last, draw the circles of this globe,
> And let there be a starry robe
> Of constellations 'bout her hurled,
> And thou hast painted beauty's world.

Mr. Granger says* " Her beauty, which was much extolled, appears to have had justice done it by all the world." Mr. Skinner had a small portrait of her by Vandyck, in which she is represented as treading on envy and malice, and is unhurt by a serpent that twines round her arm.† Here the historian and painter illustrate each other. This was a model for a large portrait for Windsor, where there is now, in the Vandyck room of the Castle, a full length picture of her, as well as a half length of her husband. Mr. Walpole had a miniature of her by Peter Oliver. There were two fine busts of her in the possession of Mr. Wright at Gothurst, Newport Pagnel, formerly the seat of Sir Kenelm Digby. There is a fine portrait of Sir Kenelm, by Vandyke, at Weston Park.

The tomb to " Anastatia Venetia, Lady Digby," stood in Christ Church, London, but was destroyed in the great fire.

---

* In the *Antiquarian Repertory* Brit: Mus:—Communicated by T. Pennant, Esq., 1808.
† In the *Anecdotes of Painting*, Vol. II., 2nd Edition, p. 102.

The inscription was:—

*Mem : Sacrum, Venetiæ Edwardi Stanley Equitis Honoratiss.
Ord. Balnei (Filii Thomæ, Edwardi Comitis Derbiæ Filii)
Filiæ ac cohæredi, ex Lucia Thomæ Comitis Northumbriæ Filia et
Cohærede ; Posuit Kenelmus Digby Eques Auratus Cui Quatuor
Peperit Filios Kenelmum Nat. vi Octobr. mdcxxv ; Joannem Nat.
xxix. Decemb. mdxxvii ; Everardum (in cunis Mortum) Nat. xii.
Jan. mdcxxix : Georgium Nat. xvii. Jan. mdcxxxii. Nata est
Decemb. xix., mdc. Denata Maii i. mdcxxxiii.*

Quin lex eadem monet omnes
Gemitum dare sorte sub una
Cognataque funera nobis
Aliena in morte dolere.

TRANSLATION :—

Sacred to the memory of Venetia, daughter and coheiress o Edward Stanley, Knight of
the Most Honble. Order of the Bath, (son of Thomas [who was] the son of Edward, Earl
of Derby). Erected by Kenelm Digby, Knight, tɔ whom she bore four sons, Kenelm, born
6th Oct., 1625; John, born 29 Dec. 1627; Everard (died in his cradle) born 12 Jan., 1629;
George, born 17 Jan. 1632. [She was] born Dec. 19, 1600. Deceased May 1, 1633. How
the same law warns all to break forth into weeping under one fate and to deplore in
another's death the death which we ourselves are born to undergo.

Sir Kenelm Digby, Knight, son of Sir Everard Digby, executed on account of his participation in the Popish plot, was
one of the most faithful adherents of Charles I. in the Civil
War, and an exile in consequence during Cromwell's usurpation.

This " Ornament of England," as Sir Kenelm has been
styled, wrote several learned books, and was a great benefactor to the Bedleian library by presenting it in 1633 with a
large collection of MSS. ; he recovered the reputation of his
family, and rendered it famous throughout the Christian
world. He was born at Gothurst, 1603, and married in 1625.
He returned to England in 1661, was appointed one of the
Council on the first settlement of the Royal Society, died at
his house in Covent Garden, 11th June, 1665, (his birthday)
leaving, by his wife Venetia, two sons and a daughter. He
was descended from Edward Digby, Esq., High Sheriff of co.

Rutland, and M.P., 1434. The ancient name was Tilton of Tilton, co. Leicester, but that abode was abandoned for Digby, co. Lincoln.

He wrote two treatises of " Choice Receipts in Physick and Chirurgery and of Cookery," published in 1669, which contained receipts for the celebrated aurum potabile or digest of gold, bites of a mad dog, serpents, vipers, &c., spirits, sweet waters, for Scotch ale, Metheglin, Morello, currant, cherry, and strawberry wines, and many other curious receipts which are now obsolete.

He wrote the " Broadstone of Honour, or True Sense and Practice of Chivalry," which Julius Hare characterises " as that noble manual for gentlemen ; that volume which, had I a son, I would place in his hands, charging him, though such admonition would be needless, to love it next to his Bible."

The Stanley Tomb, No. 19, bears the name of Venetia, and a long account of her parents and grandparents is given under the description of that monument.

It may not be out of place to give here the portrait of King Charles I., the unfortunate prince whose queen's violent spirit and foreign temperament conduced so much to the disasters of his troublesome reign, and during whose time Tong Castle was burnt, and other memorable incidents are recalled to the minds of Salopians.

He was a good rather than a great man ; one of the most powerful and elegant writers of the English language, a liberal patron of the fine arts, and but for the evil counsels by which he suffered himself to be guided, might have escaped the untimely end to which he was brought by the offended judgement of a people determined to be free.

Charles I., 1642, Sept. 20, Tuesday, came to Salop with his army, where he and the court were joined by Prince Rupert,

Prince Charles, and the Duke of York, and generously condescending to consider the worthy services of Sir Richard Newport, he advanced him to be a baron of England by the title of Lord Newport of High Ercall*; and Feb. 22, 1644, the enemy quitted and burned Tong Castle.*

During the last few days a silver pound piece, coined at the mint of Charles I. at Shrewsbury, realised £27.

The original painting of Charles I. belonged to the famous John Mytton, of Halston, Co. Salop, and appears to be a hitherto unknown portrait of the King, which does not seem to have been engraved, the print room of the British Museum affording only two of any similarity, one of which, very rare, is after Rubens, and the other, a French one, by Daret. " Monsieur Hymans, Curator of the National Gallery, Brussels, the great authority on all that relates to Rubens, writes that we know very little of the meetings between Rubens, Gerbier, Buckingham, and probably Charles when prince. It is not known that Charles ever was painted by Rubens. Rubens however accompanied him in Spain, when he went fruitlessly to woo the Infanta.

> Oh happy he, who with good address,
> Knows how and when and where his suit to press
> Unto attainment of assured success;
> But, oh! unhappy he, who not possessing
> The art of fluently his thoughts expressing,
> Addresses him in vain to his addressing.

Unlike the happy coster or the rural swain, who, after a more successful errand—

> Now fitted the halter, now travers'd the cart,
> And often took leave, but seemed loth to depart!

ISABELLA FORSTER, LADY STAFFORD. I am unable to learn much about this lady, a member of a Tong family, branching from the ancient Shropshire family of Forester, Foster, or as it was often spelt Forster, for a not too diligent regard was paid to spelling two or three centuries ago.

Isabel married the young son of Edward, 2nd Baron Stafford, whose mother was heiress of the Duke of Clarence,

---

and thus direct legal heir to the crown. Edward was grandson of Edward, the attainted Duke of Buckingham. Her father was Thomas Forster, of Tong, the younger of two brothers, the elder being Robert Forster, of Barton Green (who married Joan Mytton, of Weston), descended from John Forster, of Evelith. Her brother, Humphrey Forster, of Tong, occurs 1614.

It seems that the attainted Duke's daughter, Elizabeth, married the Duke of Norfolk. Their son Henry was beheaded 1572. His son, Thomas, Duke of Norfolk, was beheaded the same year, and his son Philip died in the Tower, 1595. His son, Thomas, Earl of Arundel,* died 1646, and his son William married Mary, the granddaughter of Isabel Forster, of Tong.

Isabel's husband, Edward, was, as 3rd Baron Stafford, heir to the crown, but died in 1625, his son Edward having died before him, leaving a son, Isabel's grandson, Henry, 4th Baron Stafford, who died under age, in 1637, and a daughter Mary.

She herself is variously described once as the " beautiful Isabella," and in another place, as of " prepossessing appearance." Doubtless the features were duly committed to canvas, but like other portraits adorning the walls of many county houses, the identity has been unpreserved, and a lamentable loss arises: " Tis pity that in many galleries the names are not writt on or behind the pictures, though it could be done with very little trouble," says an old writer.

The heir *de jure* of this Henry in the male line was—through an uncle of Isabel's husband, Richard, who was " very poor " —a cousin, Roger, born 1572, who died about 1640, leaving a sister, Jane, born 1581, described as a widow, living 1637. She married a joiner at Newport, Co. Salop, and left a son, a

* This was the great patron of the Arts the Collector of the Arundelian Marbles, and portraits of him holding a baton over his grandson are at Weston and Arundel.

cobbler at Newport, 1637. King Charles I. created William Howard and his wife Mary, baron and baroness Stafford, of Stafford Castle, "with such precedency as Henry, brother of Mary, did enjoy." This was an instance of the improper and undue Court influence of Thomas Howard, Earl of Arundel which was quite reprehensible.

Roger claimed the honor that had become his by right of law, but "was unjustly denied the dignity on account of his poverty." Roger presented a petition to the king, who, however, declared "his royal pleasure that Roger, having no part of the inheritance of the said Lord Stafford, nor any other lands or means whatever, shall make resignation of all claims and title to the said barony of Stafford, for his majesty to dispose of as he shall see fit." In obedience to the King's command poor Roger duly surrendered his claim by Deed enrolled 7 Dec., 1639. In 1640 the lords in parliament were too regardant of their privileges to allow the "melancholy precedent" of the Lord Stafford to remain uncondemned, and they afterwards resolved to obviate so dangerous an example.†

MARGARET and DOROTHY VERNON, daughters of Sir George Vernon, Lord of Tong, and King of the Peak, must not be omitted from mention again here among the Ladies of Tong,—though an account is given of them under Tomb 19, page 71,—as the story of their lives is interwoven with the annals of their time. Mr. New's sketch of Margaret is taken from her effigy at Tong, and the portrait of Dorothy is sketched by Miss Bradley, from a painting in the Porter's Lodge at Haddon, by kind permission given to me by the Duke of Rutland.

> " Where are the high and stately dames
>   " Of princely Vernon's banner'd hall,
> " And where the knights, and what their names,
>   " Who led them forth to festival ? "
>
> " Arise ye mighty dead arise !
>   " Can Vernon, Rutland, ·tinley, sleep ?
> " Whose gallant hearts, and eagle eyes
>   " Disdjin'd a ike to crouch or weep."

---

† The *Howard Papers*, by H. K. S. Causton, 1862.

X

BOSCOBEL AND THE ROYAL OAK.

AM loth to bring to a conclusion the History of Tong without mentioning some few particulars of historic Boscobel and its neighbouring Convents known as White Ladies and Black Ladies.

Many have formed conclusions on the question of the identity of the Oak, based upon very fragile and chimerical data, and the sincere conviction that this tree, happily protected from the ravages of enthusiasts, is one and the same tree which sheltered the royal and jovial, if unworthy, king, prompts me to commit to paper some notices and notes to quell the storms of detraction which gather round this and similar marks of antiquity.

The King's wanderings in Tong and neighbourhood are related by His Majesty himself, and his flight, and seclusion with the notoriety of the humble Penderells, born and bred at the house at Hubball in the parish of Tong, in the depths and secluded part of the Forest of Brewood, are ably related by Thomas Blount, a Catholic lawyer and sufferer in the royal cause, in which also he is said to have borne arms. His account runs thus :—

The battle of Worcester* took place on Sept. 3rd, 1651. At one time so resolute was the onset of the Royalists, led by Charles II. in person, that the Republicans at first gave way before them, abandoning a part of their cannon. "One hour of Montrose" at the head of the 3,000 horse, whom a few minutes might have brought to the charge, had perhaps retrieved the fortune of the day ; but Lesley, who commanded this important force, induced either by treachery or distrust,

---

* The writer has an interesting painting of this.

Royal Oak. 1894.

Black Ladies.

kept them stationary in the rear, until the infantry, having expended their ammu-
nition, and reduced to fight with the butt-ends of their muskets, gave way before
the reserve poured in by the Protector, and fell back into the city with the loss of
their best leaders. The Republicans followed closely, and the King finding his
entrance on horseback impossible, got into the City on foot; and putting off his
heavy armour rode up and down the streets on a fresh horse, calling the officers
and men by their names, and in vain urging Lesley and his cavalry to face the
enemy for the first time. At six in the evening, Charles II., surveying
the still unbroken appearance of Lesley's horse, who had taken little or no share in
the struggle, faced about, and meditated a fresh charge to retrieve the fortune of
the day. From this hazardous step he was soon dissuaded, as his infantry were
nearly annihilated, and Lesley's horse had begun to show symptoms of mutiny and
desertion. Nothing, therefore, now remained but the alternative of escape.
Accordingly Charles rode off, accompanied by about 60 most trusty adherents, in-
tending to reach Lord Derby's place of refuge at Boscobel House, whither Mr.
Charles Giffard undertook to conduct them. At day-break next morning they
reached White Ladies, a house belonging to the Giffard family, bringing the king's
horse by way of precaution into the hall. Here news was brought to him that
Lesley's cavalry had rallied in full force on the heath near Tong Castle (*i.e.*,
between Tong Norton and Lizard Grange), and it was suggested to the King to
join this force with the view of ensuring his retreat to Scotland. This advice
Charles absolutely rejected, indignant at their recent conduct, and "knowing," in
his own words, "that men who had deserted him when they were in good order
would never stand to him when they had been beaten": an opinion which the
event fully justified. He was recommended by Mr. Giffard to the good offices of
his retainers, Richard and William Penderell, whose fidelity Lord Derby had
already experienced. Being divested of his buff coat, his George, and other ornaments, and disguised in a leathern doublet and woodman's suit belonging to those
honest yeomen, the king parted from his devoted band of followers. Under the
guidance of the brothers Penderell, Charles quitted White Ladies by a back door it
being now broad day, and took refuge in a wood called Spring Coppice,* on the
Boscobel demesne. The noblemen and gentlemen rode off with the intention
of joining Lesley's horse on the northern road. In this attempt most were taken
prisoners. The horse under Lesley, as in-fficient in retreat as in battle, were
shortly dispersed by a comparatively trifling force of republican cavalry.
In the meantime the King enjoyed comparative security under the protection of
the Penderel family. This loyal brotherhood consisted of 6. George and Thomas,
the latter of whom fell at Edgehill, had served in the army of Charles I. At the
time of the battle of Worcester the 5 survivors were living as tenants of the Giffard
family, on the demesne of Boscobel and White Ladies, then annexed to the
principal mansion of Chillington. William Penderel resided with his wife in
Boscobel House; Richard with his mother at Hubbal Grange, now a little homestead, and where all the brothers were born; Humphrey at the mill of White
Ladies, and John and George in neighbouring cottages, occupying small portions
of land in payment of their services as woodmen. On Thursday night, when it
grew dark, his Majesty resolved to go from those parts into Wales, and to take
Richard Penderell with him for his guide; but before they began their journey his
Majesty went into Richard's house at Hubbal Grange, where the old good-wife
Penderell had not onely the honour to see his Majesty, but to see him attended by
her son Richard. Here his Majesty had time and means better to complete his

disguise. His name was agreed to be " Will Jones." and his arms a wood-bill. In this posture, about 9 o'clo k at night (after some refreshment taken in the house), his Majesty, with his trusty servant Richard, began their journey on foot. At Evelith Mill, near Shifnal, they met with an ill-favoured encounter. The miller had been protecting in his mill some loyal soldiers, and " Trusty Dick," un- happily allowing a gate to clap, caused the miller to be alarmed, and the fugitive and his guide, thinking themselves pursued, hurried away by an unusual route, and waded through a brook, causing the king some discomfort, and here he would have lost his guide that dark night but for the rustling of Dick's calveskin breeches. They arrived at Madeley about midnight, but the Severn was so guarded as to make a passage of it impossible. After spending a night in a barn, and a day in a hay mow, the king and his guide determined to return to Boscobel, the king previously discolouring his hands with walnut leaves. They started on the return journey about 11 o'clock that night, and arrived at Boscobel about three in the morning, the king remaining in the wood. Here Richard found Colonel Carlis,* and William and Richard subsequently assisted the King and the Colonel to get up into a thick-leaved oak, the famous Royal Oak of Boscobel.

That night the King spent in Boscobel house, in the secret place where Lord Derby had been secured. And here Wm. Penderell shaved him, and cut his hair, leaving some about the ears, according to the country mode. Humphrey Penderel went this day (Saturday) to Shefnal to pay some taxes, where a colonel of the rebels offered him £1000 for discovering the King, and threatened him with death for concealment. Humphrey, however, pleaded ignorance, and returned to Boscobel, and related his adventure. Sunday the King got up early (his dormitory being none of the best, nor his bed the easiest†), and having spent some time in devotions, surveyed from a window the road from Tong to Brewood. In the arbour on a mount he spent some time in reading on Sunday. Mr. Huddleston, the Catholic priest, now did some good service ; and arranged that the King should go to Moseley, *en route* for Bentley.‡ The King being very foot-sore, it was arranged that he should ride upon Humphrey's mill-horse (for Humphrey was the miller of White Ladies mill). The horse was taken up from grass, and accoutred with a pitiful old saddle, and a worse bridle, " the heaviest dull jade he ever rode on," as the king remarked, to which Humphrey rejoined, " My liege can you blame the horse to go heavily, when he has the weight of three kingdoms on his back!"

This scene, sketched by Miss Bradley, where the King, accompanied by the five Penderell brothers, sets out for Moseley, is represented in the picture on the black marble chimney-piece at Boscobel house; being an accurate copy of Blount's print in the Bodleian library.

*A name still retained by the plantation at Tong Hill.

* A family seated at Albrighton temp Rich. ii. H.F.J.V. says.

† A hole or hiding place in the floor, where the King squeezed himself in, and some very precipitous steps remain, all of which have been duly tried by H.R.H. the Duchess of Teck and many royal and noble personages with much amusement.

‡ Mr. Hodleston was tutor to Sir John Preston (a young man), a guest at Moseley, under the assumed name of Jackson, to protect him from the Puritans, who had sequestered his father's property ; and Mr. Whitgreave had taken the opportunity of placing his two nephews, Palyn and Reynolds under Father Hodleston's care. It was on Monday, Sept. 8, that Father Hodleston, under pretence of personal apprehension as a Catholic priest, set his pupils, Palyn, Reynolds, and Sir John, to watch from the garret window of Moseley the approach of any rebel parties.

The gigantic figure immediately behind the King is meant for William, whom Hodleston describes as so tall a man that his breeches hung below the knees of Charles, himself a person above the middle size.

The King arrived at Bentley, where, availing himself of a pass to the west, that Mistress Jane Lane had obtained for herself and man, he performed the part of page, and rode before her, in which journey Mistress Lane acted as a most faithful and prudent servant to his Majesty, shewing her observance when opportunity would allow it, and at other times acting her part in the disguise with much discretion. The King's narrative says:—" Memorandum, that one Mr. Lassell's, a cousin of Mrs. Lane's, went all the way with us from Colonel Lane's on horseback, single, I riding before Mrs. Lane." Thence the King proceeded to Stratford, Long Marston, Cirencester, and Bristol, and eventually to Brightelmstone, whence he sailed to France.

The Watch, given by Charles II. to Jane Lane, was exhibited at the Stuart Exhibition recently. She became Lady Fisher, and died in 1689. A pretty picture of her is in the Staffordshire Archæological Collection; as also one of Charles II. as a youth.

The day after he left Boscobel the rebels called and made diligent search for him there in vain.

The name of Trusty Dick is said to have arisen from a dialogue (related by Mrs. Penderel, a maiden descended in a direct line from Richard Penderel), which took place between him and his wife, in the silence of the night, and overheard by the King when at Hubbal Grange. The dame passionately reproved her husband for the danger he had incurred for himself and family by concealing Charles, held out to him the certainty of the splendid reward offered for his apprehension, and conjured him to seize the golden opportunity, hinting her readiness to be herself the informer. Her husband replied with much indignation, assuring her that no money should bribe him to desert his sovereign, and charging her, in good set terms, as she valued his future affection, to be secret and faithful to the trust imposed upon them. Next morning the King acquainted Richard with his having overheard the conversation, and ever after distinguished him by the name of Trusty Dick. After King Charles' restoration the brothers Penderel were received at Court, and had substantial pensions for their fidelity. Penderell rents are still paid by Lord Bradford, Mr. Giffard, and others, to the descendants of this loyal family.

The Penderell, who lived at Weston in the cave there, hewn out of the sandstone rock, was probably an idle relation (perhaps a brother) of the loyal band.

It was King Charles II. who advanced Viscount Newport, of the Newport family, to the Earldom of Bradford.

In person, Charles II. was tall and well proportioned, his complexion swarthy, his features singularly austere and forbidding. The disposition of his mind presented an extraordinary contrast to the harsh lines traced on his countenance. "Whatever might have been his failings (and they were too glaring to escape observation), few monarchs were more beloved by the people. During his reign, arts improved, trade met with encouragement, and the wealth and comforts of the people increased. He entered London 29th May, 1669, his birthday, amidst the most universal and extraordinary demonstrations of joy."

Oak-ball day, or oak-apple day, is named from this circumstance, and the school-boys' local rhyme is never forgotten :—

> Oak-ball day,
> The twenty-ninth of May,
> If you don't give us a holiday
> We'll all run away!

A poet, Thomas Shipman, more gracefully alludes to the subject :—

Let celebrated wits with laurels crown'd,
    And wreaths of bays, boast their triumphant brows.
I will esteem myself far more renown'd
    In being honoured with these oaken boughs.

Charles II. issued a proclamation dated at Tong Norton, 20th August, 1651.

The portrait of Charles II., which is given here, is a contemporary painting in the possession of the writer, and " much resembling Sir Peter Lely's, picture of the King at Bridewell Hall, and may be by an equally able artist of the time, such as Riley."

MEASUREMENTS OF THE ROYAL OAK.

1881.	Girth 1 foot from ground				14 feet 1 inch.	
Nov. 11th	„ 4	„	„	„	12 „ 2	„
	„ 5	„	„	„	11 „ 6	„
	„ 10	„	„	„	11 „ 0	„
	Length of trunk or butt, 21 feet.					
1883.	Girth 1 foot from ground				14 feet 1 inch.	
Dec.	„ 4	„	„	„	12 „ 2	„
	„ 5	„	„	„	11 „ 6	„
	„ 10	„	„	„	11 „ 0	„
1885.	Girth 1	„	„	„	14 „ 1	„
Jan. 21st.	„ 3	„	„	„	13 „ 2	„
	„ 5	„	„	„	11 „ 7	„
1886.	Girth 1	„	„	„	14 „ 1	„
July 24th.	„ 4	„	„	„	12 „ 3	„
	„ 5	„	„	„	11 „ 7	„
	„ 10	„	„	„	11 „ 0	„
1889.	Girth 1	„	„	„	14 „ 1½	„
May 2.	„ 3	„	„	„	13 „ 2	„
	„ 5	„	„	„	11 „ 7	„

It is from data, such as appeared in an article in a local paper in January, 1890, that wrong impressions are formed. Some of the reports upon the Royal Oak (of which I have a collection) bristle with inaccuracies and contradictions, and these arise from the writers not having verified their statements, but having written from " hearsay," I have no doubt.

Preferring as I do to rely upon the well-weighed opinions of those who live in the neighbourhood, and who make trees a study of their lives, and form their conclusions from frequent observations at various seasons of the year, rather than on the hastily-conceived ideas of hurrying tourists who devote half-an-hour to the inspection of a celebrated tree, I unhesitatingly advise my readers that this tree cannot be a *sapling* of the Royal Oak.

It is a tree of no mean dimensions, as the above measurements shew, and has indications of numerous branches having been lopped off its sides. It is decaying in the butt, though so vigorous and fair to view ; but a large sheet of lead hides the hole in the trunk.

Partly from the Rev. H. G. de Bunsen's little *History of Boscobel*, and partly *viva voce*, we get the Earl of Bradford's account, 1878, as related to him by his father, which is generally thus :—

"The trees and underwood were in full leaf in September, when the King hid in the Oak, not decayed, but a growing tree. It became well known to Mr. Giffard, the owner, and other loyalists. After the restoration (nine years after) numbers visited it. The idea of its being a substitute, least of all an acorn from the tree, his lordship discards as ludicrous and absurd. Known it himself half a century. Looks same now as then. His father spoke of the absurd stories of the owl, the acorn, &c. He used to say his father and grandfather spoke in the same sense, which would carry him back to 1740, less than 90 years after the King sat in it. Trees in the park at Weston estimated at 1,100 or 1,200 years old; others at 600, 500, and 400; sometimes a smaller tree is considerably older than a larger one. Estimates it at 400 or 450 now, *i.e.*, 220 then. His father, the late Earl, spoke of hearing from those who went before him, the labouring men had pointed out the tree from father to son as *the* Royal Oak."

Mr. J. S. Hooker, who has care of the National Gardens at Kew, writing on this subject, says he is of opinion that the maximum age of oaks may be between 800 and 1,000 years, and he judges by the rapid growth of trees of known age, and from the fact that the insects and fungus ravages on old oak wood are so multifarious and great. . . . . . He is astonished to see the size to which trees have attained, which he himself planted at Kew since 1865.

At the Edinburgh Forestry Exhibition, about 9 years ago, much interest was shewn in sections of two Scotch firs, one

THE ROYAL OAK.

THE TREE IS FROM A PHOTOGRAPH IN 1879.

23 feet in circumference, distinctly vouching its own age to be
217 years; the other, a lesser tree, 18 feet in circumference,
shewing a clear record of year-circles to the number of 270.
The site of both was known, as well as the dates of the felling
of one, and the blowing down of the other.

The above measurements of the Royal Oak have been
taken by Mr. James Craig, the Earl of Bradford's head
forester, whose careful study of this and other trees for many
years firmly convinces him that this is no two-century
" sapling " as some suggest. He further says that Mr. H. S.
Cumming's Paper on the Royal Oak, read before the British
Association, is written in a sensational and romancing spirit;
and any relics that it mentions might all have been made out
of the many boughs and limbs that have been taken from the
tree. Mr. Craig points out some errors made by Mr. Collins,
forester, of Trentham, and says the girth of the tree round the
surface of the ground is only 15ft. 7in. (instead of 16ft. 3in.,
as Mr. Collins says), and the girth at 5ft. from the ground
11ft. 7in. This is a little more than it used to measure,
because the sheet of lead has been fastened on lately, and
bulges out more than it used to do. Also the tree shows scars
all up the stem, where branches have been cut off from time
to time ; and records bear testimony to this fact, that at one
period of its existence it would have been difficult to find a
tree in the Forest with more leafy surface. The heart is
quite rotten at that large hole in the stem that is covered over
with a sheet of lead about 3ft. by 2ft.

Mr. James Hope, head gardener at Weston for 35 years,
writes me : I do not think the Oak at Boscobel a sapling. I
have no doubt but it was a good sized tree when the King
was there, and quite large enough to hide anyone, with the
foliage on.

Y

It shews marks on the bark of the trunk, where low branches have been removed. It may easily have been a pollarded tree, and from the accompanying reproductions of photographs anyone will perceive that conclusions, quite at variance, may be arrived at respecting it.

Mr. Barnett's dimensions of the Royal Oak, taken in presence of Mr. Brooke and Mr. Botfield in 1857 :—Girth just "above the ground" (too indefinite to rely on), 15ft.; at 4 feet above the ground, 11ft. 4in. This must have included the large piece of lead shewn in one of the views where the trunk is rotten in the side, hence the discrepancy with the recent measure.

Charles II. (in *Pepys' Diary*) said :—

"A great oak in a pretty plain place, that had been lopt some three or four years before, and, being grown out again very bushy and thick, could not be seen through."

The tree readily accords with the King's description in *The History of His Sacred Majesty's Preservation* (1809), " Boscobel " pt. 1. " Where the Colonel made choice of a thick-leav'd oak."

Blount in his *Boscobel*, published in 1660, says :—

"Hundreds of people have flock'd to see the famous Boscobel . . . but chiefly to behold the Royal Oake, which has been deprived of all its young boughs† by the numerous visiters of it, who keep them in memory of His Majesty's happy preservation ; insomuch that Mr. Fitz-herbert has been forced in due season of the year to crop part of it for its preservation, and has lately been at the charge to fence it about with a high pale."

The Rev. Geo. Plaxton, vicar of Sheriffhales, 1673, rector of Donnington, 1690-1703, says in a paper of 1707 :—

"I had nothing very remarkable at Donington, save the Royal Oak at Boscobel. The Royal oak was a fair spread thriving tree. The boughs of it were all lined and covered with ivy. Here in the thick of these boughs the King sate . . . they are strangely mistaken who judged it an old hollow oak, whereas it was a gay and flourishing tree, surrounded with a great many more."

This is a very natural description. It would have been mad folly to choose a large tree standing alone, or one that would call attention to itself.

---

† Probably the lower boughs easily reached, which have evidently been cut off, as the bark shows now.

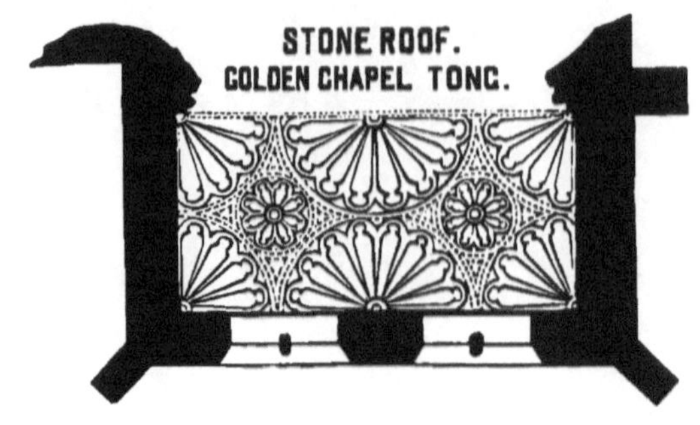

(page 53).

WILLIAM PENDERELL

(page 179).

SIR KENELM DIGBY

(page 173).

ROYAL OAK: THE BRICK WALL.

(page 187).

Mr. Plaxton further says :—

"The poor remains of the Royal Oak are now fenced in by a handsome brick wall . . . put up 20 or 30 years ago by Basil and Jane Fitzherbert."

The view of this in the *Gentleman's Magazine* shews the tree much as at present, and the brick wall surrounding it.

Evelyn (born 1620, died 1706) "*Silva,*" published 1729, edition reprint of 1714, speaks of remarkable oaks, bearing strange leaves, &c. :—

"The people never left hacking the boughs and bark till they' kill'd the tree [in New Forest]; *as I am told* they have serv'd that famous oak near White Lady's."

Mr. Thos. Arnold, who transcribed it, remarks this sentence was *not* in the edition of 1679, being an insertion of later editions. The first edition was 1664. This "as I am told," is only hearsay evidence, and not reliable, as he was writing without local knowledge.

Dr. Charlett, writing in 1702 to *Pepys* :—

"The trunk of the Royal Oak is now enclosed within a round wall, with an inscription having no date."

Dr. Stukeley, in a letter, Dec. 1713 :—

"A bow shot from the house, just by a horse track passing through the wood, stood the Royal Oak. The tree is now enclosed within a brick wall, the inside whereof is covered with laurel . . the oak is in the middle, almost cut away by travellers, whose curiosity leads them to see it. Close by the side grows a young thriving plant from one of its acorns."

This gentleman relates the story of the owl as they related to us, which formed valuable material for Ainsworth's Novel ; but is a pretty fiction, finding no basis in fact. He does not say that he saw the tree himself, and Mr. Dale wrote, not many years after, that "it *is going* to decay."

Mr. Charles Dunster, M.A., writes, in a work dedicated 1791, whether from hearsay or not he does not say. It does not appear that he had seen the place :—

"The old tree in which the King was hid was soon after cut down and carried off, but one is still shewed as the Royal Oak, having been raised (it is said) from an acorn of the old tree. The present tree is a large one, and appears to be about four score years old. The bark and sides are much torn and cut by the curiosity of its visitors."

The Rev. J. Dale, 1845 :—

"The site of present tree accords with that on which the old tree is represented in the engraving [Blount's Boscobel] to have stood. Old persons had indistinct recollections that present tree did not stand in centre of the plot enclosed by a wall earlier than Miss Evans', but nearer to an angle of it."

Plaxton makes no mention of the sapling or successor ; but his description accords with the King's.

Mr. Dale gives opinions to Mr. Botfield and Mr. Brooke, *later*, against the identity : (saying 50 years ago *he was told* it had been rooted up, writing in 1857) : this is " The Bishton Legend ! " He also, writing in 1845, said, " The present Royal Oak is now rapidly going to decay," and attributes it in some part to the removal of the wall, and consequent exposure to storms, &c.

Mr. Dale also said it was a shy bearer, not bringing acorns to perfection oftener than once in 8 or 10 years.

Mr. Stubbs, old gardener at Boscobel, again refutes this in 1878, saying it only *failed to bear* acorns once in 10 years, and that was last year, 1877.

Rev. J. Dale, curate of Donington, found the broken stone (blue gold letters) broken, and a new inscription " restored by Basil and Eliza Fitzherbert about 33 years ago, *i.e., 1812.*" Mr. Evans soon after bought Boscobel.

The brick wall and the brass inscription were removed in 1817, when iron pallisades were put at Miss Frances Evans' cost.

The Rev. H. G. de Bunsen notes in 1878 :—

"Mr. Dale's anticipations have not been realized ! The Oak still looks like a flourishing tree, and has no appearance of decay about it at the present time."

There are two inaccuracies in the article of January, 1890, before referred to. First, there is the trifling error of 10 feet in the height of the tree (57 should be 67ft.) ; secondly, the soil in which it grows, Mr. Brown, who occupies the land, says is certainly not marl, as stated therein.

Mr. Ralph said in a paper, *re* Boscobel, that the King's account and Lord Clarendon's account are inaccurate, quoting Stukeley's as correct, who gave the account "as they related to us." Mr. Ralph says it is *not* a pollard tree! also that there are *no* records of White Ladies!

The following are Mr. Craig's measurements of large local trees, which may interest arboriculturists :—

	Girth at 1 ft. ft. in.	Girth at 4 ft. ft. in.	Date Measured.	Remarks.
The larger Oak of 2 at Aqualate	28 6 ..	25 7 ..	Oct. 1883	
Great Oak in Weston Park	31 2 ..	22 9 ..	Nov. 1884	..
Large Oak near Weston Hall Stables	27 0 ..	26 6 ..	„	.. Including ivy
Oriental Plane on Weston Hall Lawn	27 3 ..	19 2 ..	„	..
Lime (N) near Pendrill's Cave......	23 6 ..	18 7 ..	„	..
Lime (S) „ „	23 10 ..	17 5 ..	„	..
Oak in Forge Croft	22 4 ..	20 0 ..	„	..
Oak near Black Fir Clump..........	25 0 ..	20 1 ..		
Wellingtonia near Temple	11 0 ..			..Height 47ft. 6in.

" Weston and its glorious Oaks " are mentioned in Lady John Manners' (now Duchess of Rutland's) Life of Lord Beaconsfield, as one of the places where that great statesman enjoyed a quiet retreat from the bustle of political life.

White Oak (see page 139)	18 2 ..	14 1 ..	Nov. 1884 ..
Brewer's Oak, at Crackley Bank (named from a suicide, Brewer)...	14 2 ..	13 4 ..	
Pine, in front of Tong Castle	16 6 ..	13 6 ..*	
*Girth at 3 ft. Height 97 feet.			
Alder at Woodlands	21 9 ..	17 7 ..	
Oak at Brockhurst	24 0 ..	24 3	
(hole inside, 5ft. 3in. by 4ft.)			

The following are dimensions of an oak, felled in 1881, in Lady Wicket field, on Weston Estate, half-a-mile from Boscobel, but within the area of the same old forest of Brewood, taken Nov. 11, 1881 :—Girth at 1ft. from ground, 14ft. 9in.; at 4ft., 11ft. 8in.; length of trunk, 22ft. This tree had 215 concentric rings, and its dead tops or stag-horns were cut off about 30 years ago, evidenced by woodmen now living, and bore the marks of having been so dealt with. The age of this tree, allowing for the time between which it ceased to

form wood, and commenced to shew signs of decay, would
bring its age to 300 years at least, and probably nearer 400.
And this tree threw out considerable foliage.

The following sizes are from *Sylva Britannica*, 1822 :—

Swilcar Oak, in Needwood Forest, is known by historical documents to be 600
years old—girth at 6ft., 21ft. 4½in.

The Beggar's Oak in Bagot's Park—at 5ft., 20ft. girth.

Great Oak of Panshanger, Earl Cowper's, is 19ft. girth at 3ft.

At Tutbury, the Wych Elm or Wychhazel, formerly used for the longbow, is
16ft. 9in. at 5ft.

> In this once favor'd walk beneath these elms,
> Oft in instructive converse we beguil'd
> The fervid time, which each returning year,
> To friendship's call devoted. Such things were :
> But are alas ! no more.
>
> *S. Dunelm.*

The Yew at Ankerwyke is supposed to be 1000 years old.

> "The Eugh obedient to the bender's will."
>
> *Spenser.*

It was formerly much used in Queen Elizabeth's time for hedges, when it was
enjoined to be planted in all Churchyards partly to ensure its cultivation, partly
to secure its leaves and seed from doing injury to cattle, and partly its unchanging
colour made it a fit emblem of immortality, and its dark green gave the solemnity
of the grave.

Of Ash, "the Venus of the Forest," at Woburn, is a great Ash, 15ft. 3in. at 3ft.
from ground.

The B ack Poplar (held sacred to Hercules), at Bury St. Edmunds, is 15ft. girth
at 3ft.

The Tortworth Chestnut is the oldest in England : and the Plane at Lee Court is
14ft. 8in. at 6 feet.

The contributions of zealous opponents of the Royal Oak's
identity as the king's refuge are marked by many contradictions and prejudiced views.

It will be as well here to mention the comparisons quoted
by Jarco (see Bygones, May, 1877) of certain trees in a timber
merchant's yard, which happened to be of the same size, and
from which he concluded that the present oak is 110 years old,
or perhaps 150 !

Among papers sent me by Lady Evans in 1888, reference is
made to the M.S. in Mr. Thomas Whitgreave's handwriting
on six separate sheets ; and marked with genuine features of

the facetious monarch. She also sent other remarks of
" Philarchus" and " Observator." Philarchus wrote, in 1789,
to the *Gentleman's Magazine*, viz.: that a maid servant pointed
out the field where the tree once was, and says there stood the
tree, which is now gone, and was a lone and pollarded tree,
and other notes upon the House, &c. Observator, writing in
1790, June 12, says " descriptions should be just and accurate,
and conjecture only permitted where facts cannot be ascertained. How can we excuse the negligence and impropriety
of your correspondent Philarchus, a person who pretends to
write from personal observation, who has given such a loose
and erroneous account . . . . which is highly reprehensible." . . . . . " The object of your miscellany ought
to be the recording matters of fact, not the repository for
groundless and ridiculous conjecture "; and he points out
other numerous errors of Philarchus.

An inscription (embodying the older ones of 1677 and 1787)
prepared by Rev. R. P. Thursfield, and affixed to the tree by
the Rev. Joseph Dale, 29th May, 1845, bore in Latin words,
after reciting the previous inscription one thus rendered " *The
present oak sprung, it is said, from the above-named tree*, Frances
Evans . . . . has fenced in with the present iron railing,
1817.

This brass plate was removed soon after, and the words in
italics were altered into " Hanc Arborem " (this tree), she
being persuaded that the present tree is the identical tree
which had sheltered the King.

There was also an English inscription placed there by her
desire.

The Misses Evans, who owned Boscobel, had another
house at Allestree, near Derby. On the survivor's decease
Boscobel passed to Mr. T. W. Evans, who was afterwards
created a baronet, but dying without issue the estate passed
to the Rev. E. Carr, the present owner.

It is a matter for public congratulation that the Evans Family and their successor, the Rev. Canon Carr, so kindly allow this historic spot to be viewed by the public daily (Sundays excepted), a privilege which H.R.H. the Duchess of Teck, the Duchess of York, and many noble personages, including M. de Waddington, a descendant of the Pendrills, gladly availed themselves of. The Visitors' Books, under the care of Miss Brown, are a delightful record of loyalty and autography.

Of single trees, relics of primeval forests, which have been preserved to our own times, Mr. Beriah Botfield mentioned :—

"Christ's Oak once at Cressage, a name recalling the period when Christian Missionaries first taught the Gospel to heathen Saxons under the tree."

"The Lady Oak, which still exists at the same place, was clearly so called in honour of the Virgin."

"The ancient and gigantic Lime which adorns the precincts of Pitchford Hall."

" Owen Glendwyr's Oak (the Shelton Oak) whence that chieftain is said to have witnessed the Battle of Shrewsbury, 1403, still standing near Shrewsbury. This was described as a "great tree" in 1540. Though now hollow and decayed, it girths upwards of 44 ft., and has some branches still fresh and vigorous."* It is mentioned by Shakespeare—

" How the grette oake at Shelton standeth on my grounds."

When so eminent an authority as Mr. Botfield describes these trees as relics of primeval forests, how easily may less experienced people be mistaken in their views of the age of trees at the present day.

The Lapley Oak was mentioned by Plot in 1686 :—

"Thus out of a great Oak, that grew at Lapley, of about 6 Tunns of Timber [about 240 feet], brought to Elmhurst for the new building the house, there was a great Toad sawn forth of the middle of the tree in a place which, when growing, was 12 or 14 foot from the ground, the tree being sound and intire in all parts quit round, saving just where the Toad lay, it was black and corrupted and crumbled away like sawdust."†

Mrs. Baldwyn Childe says that at Kyre Park are some enormous oaks, no doubt planted in Norman times, for the licence to plant them is dated 1275.

In conclusion, let me quote some lines of Proverbial Philosophy, written by a negro, who, rather bold and severely, sums up in a comical manner his lessons of a lifetime :—

> Dar's a heap o' dreadful music in de very finest fiddle :
> A ripe and mellow apple may be rotten in de middle ;
> Dar's a lot of solid kicking in de humblest kind o' mule :
> De wisest-looking trabeller may be de biggest f—— ;
> De preacher ain't de holiest dat wears de meekest look,
> And does de loudest banging on de kiver o' de book.

All lovers of historical treasures are wary of historical fiction, and I advise them to defer still longer from arraying themselves on the side of those who declare for the imposture of a Royal historical tree.

z

WHITE LADIES.

Not far from this Town (Tong) and Castle is Whitladyes, the seat of Mr. Gifford and Boscobel so famous for the Oak.—*Cox's Magnu Britannia, 1720*.

THE Convent of White Ladies was so-called from the habit of that colour worn by the Cistercian Nuns, who occupied it. It is supposed to have been founded or established in the reign of King Richard I. or King John possibly by Herbert Walter, Archbishop of Canterbury, about 1195 ; but J. C. Anderson, in his *History of Shropshire*, says that Mr. Eyton finds that Ema de Pulverbatch having granted a virgate in Beobridge to these White Nuns earlier than 1186, granted the remainder in 1186 to Haughmond Abbey, so he concludes that the foundation may be as early as 1185. All antiquarians are silent upon it, and "no Chartulary or even a legend exists to throw a light upon its origin," says J. C. Anderson in his *History of Shropshire*. Dedicated to St. Leonard, it was a house parochially and manorially independent, whose property was acquired by gradual instalments, each representing the consignment of some female member of a wealthy or powerful family to the service of religion ; these, in time, came to be represented by a large aggregate, and in 1536, the Prioress returned the gross annual value of this Convent, derivable from demesne lands at White Ladies, and from various rents in Notts, Staffordshire, and Salop, at £31 1s. 4d.

Leland says in his Itinerary :—" Byrwoode, a Priory of White Nunnes, lately suppressid, in the very Marche of

Shropshire toward Darbyshire."* It was within the Forest of Brewood, whose boundaries described by Mr. Botfield, were: Weston and Bishop's Wood on the North, Brewood and Chillington on the East, and Albrighton, Donington, and Tong on the South and West.

The Bishop's Wood, reference to which has already been made on pages 10, 139, and 140, as also to White Ladies pages 12 and 139, was granted by Henry II. in 1153, to the Bishop of Lichfield.

Bishop's Wood was in Brewde, in Domesday. Brewood belonged exclusively to the Bishop of Chester,. *i.e.*, Coventry and Lichfield styled Chester, in 11th and 12th centuries ; the White Nuns being called of Brewood because they were in Brewood Forest. So far from the two Convents constituting one foundation they had nothing to connect but their propinquity and nothing in common but the spirit of rivalry which was mutual, Mr. Eyton says.

In 1200, the Bishop was to enclose from the forest, a park in his wood of Brewude, which was to be two leagues in circumference, Weston being the forest's northern boundary.

In 1204, the King has altogether disafforested his forest of Brewude, and the men who dwelt therein for ever.

In 1206, the King gives the Bishop license to make a decoy saltatorium in his park of Brewde. A saltatorium is a deer-leap, so constructed that the deer could jump over the park pales from the forest into the Bishop's Park, but not back again. There was one near Shifnal, not far from the Manor-house of the King's Forester of Wellington Forest.

In 1209, Hamo de Weston and John Bagot were indicted for receiving marksmen and hounds at Blymhill and Weston, but the result was not given, as the illicit objects were undecipherable.

* Error for Staffordshire.

1315.   Hugh de Beaumes, wishing to benefit this Convent, inquired for the King's permission to grant 30 acres in Donynton to the Prioress.   The Jurors sat at Donynton, and held that the grant would be harmless.   The same Hugh grants a messuage in Shakerlew, which John atte Syche* held to John, his brother, and wood for fire and fence and common right for own stock, and 240 sheep of other people.

Undertenants of the Nuns were at Neachley, Shackerley and Kilsall.

In 1212, King John granted to the White Nuns—he may have been at Brewood at the time, a Weir called " Withlakeswere " in River Severn, near Bridgnorth ; and in 1225, Alditha Prioress, and her Convent of Brewe, and Cecilia, another Prioress, each granted half the rent of the Weir to Henry of Brug.

By Inquisition, 1255, the Nuns of Brewood are in receipt of 6/8 rent in Brug, and a few years later of other income in that Borough ; Agnes was Prioress about then.

In 1288, the Prioress had right of Common Pasture in Rugge.

In 1292, Sarra, Prioress, complained that she had not enough of pasture, and defeated William de Rugge, in a suit.

1286.   In the Pleas of Cannock Forest, the *Staffordshire Archæological Society's Transactions*, Vol. V., page 163, expublic records occurs :—

It was presented that when the huntsmen of the King were hunting in the bailiwicke of Gauel-ye 4 E. I., they put up a stag with their dogs, and followed it as far as the Park at Brewode into a wood there, and John dela Wytemore came up with a bow and arrow and shot at it, and it fled out of the forest as far as the fish pond of the Nuns of Brewode, and the said John followed it and dragged it out dead from the said fish pond (vivarium) ; and John Giffard, of Cbyl'yngton came up and stated he had pursued the stag, and claimed the whole of it ; and they skinned it and the said John took half of it and carried it to his house, and

---

the Nuns of Brewode had the other half. As they are poor they are pardoned for
the good of the King's soul, and although the said stag was taken outside the forest,
yet it was the chasia of the King, and put up by his dogs within the forest, and
taken in front of them against the assize. The Sheriff is ordered, therefore, to
arrest the said John and John, who being convicted of the above were committed
to prison.   John de la Wytemore was fined 1 mark, and John de Chilinton
(sic) 20s.

And the same Bishop [Roger] has a saltatorium [deer leap] against the forest, in
his part of Brewode which adjoins the boundaries of the forest, to the injury of the
said forest. It is not known by what warrant. He, being infirm and weak,
appeared by his attorney, Robert de Pype, at Lichfield. Said he was not bound to
answer except by the King's writ, nor without his peers, the Barons of England,
said he found his church in seisin of the woods with power of taking venison, &c.
The Bishop commanded to appear before the King at the Parliament. Nothing
was done, but later the forest was taken into the King's hands, the Bishop showing
no warrant. Bishop subsequently took proceedings to recover, and produced
charters, and showed his predecessors had been accustomed to hunt and take in the
woods at will, beasts which came from the forest of the King.

After further proceedings, Bishop came before King at Westminster, 18 Ed. I.,
and gave up all his woods, etc., in Cannock Forest, and the King of his special
favour conceded and granted again to the Bishop the same woods, to hold in free
and perpetual alms as his free chase for ever, and so that it may be lawful for him
to inclose his woods and make parks in them at his will, sc long as he and his
successors made in them no saltaries or used nets to capture the King's deer—
and for this concession the Bishop gave to the King £1,000.

1304.   Inquest whether it would injure the King if it be
allowed John de Beaumeys to grant 10 acres of land and 10
acres of wood in Donynton, to the Prioress of White Nuns of
Brewod.   Inquest in favor.

1318.   Submission of the Priory of White Nuns to the
Papal Ordinance—as to Church of Tibshelf, Co. Derby.

Elizabeth la Zouche, great granddaughter of the loyal
Alan, (see page 11) caused a flutter of excitement by escaping
from White Ladies Nunnery in 1326, with Alice de Kallerhal,
Nuns regularly professed of this house, who had left their
Convent.

The Bishop causes publication to be made in Churches ;*
all who aided or abetted to be severely punished.

Bishop Norbury's Register (Lichfield), says in 1331, Elizabeth la Zouche makes her confession before the Bishop in Brewood Church, her petition before the Convent Gate for re-admission, after which absolution by the Bishop, and admission to penance.*

Also 1338: An Order falling heavily on the Prioress for *expensæ voluptariæ*, dress and laxity of rule; *Canes Venatici* (dogs of the chase) were found in the Convent.

1332. The Priory was vacant by the resignation of Dame Joan de Huggeford, last Prioress. On the third day of the vacancy, the Sub-Prioress and Convent met, and agreed to elect a Prioress by scrutiny, whereon Agnes de Weston, Sub-Prioress, and two others collected and announced the votes of the Convent. The result was the election of Dame Alice Harlegh, which was quashed by the Bishop, who appointed Dame Alice, because he had heard of her many virtues. She died 1349.

> Then she for her good deeds and her pure life,
> And for the power of ministration in her,
> And likewise for the high rank she had borne
> Was chosen Abbess; there, an Abbess lived,
> For three brief years, and there an Abbess, past
> To where beyond these voices there is peace.
>
> *Tennyson.*

when Beatrice de Dene was appointed, when the site and local possessions were three carucates in Donington.

William de Ercall III. gave a ninth of the tithes of Ercall to the White Nuns of Brewood, and land near his Court of La More on which to make a weir.‡

1535-6. At the Dissolution, besides £6 13s. 4d. at White Ladies, there were rents in Notts, Staffordshire, and Shropshire, at Higley, Chatwall, Rudge, Bold, Sutton Maddock, Ronton, High Ercal, Berrington, Shrewsbury, Bridgnorth, Ingardine, Tedstill, Beckbury, and Humfreston, and the Advowsons of Muntford (Salop), and Tydshull (Derby), and

---

* See Notes by W. Salt Archæological Society Publications, and Eyton's Antiquities.
‡ *Shrop. Trans.*

a pension from Bold Chapel. They had to pay a chief rent of 10/- to the Lord of Donnington, and 16/8 annual fee to Thomas Giffard, Esq., their Seneschal ; a salary of £5 for the Chaplain, appointed by the Nuns, to pray for the souls of the Founders.

The following descriptive letter was sent me by Dr. Knight, in reply to my enquiries :—

Letter from Francis Whitgreave, Esq., to the Right Rev. Dr. Knight, D.D., Roman Catholic Bishop of Shrewsbury.

Burton Manor, near Stafford,
August 24th, 1886.

MY DEAR LORD,—

In answer to your kind note just received, enclosing one from Mr. George Griffiths and which I now return, I am sorry to inform you that but little is known with regard to the Convent of White Ladies, near Boscobel. We have, perhaps, the best collection of books and manuscripts in England relating to any County, at the Salt Library, in Stafford, and if Mr. Griffiths, on his next visit to Stafford, which is only a very moderate distance from what I presume to be his residence— Weston Bank—will call there, the Librarian, on his application, will show him all that is known with regard to the Cistercian Convent in question.

Please to tell him to ask to be shown a small engraving representing "White Ladies" as it existed in the time of Charles II.

A half timber house, with a curious gate-house of the same materials, existed at that time attached to the ruins, which were then in much the same state as they are now ; the Convent itself having been swept away and only a portion of the Church remaining. The more modern house mentioned was the residence of a younger branch of the Giffards's, of Chillington, and it was to this house that Charles was first conducted by Captain Gifford after having ridden with him and other attendants all night on his flight from Worcester.

As you are perhaps aware, the house has now entirely disappeared, leaving only the ruins of the Church.

The property of the Convent, and also that of the Benedictine Nuns at Black Ladies, was granted by the infamous Tyrant who suppressed them to the Gifford of the time. White Ladies passed by marriage to the Fitzherberts.

Black Ladies still continues the property of the Giffords.

But I will not add more, as you and Mr. Griffiths proba ly know all this.

I shall be much obliged to your Lordship if you will ask Mr. Griffiths to let me know where his "Guide to Tong Church" can be procured, and the value of the same.

I need hardly add that Mr. Griffiths will find ample materials relating to Boscobel at the Salt Library.--Believe me, my dear Lord, yours very sincerely and respectfully,

(Signed)   FRANCIS WHITGREAVE.

P.S.—The house which now exists at Black Ladies was built by the Giffords in the reign of James I. upon the foundations, however, in part, at least, of the Benedictive Convent.

The Convent ruins were described in 1550, as in the Parish of Tong, but they now are in Boscobel extra-parochial district in Shropshire. They exhibit some Norman features, particularly a circular-headed doorway.

It is a cross Church without aisles. There are indications of a pent roof on the north wall, and looking into the cloister on that side were four windows. A tiny south window indicates the centre of the south transept ; a large circular one on the north, the north transept, while three more, further east are in the north Chancel wall.

The caps to the south door and arch of the north transept are beautiful and characteristic. Generally, there are indications of great simplicity and much refinement. The ancient vestment in Tong Church (see page 97) is believed be the work of the Nuns here or at Black Ladies. Probably, Neachley was the Grange of the Convent. Is it possible that the Mill at Shackerley was the Mill of this Convent ?

In 1785 Mr. Parkes found at White Ladies, a triple head carved in stone, and at seven feet deep several ancient tiles, green, yellow and red, with simple designs of circles and quatrefoils. Within the ruins are some old monumental slabs, commemorating I suppose conventual or church dignitaries, viz. : —

One a cross with quatrefoil and circle head, a cup and J. T.

One a sunk quatrefoil with circle near south wall, on a tapering slab.

One on a similar slab, with Latin cross, having each limb trefoiled, and a cup on the right side.

One a circle with four anchor-like arrows radiating to the angles of the square at the head of the slab.

Winifred White's tomb is still here; her " miraculous " cure of permanent lameness was attributed to the healing virtues of her namesake's well at Holywell.

The site consists, I believe, of two acres of land, at present unfenced, but defined, the property of the Fitzherbert Family,

WHITE LADIES, FROM THE S.E. CORNER OF RUINS.

(Photographed by G.G., 1894.)

UPRIGHT SLABS AT WHITE LADIES.

and the records are kept by the Rev. Lewis Groom, Roman Catholic priest of Brewood, of which place it was the Roman Catholic Cemetery until recently.

In recent times, comparatively, the spot has earned notoriety as the burial place of King Charles II's protectress, Dame Joane wife of William Pendrell, for a headstone, seen there in 1792—and a copy of which still is *in situ*—bore the following inscription :—

Here lyeth The bodie of a
Friende The King did caLL Dame Joane,
But Now Shee is Deceast and Gone.
Interred Anno Do. 1669.

Here grew the yellow saffron or autumn crocus, which an old herbalist informs me, grew at Tung and all Romish places ; and here still grow the Myrrhis Odorata, a relic of the Nuns' herb garden, and other rare plants.

This Nunnery is in Shropshire, and that of the Black Ladies is in Staffordshire. White Ladies was the more important of the two. It was a larger establishment than that of the Benedictine Nuns, 2 miles distant.

The perplexities of an Abbess at the time of the Dissolution may be gathered from the following curious letter to Thomas Cromwell, afterwards Earl of Essex, and as it may be from Margaret Vernon of Tong it is interesting :—

A.D. 1535.   MARGARET VERNON to SECRETARY CROMWELL.

After all dew commendacyons had unto yowre good maystershyp with my most umble tiankes for the greate coste mayd on me and my pore maydyn at my last beyngs with yowre maystershyp, furthermore plesyth yt yow to understonde that yowre vysytors hath bene here of late, who hath dyscharged iij. of my systers, the one ys dame Catheryn, the other ij. ys the yonge women that were last professyd, whyche ys not a lyttll to my dyscomforte ; nevertheles I must be content with the kynges plesure.

But nowe as touchynge my nowne parte, I must humbly besech yow to be so specyall good mayster unto me yowre pore bedwoman, as to give me yowre best advertysment and counseyle what waye shalbe best for me to take, seynge there shalbe none left here but myselfe and thys pore mradyn ; and yf yt wyl plese yowre goolnes to take thys pore howse into yowre owne hondes, ether for yourselfe, or for my nowne [maister] yowre sonne ; I woylde be glad with all my hart to geve yt
AA

into yowre maystershypes hondes, with that yewyll commaunde me to do therin Trustynge and nothynge dowptynge in yowre goodnes, that ye wyll so provyd for us, that we shall have syche onest lyvynge that we shall not be drevyn be necessyte nether to begge, nor to fall to no other unconvenyenca

And thus I offer my selfe and all myne unto your most hygh and prudeot wysdome, as unto hym that ys my only refuge and comfort in thys world, besechynge God of hys holy goodnes to put in yow hys holy sprete, that ye maye do all thynge to hys lawde and glory.

By yowre owne assured bedewoman,

MARGARET VERNON.

Mr. Thomas Wright, F.S.A., says he had not ascertained of what Nunnery, Margaret Vernon, the writer of this letter, was Abbess.   There was a Margaret Vernon, Abbess of West Malling, 1511, daughter of Sir Harry Vernon ; probably it is the same person (see page 52).

Mr. Wright adds that the visitors, by putting in force the injunctions already alluded to, seem to have nearly emptied the house, all the sisters but one having quitted it voluntarily or by force, and the Abbess herself seems to have been not unwilling to follow their example.

Here is another curious letter, and of local interest, written about the same period as the one from Margaret Vernon :—

JOHN FOSTER to CROMWELL.

[from M.S. Cotton Cleop. E. IV., fol. 116.]

In my moste humblyst wyse, I beyng not so bold as to appere before your lordschyp untyll your plesure is knowyn, feere sett aptartt, nede compellythe me to wrytt.   Thys last Lentt I dyd no lesse then wrytt, and also to your presence I dyd approche, suyng for your lordschypps gracyous servyce ; but now my sute ys muche other, for my dysfortune hathe byn to have conceyvyd untruly Goddys Wordo, and not only with yntellectyon to have thought yt but externally and really I have fulfyllyd the same.   For I as then beyng a presste have accompleshyd maryage, nothyng pretendyng but as an obedyentt subject ; for yf the kyngys grace could have found yt lanfull that prestys myght have byn maryd, they wold have byn to the crowne dubbyll and dubbyll faythefull ; furste yn love, scondly for fere that the byschoppe of Rome schuld sette yn hys powre unto ther desolacyon.   But now by the noyce of the peopull I perseyve I have dunne amysce, which saythe that the kyngys erudyte yugement with all his cowncill temperall and spyrytual bathe stableschyd a contrary order, that all prestys schalbe separat by a day ; with which order I have contentyd my selfe, and as sone as I herde yt to be tru I sent the woman to her frendys iij score mylys from me and spedely

† From Letters relating to the suppression of the Monasteries Camden Society,—from M.S Cotton Cleop., E. IV., cap. 55.

HINGE.

WHITE LADIES.
NORMAN DOORWAY.

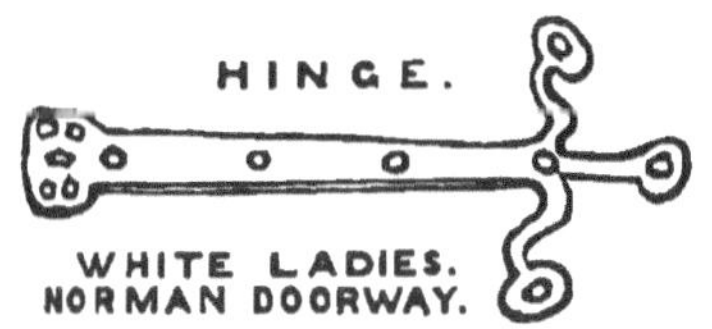

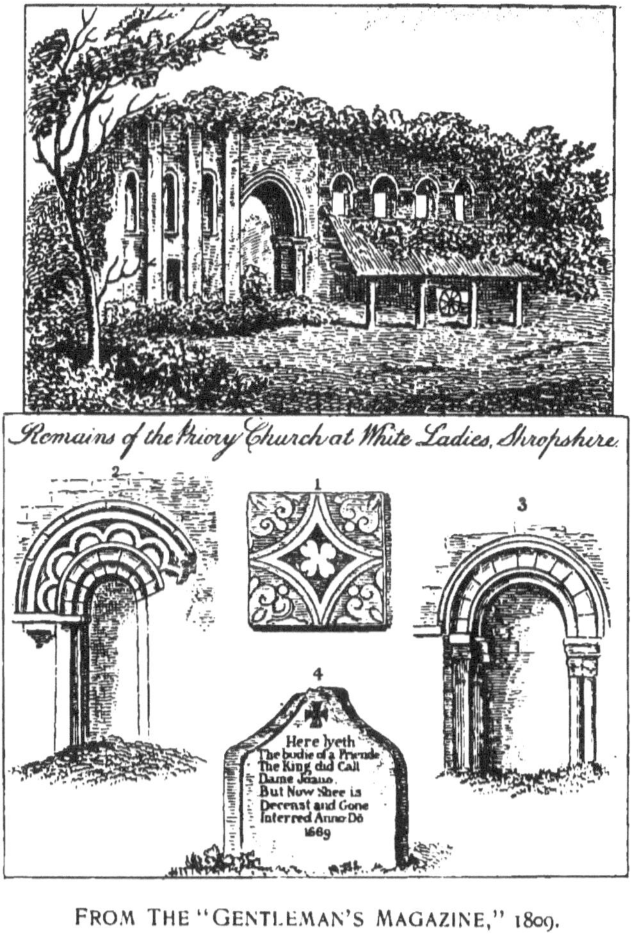

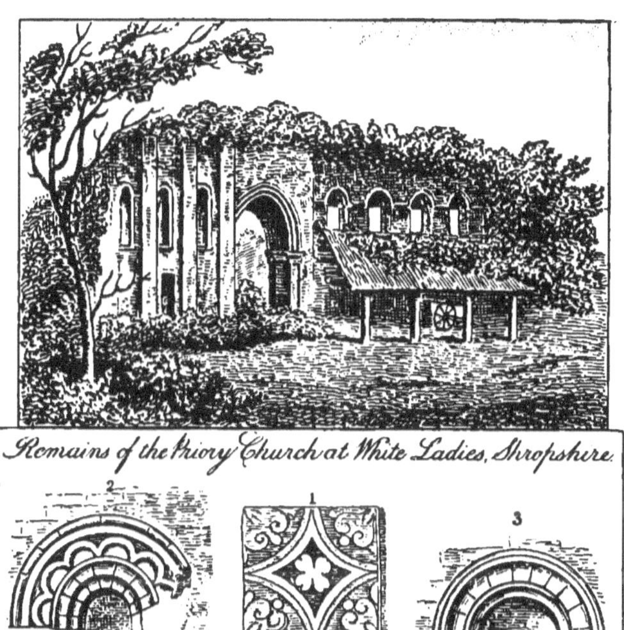

FROM THE "GENTLEMAN'S MAGAZINE," 1809.

and with all celeryte I have resortyd hether to desyre the Kynges hyghtnes of hys favour and absolucyon for my amysce doyng, prayng and besechyng your lord-schypps gracyous cumfort for the optaynyng of hys gracyous pardon, and I schal be your bounden servauntt yn hartt and also yn contynual servyce, yf yt schall please your gracyous lordschypp to accept yt, duryng my lyfe·

Wryttyn the xviij day of June.

Youre bounden for ever,
John Foster.

Cromwell was the son of a blacksmith ; some time after being a clerk in an Antwerp factory, he was taken into the service of Cardinal Wolsey, and on the fall of the Cardinal became chief adviser to Henry VIII. He was instrumental in the dissolution of the Monasteries, and was created Earl of Essex, but for having advised the King's marriage with Ann of Cleves, he was accused of treason and heresy, and executed on Tower Hill, 1540.

At White Ladies Lord Derby committed the King to the care of the Pendrill's, having ridden 26 miles. Of Richard Penderel's Mill, itself, at White Ladies, if it were there, no trace can be found. Near the Abbey were found an old hollowed piece of oak, and an ancient water pipe, and traces of a pool were visible nearer the brook. George Penderel was servant at White Ladies, and opened the door for the King, who had hardly arrived before he was advised to go into the Woods. One of the Penderels, William was a farmer at Hubbal Grange, Richard, or " Trusty Dick," a retainer at Boscobel House and two had lately fallen in the Civil War.

Mrs. Yates of the Wood was a sister of Richard Penderel's wife. She lent the King a blanket, provided eggs, milk, butter, &c.

At the time of the Reformation, Sir John Giffard who lived at Chillington, and was one of the Commissioners for the seques-tration of Church property, received for his own part the property of Black Ladies at Brewood. His grandson Edward was seated at the White Ladies, another sequestrated religious, house. Edward's grandson Peter was an active partizan for the King during the Civil War, and it was his nephew Charles who attended on that Monarch at Boscobel.*

Dame Margaret Stamford was Prioress at the Dissolution, and she had £5 allowed her yearly out of the Revenues £17 10s. 8d., and the other Ladies in proportion. Henry VIII. gave it to Sir Thomas Giffard, 10th Lord, 1560, who was Bailiff and Keeper of the Bishop's Park, and Seneschal of the Priory of St. Leonard's. He was High Sheriff and a Royal Commissioner to obtain inventories of Church Revenues, 1552. Doubtless his loyal descendant the Squire of Chillington could throw much light upon the history. It passed through females to the Fitzherberts, of Swynnerton, who still own the ruins, and a right of way thereto. The Skeffingtons lived here in the 16th century, and there exist 3 tablets with exceedingly quaint lines to their memory, two (to William Skeffington and his mother) in Tong Church (Nos. 28 and 29), and one to his wife Jone in Brewood Church, and some account of that family is given on page 88.

Hubbal Grange is a little old brick and timber homestead in Tong Parish, on the side of the Green Lane from Tong to White Oak. (See illustration.) In Hartshorne's *Salopia Antiqua*, a suggestion is made as to the derivation of this place's peculiar name. "Brompton, in his Chronicle, speaks of Hubbelow, or Hubba's Grave, and there is scarcely a place in England where there is not some spot thus nominally consecrated by a Briton's or a Saxon's grave, *low* meaning a tumulus, or grave. To the present day the first syllable indicates the name of the person so interred. In an old Chronicle cited by Hearne, speaking of Hubba, the writer says : And when the Danes fond Hungar and Hubba died, thei bared theym to a mountain ther besyde, and made upon him a logge, and lete call it Hubbslugh."' Samuel Hubball, a local tailor, says his family came from Hubbal.

BLACK LADIES.

BLACK Ladies in Staffordshire, was a Convent of Benedictine Nuns dedicated to the Virgin Mary, and so-called from their black habits, the Nunnery being three miles from White Ladies. It was valued at the Dissolution at £17 10s. 8d. (or £11 1s. 6d.) per annum, and was styled the Convent of Brewood. It only had six religious persons in it at the dissolution. One seal of the House bore :—S. CONVENT S. MARIE NIGRAR D'NARVM, and another, if we may believe Bagshaw :—SIGILLUM COMMUNE NIGRARUM MONALIUM D'BRE. This second seal is thus described in the Brit. Mus. Catalogue :—A pointed oval, the Virgin, seated in a canopied niche on the left arm the Child with cruciform nimbus, in the right hand a sceptre fleur de lizé.

Henry II. founded Black Ladies, and in 31 Hen. VII., it was conveyed to Wm. Whorwood.

King John, 1199—1200, bestowed the year's rent of* Brom, 2½ merks on the Nuns of Brewood—probably when he visited it, as he did also and in 1204, when he gave it a Charter. In 1203-4 he gave Brewood Nunnery and five others an almoign of two merks each.

Isabel, Prioress of the Black Nuns at Brewood, granted lands at Brewood to Bishop Roger Meyland. Bishop elected 1265.† 1283, a Papal Bull addressed through the Bishop to the Black Nuns of Brewood.

Staff.—Clement de Wolvernehampton, Clerk, sued Alice, Prioress of the Black Nuns of Brewode, Robert de Stafford. and Robert atte Hyrst, for taking by force

---

two oxen belonging to him at Horsebrok, worth 40s.   The defendants did not appear, and the Prioress was attached by Ralph le Messager and another, and the others could not be found.   The Sheriff was therefore ordered to distrain the Prioress and to arrest the others, and produce them at the Octaves of St. John the Baptist.   m 38.

Staff.—Clement of Wolvernehampton, Clerk, sued Alice the Prioress of the Black Nuns of Brewode, and Robert atte Hyrst and another for forcibly breaking into his house at Horsebrok, and taking his goods and chattels to the value of 100s.   The defendants did not appear, and the Sheriff had been ordered to distrain, and he now returned 10s. distrained from the chattels of Alice.· He was therefore ordered as before to distrain and produce the defendants at the Quindene of St. Michael.   m. 138.

1394.—Petronilla, Prioress of the Black Nuns of Brewode and the Convent there, acknowledges £100 at the hands of Thomas lech (de Newport, of High Ercall, Esq., who married Isabel, sister of Sir Adam de Peshali, Kt. of Weston) to pray for the soul of Thomas de Brumpton, Isabel's first husband, formerly Lord of Eyton, and the souls of all his ancestors; dated in their Chapel at Brewode on Tuesday' in the Feast of St. Michael the Archangel, 18 Rich. II.—Thomas de Brnmpton died 1382 Isabel was dead 1438.

Brewood Nunnery ex Dugdale's Monasticon; but whether relating to White Ladies or Black Ladies, I cannot tell :—

The Church, the Vestrye, the Chapter Ho., Bells in Stepull (iii.), the Hale, the Parlore (includes i Folding Tabull, the Forme, the Chayre, the Cuborde, and the Hangings of the Payatyd Cloth).   The Chaffe Chamber, the Baylyff's Chamb., the Keichyn, the Larder, Brewhouse, Kelyng House, Boylyng Ho., Cheslofte, Kylhouse, Grayne (1 qart of whete 6s., 2 qt. of munke corn 8s., 1 qt. of oats xxd., 1 qt. pese 2s. 8d.)   Catell (1 horse 4s.)   Waynes (1 wayne and 1 dungcart)   Heye xvs.   Plate (1 chales and 4 sponys).

Given to Abbess and Convent ther at ye deptun.

First to Isabell Launder	xls.
It to Christabell Smith	xxs.
Alin Beche	xxs.
Felix Baggshawe	xxs.

Rewards gyvene to the Sarvente ther at ther lyke deportun.

It. to Wm. Pker chapelon	xxxs.	
Robt. Baker	xiii.	ivd.
Margt. Burre	ii.	
Thos. Bold	iii.	
Wm. Morre	ii.	xvi.
Thos. Smith	x.	
Kateryn Alate	xiii.	iiii.
Php. Duffelde	iiii.	

Owing by Bailiff of Tonge iis. rent.

Churchwarden of Brewood iijd.

There were Roman Catholic Chapels at Long Birch and Black Ladies in 1834, the Rev. R. Hubbard being priest at the former, and the Rev. John Roe, assisted by the Rev. Henry Richmond, incumbent of Black Ladies. Services were discontinued in 1840.

Here in 1834 one report says, "The choir for these latter nuns, that for lay sisters, the images on the altar, &c., are in the same condition they were left in at the dissolution." Where are these now? It is strange how they escaped so long when we find other Commissioners' reports tell how the contents of various Religious Houses in Lincolnshire were disposed of as mentioned below, the sacred objects having to be deliberately put " to profane use," as the report quaintly expresses it.

1566 Images of Rood, Mary, and John, burned III Eliz.

1566 Itm. all mas bokes and all bookes of papistrie torne in pces, and sold to pedlars to lap spice in.

Itm. one handbell broken, the start of it sold to J. C. and he hath made a morter of yt.

Itm. one crewett cruste in peces and sold to plumer for sawdar.

Itm. copes ve-tments amisse, towelles, one vaille sold to Johnnie ffoster and George verna' 1565 and they have defaced same.

Itm. all brassen things sold and George Verna' haith sold them to a pewterer of Lincoln.

Itm. crosse cloth, banner clothes, one cannabie, one veal, one crewitt, one sacring bell, one paire of scissors, and one hally water ffatt wee know not what was doue wt theim and that wee will depose upon a book.

Itm. iiij altar stones Remayneth vnbroken but at or retorne wee will put it (sic) to pfane use.

Itm. candlesticks, &c., which we have to make awaie and breake afore Easter nexte; one sacring bell, Will Eland had and hong it by his horse eare a long tyme and now yt is broken.

Itm. a pix defacid and made a salt cellar for salt.

Itm. a roodloft sold to Langlands who haithe made a bridge for his sheep to go over into his pasture.

Itm. altar stone Pennell made a fyreherth of it in his hall.

To Robt. Rellamee ij corporax' whof his wief made of one a stomacher for her wench and of thother being ript she will make a purse, the covering of the pix sold to John Storr and bis wief occupieth yt in wiping her eies.

I visited Black Ladies in 1881 when there seemed scarcely to be a vestige left of the ancient nunnery; yet the place has an old world look.   A rather bold head, carved in stone, is set in the chimney stack in the attics.   The Chapel between the pool and the stackyard is now used as stabling ;   in one wall is a stone cross, perpendicular, let into the wall.   It was disused as a chapel in 1844.   Small and poor though this chapel was, it seems to have at one time possessed among other vestments, " a beautiful cope of crimson velvet."   Is this the one now at Tong ?

The late Mr. Hicks-Smith wrote a little account of Brewood, with notices of these nunneries, and the letters from Mr. W. Parkes to him on the subject, which I have recently purchased, are full of interest.   There are pictures of Black Ladies and White Ladies in the Salt Library, Stafford.   In the Gentleman's Magazine the White Ladies' Abbey is shewn as being used for a cart shed, and drawn, I think, by Mr. Parkes ; of him and another correspondent in that old magazine, the inimitable Tom Hood makes sorry jest :—

> B asks of C if Milton ere did write
>   "Comus" obscured beneath some Ludlow lid,
> And C next month, an answer doth indite,
>   Informing B that Mr. Milton did !
>
> X sends a portrait of a genuine flea,
>   Caught upon Martin Luther years agone,
> And Mr. Parkes of Shrewsbury, draws a bee,
>   Long dead, that gathered honey for King John.

If time and space permitted there are many more notes, including some on the patronage of the Church of Montford, which could be added, throwing light on and relating to these Nunneries, but these and many other interesting notes must be omitted, as the limit of pages is reached, and I now conclude a work which has been full of interest to write, and will, I trust, be perused and accepted by an indulgent public as a volume which aims at being nothing more than an earnest attempt to contribute an humble page to the glowing records of my native County.

Mr. Eyton, in his " Antiquities of Shropshire," tells us that the Advowson of Montford had passed to the White Nuns of Brewood in the 13th century ; but whether by grant of a Lacy or a Fitz-Alan he cannot learn. They had the appropriation of the Rectory soon after 1291. In 1341 the Assessors quoted diminished revenues of Montford, and therefore of the Nunnery, because there had been a murrain among the sheep, and a Severn flood had destroyed most of the growing corn.

In 1535 the Nuns' Ferm at Montford produced £8 per annum, but 10s. pension they had to pay out of it to the Prior at St. Guthlac at Hereford. The Priory and Convent of the White Nuns of Brewood presented the following Vicars—Sir R. de Audla, d. 1331 ; W. de Redenhull, d. 1342 ; Richd. Morys, d. of the pestilence 1349 ; Robert de Wythington, 1349 ; Sir John de Brehull, 1373 ; and others, the concluding name being Sir Richard Hamon, 1418.

The following extract from " Forest Pleas," 14 Edward I.. †Stafford, relates to the Nuns of Brewood :—

" It was presented by the reguardors of Cannock that when the huntsmen of the Lord the King were hunting in the said Forest, in the Bailiwick of Gauley [Gailey], in the fourth year of the present reign, they put up a stag with their dogs, and followed it as far as the Park of Brewood, and into the Wood there, and that John de la Wytemore came up with a bow and arrows and shot at it ; that it fled out of the Forest as far as the Vineyard of the Nuns of Brewood, and the aforesaid John followed it, and drew it out dead from the said Vineyard. And thereupon came up John Giffard, of Chylyngton, saying he had followed the same stag, and claimed it ; so that after they had skinned it together, the same John Giffard took half of it with him, and carried it to his house without warrant, and the other half the Nuns of Brewood had ; and because they are poor, let the same be pardoned to them for the soul of the King. And notwith-

---

standing the same stag was captured outside the Forest, yet was it the chase of the Lord the King, being put up by his dogs within his Forest, &c. It is, therefore, ordered to the Sheriff to produce the aforesaid John and John. They were fined, the sureties being Will Fitzmargery and Adam of the Gate."

A Convention is mentioned by Mr. Hicks-Smith, without date, between the Prioress and Nuns of Browde and the Lady Ysabel of Patingham, by which " the said Nuns released to " Ysabel all their right in half a virgate of land in Pattingham " of the demesne of the said vill, and which they held in free alms " of the gift of Ralph Bassed, and for which the said Ysabel " released to the same Nuns an assart in Chylintun. " Witnesses, the lord Ralph Abbot of Lylleshull, Ralph " Bassed the younger and Richard his brother, Ralph de " Perton, William de Wrotesle, and Yva de la Yde."

It may be that Lady Isabel's Well, on the road near Boscobel, mentioned on page 140, is named after this lady.

Here is another Grant, given by Mr. Hicks-Smith, but from what source is not said, relating to Brewood Nunnery.

" A grant by Margery, formerly daughter of Ralph de Coven, to the Black Nuns of Brewde, of 16 pence rent in the vill of Horsebroc, from the heirs of Richard Bromhale. Witnesses, Richard de Stretton, Kt., Hugh de Weston, Hugh de Bolinghale, William Giffard, Robert de Somerford, John de Sempiham, Walter [serviente] Peter de Brewode, and W. D. Bromhall." It is without date.

Brewood means frightful wood, and the lane near Kiddermore Green, which is on the way for Black Ladies Nunnery, was called Spirit Lane. There were two healing wells in Brewood parish, one of which was, I think, in the fields adjoining Black Ladies at Stinking Lake, near the Watling Street road; was the other the Leper Well, in the direction of Codsall, just outside the Chillington Woods ?

A view of the present interesting domestic structure, known as Black Ladies, now used as a farmhouse, is given.

DEEDS RELATING TO TONG, &c.

IT should be premised that I have obtained these ancient Charters chiefly from the British Museum, from time to time, and the principal ones of them have been translated by Mr. Walter de Gray Birch, F.R.S.L., author of "Vita Haroldi" or the "Romance of King Harold," the "History of the Utrecht Psalter," the "Heads of Religious Houses in England," and many other works. Two of the Charters with seals were transcribed by Mr. R. Sims, author of the Handbook of the Library of the British Museum. I am aware that antiquarians generally like old documents, such as these printed in the Norman-French or Latin, as the case may be ; but making a choice of difficulties I have thought it best to give them in English only, hoping that Mr. Birch's translations will satisfy the most exacting readers, and not forgetting that there is a growing number of students of antiquity, who, charmed by the subject, have regretfully to confess to a similar situation to that expressed in the " Shipmannes Prologue " in *Chaucer's* " Canterbury Tales " :—

> My joly body shal a tale telle
> And I shal clinken you so mery a belle,
> That I shal waken all this compagnie:
> But it shal not ben ot philosophie,
> Ne of physike ne termes quiente in lawe:
> Ther is but litél Latin in my mawe

Grant in Norman French by Fouke of Pennebruge, Lord of Tonge, to William, son of William de Pres, 1323.

To all the lawful ones in God who shall see or hear this present writing Fouke de Penebrugge (a) Lord of Tonge greeting in God. Know ye that I have given and granted and

---

(a) Probably Fulco de Pembruge II., Lord of Tonge, died 1326.

by this present writing confirmed to William son of William de Pres and to his heirs of his body lawfully begotten one acre of land in the town of Nortone (b) within my Manor of Touge lying within the field which is called the Watecroft (c), between the land of Harlewyne on the one side and the land of the aforesaid William on the other side. And if the aforesaid William die without heirs of his body lawfully begotten, then I will that the aforesaid acre of land remain to Richard son of Richard Haligode of Schuffunhale [i.e., Shifnal] and to the heirs of his body lawfully begotten, and if the aforesaid Richard die without heir of his body lawfully begotten, then I will that the aforesaid acre of land remain to Alice sister of the said Richard and to the heirs of her body lawfully begotten. And if the aforesaid Alice die without heir of her body lawfully begotten, then [I will that] the aforesaid acre of land remain to Gralan brother of the aforesaid William and to the heirs of his body lawfully begotten. And if the said Gralan die without heir of his body lawfully begotten then [that] the aforesaid acre of land remain to Ralph brother of the said Gralan and to the heirs of his body lawfully begotten. And if the said Ralph die without heir of his body lawfully begotten, then I will that the aforesaid acre of land with its appurtenances revert to me the aforesaid Fouke and to my heirs or to my assigns. To have and to hold all the aforesaid acre of land with its appurtenances easements and approachments inclosed (?) and in defence each hour of the year, of me and of my heirs or of my assigns, to the aforesaid William, Richard, Alice, Gralan, Ralph, and to their heirs of their bodies lawfully begotten in form above-mentioned, freely, quietly, well, and in peace, for ever, yielding therefor yearly to me and to my heirs or to my assigns fifteen pence sterling at the two terms of the year usual, by equal portions, and two appearances at my Court of Tonge, for all manner of other secular services, exactions, customs or demands. And I the aforesaid Fouke and my heirs will warrant and defend all the aforesaid acre of land with its appurtenances aforesaid to the aforesaid William, Richard, Alice, Gralan, Ralph, and to their heirs of their bodies lawfully begotten according to the form above-mentioned, against all mortal persons for ever. In witness whereof I have set my seal to this present writing. By those witnesses John the Ward of Tonge (d), John the Parker (e), William de Hethui (f), Nichol the Tailor, Robert Lefevre [the smith] (g), and others. Given at Tonge, on Sunday next before the feast of St. Barnabas the Apostle, in the sixteenth year of the reign of King Edward son of King Edward. [A.D. 1323.]

Grant in Norman French by Fouke of Pennebrugge, Lord of Tonge, to John the Parker, of Tonge, and Cecilia his wife, probably about the same date as preceding. Many of the earliest deeds are undated.

Know all men who are and who are to come, that I Fouke of Penebrugge, Lord of Tonge, have given and granted, and by this present writing confirmed to John the Parker of Tonge and to Cecilia his wife, all the land which John Brid lately held in the manor of Tonge excepting the Messuage with the curtilage, that is to say, that three acres lie in hollefeld, and one acre lies on the mill hul, and one acre lies in the hullefeld, and a " place " in Cole-winescroft between the land of William atte Wode (h) of Ampart, and an assart atte Ivy hattes between the highway and the land of Thomas de la Hulle, and an assart Breryhurst (i) between Matheus Mor and the land of Thomas de la Hulle.

I have also given and granted to the aforesaid John and to Cecilia his wife three acres of land in the lyhte outside the Town of Tonge, that is to say, lying between the fields called presteleye (j) on the one side and the way leading towards Brewood from Tonge on the other side.

I have also given and granted to the aforesaid John and Cecilia his wife a " place " of land containing six acres in the hyewood, that is to say lying along the highway near the assart of Thomas de la Hulle towards the highway near the assart of Edith Rogers enclosed between the land of William Robyns on the one side and my demesne land on the other side.

To have and to hold all the aforesaid land of me and of my heirs to the aforesaid John and Cecilia his wife for the term of their lives, and after their decease I will and grant for me and

---

(b) Tong Norton.

(c) Is this the Water-croft, or wet-croft, or wheat-croft ?

(d) Le Ward, the Warden, or one who takes care of. The same name occurs on the old slab mentioned on page 28.

(e) Or park-keeper, a name still lingering in Tong Parish.

(f) Heathill in Sheriffhales.

(g) The smith or blacksmith, the forgeman.

(h) Is this The Wood, now Mr. F. W. Yates's ? An assart is part of the forest cleared of wood.

(i) Briery Hurst, mentioned on page 140.

(j) Priest-ley or pasture.

for my heirs that all the aforesaid land revert to John their son and to the heirs of his body lawfully begotten.

And if the aforesaid John [die] without heir of his body lawfully begotten alive all the aforesaid land shall return to Oliver his brother and to the heirs of his body lawfully begotten.

And if the said Oliver [die] without heir of his body lawfully begotten alive all the aforesaid land shall return to Avore his sister and to the heirs of her body lawfully begotten.

And if the said Avore die without heir of her body lawfully begotten all the aforesaid land shall return to Amice his sister and to the heirs of her body lawfully begotten.

And if the said Amice die without heirs of her body lawfully begotten all the aforesaid land shall return to Edith her sister and to the heirs of her body lawfully begotten.

And if it shall by chance happen that the said Edith [die] without heir of her body lawfully begotten alive all the aforesaid land shall return to me the aforesaid Fouke, and to my heirs without any contradiction.

Yielding therefor yearly to me and to my heirs and to my assigns thirteen shillings and ninepence sterling at the terms of the year usual in the town of Tong, and making two appearances at my Court of Tonge for all other services, exactions and demands.

And I the aforesaid Fouke and my heirs and my assigns will warrant acquit and defend all the aforesaid land to the aforesaid John Cecilia, John, Oliver, Avore, Amice, and Edith and to their heirs of their bodies lawfully begotten in the form aforesaid against all people for ever.

In witness whereof as well the aforesaid John on the one part as I the aforesaid Fouke by the other part, to this present writing indented and partite among us, have put our seals on these witnesses :

Hugh de Beaumes (d)
Roger de Pulesdone
William de Preez
John le Warde
Roger Hadham and others.

Seal. A shield of arms; Barry of six, between two wyverns.

..........DE . PENBRIGG..........

A similar seal was in the Shrewsbury Museum of the Shropshire Archæological Society before its removal to the Corporation Museum, but cannot now be found.

Receipt in Latin by Robert de Penbrugge, Lord of Tonge, to William le Harpour, 1351.

Let it be manifest to all by these presents that we Robert de Pennebrugge (a), Lord of Tonge, have received by the hands of William le Harpour all the moneys due to us for ward and marriage of all the lands and tenements formerly belonging to John le Ward (the Warden) of the said Town of Tonge. Whereof we confess that we are fully paid and the said William quit and absolved. In witness whereof our seal has been appended to these presents. Given at the Castle of Tonge. on Thursday next before Palm Sunday in the twenty-fifth year of the reign of King Edward the Third after the Conquest. [A.D. 1351.]

(a) Robert de Pennebrugge being described as Lord of Tonge, sets at rest the doubt of Mr. Eyton in his *Antiquities of Shropshire*, as to whether he was ever owner of Tong, see page 12
Seal, a shield of arms in tracery as before : SIGILL . . . . .

Indenture in Latin by Sir Fulke de Pennebrugge, Knight, Lord of Tonge, to William the Smith, of Tonge, 1377.

This Indenture witnesses that I, Fulke de Pennebrugge, Knight, Lord of Tonge, have given and granted to William the Smith of Tonge, and to Joan his wife, those two messuages with their adjacent curtilages and appurtenances which John Bysshop formerly held in the town of Tonge.

To have and to hold the aforesaid messuages with their curtilages and appurtenances to the aforesaid William and Joan and to the heirs issuing lawfully from the body of the same William, of me and my heirs freely, quietly, well, and peacefully. Yielding therefor yearly to me and my heirs two shillings of silver at the usual terms within the Manor of Tonge, and suit of Court as the other burgesses do. And also I, the aforesaid Fulke, and my heirs will warrant the aforesaid messuages with their curtilages and appurtenances to the aforesaid William and Joan and to the heirs issuing lawfully from the body of the same William in the form above mentioned against all people for ever. In witness whereof as well I, the

---

(d) Or de Belmeis, a family who a century earlier had so much to do with Tong.

said Fulke, as the aforesaid William have to these indentures alternately appended our seals. These being the witnesses:

> Fulke the Smith of Tonge,
> Thomas Harlewyn of Norton,
> Roger de Hatham,
> William Hynkeley, and others.

Given at Tong, on Sunday next after the feast of St. Hilary the Bishop, In the fiftieth year of the Reign of King Edward the third after the Conquest. [A.D. 1377.] Broken seal: a hare or rabbit.

Release in Latin by Sir Fulk de Pembruge, Knight, of claim in Weston to Sir Adam de Peshale, Knight, 1399.

Let all men know that I, Fulk de Pembruge (a), Knight, have remitted, relaxed, and absolutely quitclaimed from me and my heirs, to Adam de Peshale(b), Knight, to the end of his life, all my rent which he was accustomed to pay me namely, thirty-three shillings and four pence, for a fifth part of the Manor of Weston-under-Lizard [Co. Staff.] which he holds from me for his lifetime, reserving to me and my heirs free entry and exit to the wood within the said fifth part of the said Manor . . . . according to my will and to my heirs (?).

Dated at Weston Thursd. after Feast of Conception of the Blessed Virgin Mary [8 Dec] in the first year of Henry [IV.] [1399].

Grant by Sir Adam de Peshale, Knight, of lands in Weston, to Roger de Aston, William Lee and Thomas de Walton, excepting those held for his life from Sir Fulk de Pembrug, Knight, 1406.

I, Adam de Peshale, Knight, have given and by this my indented Charter confirmed to Roger de Aston, parson of the Church of Weston, William Lee, and Thomas de Walton, my Manor of Weston-under-Lizard [Co. Staff.] and the advowson of the same Manor, with all its appurtenances, excepting those lands and tenements with appurtenances which I hold in the same town to the end of my life from Fulk de Pembruge, Knight.

Dated at Weston, Thursday before the Feast of the Purification of the Blessed Virgin Mary [2 Feb.] in the 7th year of the reign of King Henry the Fourth after the Conquest. [1406].

Indenture by Isabella de Penbrigge, lady of Tonge, and Sir Richard Vernon, Kt., to William Wixstone, 1436-7. Campbell Chart. April 14, 1436-7, 14 Hen. VI., L.F.C. xix. 13.

This indenture made between Isabella Penbrigge, lady of Tonge, and Richard Vernoun Knt., upon the one part, and William Wixstone, upon the other part, witnesseth, that the aforesaid Isabella and Richard, have conceded, delivered and to farm let, to the aforesaid William, a cottage called le Bakhous and a toft in which a cottage called le Hallehous was lately built, which said toft is called le hallehous yarde, and three acres of waste land, of land existing in the hand of the lady and one half acre of meadow lying next a meadow called Fysshermedowe. To have and to hold, the aforesaid cottage, toft, three acres of land and half an acre of meadow, with appurtenances, to the aforesaid William and his assigns, from the day of the making of these presents, until the end of a term of sixty years, then next following and fully completed. Rendering thence annually, to the aforesaid Isabella, or to her certain attorney, or to her executors, during the life of the said Isabella, three shillings of lawful money of England, and after the decease of the said Isabella, if she should die within the term aforesaid. Rendering thence annually, to the aforesaid Richard, his heirs or executors, or to his certain attorney, three shillings of the lawful money of England, at the three terms of the year, there usual, by equal portions. And if it should happen that the aforesaid rent of three shillings be in arrear, in part or wholly, and not paid for the space of fifteen days, after any Term in which it ought to be paid, then it shall be lawful for the aforesaid Isabella and her assigns, and for the aforesaid

---

(a) Fulke de Pembruge IV. who died 1499.
(b) Lord of Weston.

Richard, his heirs and assigns, if the aforesaid Isabella should happen to die within the said term, to distrain upon the aforesaid cottage, toft, three acres of land, and half an acre of meadow, with appurtenances, and upon any parcel thereof, and to abduct, carry away, drive away, and take possession of, the distraints so taken, until the aforesaid rent together with the arrears of the same, if there shall be any, shall be satisfied and paid to them. And if it should happen that the aforesaid rent of three shillings, be in arrear, in part or wholly unpaid for forty days after any term in which it ought to be paid, by default of the aforesaid William, and that sufficient distraint upon the aforesaid cottage, toft, three acres of land and half an acre of meadow, with appurtenances, cannot be found, then it shall be truly lawful for the aforesaid Isabella or her certain attorney, and to the aforesaid Richard, his heirs and assigns, provided that the said Isabella should die within the term aforesaid, to enter upon the aforesaid cottage, toft, three acres of land and half an acre of meadow, with appurtenances, and to repossess the same, and to hold them in their original state, the present indentures notwithstanding. And the aforesaid William shall build upon the said toft, next the said cottage called le Bakhous, a certain house of two spaces, and a sufficient oven in the said house, such as may satisfy the tenants of the lord there. And the aforesaid William shall build, upon the said toft, called the "Hallehous yarde," a certain house of three spaces in which the said William shall dwell, within two years of the term aforesaid. And the aforesaid William his heirs or assigns, shall well and sufficiently repair, sustain, and main-, tain, the said tenement so erected, as often as it shall be necessary, during the term aforesaid, and shall restore it, sufficiently repaired, at the end of the term aforesaid. And the aforesaid Isabella and Richard, and their heirs, shall warrant, in form aforesaid, the aforesaid cottage, toft, and three acres of land and half an acre of meadow land, with appurtenances, to the aforesaid William and his assigns, during the whole of the term aforesaid, against all people. In testimony whereof the parties aforesaid, have alternately affixed their seals to those Indentures. These being witnesses, Thomas Merstoue, William Glever, Henry Benet, John Jowe, John Cat, of Aylestone, and many others. Dated at Aylestone, the 14th day of the month of April, in the 14th year of the reign of King Henry, the sixth since the Conquest.

A small circular seal of red wax impressed with the letter I. surmounted by a crown.

This seal is sketched on the plate at page 27, and an account of Isabella, the Foundress of Tong College and Church, is given on page 32.

Grant, in Latin, by Isabella (formerly wife of Sir Fulco Penbrugge, Knight), lady of Tonge, and Sir Richard Vernon, Knight, to Thomas Skot and Johanna his wife, at the rent of a red rose, 1446.

To all the faithful in Christ to whom this present indented writing may come Isabella (a) formerly wife to Fulco Penbrugge, Knight, lady of Tonge, in the County of Salop, and Richard Vernon, Knight, greeting in the Lord. Since I the aforesaid Isabella may have and hold for term of my life, a burgage with croft at the end of the town of Touge towards Culsale (b), situated next the high way, the reversion and remainder of the said Burgage and Croft belonging after the death of the said Isabella to me the said Richard Vernon and my heirs. Know that we the aforesaid Isabella and Richard Vernon by unanimous assent and will, have delivered, conceded, and by this own present indented writing have confirmed to Thomas Skot (c) and Johanna his wife the aforesaid Burgage with croft, for the good service of the said Thomas, paid to me the said Isabella and also for the laudable service to be hereafter paid to me the aforesaid Isabella and to Richard, and to the heirs of the said Richard. To have and to hold the aforesaid Burgage with Croft, to the aforesaid Thomas and Johanna his wife for the term of their lives and of the longest liver of them. Rendering thence annually to me the said Isabella during my life and after the death of the said Isabella to me the said Richard and my heirs during the life of the said Thomas and Johanna and the longest liver of them, a red rose on the feast of St. John the Baptist suit at Court and of the mill for all other services and demands. And the said Thomas and Johanna shall well and truly maintain repair and sustain the said Burgage with croft during their lives and the longest liver of them, at the expense of 16s. to them, and after the death of the said Thomas and Johanna the said Burgage with croft shall wholly remain to me the said Richard and to my heirs for ever. And we therefore the aforesaid Isabella and Richard and my heirs will warrant and defend the aforesaid Burgage with croft to the aforesaid Thomas and Johanna during their lives and the longest liver of them in form aforesaid against all people. In testimony whereof the said Isabella and Richard Vernon have affixed their seals

---

(a) Same as in preceding deed. The Foundress of Tong College—see page 32. Date 1446, 24 Hen. VI.

(b) Kilsall.

(c) Name mentioned on page 107.

to the one part of the indented writing remaining in the possession of the aforesaid Isabella and Richard, the aforesaid Thomas and Johanna have affixed their seals. Dated at Tonge on the feast of All Saints in the twenty-fourth year of the reign of King Henry the Sixth since the conquest.

(Without Seal.)

Charter, in Latin, by Sir Richard Vernone, Knight (see page 37) to John Vernone, his son, of all his lands at Trusseley, Co. Derby, 1447.

Know men present and to come that I, Richard Vernone, Knight, have given granted, and by this my present charter confirmed to John Vernone my son, all my lands and tenements, rents and services, meadows, fields, and pastures, with all their appurtenances in the town and fields of Trusseley in the County of Derby. To have and to hold all the aforesaid lands and tenements, rents and services, meadows, fields and pastures, with all their appurtenances, to the aforesaid John, his heirs and assigns for ever of the chief lords of that fee for the services there for due and of right accustomed : And I also the aforesaid Richard and my heirs will warrant and for ever defend all the aforesaid lands and tenements, rents and services, meadows, fields and pastures with all their appurtenances aforesaid to the above said John his heirs and assigns against all people. In witness whereof to this my present charter I have appended my seal. These being the witnesses :

Thomas Blount, Sampson Meverell, Knights:
Nicholas Mountegomery, John Cokayn,
Henry Bradborne, esquires, and others

Given at Harlastone, on the fourteenth day of the month of September In the twenty-sixth year of the reign of King Henry the Sixth after the Conquest. [A.D. 1447.]

Seal in red wax : A Shield of Arms ; Fretty, a canton, etc.
SIGILLUM. RICARDI. VERNOUN. MILITIS.

Mr. Charles Wrottesley writes to the Rev. J. H. C. Clarke, vicar of Tong :—" General Wrottesley copied for me John Mitton's will, dated 1499, from a manuscript of 'Huntbach,' now at Wrottesley. I should have sent it to you before, but I mislaid it. You will see in his will John Mitton of Weston bequeaths 2/6 to the 'forming of Tong Church,' which I suppose is the ancient way of naming the seats in a Church."

Huntbach M.S. at Wrottesley, p. 153, Oct. 12, 1893.

In the name of God Amen,* 21 Dec., 1499, I John Mitton of Weston make my testament in this wise. First I bequeath my soul to God and to our Lady and all the company of heyven and my body to be buryed in the Chancell of St. Andrew of Weston, and 40/s to the said Church and XIIlb of wax to burne about my body the day of my buryall to our Lady of Coventry 12d. to St. Chad of Lichfield 12d. I give to my wife the Manor of Weston for 6 yeares to find a preist to sing for my soule in the Church of St. Andrew of Weston for 7 yeares, to Griffith my son 6 marks of land for his life and 10 marks in monye, 6 kine, 2 gownes, and 2 doubletts. I will my servant John Brokes goder (gather) my rents in Bobinton and have 20/s per annum for his life. Item to my servant Thomas Steventon 6s 8d, to William Fowke of Brewewode a gowne of black and penke furred with martennes, to Bobinton Church 3s 4d, to the forming of the Church at Tong 2s 6d. To my cozen Joyce Jacks the farm of Donnetione for her life. Executors Jane his wife and Mr. Docter Salter and the Lord Shrewsbury, overseer. Proved 12 February, 1499.*

Fulke Eyton's Will, date 1454. See referred to on page 36.

" In dei nomine, Amen; and of oure Lady and of alle the Holy Company of Heven, Amen. I Fooke Eiton, Esquire, hole of body and mynd, make my Testament in this wise. First I bequeath my sowle to God, and to our Lady, and to alle the Company of Heven, and make myn Executors Sir Richard Eiton Prest my brother, Warden of the College of Tonge, and Sir Roger the Vicar of Welyngton, and Isabella Englefield. First I will that my body be laide in Tonge, by my Godfadre, Sir Fowke of Penbrege,

---

* One of these dates is an error.

withinne the Chapell of Oure Lady; and after that, I will that there be take of my best goods for to say V thousand placebos and dirigies and V thousand masses; and for every dirigie and masse iiijd., add I bequeth to the almeshouse of Tonge X Li of money, for the which money the said almesman should be charged for to sey at my grave De profundis, thei that canne, and thei that cau not a Pater noster—and for mo sowle and Thomas of Eiton my fadre and Katherine my modre's sowles; and also thei should pay a prest to cast holy water on my grave. Also I bequeth to the Warden and to the Prestes of the saide College of Tonge my best Basin and Eure of Silver; and the saide Warden and Prestes shall have in charge, every daie when thei wesch, to sei a Pater Noster and Ave, and so to have me in perpetuall remembrance.—Also I bequeth to the saide Collage a Bed called a fedrebed, with the honging thereto of blew worstede; wherefore the saide Warden and Prestes should be charged and bounden for to seie withyn the same yere XV Placesbos and Dirigiees, and V Masses of the Trinitee, and V of the Holy Ghost, V and of our Ladye, and while it pleasith him to seie a mass of Requiem every yere, on that same day that I dide upon. Also I bequeth to a prest to synge V yere as my Executor may accorde with him for my fadre sowle, and my modere's and myn, and I charge you that he be a clene man ot his body. Also I bequeth to John Eiton alle myn horse and riding harnes, reservyd to me all my trapers and harnes of Goldsmythes worke; and I will that Luce his wife have X.li so that she kepe here a clene woman and a good till the daye of here mariage. I bequeth also to John the boy an horse and XL.s : and also to John de Labowley XL.s.; and to my page Hermon XX.s,: for thei both came with me out of Normandye. Also I bequeth to the Chapell of our Lady of Tonge my masse boke and Chalice, and my blew vestiment of damaske of my armes; and another vestiment to Wembrege, to pray for my fadre's sowle and my modere's. I bequeth also to John Eiton XX.li to his mariage; and to Fowke Eiton, Roger Eiton son other XX li of the summe the which Roger Eiton oweth me; and he to be alowed of all that he paide me.—Also I wille that the said Roger yeve to every frere house of Schropbery a centayn ot corne for to pay certain eires (years) for my soule, after the disposition of myn Executours: and that if he woll not I charge you that ye lawfully sue him till he doe it. Also I woll that my Lord of Arundell, that now is aggre ar.d compoune with you my seide Executours, for the bon (bones) of my Lord John his brother, that I broughte oute ot France; for the which carriage of bon and oute of the frenchemennys handes delyveraunce, he owith me a ml, marc and iiij c, and aftere myn Executours byn compouned with, I woll that the bon ben buried in the Collage of Arundell, after his intent; and so I to be praide for in the College of Arundell and Almeshouse perpetually. Also I bequeth to Nicholas Eiton one of the good fedre beddis and a chambre and a bedde of lynne cloth, styned with horses. I bequeth also to Isabelle Englefield another goode feder bedd, and a pair of fustians and a sparner of selke, the which myn armes beth ynne; and after her decosse, to yeve it to John Englefeld here sone.—and as towchinge the goodes to fulfille my Testament, Sir Wiliam Iynsey my prest can teile you where thei ben and more overplus. Wherefore I charge you as ye will answer afore God at the dreddfull day of Dome and that ye fulfill and ccmplete this my Testament here and afore God, I geve you full power of all my goodes, so for to do; and wille that my brothers Nicholas and Roger, have the oversight of the fulfilling of my Testament. In to the witness of alle this, I have sett to the seigne of myn armes and the seigne of myn devise. I wreten atte Schrawardyue the VLij day of Februarie the yere of our Lorde a.m.l. ccccli."
(Proved 12th Dec., 1454, by Richard Eiton and Isabella Englefield).

Ex Shreds and Patches.

A curious letter of Margaret, Lady Stanley (see pages 64 and 177), to her brother-[-in-law], John Manners.

1594, Sept. 16, Tonge. I spoke to you before of a lease my father made of a tenement at Harleston to Harry Vernon and Dorothy his wife and George their son for their lives; but virtue of which they lived and died in that tenement. Now comes Maud Vernon and claims it by virtue of a prior lease granted to her father and mother and her, by my father. She can shew no lease, but tries to prove it, by witnesses. As these witnesses fail, they vaunt that Lady Vernon "will knocke yt deade, and that in her ys all there truste.' It would be very bad if my lady should do so, as she cannot justify Maud Vernon's title, without touching my father's credit. I beg to be commended to my nephew George and his wife.

Signed.

Indenture between Sir Edward Stanley, K.B., Sir Baptist Hickes, and Dame Elizabeth, his wife, of the one part, and Thomas Crompton, of Stone, Esq.; Robert Challenor and

CC

Richard Barbour, of Stone, gent. ; George Bennett, the elder, of London, and George Bennett the younger ; and John Daintry, of Spott Grange, yeoman, of the other part. A.D. 1613. (L. F. C. xi., 30, Brit. Mus.)

This Indenture made the three and twentieth daye of June in the yeres of the Raigne of our Soueraigne lord James by the grace of God king of England Scotland ffraunce and Ireland Defendor of the ffaith etc. That is to saye of England ffraunce and Ireland the Eleuenth, and of Scotland the Sixe and ffouretieth, Betweene Sir Edward Stanley of Eusham in the Countie of Oxon Knight of the Honorable order of the Bath Sir Baptist Hickes of the City of London Knight and Dame Elizabeth his wife of the one partie, And Thomas Crompton of Stone in the Countie of Stafford Esquire, Robert Challenor and Richard Barbour of Stone aforesaid gent, George Bennett the elder Citizon and Salter of London, and George Bennett the younger Sonne of the saide George Bennett the elder. And John Daintry of Spott grange in the said Countie of Stafford yeoman on the other partie, Whereas the saide Sir Edward Stanley and Sir Baptist Hickes, by diverse and sundry deedes Indented bearing date the second day of November last past before the date of these presents, and enrolled in his Majesties High Court of Chauncery, as also by diverse and sundry other deeds bearing date the Tenth day of November last past before the date of these presents, Have for the Consideracions in the saide Deeds expressed graunted bargained sold assured Conveighed vnto them the aforesaid Thomas Crompton Robert Challenor Richard Barbour and John Daintry theire heires and assignees, And vnto the said George Bennett the elder and George Bennett the yonger and the heires and assignees of the saide George Bennett the elder diverse Messuages Cottages ffarmes lands Tenements Commons and Hereditaments scituate lying and being or to be had Received or taken within the Manor or Lordshipp of Cublaston *alias* Kibbulstan *alias* Kebleston, *alias* kebulston *alias* Cubleston, and in Stone in the aforesaid Countie of Stafford : as by the said severall deeds more at larger appeareth, And whereas also the saide Sir Edward Stanley, Sir Baptist Hickes and Dame Elizabeth his wife have in the Octaves of Saint Martin last past before the date of these presents leuied and acknowledged one ffine before his Majesties Justices of the Common Pleas at Westminster vnto the aforesaid Thomas Crompton and Robert Challenor and to the heires of the saide Thomas of Thirty Messuages, Tenne Cottages, ffourety gardens three hundred acres of land, two hundred acres of meadow ffoure thousand acres of pasture a hundred acres of wood ffoure hundred acres of ffurces and Heath, and one Hundred acres of Moore with the appurtenaunces in Cublaston *alias* Kibbulston *alias* Kebleston *alias* Kebulston *alias* Cubleston Meyford *alias* Meyforth Outonne *alias* Oulton Cotwalton Woodhouses *alias* Woodhousen Spott and Stone, and of Common of pasture for all manner of Cattle in Outoune *alias* Oulton and Meyford *alias* Meyforth as by the Record of the saide ffine more at large appeareth : Now these present witnesse that the entent and true meaninge of the parties to the said ffine at the tyme of the acknowledging thereof was, That the Messuages Cottages lands Tenements Commons and other the hereditaments in the saide ffine Conteyned were, And it was ment and entended they should be the Messuages Cottages lands, Tenements and hereditaments by the aforesaid deeds enrolled and other the Conveiances aforesaide graunted bargained sold assured and Conveighed or thereby mencioned to be graunted bargained sold assured and Conveighed, And all and every the parties to these presents doe further by these presents declare, And for them and every of them theire and every of theire heires and assignes doe Covenantg graunt and agree that the saide ffine shall be an envre, and shall be deemed and taken to be an envre, And that they the saide Thomas Cromspton and Robert Challenor theire heires and assignes shall stand and be seised of the premisses in the saide ffine mencioned and Conteyned vnto the uses entents and purpose hereafter followinge. That is to say that as to the Messuages [etc., etc.] . . . . . .

In witness whereof the parties above said to these presents have interchangeably put theire handes and scales the day and yere first above written. [A.D. 1613.]

Seals of the arms of

Sir Edward Stanley and
Sir Baptist Hickes.

Edward Stanley   Baptiste Hickes.

Sealed and delivered in the presence of ⎫   Sealed and delivered
      John Lathu. (*a*) ⎬   per Sir Baptist Hickes
      Simon Smith. ⎭   in the preseutes of vs.

                                           Robt. Grigg.
                                           Ælcocke.

(*a*) It will be remembered that this man wrote the coffin plate recently found in the vault in Tong Church. See page 65.

Deed—John Giffard, of Boscobell, and his three daughters, Frances, Dorothy, and Phillip, 1632.

To all Christian people to whome theis presentes shall come I John Giffard of Boscobell in the Countie of Salop Esquier doe send greetinge in our Lord God everlastinge. Whereas I the said John Giffard by Indenture bearing date the Ninth day of May last past before the date of theis presentes made Betweene me the said John Giffard of the one parte, And ffraunces Giffard, Dorothie Giffard and Phillip Giffard three of the daughters of me the said John Giffard on thother parte, for and in consideracion of the naturall Love and Affeccon which I have to my said daughters And for the Continuance of the Lands thereafter expressed in my bloud And for other Consideracons me the said John Giffard especially thereunto moving did for me and my heires thereby covenant and graunt to and with the said ffraneces Giffard Dorothie Giffard and Phillip Giffard their heires and assignes That I the said John Giffard and my heires and every other person and persons and his and their heires whoe then stood and were seised or hereafter should stand and be seized of any estate of Inheritance in all or any parte of the Scite of the dissolved Monastery Priory or Nunnery of the White Ladies of Brewood otherwise called the Scite of the late howse and Church of Maint Leonard of Brewood in the Counties of Salop or Stafford or either of them And of the Scite of the howse now Called or knowne by the name of Boscobell And of all or any parte of the howses Buildings Barnes gardens orchards dovecotes hoppyards Lands Tenements Meadowes Leasowes pastures profitts Comodities Rentes Revercions quitt rents and all and singular other the hereditaments to the said dissolved Monastery Nunnery or Howse and Church in any wise belonging which was or were theretofore the inheritance of Edward Giffard Esqro deceased father to me the said John Giffard And of all that the Grange Farm or Tenemente called Necholes with the appurtenaunces in the parishes of Tonge and Donnington or either of them in the said Countie of Salop—and of all howses Buildings Lands Tenements and other hereditaments to the said Grange or farme or Tenement in any wise belonginge or then or late to and with the same occupied or enjoyed or was reputed to be parte or parcell of the said Grange or farm called Necholls And alsoe of all that the Mannour of Plordweeke with the appurtenaunces in the said Countie of Stafford and all the Lands Tenements Rents Revercons and other hereditaments being and arisinge in or out of the Townes feilds or precincts of Plordweeke which herotofore were the inheritance of the said Edward Giffard deceased should and would stand and be seised thereof and of every parcell thereof to the severall uses intents and purposes thereafter expressed That is to say of the Scite of the said dissolved Monastery Priorie or Nunnery of White Ladies of Brewood otherwise called the Scite of the howse and Church of St. Leonard of Brewood the house called Boscobell and of all and singular other the premisses with their and every of their appurtenaunces to the said howse Priory Nunnery or Church belonging or to or with the same used or enjoyed And alsoe of the saide Grange or ferme called Necholls and all other the premisses with their appurtenaunces to the said Grange or farme belonging or to and with the same used or enjoyed TO the use and behoofe of the said John Giffard for and during his Naturall life without impeachment of or for any manner of Wast whatsoever and from and after the decease of the said John Giffard then TO [the use and behoope of the said] ffraunces Giffard and her heirs &c. 1632.

(Signed)   Jhon Gyfford.

Seal of his arms well preserved.

Endorsed.—Subscribed. sealed and delivered in the presence of—

         Jephson Jnell
         Thomas Cotton
         Edward Bariff

Deed—John Giffard, of Boscobell, and John Cotton and Frances Giffard, on their marriage, *re* White Ladies, Boscobell, and Neachley Grange, 1633.

This Iudenture made the Twentith daie of June in the Eight yeare of the raigne of our soveraigne Lord Charles by the grace of God of England Scotland ffraunce and Ireland King Defender of the faith etc. Betweene John Giffard of Boscobell in the Countie of Salop esquire of a th'one parte and John Cotton Sonne and heire apparent of Thomas Cotton of Gidding Abbotts in the Countie of Huntington esquire and ffraunces Giffard daughter of the said John Giffard of th'other parte Witnesseth that the said John Giffard for and in Consideracon of a marriage by the grace of God shortly to be had and solempnized by and betweene the said John Cotton and ffraunces Giffard And for the naturale love and affeccon which the said John Giffard beareth unto his said daughter and unto the said John Cotton his intended sonne in lawe and for the Continuance of the lands hereafter menconed in his blood and for other good causes and consideracons him the said John Giffard thereunto specially moveinge Doth for him his heires and assignes and everie of them Covenaunt

graunte and agree to and with the said John Cotton and ffraunces Gyffard and either of
them their heires executours administrators and assignes and every of them by theis presents
That hee the said John Giffard and his heires and every other person and persons and his and
their heires whoe nowe stand or bee seised or at any time hereafter shall stand or bee seised
of any estate of inheritance of or in all or any parte of the Scite of the Manuour or disolved
Monastery Priorye or Nunnerye of the White Ladies of Brewood otherwise called the Scite
of the late howse and Church of St. Leonard of Brewood with th' appurtenaunces situate
lyeing or being in the Counties of Salopp and Stafford or one of them And of the Scite of the
howse nowe called or knowne by the name of Boscobell. And of all that the Graunge ffarme
or Tenement Called Nechells with th'appurtenaunces situate or being in the parrishes of Tonge
and Donnington or either of them in the said Countie of Salopp with th'appurtenaunces
scituate lyeing and being in the said Countie of Salopp and Stafford or one of them And of
all or any parte of the howses buildinges Barnes stables Courtes Backsides gardens orchards
dovecotts hoppyards lands meadowes leysures pastures feedinges waters pondes fishpooles
profitts Comodities services Rentes quitrents reversions and all and singular other the
hereditameuts with their and every of their appurtenaunces unto the said Mannour or
disolved Monastery Priorye Nunnery howse or Church Graunge ffarme or Tenement in any
wise belonginge or apperteyning or now or late vsed occupied or enjoyed with the same or
knowne reputed or taken to be part or parcell thereof and of all other the Landes and
tenementes of inheritance of the said John Giffard lyeing and beinge in the said Counties of
Stafford and Salope or either of them (except all that Tenement with th'appurtenaunces
commonly called Hedgford lyeing in the said Countie of Stafford) shall and will imediately
from and after the said Marriage had and solempnized Betweene the said John and ffraunces
stand and be seised thereof and of every parte and parcell thereof and of all and singular the
premises with th'appurtenaunces (except before excepted) unto the several uses intentes and
purposes hereafter in and by theis presentes menconed expressed limitted or declared and vnto
none other use intent or purpose whatsoever that is to saie unto the use and behoofe of him
the said John Giffard and Dorothy Giffard wife of the said John Giffard for and dureing
their naturall lives and the naturall life of the longest liver of them And from and after the
deathes of them the said John Giffard and Dorothie his wife vnto the use and behoofe of the
said ffraunces Giffard. &c., &c., provided allwayes and it is mutually agreed Betweene the
said parties that the sale of the said tymber and tymber trees be ffirst of all Tendred for the
said somme of Three Hundred pounds vnto them the said John Cotton and ffraunces his
intended wife or to the survivor of them before any sale thereof be absolutely made unto any
person or persons whatsoever. And the said John Giffard for himselfe his Executors
administratours and assignes and every of them Doth Covenaunte graunte promise and agree
to and with the said John Cotton and ffraunces Giffard his intended wife and either of them
their executours administratours and assignes and every of them by theis presentes That hee
the said John Giffard or his assignes or any other person or persons by or with his consent or
procurement dureing the naturall life of him the said John Giffard shall not nor will not fell
or cutt downe or cause to be felled or cutt downe any wood Underwood or Copice wood
standinge or groweinge in the vpward parte of the wood Commonly Called or knowne by the
name of Cawdle wood the same wood being parcell of the foremenconed premisses and the
said vpward parte thereof in and by this covenaunte intended doth conteyne and is to be
esteemed the greater parte of the said Wood and leadeth from the dwelling howse there
called Boscobell to the Lawnde there belowe In Wittnes whereof the parties ffirst above
named have vnto theis presentes Interchangeably putt their hands and seales the day and
yeare first above written.

(Signed)   Jhon Gyffard
Seal of his arms : well preserved.
Endorsed :—Sealed and delivered in the presence of

Thomas Cotton
Thomas Cotton
Jephson Jnell
Edward Husbands

[British Museum. Cotton Charters, iv, 13—2.]

Deed—John Giffard to John Cotton, *re* White Ladies, 1632.

Memorandum quod Johannes Gyffard de Boscobell in Comitatu Salopie Armiger (blank in
MS) Junii Anno Regni Domini nostri Caroli Regis Anglie Scotie Frauncie et Hibernie etc :
Octavo Coram Domino Rege in Cancellaria sua personaliter constitutus Recognovit etc.

The Condicon of this Obligacon is such that yf thabovebounden John Cotton doe or shall
from time to time and at all times hereafter peaceably and quietly permit and suffer thabove
named John Gyffard and his asgs to have hold possesse and injoye All that Mannor Scite of
the Mannor or dissolved Monastery or Nunnery of the Whiteladyes of Brewoode otherwise
called ye Scite of the late bowse and Church of Sct Leonard of Brewood with thappurtenaunces
scituate lyinge or beinge in the Countyes of Salope and Stafford or one of them And alsoe
all that Scite of the howse nowe Commonly called or knowne by the name of Boscobell with
thappurtenaunces scituate or beinge within the saide County of Salop And likewise All

that Graunge Ferme or tenement called Necholls with thappurtenaunces scituate or beinge in ye parishes of Tonge and Donnington in the said County of Salope And all the howses buildings barnes stables Courts backsides gardens orchards dovecotes hoppyarde lands meadowes leasowes pastures fee inga waters ponds fishpooles profitts Commodityes services Reuts quitrents Reversions and all and singular other the hereditaments with their and every of their appurtenaunces vnto ye said Mannor or dissolved Mouastery Priory Nunnery house or Church Graunge Farme or tenement in any wise belonginge or appertayninge or now or late vsed occupied or injoyed with ye same or is knowne reputed or taken to be part or parcell thereof for and duringe the naturall life of him ye said John Gyffard without the let molestacon disturbance hinderaunce or denyall of him the salde John &c. &c.

Brewode Priory. Dissolution of Monasteries. White Ladys.

BREWODE PRIORY.

Hereafter ensueth the names of all and every suche Person and Persons as was by Thomas Bigg Doctor in the Lawe and William Cavendyshe Auditors Commissioners appoynted by the kyng our Soveraigne Lorde for the dysolucon of these Monasteryes followeng by them indiferently chosen and sworne of and for the valuyng and ratyng and appresyng of all and singlor the Gooddes and Chatells cumyng and being found at the Surrenders taken in the same late dysolyed Monasteries and priories within the Countie of Stafford the names as well of the seyd Howses as of the Persons so sworne foloweng hereunder wryghten in order.

THAT YS TO SAY

Brewode	John Browne William Barnes Henry Halt Thomas Wills	Jur	Richard Wayt John Baker William Turner William Atwill	Jur	John Shyrborne Jhones Clarke Anthony Palmer George Wilkayns	Jur

The late Priory of Brewode in the County of Stafford.	Hereafter folowyth all suche parcells of implements or houshold Stuff Corne Catel Ornements of the Church and such other lyke founde within the late priory ther at the tyme of the dissolucon of the same House Solde by the kyngs Commisioners to Thomas Gyfforde Esquire.

The Churche	Fryst one Table of Alebaster owlde formes and Settes 2 Particions of Carvyd Woode pavyng of the Church and Quere 28 panes of Glas and one masboke	20s.
The Vestrye	Item 2 payr of grene Dornyx Westments 1 olde Cope of Sendall one Serples 1 Altercloth and 1 Towell 1 litell Bell and a Sensure of latynne...	4s.
The Chapter House	Item 3 panys of Glasse and 2 long Formes soulde for	12d.
Bells in the Stepull	Item ther Remeyneth unsolde in the Stepul 3 Bells................	
The Hale	Item there 2 Tabulls and a Forme soulde for........................	12d.
The Parlore	Item 1 foldyng Tabull 1 forme 1 chayre 1 Cubborde and the hangyngs of payntyd Clothe	2s.
The Cheffe Chamber	Item one fetherbedd 2 oulde Coverletts 1 oulde blankett 1 Tester of whyght Lynen Clothe 2 bedstedds 2 formes 1 Cobborde one Joynt Cheyre 2 oulde Coffers 1 Boulster 2 pyllowis and 4 payre of Shetts	10s.
The Baylyffs Chamber	Item one mattres 1 coverlet one blanket and one axe	12d.
The Buttery	Item 2 ale tubbs 1 oulde chest 1 borde 1 table clothe and 2 candle stykys of latten	12d.
The Kechyn	Item 2 dressyng bordes 2 stoles 1 forme 1 ladder 1 (blank) of salt 4 porrengers of peuter 4 platters 2 saucers and 2 braspottes...	5s.
The Larder	Item one great chest 1 troffe and 2 little barrels....................	6d.
The brewhouse	Item 5 tubbs 1 Keler 1 olde tubbe 1 olde table 1 olde whete and one chese presse	16d.
The Yelyng house	Item 5 colyng ledes 2 brasse pannes and 7 olde tables............	5s.

The Boultyng house	Item 3 troffes 1 watering fate 1 boultyng Huche, one bushell and 2 tables soulde for............................	8d.
The Cheslofte	Item 2 little tubbes 2 cheese rakkes 2 charnes 1 lytell whele and 2 shelves	8d.
The Kylhouse	Item 1 Hercloth and 1 ladder hangyng upon the Walle of ye seid house............................	11d.
Grayne	Item one Quarter of Whete 6s. 2d. quarter of Monck Corne 8s. one Quarter of Ottes 2od. a Quarter of pese 2s. 8d. in all...	18s. 4d. ex
Catell	Item one horse 4s. soulde to the seid Thomas .a.................	4s.
Waynes	Item 1 wayne and 1 Dungcarte sould for	16d.
Heye	Item for 10 lode of Hey	15s.
Plate soulde	Item soulde to George Warren 1 Chales and 3 sponnys all whytt weing 8 ounces at 3s. 4d. the ounc	26s. 8d.
Dette Receyved	Item Reseyved of an olde dett dwe to ye seid late Priorye......	26s. 8d.
	The Sume totall of all the Guddis of thys seid late Priory with 26s. 8d. for Dett receyvyd and 26s. 8d. for Plate............................	£7 6s. 1d.

Rewardes gyvene to the late Abbes and the Convent ther at yer Departure	Fyrst to Isabel Launder	40s.	
	Item to Cristabell Smith	20s.	100s.
	Item to Alice Beche	20s.	
	Item to Felix Baggshawe............................	20s.	

Rewardes gyvene to the Servants ther at theyr lyke Departure	Item to William Parker Chapelen............................	30s.	
	Item to Robert Baker	13s. 4d.	
	Item to Margarett Burre	2s.	
	Item to Thomas Bolde	3s.	78s. 2d.
	Item to William Morre............................	2s. 6d.	
	Item to Thomas Smith	10s.	
	Item to Keteryn Slate	13s. 4d.	
	Item to Phillip Duffelde	4s.	

	Item in Cates boughte and spent at the tyme of the Comissioners being there for the Dissolucon of the said late Priory and for the saffe kepyng of the Gudds and Catell there founde duryng the said tyme............................	60s.
	The Sum of the payments aforeseid is	£11 18s. 2d.
	And so remayneth in the seid Com[m]issioners handes for they have payd more then they for the Goodes of the seid late Priory have receyd by............................	£4 12s. 1d.

Memorandum that the Prioress of the seid late Priory hath receyveyd of Michaelmas qrth rents due to the seyd Priory thes parcells folowyng And none other as sche sayth.

Fyrst of Mr. Thomas Gyfford for blythebery for halfe a yere	33s.	4d.
Item of Mr. Thomas Moreton for le feldes for half a year............	26s.	8d.
Item of T Tunks for the Rents of hys farme for halfe a yere......	6s.	8d.
Item of John Penford for half a yeres Rent............................	8s.	
Item of Thomas Pitt for a hole yeres rent	2s.	
Item of Cristofer Alatte for one quarters rente	6s.	8d.

Summa £4 3s. 4d.

Memorandum that ther ys owyng to the said late Priory of Michaelmas rente by the Confession of the foreseid theis parcells.

Fyrst of Barnaby Clarke for 3 yeres quietrente............................	18s.
Item of the Balyff of Tonge for 1 yeres rente	2s.
Item of William Wydowes for 1 yeres rente	12d.

Item of the Lordshype of Brome for 1 quarters rente .... 9s.

Item of Richard Gowgh for halfe a yeres rente .... 8d.

Item of Mathew Parker for halfe a yeres rente .... 15d.

Item of John Staunton for halfe a yeres quietrente .... 6d.

Item of   Blakeman for halfe a yeres rente .... 12d.

Item of   Whytemore for 2 yere .... 6d.

Item of Thomas Johnson for halfe a yeres rente .... 3d. ob.

Item of the Churchwardens of Brewode for 3 yeres rente............ 3d.

Item of Robert Bromhall for halfe a yeres rente .... 4d.

Summa 34s. 9d. ob.

Pencions and Porcions grauntyd and allotted to the late Prioresse and Convent there by the seid Commissioners.

Fyrst to Isabell Launder late Prioresse	66s. 8d.	
Item to Cristabell Smyth	33s. 4d.	£8 6s. 8d
Item to Alys Beche...	33s. 4d.	
Item to Felix Biggeshawe	33s. 4d.	

[British Museum. Additional MS. 6714, f. 183; and Additional MS. 6698, f. 248b.]

Sir Arthur Vernon's Will.

Prerogative Court of Canterbury.
Book, Holder, folio 35, b.

Testamentum Domini,   In the name of God amen.
Arthuri Vernon,   In the yere of our Lord mt vᵉ and xvij. The last day of Septembre,

In the yere of the Reign of Kyng Henry the viijᵗʰ the viijᵗʰ yere. I Sir Arthur Vernon prest hole of mynde and of body being in clene lyfe at the making of this my last will and in good prosperiie often tymes thinking of this wreched lyfe seyng by circute of daies and revolucion of yeres the day of deth to fall which nothing lyving may passe therfor of this helefull mynde thus I make my testament. First I bequeth my soule to god almighty and to all the holy company of hevyn and to the blissed saint Petyr and saint Mighel and to be detended ayenst all wyked spirits. Item I bequeth my body to be buried in the same pisshe church where I dye and to have a stone what myn executours thinke best for me and my picture drawen therupon and for making of my stone I bequeth xxxs. and for asmoche as with good prayers and almes dedes the soule is delivered fro everlasting deth and payne therfor I will that at the day of my burying I may have a trentall songe for my soule my fadre soule my moder soule and for all my brethern and sustern soules and for all xpen soules yf it may be. And of this my testament aforewriten and after to be truely doon I ordeyn constitue and make my true executours my brother John Vernon Rauf Gilbert and Thomas Wagstaff my servants the which executours all thinges aforewriten and after shewed truely to be executed after myn entent in this my wille shewed as they will answere afore the high Juge at the dredfull day of Dome. Item I will that at the day of my burying ev'y poren man that cometh have a peny and a loffe to pray for my soule and the soules afore rehersed yf it may be at that tyme and yf not therefore to tarye unto the tyme convenient. And yf my goods will not reche to that I will that myn executours do as they thinke most best for me. Also that I have Torches and Candelles about myn herse the day my burying as myn executours thinke necessary for me. Item to ev'y preest that comyth to my burying and saith masse for my soule and the soules afore rehersed shal have iiijd ev'y clerk id. Item I will that at my moneth mynd there be songe a trentall for my soule and the soules afore rehersed and for asmoche as this my will may be taken doubtfull in many poynts therfore I will that yf any ambiguite contrariosiie or mys-rehersall or doubtfulnes be founden in this my last will I wille therefore that it be correcte by one or ij of myn executours also my reyment I will that it be evynly devided betwixt Raut Gilbert and Thomas Wagstaffe my servants and also yf they be good of demenure toward my brother John I will that they have xljli. evynly devided betwene them and their wages to be content in the said sume aforewriten. And yf the be not of good demenure I will that they be at my brother John Vernon limitacion. Also all my good not bequethed my will perfourmed I will my brother John Vernon have them. Also the Reversion which I had besett me by my fader bequest I will my brother John Vernon have it. Item I will that my brother John Vernon have all my naprye ware and also all my beddinge and my boks wt the chests and coffers. Item I will that Robert Neyll have for paying of subsidies and Dymes and other ducties which I have cawsed him to paye xljli and to be forgevyn of him for it. Writen the day and yere aforsaid. These beign witnesse Sir Roger Lyne maister Harry Bullock maist' Harvy Sir Thomas Rowson and maister Browne. Item I will that my Skarlet gown and my murrey gowne and my Jaket of velvet may paye suche dettes to the Church of Schele and of Bogeston yf there be any asked as owght to be And all other stuffe of silk or velvet I will my brother John Vernon have it. Item I will that all my linnen clothes my brother John Vernon have them and all my plate of silver Also I will that x marcs be distributed for to pray for my soule and the soules afore rehersed that it be distributed in the parishe of Schele.

Church Goods at the Dissolution.

DONYNGTON.

This byll indented mad the xvij^th day of May in the seventh yere of the Raigne of o^r most dread sov'aign lorde Kyng Edward the syxth betwyxt Andrewe Corbett Rycc Manweryng Knyghtes Rycc Cornwall & Rycc Newport esquires on thon ptie & Rycc Hyll pson Thomas Boscoke & john Dossett church wardens on thother ptie wittnessith that we the sayd Rychard Thomas & John do bynd o^r selves by these p'sentes to save kepe unstollen unsold & unembesellyed one chalys of sylv' withe pattent there unto ij smale bell[s] nowe remaynynge within the church & steple of Donygto' as we wyll answere therefor In wyttnese wherof we have putte o^r handes the day & yere above sayd.

Rychard Hyll   Thomas Bosschock.

Church Goods, Salop.

TONGGE.

Thes byll Indentyd made the xxv^th of Maie in the vij^th yer of the reygne of our moste dreade Sov'aygne lorde Kyng Edward the syxte betwyxt Andrewe Corbett Rychard Cornewaylle & Rychard Newport on thon ptyee & Robt Foster Roger Wysston & Henrye Harryson on the other ptyee wyttnessythe that wee the sayd Robt Roger & Henrye do by these p'sens confesse & bynd our selvys to saive & kepe unstollen unsolde & unembessallyd three bellys att these p'sens remaynyng wythin the steeple of Tonnge & in wytnes heroff wee have putte our handes the yeer & dey above seyd.

Robert Forster.

HENRY VII. to [SIR] HE[NRY VERNO]N, knight.

1492, April 13. Sheen.—"Trusty and right welbeloved we grete you wele, ascertaynyng you that for the singulier trust that we have in your approved trouth and wisedom, we have appointed you to be Comptroller of houshold with our derest son the Prince, entending by Goddes grace that he shal procede to the begynnyng of the same the vij. day of May next commyng. Wherfor we pray you that ye wilfully dispose you to take uppon you the said rowme and auctoritie, and to yeve your attendance in be begynnyng of the said housholde for the good ordering and establisshing of the same, desiring you that somwhat bifor the said tyme ye wol addresse you unto us to thentent that uppon convercacion we may shewe unto you our minde concernyng the premissez more at large, not failling herof in any wise, as we specially truste you. Yeven under our signet at our manoir ot Shene the xiij day of April the seventhe yer of oure reigne." *Sign manual.*

HENRY VII. to SIR HENRY VERNON, knight.

[1492?] April 26. Greenwich.—"Trusty and welbeloved we grete you wel, lating you write that as wel by our espies that we have in the parties beyond the see, as othrewise, we undrestande that our ennemyes of Fraunce prepaire theymsilf to do all the hurt and annoyance that they can compasse and devise to this our reame and subgiettes of the same, for the [resi]sting and subduyïng of whoes malicious purpos we shal, with Goddes grace suffisantly provide and putte us with a good multitude of our subgiettes in defensible redinesse for the same entent, which can in noo wise be doon without grete substance of good. Wherfor we holding for undoubted. that ye bere a singulier tendrenesse to suche thinges as concerne the suretie and universal weale and tranquillite of our saide reame and subgiettes desire and hertily praye you that ye wil lene unto us the somme of an c^li, and to sende it unto oure Tresourer of England by some trusty servauntes of yours to thentent that theye maye recyve bills of hym for contentaccion therof ayen. And we felthfully promitte you by these oure lettres that ye shal have repayment or suffisant assignment upon the half quinzame payable at Martilmasse next commyng, wherunto ye maye verraily truste, wherin ye shal not oonly doo unto us thing of [grete?] and singulier pleasir, but also cause us to have you therfor moore specially recommended in the [ho]nor of oure grace in such thinges as ye shal have to poursue unto us heraftre. Yeven undre our signet at our manoir at Grenewiche the xxvj day of April." *Sign manual.*

Henry VII. to Sir Henry Vernon, knight for his body, Controller with the Prince.

1492, August 31. Windsor.—"Trusty and welbeloved we grete you wel. And inasmoche as we have appointed you to be Comptrollour of houshold with oure derrest son the Prince, and that we departe in all hast on oure voyage over the see, we therfor desire and praye you that ye wol geve your personall attendance uppon our said derrest son for the tyme we shalbe out of this oure reame, and that ye faille not herof, as we truste you. Yeven undre our signet at our Castel of Windesor the last day of August, the viij^th yer of our regne." *Sign manual. Signet*

Henry VII. to Sir Henry Vernon, Controller of the Household of the Prince.

[1494?] June 2 Sheen.—"Trusty and welbiloved we grete you wele. ' And for the true and acceptable service that ye have doon to our derrest son the Prince we can you special thanke, and considre wele that by your wise and poletike meanes his houshold is the better conducted and governed, which is greatly to your laude a praise. And therfore we pray you to dispose you to contynue and yeve your personal attendance there at such seasons as the counsail of our said son shal thinke necessarie and expedient, for then-creace of your said thanke. And elles we must of urgent necessite appointe oon of our bede officers to exercise your saide rowme, and calle you to serve us in his stede. Yeven undre our signet at our manoir of Shene the secund day of Juyn." *Sign manual.*

Henry VII. to Sir Henry Vernon, one of the knights for his body, and Treasurer of Household with the Prince.

N.Y. March 2. London.—"Trusty and welbeloved we grete you wele. And for certain causes and matiers concernyng as wele our derrest sonne the Prince as youreself, we wol and desire you to comme unto us some day this Lent tyme, and that ye ne faille [so] to doo in any wise, as we trust you. Yeven undre our signet at oure Citie of London the ij^de day of Marche." *Sign manual.*

The Townsmen of Walsall to Sir Henry Vernon.

N.Y. January 18.—We have a chaplain and true bedeman of yours amongst us, whose name is Sir John Staple. We hear that you intend to take him away from us. He has always been ready to maintain the service of God. He has caused charity amongst the people, where else there would have been much discord and debate. He has kept a school, and taught the poor children of the town of his charity, taking nothing for his labour. He has done many more good deeds, specially to the poor people. That he should thus depart were the greatest loss to the poor town of Walsall that it has ever had by the departure of any priest. If you will suffer him to continue with us, you shall have the prayers of him and of us all. "Wryttan [at] Walsale the morou next after Scent Antonyys day be the cowencelles of the mere masters of the yeld (guild) and the xxiiij^ti with all the best of the commyns asemblede at the same tyme, and selyd with the commyn seall o the towene.'

Henry VII. to Sir Vernon, knight for his body.

[1503.] May 6. Richmond.—"Trusty and welbiloved we grete you wele. And forso-mouche as according to the treatie and convencion passed bitwene us and oure derrest sonne the King of Scottes, and of late at his special desir and instance, we have ordeyned and determyned oure moost dere doughter the Quene of Scottes to be delivered into Scotland for her traduccion and the solempnisacion of matrimony betwixte the said King and hir by the furst day of August next commyng, We willing as wel for the perfourmance of oure promyse made in that behalve, as also for the honnour of us and this oure realme oure said doughter to bee honorably accompanyed as in like caas it hath been hertofor accustumed not oonly for hir conveyance thoroughoute oure said reame and at hir entree into Scotland, but also during the feest and solempnisacion of the said mariage, have appoincted you amonges othre nobles and estates to yeve youre attendance upon hir at hir commyng to oure Citie of Yorke, and from thens to contynue the same til the said mariage and feest bee doon and finisshed. Thefor we wol and desire you to prepaire youre self for this entent with as smal a nombre as ye shal thinke convenient, soo that ye maye bee in arredinesse to entre into your said attendance upon oure said doughter at hir commyng to Yorke forsaid, withoute any youre failing as ye tender the honnour of us and of this our reame. Over this insomoche as it is thought unto us and oure counsaill inconvenient and not mete that any mornyng or sorofull clothinges shuld be woran or used at suche noble triumphes of mariage, We therfor wol and desire you tattende upon oure saide doughter in youre best arraye as in suche caas it apperteigneth. Yeven undre our signet at oure manouur of Richemounte the vjth day of May." *Sign manual. Fragment of signet.*

Miss Lane to the Queen.

I was infinitly glad to have the honour to reseave a letter from your Matie for it was reported here that you ware not well and indeed I was in much pane till I heard from my cosen Broughton, God be praysed the King is well out the Duke is in phisick still and soe is the Duches she is very gratious to me but I doe not goe oft up to wait on her. The King has now given order for the setling of a thousand pounds a yeare upon me I am very much bound to his ma^{tie} for his gratious favour to me I hope in time he will doe what is fit for ma^{ties} to expect from it tys the opinion of many heare that your ma^{tie} should com into England without an invitation but I confes I cannot tell how to advise your ma^{tie} in this point I think your ma^{tie} the best judg on it your selfe what is most proper for you to do, if I may be so happie as to know when your ma^{tie} will come I will not faile to paye my duty in waiting of your ma^{tie} for noe soule a live is more

Your ma^{ties} most obedient most humble servant

J. LANE.

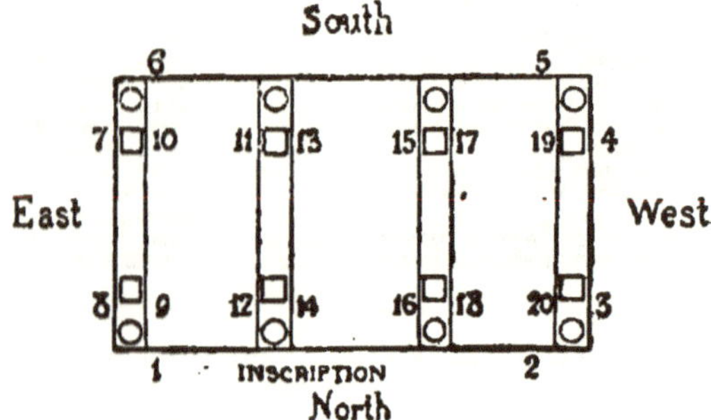

Stanley Tomb : Shields.

See Page 67

ADDENDA, ERRATA, &c.

Page 15.—Lieut,-Col. should be Col.

Page 45.—Last line--aucerlis should be Saucerlis.

Page 88.—The * and † Notes should be on page 87.

Page 108.—Page 60 should be 83.

Page 132.—Thomas Row should be How.

Page 133.—Ati⁚ should be ali(a)s,

Page 142.—Idd's hall should be Ida's hall.

Page 143.—Line 11, *where* not when.

Page 163.—Dorothy Giffard, 1634 not 634.

Page 179.—The * note is on page 180.

Eage 180.—The second * note refers to Col. Carlis.

Page 182.—King Charles II. advanced Lord Newport to a Viscountcy in 1675; the Earldom of Bradford was given by William and Mary in 1694.

Page 206.—Lech should be Gech.

Page 206.—Peshali should be Peshal.

Page 208.—The additional notes as to the Nunneries were subsequently printed. See pages 209 and 210.

Page 213.—The note (a) to Robt de Pennebrugge deed should have been a footnote, not to have been printed as part of the deed.

Page 214.—Note (a) 1409, not 1499.

The View of the Pulpit (page 26) shews position it occupied before the Restoration in 1892.

The View of Stanley Tomb (page 20) shews position it occupied before the Restoration in 1892.

Richard de Pembruge, *i.e.*, Sir Richard de Vernon, the Speaker.

INDEX.

	Page
Abertanat	17
Acorn Lodge	140
Acreage	5
Æolian Harp	160
Albrighton	51, 136, 139, 195
Alderton	131
Alditha	196
Ale and Alehouses	105, 115, 128, 152
Almshouses	25, 95, 116
Altar	55, 85
Ambling Meadows	132, 147
Andrews, Bemjamin	150, 151
Ankerwicke	190
Appuldercombe, Heiress of	16
Aqualate	189
Architectural Details	22, 23, 26, 30, 43, 47, 53, 54, 57, 66, 73, 77, 78, 96, 108, 109, 110, 156, 157, 200
Armour	40, 41, 48, 58, 60, 65
Arms	33, 34, 36, 45, 46, 47, 48, 54, 63, 66, 67, 80, 86, 87, 115, 130, 156, 157, 159, 160
Arms, Shields of—	
Bermingham	34, 36
Camville	46, 48, 55
Childe	86, 87
De la Bere	78
Doyle	86
Dureversale	45
Durant	89
English	86
Fitzalan	78
Forester	14
Forster	130
Harries	80
Isle of Man	67
Latham	67
Lingein, Lingayne, or Lingaine	34, 78
Ludlow	34, 37, 45, 55, 63, 67, 78
Ouldbelf	86, 87
Peche or Peeke	87
Pembruge	34, 36, 37, 45, 48, 54, 55, 67, 78
Peter de Sancerlis	45
Pype	45, 48, 55, 59, 67, 78
Reymes or Rheims	54
Royal	25
Skeffington	86, 87
Stanley	67
Strange	67
Talbot	48, 54
Trumpington	55
Trussel	34, 78
Vernon	33, 34, 36, 45, 47, 48, 54, 55, 59, 63, 67, 78
Warren	67
Willoughby of Middleton	79
Willoughby of Parham	79
Wylde	80
Umfreville	67
Unknown	46, 47, 67, 80, 86, 87, 92
Arthur Tudor, Prince	47, 48, 49, 56, 99, 224
	Page
Arundel	9, 176, 177, 217
Aston, Roger de	214
Audley Barons	71
Aumbry	57
Babyn, John	29
Baddeley, John	151
Bagot, John	195
Bagots Park	190
Bailifie of Tong	206, 222
Bakewell	12, 59
Barbour, Richard	218
Barretors or Scolds	128
Beaufoy	89, 155
Bedall, Roger	148
Beighterton, or Betterton	145
Belfry	29, 73, 99, 224
Belle Isle	159
Bells, Bell-founders, and Ringers	101, 102, 103, 224
Bell, "The Great"	22, 49, 99, 100, 103
Belmeis or Beaumes, Alice de	10
,, ,, Bishop de	2, 135
,, ,, Philip de	10
,, ,, Ranulph de	10
,, ,, Richard de I.	10, 20
,, ,, Richard de II.	10
,, ,, William de	10
,, ,, William de alias La Zouche	2, 10
,, ,, Robert de Belesme	10
,, ,, Hugh de	196, 213
,, ,, John de	197
Benet, Joy	215
Bennett, George	218
Bentley	180
Bermingham, Matilda de	12
Berestord, Jas.	152
Bishops	10, 11, 166, 195, 198
Bishop's Marks	56, 76
Bishop's Wood	10, 139, 140, 195
Black Ladies	125, 139, 199, 200, 201, 205, 210
Blodwell	16, 17
Blount, Thos.	178
Blymhill	128, 132, 195
Bobbington Church	216
Boden	19
Body-ring (iron)	114
Bordesley Abbey	148
Boscobel	144, 178, 203
Bosschock, Thos.	213
Botfield, Mr.	97, 106, 144, 178, 192, 203
Boundary	132, 134, 135, 136, 151
Bourne, W.	152
Bradford, Countess of	13, 14, 101
,, Earls of	12, 13, 16, 23, 52, 100, 140, 147, 151, 153, 182, 184
Bradley, Miss	177, 180
Braose de	11
Brasses	43, 45, 55, 84, 85, 86, 87, 96
Brewers Oak	189

Page

Brewood, Brewde...10, 11, 12, 136, 145, 194, 196, 205, 219
Brewood Forest...... 99, 139, 140, 178, 189, 195 209, 210
Bridgeman, Lady Anne ... 16
" Bishop ... 13, 18
" Hon. Beatrice Adine ... 15
" Lady Florence K. ... 15
" Hon. Florence Sibell ... 15
" Col. Hon. F. C., M.P....15, 19, 153
" Frederick Paul ... 15
" Hon. and Rev. Canon... 39, 130
" Hon. Mrs. F. C. ... 15
" Hon. Helena Mary ... 15
" Hon. Henry George O. ... 15
" Humphrey H. O. ... 15
" Lady Mabel Selina ... 15
" Hon. Margaret Alice ... 15
" Hon. Orlando... 15
" Sir Orlando ... 13, 17, 18
" Hon. Richard O. B. ... 15
" Reginald Francis ... 15
" Selina Adine ... 15
Brid, John ... 212
Bristol, Marchioness of ... 14
Brockhurst ... 189
Brodmore ... 145
Brokes, John... 216
Bryery Hurst ... 132, 140
Buccleuch, Duke of ... 15
Buckeridge, Chas. Thos. Margtta. Eliz... 19 94, 96, 163
Bullock, Harry ... 223
Buckingham, Duke of ... 175, 176
Buildwas Abbey... 10
Burials ... 162, 163
Burlington ... 7, 133, 141
Burnal, Lord of ... 72
Bush Inn ... 153
Butters Brook... 151
Bysshop, John ... 213
Calais, Treasurer of... 37
Camp of Refuge... 9
Camville ... 46, 48
Cannock ... 196
Cannon Ball Marks ... 105
Carnac, C. R. ... 19
Carved Stone (early) ...
Carr, Rev. Canon... 191, 192
Castle Bromwich ... 16
Castle, Tong ... 11, 49, 50, 83, 90, 91, 137, 153
Celcilia ... 196
Celerer ... 124
Chairs, Old Oak... 85
Challenor, Robert... 217
Champions ... 149
" The King's ... 59, 60
Chapel, The Lady... 23, 36, 55, 57, 73
" Golden... 36, 53, 2
Chaplet of Roses ... 11, 32, 147
Charities ... 83, 97
Charles I ... Frontispiece, 93, 174, 175, 182
Charles II....81, 89, 114, 137, 141, 178, 181, 183, 186, 201
Charlett, Mr. ... 187
Childe, Mrs. Baldwyn... 192
Chillington... 179, 195, 209, 210
Choir Screen ... 73, 76
" Stalls ... 74, 75 76
Christian, H. R. H. Princess... 15, 101
Chrysom's, St. Cemetery ... 104

Page

Chudleigh, Miss (Duchess of Kingston) ... 12, 22, 166
Churchwardens' Accounts... 97, 100
Ciborium... 82, 83, 108, 115
Cilin-ap-y-Blaidd Rhud ... 17
Cirencester ... 181
Clarence and Avondale, Duke of... 101, 175, 176
Clarendon, Lord ... 189
Clarke, Rev. H. C.... 19, 100, 216
Clay, W. ... 27, 107
Clergy, Clerks, Chaplains of Tong... 19
Clews, Mr. ... 152
Clockmaking ... 151
Cocking... 152
Codsall Wake... 152
Coffins ... 64, 159
Coiffure... 42
Coins ... 25
Cole, Mr. ... 47, 55, 65, 95, 116, 124
Colemere, W. Esq. ... 132, 144
College 19, 21, 36, 38, 54, 83, 96, 111 to 124, 216, 217
College Chapel ... 124
Commandments... 75
Communion Plate ... 83, 108
" Contoise " ... 31
Consecration Marks ... 55, 56, 76
Constable's Office ... 44, 45, 60, 128
Convent Lodge ... 156
Coppice Green ... 134
Coracle... 149, 150
Corbet, Andrew... 224
Cornwall, Ryce ... 223
Coronation-day ... 52, 60, 72
Cotton, John... 132, 133, 218, 219
Cotton, Wm. ... 19
Court of Tong ... 11, 212
Cow Haye ... 132, 141
Cowper, Earl ... 190
Craig, Mr. Jas. ... 185, 189
Cressage ... 192
Crest ... 73
Crompton, Thomas ... 217
Cromwell, Oliver ... 81, 105, 174, 203
Cromwell, Thomas ... 162, 201
Crosses ... 55, 56, 74, 103
" (Rood) ... 74
Crowther ... 152
Crucifix ... 74
Cublesdon ... 32, 39, 218
Cummings, Mr. ... 185
Cynllaeth ... 17
Daintry, John... 218
Dale, Mr.... 187, 188, 191
Dalkeith, Earl of ... 15
Dame Joan ... 201
Damer, Hon. Mrs. Dawson ... 169, 171
Daret ... 175
Darfield ... 72
Daunsey, Dame Elizabeth, Lady... 86, 87, 88
" Sir John ... 87
Deacon ... 74
Dead Woman's Grave... 127
Dean or Den ... 54
Done, Beatrice ... 198
De Belmeis ... See B
De Bunsen, Rev. H. G. ... 133, 184, 188
Deeds, Ancient ... 146, 211 to 226
Definitions 8, 10, 21, 29, 41, 42, 45, 85, 88, 103, 126, 127, 134, 138, 139—141, 150
De Hugefort ... 146, 198

	Page
"Dennis Field"	132, 139
Derby, Earls of	64, 65, 67, 72, 179
,, The	147
Devonshire, Duchess of	171
Digby, Sir Kenelm	69, 172, 173, 174
Digby, Venetia	See Stanley
Domesday	7, 8, 10, 20
Donnington	94, 124, 133, 148, 195, 227
,, Monks Pasturage at	12
Dove-cote	10, 11, 160
Draycot	44
Dress	46, 50, 51, 55, 59, 65, 79, 124, 131, 168
Dropping Well	160
Duchess of Teck, H.R.H.	101
Dugdale, Sir William	32, 33, 68, 69
Dunham, Massey	72
Dunster, Mr. Chas.	187
Durant family	91
Durant, Edwin Mr.	155
,, F. O. Mrs.	154
,, G.	75, 89, 116
,, George	12, 91, 155
,, George Chas. Selwyn	12, 91, 155
,, George Stanton Eld.	12, 155
,, Mr.	65, 75, 82, 90, 108, 158, 159, 161
,, Mrs. Celeste	91, 155, 160, 171
,, Richard	89
Dureversale, Wm.	44, 45
Dymoke, Sir Edward	61
,, Margaret	(See Vernon)
,, Sir Robert	58, 59, 60
Easthope	14
East Window	77
,, ,, of Chapel	43
Eclipse	164
Edric	45
Edward, The Confessor	8
Edward VI.	19, 74, 115
Edwin, Earl	8, 9
Effigies	29, 40, 41, 42, 64, 65
Einion-Efell	17
Eiton, John	36, 217
Eiton, Sir Richard	19, 216
Elcock, Ralph	19, 96
Eld, Miss	91
Englefield, Isabella	36, 216
,, John	217
Ercall, William de	198
Ernulf, Chaplain	19
Evans, Thomas Mr.	148, 191
,, Miss Francis	188, 191
,, Lady	190
Evelith	131, 180
Eynsham	64
Eyton, Fulke	36, 216, 217
,, Nicholas	36, 216
,, Roger	217
Factory	150
Fair	11, 123
Famous Ladies	166, 167, 168
"Fermor"	138
Figure of Priest	55
Fisher, Lady	181
Fisherwick	88
Fishing	11, 147
Fitcherbot, Esq.	144
Fitzherbert, Mrs.	166, 169, 170
,, Sir Anthony	146
,, Thomas	169
,, William	103
Fitzherberts	132, 188, 200, 204

	Page
Font	27
Forest Laws	7, 14
Forester, Edric the	45
,, family	13, 107, 130, 131, 176
,, Col. Hon. Henry Townsend	14
,, Hon. Selina L. Weld	13
,, John	14, 176, 202
,, Lord	13, 131
,, Richard	14, 131
,, Robert	176, 224
,, Thomas	176
,, Mary	176
Forster, Anthony	131
,, Humphrey	176
,, or Forester, Isabella	131, 166, 175, 176
,, Thomas	19, 130, 179
Forge, Tong	133, 142, 150, 151
,, ,, Bridge	144
,, ,, Brook	142
,, ,, Hammer	142
Fortescue, Frances	72
Fowke, William	87, 88, 216
Fowl House, pyramidal	159
Fox	23
Frontal Pulpit	83, 98
Gailey	196, 209
Gallery	74
Gallowses	152
Gamble	152
Gargoyles	110
Gerbier	175
Giffard, Charles Mr.	87, 179, 182, 194, 196, 200, 210, 217, 218
Giffard family	80, 163, 179, 199, 218, 219, 220
Giffard, Sir John	203, 217
Giffard, Sir Thos.	204
Gilbert, Ralf	222
Gildenmorton, Manor of	112
Glass, Stained	77, 96
Glever, Wm.	215
Golden Chapel	22, 36, 47, 49, 53, 54
Gospel Road, Gospel-trees	136, 144
Granges	10, 11, 37, 123
Grafton	51
Greatbatch, Sam	151, 152
Great Ness	131
Grey, Sir Richard	63
Groom, Rev. L.	201
Grosvenor, The Countess	15
Gunpowder Plot, Proclamation Tong	164, 165
Gwenwynwyn	17
Griffith of Cae Howell, Kynaston, &c.	17, 18
Griffiths, Ap Griffith	39, 127, 236
Haddon	12, 42, 45, 46, 49, 51, 63, 71, 177
Haighway Road	152
Hadham, Roger	213
Haligode	212
Hallelujah Victory	3
Hall, S.	19
Hall The, Tong	160
Hall, Thos.	19
Halston	175
Hamilton, Duchess of	168
,, George	159
Hanaper	21
Hanbury, George	15
Harcourt, Margery	11
,, Orabel	11
,, Wm. de	2, 11, 145
Harding, Revs. G. and J.	16

	Page
Harding, Mrs.	108
Hare, Lucy	107
Harewood, Countess of	15
Harlaston	52, 216
Harlegh, Alice	198
Harlewyn	212, 214
Harpour, William le	213
Harries, Ann	12
,, Elizabeth (see Pierpoint)	12, 80
,, Lady	46, 158
,, Lady Eleanor	80, 82, 83, 98, 108
,, Sir Thomas	12, 65, 80, 83, 92, 158
Harrington, Lord and Lady	41
Harrison, George	99
Harriot or Herlot	127
Hartley, John	153
Harryson, Henry	223
Hatchments	92
Hatham	214
Hatton, John	130
Haughton	160
Havannah	12, 90
Hawarden	135, 144
Hay	14
Heathill or de Hethull	212
Hell Meadow	122
Hempenstall, A.	149, 150
Henry-de-Hugefort	11
Henry I.	2, 10, 45
,, III.	11, 40
,, IV.	111, 112
,, V.	19, 112, 115
,, VI.	54
Hengist	2
Henry VII.	59, 224, 225
,, VIII.	13, 49, 59, 114, 115
Hereward	9
Hermit of Tong	156
Hermon	217
Herons	153
Hickes, Sir B.	217
Higgs, Daniel and Maria	57
High Ercall	174
Hilton, Robert	19
Hodnet	43, 52, 63
Hogs	11, 147
Holbein	114
Holmes, George	133
Holy Rood	74
Holywell	200
Homilies, Book of	25
Hooker, J. S.	184
Hope, Mr. Jas.	185
Hops	115
Horse Brook	206, 210
Horse Shoes Inn	153
Horton, John	133, 151
Hospital	95
Hotspur	38, 72
How, Mr.	132, 140, 145
Howard, Thomas	177
,, William	177
,, Roger	177
Howe, Countess	14
Hubbal Grange	10, 37, 137, 179, 203, 204
Huddleston, Mr.	180
Hulle, Thos. de la	212
Hulter, John	19
Hugefort	11, 32, 146, 198
Hunt, Will	164
Hurst, A.	140
Hyde (or Yde)	210
Hyll, Richard	224
Hynkeley	214
Idsall	19, 130, 133, 142
Image of Blessed Virgin	11, 73, 147
,, of St. Bartholomew	11, 73
Iynsey, Sir Wm.	217
Inscriptions	43, 53, 57, 63, 64, 67, 88, 91, 93, 94, 157, 158, 159, 160, 161, 169, 173
Isabel's, Lady, Well	140, 210
,, ,,	205
Iron Ore	142, 143
Jacks, Joyce	216
John, King	2, 11, 196, 205
Jowe, John	215
Jones, "Rosy"	151
Jones, Mr. W.	151
Jones, Lancet	133
Jorwerth Goch	17
Jury	151
Katherine of Arragon, Princess	49, 236
Keepers' Meadows	144
Kenyon Slaney, Lady Mabel	15
,, ,, Robert O. R.	15
,, ,, Sybil	15, 149
,, ,, Colonel, M.P	15
Kilsall	132, 135, 196, 215
Kingston, Earl of, Evelyn 1st Duke	12, 57, 82, 90, 116, 135, 166, 167
,, Earls of	12, 81, 82, 93
King of the Peak	71
Kitcat Club	167
Knight Constable of England	44
,, of Mawddy	17
,, Doctor	199
Knockyn	72
Knoll	137
,, Tower	161
Knowsley	71
Kynaston, Humphrey	17
,, Judith	17
Kynton, Viscount	72
Lascelles, Henry Viscount	15
Lascelles, Hon. Edward Cecil	15
,, Lady M. Selina	15
Lacy, Lord of	72
Lady Wicket Field	189
Lafefvo, Celeste	91, 155
Lance	150
Lane, Mistress Jane	181, 226
Langefofot, Mawde, dau. of Sir Ralph	59
Llanfyllin	127
Lapley, and Priory	19, 38, 112, 115, 130, 192
Lathom, John	64, 65, 218
"Lass of Richmond Hill"	170
Lawrence, Rev. R. G.	19, 133, 147
Lawrence, Thos.	19
Lassels, Mr.	181
Lectern	46
Lee Court	190
Lee, William	214
Leofric	8
Leeke, Rev. R. H.	46
Leper Well	210
Leslie's Cavalry	141, 179
Levison, Jone	87
,, R.	88
Library, The Minister's	25, 97, 100
Lilleshall Abbey	10, 148, 210
Little Nell	155
Lime	146

Page

Lines to Bellringers 99
Lingen, Elizabeth de (see Pembruge) ...
  30, 32, 37, 38
Lingen, Sir Raffe 30, 38
Little Harriots Hays 127
" Little Nell ".................................... iv. 155
Lizard Grange 10, 11, 123, 133
Lizard Mill 136, 142
Lollards 113
Long Birch 207
Longford 83
Long Marston....................................... 181
Louvre 160
Ludlow... 45, 49
  „   Alice, dau. of Sir Richard de...... 63
  „   Benedicta de 37
  „   John 63
  „   Sir John 41, 52
  „   Sir Richard, Kt....................... 52, 63
  „   Sir Thomas 37
Lumley, Lady Ida F. H. 14
  „   Hon. Osbert 15
Lusard 10
Lye, Master John 19
Lyne, Sir Roger.................................... 223
Lyttletons... 90
Madeley 180
Man, Lord of and the Isles 72
Manners, Lady Katherine 13, 189
  „   Sir John 12, 71, 217
  „   Sir Richard 115
Manor of Tong 105, 132, 212
Manorial Courts, Leet and Baron 125, 127, 133
Manweryng, Ryce.................................... 223
Maps and Plans .... ix., x., xii., 122, 226
Margery de Harcourt 11
Market or Fair....................... 11, 105, 123
Marl 145, 146, 147
Marlpit, Methplekes................... 11, 132, 145
Marmion 59, 60
Marriages 162
Marrion Road....................................... 133
Marshal of England 60
Mary Queen of Scots 71
Masons, R. 133
Matthews, Rogers, Esq., and Ursula...... 17
Mausoleum 159
Maypole 136, 137
Meashill 11, 132, 139, 140, 145
Mears, Thomas 103
Meddings, George................................... 153
Meeson, George 19
Mercia, Earls of, Morcar and Edwin... 1, 8, 9
Meredith-ap-Bleddyn 17, 18
Merlin 5, 6, 7
Merstone, Thomas 215
Mervyn, King of Powys 17
Middleton, Lord 79
  „   Sir Thomas 79
Mill, the Water 11, 132, 133, 135
Miller, The 136
Millfield 147
Milner, Thomas 19, 162
Minerals Leasow 139
Misereres 74
Mitton, Griffith 216
Mitton, John 216
Mohun, Lady 42
  „   Lord 72
Molineux, W. H. 19

Page

Monasteries, Colleges, Hospitals,
  destruction of 114, 162, 203, 207, 219,
  220, 221
Moncreiffe, Sir Thomas 13
Monks 75
Montague, Mr. Edward 166, 168
  „   Lady Mary Wortley ... iv., 12,
  82, 166, 167, 168
Montford 208, 209
Montgomery, Earl Hugh de.............. 10, 20
  „   Earl Roger de 9, 10, 20
Montrose 178
Montrose Lucy, Duchess of 16
Monument, Knoll 161
Mountrath Diana, Countess of.............. 16
More, Sir Thomas 114, 115
"Morralls meicell" 139
Morse, William, or Mosse 19, 111, 116
Mortimer, Ralph de 45
Muckleston, J. F. 19
Murdock, Mr.. 139
Mytton, Edward, Esq................................ 88
  „   Jane 216
  „   Joan 176
  „   John 175, 216
  „   Thomas 18
Mytton Family 13, 88, 216
Nave... 27
Neachley Grange ... 15, 145, 151, 196, 218, 226
New, Mr. 177
Newport 152, 177
Newport, Geo. Cecil Orlando Viscount... 14
  „   Lady Anne 16
  „   Lord 174
  „   Margaret 112
  „   Sir Richard 175
  „   C. Ryce 224
Newport Family 13, 16, 18, 52, 182, 206
Newport, William 112
Nether Haddon 67
Neyll, Robert 222
Niches 104
North Aisle 27
Northumberland, Earl of 72
Norfolk, Duke of 176
Norton (see Tong Norton) 11, 99. 212
Norton Heath 107, 132, 141, 179
Nuts, gathering 11, 147
Nunnery of Brewood, see Black Ladies
Observator 191
Office, Constable's 44, 45
Offoxey 137
Old Castle 49
Old Mill 160
Oliver, Peter 173
Orde-Powlett, Hon. Wm. 14
Order of the Garter 35
Ore's Bank 140
Ore, Thomas 105, 133, 151
Organ.. 61
Organ, Old Gothic 27, 61, 62, 63
Oryngbere, St. Mary of........................... 111
Oswestry 127
Owners of Tong 10, 11, 12, 13
Parker, John the 212
Palfreys... 147
Parham 79
Park (Tong) 11, 137
Park Pale....................................... 132, 137, 140
Parker, John le, and Cecilia 212

Page

Parker, John, Oliver, Avice, Amore, Edith ... 212
Patingham, Lady Ysabel of ... 210
Payne, Major ... 91
Paunage of Hogs ... 11, 147
Peckes Ye, or Peche ... 87
Pedestal ... 73
Pelham, Lucy, daughter of Sir John ... 84
Pembruge, Pembrugge, Penbrugge, Pembruge or Pembridge ... 2, 11, 34, 35, 45, 50
Pembruge, Dame Elizabeth nee Lingen 12, 21, 30, 32, 37, 39, 111, 121
    " Fulco de I. ... 11, 121, 147
    " Fulco de II. ... 11 111, 112, 121, 147, 211, 212
    " Fulco de III. ... 12, 35, 213
    " Fulco de IV. ... 12, 30, 35, 36, 213, 214, 216
    " Half-brother of Fulco de I. ... 11
    " Henry ... 11
    " Isabella ... 214, 215
    " Juliana ...
    " Margaret ... 36
    " Robert de ... 12, 35, 213
    " Sir Fulke de 21, 30, 33, 36, 38, 39
Pencions ... 221
Pendragon ... 3
Pendrell, Penderel, or Pendrill ... 147, 178, 179, 182, 192, 201, 203
Pendrell Cave ... 189
Percy, Lady Lucy, daughter of the Duke of Northumberland ... 67, 70, 72
Percy, Sir Thomas ... 72
Percy, Thomas ... 72
Pertry ... 140
Peshall de ... 13, 206, 213, 214
Pew or Pew ... 126
Peynton, T. ... 100
Philarchus ... 190
Pierpoint ... 117, 152, 163, 166
    " Elizabeth, daughter of Lord Gervase de... 12, 81, 82, 84, 92, 93, 97
    " Elizabeth, daughter of Wm. and Elizabeth ... 84, 92 93, 112
    " Gervase Baron ... 82
    " Gervase Lord ... 12, 93, 150
    " Hon. William ... 12
    " Lady Mary ... 167
    " Robert de ...
Pietier, Lewes ... 19, 100, 107, 133
Pigeons ... 127
Pigs ... 142
Pillars ... 74
Pillar of Mary ... 73
Pikemere Hollow ... 141
Piscina ... 56, 85
Pitchford Oak ... 192
Plans, see Maps ...
Plate, Communion ... 108
Plaxton, Rev. G ... 186
Pochards ... 153
Pool of Tong (the Great) ... 11, 147
Pool, Church ... 135
Poole, Walter ... 27
Population ... 152
Porch ... 26
Porlock Effigies ... 23, 48
Pound ... 121
Powis, Prince of ... 17
Powys, Lord ... 63

Page

Preface to first edition ... 7
Preface to second edition ... 6
Pres, William de ... 211, 212, 213
Preston, Sir John ... 180
Prince Arthur Tudor ... 47, 48, 56, 99, 224, 225
Prince Charles ... 174
Prince Edward ... 11
Prince of Wales, H.R.H. (George IV.) ... 169
Princess Margaret ... 57, 227
Prioresses ... 196, 197, 198, 201, 204, 205, 206, 210, 222, 223
Prior's Lee ... 142
Priors Road ... 121
Proclamation ... 164, 165
Public Houses (old) ... 128, 153
Pugh, Isaac ... 127
Pulesdon, Roger de ... 213
Pulpit ... 46, 83
    " or Oratory ... 156
Puritans ... 73
Pype, Redware ... 44, 46
Pype, Sir Robert ... 43, 44, 45
Queen Anne ... 79
Queen Elizabeth ... 61, 65, 71, 72
Queen Mary ... 61, 72
"Queen of Love and Beauty" ... 149
Queen Elizabeth of York ... 224
Ralph, Mr. ... 188
Red House Inn ... 153
Registers ... 19, 115, 162, 163, 164, 165
Restoration ... 24
Rheims Abbey ... 54, 112, 115
Rhys, Prince of South Wales ... 18
Richard III. ... 51, 59, 72
Richmond ... 51, 72
Richmond Park ... 16
Riley ... 183
Rivet Carnac, Rev. G. C. ... 19, 46
Rhodri Mawr ... 17
Robyns, Wm. ... 212
Roe, Rev. John ... 207
Roger, Robert ... 223
Rogers, Edith ... 212
Roman Road ... 7
Rood Beam ... 30
Rood Cross ... 74
Rood Loft ... 30, 74
Rosary Lodge ... 160
Rouen, Captain of ... 37
Round House ... 160
Rowena ... 5
Rowson, Sir Thos. ... 222
Royal Forest (Wrekin) ... 131, 195
Royal Oak ... 178, 183
Royal Visits ... 49, 101
Rubens, P. P. ... 174, 175
Ruckley Grange ... 10, 11, 12, 133
Ruckley Wood ... 11
Rudhall, Abraham ... 100, 103
Rugge ... 196
Rungey Hale ... 72
Rupert Prince ... 174
Rutland, Duke of ... 13, 56, 71, 82, 177
    " Duchess of ... 189
    " Earl of ... 71
St. Bartholomew's Day ... 11
St. Leonard's Nuns of, see White Ladies
St. Denys ... 139
St. George, L. H. ... 19
St. Paul's Cathedral ... 10, 159
Salden ... 72

Page

Salter, George 133, 151
Salter, Doctor.. 216
Salter, Mrs.. 151
Saltworks... 148
Sarra 196
Sayings... 152
Scarbrough, Earl of 14
Scott, Wm. and Elizabeth....................... 107
Scot, Thomas......................... 133, 163
Screens 28, 29, 73, 74
Scuddamore, Mr. 148
Seats, Old Oak 26, 75, 216
Sedilia 85
Seal 27, 121, 130, 146, 205, 213, 215, 216
Seile 44, 224
Serfs 8
Seymaur, Lady Horatia...................... 171
Seymour, Miss 171
Shakerley 144, 147, 196, 200
Shakspearian Inscription 68
Shameford 111
Shaw, The........................... 11, 121, 136
Shaw, Mr. T. 141
Shaw, William 19, 111, 116, 121
Shawfield 121
Shaw Lane......................... 121, 136
Shelton Oak 192
Shields... See Arms
Shifnal 2, 7, 19, 124, 142, 212
Shireford, Robert de 19
Shottesbrook 36, 38
Shrewsbury 49, 52, 74
    „   Abbey 10, 111
    „   Battle of 38
    „   Earls of (see Talbots) ... 45,
                                47, 48, 51, 216
             Great Earl........................... 51
" Sir " 54
Sir Hugo 147
Skeffington, Cecilia 88
    „   Johanna 88
    „   John 86
    „   Sir William......................... 88
    „   William 86
    „   Tablets............................... 85
Skinner, Mr. 173
Skot Thos. 215
Slaney, Elizabeth 94
Slabs 27, 28, 63, 200
Small Ore's Bank 140
Smith, Robert the (or Lefevre) 212
Smith, William and Joan, The............... 213
Smith, Fulk... 213
Smythe, William 169
Smythe, Sir E. 169
Somerset, Lord Protector 115
Southall, Wm. 19
Souling 152
Sow and Pigs... 142
Speaker, The 37
Spernor, Spernores, Spermore 44
Spirit Lane... 210
S.S., Collar of 40, 42, 58
Stained Glass... 77
Staindrop Church........................... 41
Stafford, Lady 131, 175, 177
Stafford, Edward, Baron 175, 176
    „   Henry, Baron 176
    „   Roger 176
Stamford, Dame Margaret...................... 204

Page

Stanley, Arabella, Marie, Alice and
                Priscilla 67
    „   A. P., Dean........................... 70, 71
    „   Frances 68, 72
    „   George 72
    „   Henry 67
    „   Jane Strange de Knockyn........ 72
    „   Lady Lucy (see Percy) 67
    „   Margaret (see Vernon) ... 12, 64,
                                65, 217
    „   Petronella 68
    „   Sir Edward ... 12, 64, 65, 67, 69,
                        70, 72, 80, 173, 217, 218
    „   Sir Thomas..2, 12, 65, 67, 69, 70, 71, 72
    „   Strange, Lord 72
    „   Thomas (son of Sir Edward) 68, 152
    „   Tomb 64, 70, 174, 175, 226
    „   Venetia, Lady Digby... 68, 69,
                        72, 166, 171, 172, 173, 174
Staple, Sir John............................... 225
Stevenson, W... 151
Steventon, Thomas 216
Stinking Lake 210
Stocks 151
Stokesay 52
Stone Cross... 144
Stones, Robert 133
Stoneyford 7
Storm, &c... 164
Strange, John Lord 72
Stratford 189
Streetway... 141
Stubbs, Mr... 188
Sudbury 52
Sundial... 105, 151
Swilcar Oak 190
Swan, Walter 19
Swynfen, Jocosa 44
    „   Margaret (see Vernon)............ 44
    „   William........................... 44
Tailor, Nichol the 152, 212
Talbot, the great Earl (Shrewsbury and
        Talbot) 48, 51
Talbot, John, 2nd Earl 47, 51
    „   Lady Anne 47
    „   Sir Gilbert 51
    „   Sir John........................... 51
Tanat, Morris... 17
Taylebois, Margaret, daughter of Sir
        Gilbert 59
Taylor, William............................... 107
Teck, H.R.H. the Duchess of ... 101, 180, 192
Temple, the... 189
Tetherton, James 140, 151
Thanes 7, 8
Thonglands... 3, 7
Thoresby 81, 82
Thorneycroft, Major 153
Thorpe, Sir E. de 41
Thursfield, Rev. R. P. 191
Tibshelf... 197
Tiles, Old 56, 84, 200
Tilton 174, 175
Timlet Bridge 133, 142, 144
    „   Holloway 11, 144
    „   Site for Mill........................... 12
Tithe Barn 137
    „   Pig 138
Token 142
Tomb destroyed 34

Tong, Tuange, Twanga, Thonk, Tugge, Thonge name of 2, 5, 7, 11
Tong Castle (see Castle) 5, 49. 79, 82, 83, 84, 90, 91, 27, 153, 170, 171, 174, 189
„ Lake 128, 144. 148
„ Norton 7, 11, 105, 107, 124, 183
„ Park House 144
" Tony-fire the Fagot " 131
Tortworth 190
Tòstig 8
Tournament 148, 149
Tournay 59
Trees Famous 190, 192
Troutbek's Heire 51
Trussel, Margaret 32, 38
Trussel, Sir William 32, 36, 39
Trusseley 216
Trusty Dick 179, 181
Tumulus 105
Turner, Alice 151
Tutbury 190
Twickenham Park 16
Twiss 152
Upton 14
Urn 158
Vauxhall Cottage 159
Vernon 33, 34, 38, 39, 45, 46, 49, 52, 152
„ Alice, daughter of John Ludlow ... 63
„ Arthur 19, 51, 53, 54, 55, 222
„ Benedicta (wife of Speaker) 37, 38, 41, 43
„ Chantry ...... See Golden Chapel
„ Dorothy 12, 71, 177, 217
„ Edward and Margaret 63, 64
„ George (of Hodnet) 63, 177, 216
„ Henry 64
„ Humphrey 42, 51, 63
„ Lady Anne 47, 50
„ Lord 64, 101
„ Margaret. Abbess of West Malling 52, 61, 201
„ Margaret (wife of Sir Thos. Stanley) 12, 64, 65, 67, 72, 177
„ Margaret (daughter of Sir Robert Dymoke) 57, 58
„ Margaret (wife of Sir George Vernon) 59. 70, 11
„ Margaret (Swynfen), wife of Sir Wm. 43, 44, 45
„ Mary 52
„ Mawde (2nd wife of Sir Geo. Vernon) 59, 217
„ Richard (father of Speaker) 34, 43 112, 217
„ Richard, Esq. ... 12, 37, 39, 51, 58, 85
„ Sir Arthur 19, 53, 54, 55, 57, 223
„ Sir Edward 65
„ Sir George 12, 59, 63, 65, 67
„ Sir Harry ... 12, 46, 47, 49, 53, 54, 56, 57, 63, 90, 100, 202, 216, 224, 225
„ Sir John (of Sudbury) ... 64. 216, 223
„ Sir Richard 12. 34, 35, 37, 39, 41. 52, 54, 58, 112, 214, 215, 216, 218
„ Sir Thomas 63, 65
„ Sir William 12, 43, 45, 46
„ Thomas (of Houndshill) 63
„ Thomas (of Stokesay) 52
Vestment 97. 98, 208
Vestry 95, 98
" Vigil of Arms " 58
Vivary 11
Vortigern 3, 4, 5

Waddingham 137
Waddington M. de 192
Wagstaffe Thos. 222
Wales. Princes of 17, 18
Walk, Dorothy Vernon's 71
Walking the Boundaries 134, 135, 136
Wall, Ellinor 80
Wall, Manor of 44
Walsall 225
Walter, Herbert 194
Waltham or Walthamstow 68
Walton, Thos. de 214
Warde, John le 28, 212, 213
Warde, Richard 19
Wardens 19, 112, 116, 117, 123, 223
Watchman 128, 129
Water Tilting 149
Water Mill 11
Watling Street 7, 141
Wedges 150
Wells 136, 140, 210
Weld (sometimes Wyld), Edward 169
Wellington Forest 195
Wellington, Sir Roger, vicar of 216
Wemme 36
Wenlock, Thomas 142
West Malling 52
Weston-under-Lizard ... 19, 39, 49, 124, 128, 195, 214
„ „ „ Church 88, 216
„ „ „ Park 13, 132, 140, 173, 189
Weston, De 13, 195, 198, 210
Whalebones 158
White Ladies ... 12, 56, 86, 87, 88, 98, 139, 145, 147, 179, 189, 194, 200, 203, 209, 218, 219, 220, 221
„ "Close " 139
White Oak 137, 139, 189, 204
White, Winifred 200
Whitgrave, Mr. 180, 190, 199
White Sitch 196
Whytemore, John de la 196
Whyston, Sir Nicholas de 39
Wiche, Dame 92
Wigmore 11, 45
Wilbrahams 13
Wilkes, John 136
William I 9, 43
William (Parson of Tong) 19
Willoughby, Lord 81
„ Hon. Henry 79
Wilmot, Lord 89
Wilson, C. T. 19
Windmill or Windmills 141
Witnesses to deeds, and other persons not immediately connected with Tong 216, 218, 219, 222, 223
Woburn 190
Winwick 64, 71
Wixstone, Wm. 213
Wolsey, Cardinal 203
Wombridge 130, 217
Woodlands 141, 189
Woodshawt T. 100
Wool 150
Woolrich, James 19, 115, 116
Woolley 151
Worcester, Battle of 89, 178
Worsley, Sir Thomas 16
Wren, Sir Christopher 159

	Page			Page
Wright, Mrs.	173	York Parliament		12
Wright, Mr.	202	York, Duchess of, H.R.H.		101, 192
Wrottesley	210, 216	Ysabel of Pattingham, Lady		210
Wylde, Ann (née Harries)	12, 79. 80, 81, 158	Zetland Countess of		15
„ Edmund	80	Zouche La		2, 10, 11, 32, 198
„ or Weld, John, senior	12	„ „ Alan		10, 11, 145
„ John, junior	12, 80	„ „ Alice		11
Wysston, Roger	223	„ „ Roger		11, 146
Yate, Yates, or Gate	132, 152, 203, 210, 212	„ „ William		10
Yeames, Mr. R. A	168	„ „ Elizabeth		197

Prosperity be thy page !

—*Shakespeare, Cymbeline.*

Confiding, speed then, on life's benturous way ;

Thy sails are set—thy launch the First of May.

Queen Katherine :

After my death I wish no other herald,

No other speaker of my liding actions,

To keep mine honour from corruption

But such an honest chronicler as Griffith.

—*Shakespeare.*

THE BELL HOTEL,
TONG.

A Comfortable Country Hotel,

with Good Stabling.

Special arrangements can be made with large Parties
requiring Dinners or Teas.

Only a Few Minutes' Walk from Tong Church.

Proprietor : MAURICE DAVIES,

Bell Hotel, Tong, near Shifnal.

BRADFORD ARMS,
IVETSEY BANK.

Proprietress—MARY CARPENDALE.

GOOD WINES AND SPIRITS.

Accommodation for Cyclists, Pic=nic Parties, Tourists, &c.

Tennis Ground.   Capital Stabling.

POSTAL ADDRESS—IVETSEY BANK,

STRETTON,

Telegraph Office—WESTON-UNDER-LIZARD.
No Sunday Post.

STAFFORD.

The Nearest Hotel to Boscobel and the Royal Oak.

Jerningham Arms Hotel

SHIFNAL.

COMMERCIAL, FAMILY, & POSTING HOUSE.

Conveyances meet Trains at Five minutes notice.   3¾ miles from Tong Church.

Catering for Luncheons, Dinners, Parties, &c.

HEAD QUARTERS OF CYCLISTS TOURING CLUB.

MRS. KENT, Proprietress.

Telegraphic Address—"JERNINGHAM."

BENNION & SON,

Booksellers, Stationers, &c., Newport, Salop.

GOLF!   GOLF!!   GOLF!!!

At makers' prices.

BENNION & SON beg to call attention to their Selection of Golf Clubs:—

SPECIAL LADIES GOLF CLUBS. LEFT-HANDED CLUBS
Always in Stock.

GOLF BALLS: "Silvertown," 12/- per dozen. Made up Balls, 6/- per dozen. Repairs done by competent men same day.
Old Golf Balls made equal to new.   Price List sent on Application.

ALL REPAIRS IN FISHING TACKLE.
Trout and Grayling Flies Tied to Pattern on shortest notice.

TENNIS, CRICKET, FOOTBALL, AND ALL MATERIALS FOR OUT-DOOR GAMES
KEPT IN STOCK.

Postal Orders promptly attended to.

BENNION & SON, NEWPORT,
SALOP.

JOHN TAYLOR & CO.,

Bell Founders   Bell Hangers,

LOUGHBOROUGH,

LEICESTERSHIRE.

Founders of the great Ring of Twelve Bells of St. Paul's Cathedral; also the Bourdon Bell, "Great Paul," the largest in England, weighing 37,483lbs.; the heavy Rings in Worcester, Newcastle, and Edinburgh Cathedrals; the Imperial Institute, and many others.

⊶ HANDBELLS ⊷

A SPECIALTY.

EMPIRE AND LIBERTY.

PEACE WITH HONOUR.

PRIMROSE ✳ LEAGUE.

WESTON HABITATION, No. 854.

Dame President: **THE COUNTESS OF BRADFORD.**

COUNCIL—

The LADY MABEL KENYON-SLANEY.
Mrs. BRISCOE, Chillington Hall.
Mrs. GIFFARD, Pendryl Hall.
Mrs. H. P. SMITH, Tong.
Mrs. H. TOMLINSON, Wheaton Aston.
The Rev. ERNEST BRIDGEMAN, Blymhill.

Miss MONCKTON, Brewood Hall.
Miss HARTLEY, Tong Castle.
Mrs. VAUGHAN, Lapley.
Mrs. WARD, Rodbaston Hall.
F. MONCKTON, Esq., Stretton.
The Rev. A. TALBOT, Church Eaton.

Mr. GEORGE GRIFFITHS, Weston-under-Lizard,
Hon. Sec. and Treasurer.

THE Terms of Subscription to Weston Habitation are— 1/6 entrance fee and 2/6 annual tribute for each Knight or Dame—badge or brooch, 2/-—and 1d. annual tribute for each Associate—badge, 3d., or brooch, 4d. There is no entrance fee for Associates. The Tributes are receivable yearly, between January 1st, and April 19th (Primrose Day), the anniversary of the late Lord Beaconsfield's death. The badges and brooches are intended to be worn on every public occasion.

The Habitation has about 1,800 Members.